On Agate Hill

On Agate Hill

A NOVEL

LEE SMITH

A SHANNON RAVENEL BOOK

Algonquin Books of Chapel Hill

2006

ℝ

A SHANNON RAVENEL BOOK

Published by

ALGONQUIN BOOKS OF CHAPEL HILL

Post Office Box 2225

Chapel Hill, North Carolina 27515-2225

a division of

WORKMAN PUBLISHING

225 Varick Street

New York, New York 10014

This is a work of fiction. While, as in all fiction, the literary perceptions and insights are based on experience, all names, characters, places, and incidents are either products of the author's imagination or are used fictitiously.

LIBRARY OF CONGRESS CATALOGING-IN-PUBLICATION DATA

Smith, Lee, 1944–

    On Agate Hill : a novel / Lee Smith.—1st ed.

      p. cm.

    "A Shannon Ravenel book."

    ISBN-13: 978-1-56512-452-3; ISBN-10: 1-56512-452-9

    1. North Carolina—Fiction.   I. Title.

  PS3569.M5376O5 2006

  813'.54—dc22   2006045859

10 9 8 7 6 5 4 3 2 1

First Edition

For my son

JOSHUA FIELD SEAY

December 23, 1969–October 26, 2003

CONTENTS

On Agate Hill

TUSCANY MILLER

30-B Peachtree Court Apts.

1900 Court Blvd.

Atlanta, GA 30039

September 19, 2006

Dr. Thomas Ferrell, Director
Documentary Studies Program
Institute for the Study of the South
Carolina State University
266 College Ave.
Charlotte, NC 28225

Dear Dr. Ferrell:

Remember me? Well, I know you have not heard from me in a long time because I dropped out and all (that was so slack), but now I do want to finish and I hope you will let me back into the program and give me another extension on my thesis considering what I have been up to.

I am not going to do "Beauty Shop Culture in the South: Big Hair and Community" after all, despite my background in pageants.

I want to turn in this box of old stuff instead, see what you think! I believe you will be as excited as I am.

Also I am truly a changed person, from reading it. More on that later.

But first I guess I need to tell you how I got a hold of all this, and some things about my family, which is not normal, though we used to be.

The family was me Tuscany Miller (actually I picked the name Tuscany myself, in high school), my older brother Padgett, and my little sister Louise, the brain. My mother was an elementary school principal while my father owned and ran his own furniture store The Aesthetic in our hometown of Lookout, NC. Our grandparents live across the street. So you see what I mean by normal.

Even that name The Aesthetic did not give a clue. We were totally surprised when Daddy came home from the store one spring day bringing a young man named Michael Oliver with a spiky haircut and a black leather jacket. "I want you to meet Michael, a wonderful person," Daddy said, standing in the front door holding hands with him. Mama put down her purse, she had just come in from school. Luckily Padgett was at baseball practice. Louise was doing her homework and I was watching Jeopardy on TV, I will never forget it.

Daddy went on to say that Michael Oliver was a designer from Chicago and that they had first met in 1999 at the Furniture Market in Hickory, where Daddy went every year, and that their friendship had continued and ripened to the point where they must be together.

"I can't believe you used the word ripened," said Louise who has always been kind of weird.

As for me I did not say one thing but put the TV on mute.

"I have heard so much about all of you," Michael Oliver said.

Later my best friend Courtney would say that he is hot.

"Oh for God's sake, Wayne," Mama said walking out of the room.

Things got even worse after that. First Daddy left and went to live with Michael in Asheville, where anything goes. Mama quit her job and started running the furniture store, which has been a big success. She buys the more traditional lines, like Bassett. I won Miss Confederacy then went off to college so was not there when Daddy came back to visit one day and announced that he was now becoming a woman so he could marry Michael.

"Oh Wayne, why don't you just be gay?" Mama asked him. "It would be a lot easier and not hurt." But Daddy said he has been a woman all along deep inside of himself. A woman just waiting to happen.

"Well I give up!" said Granddaddy who was over there bringing us some tomatoes.

Anyway Daddy did become a tall thin woman named Ava because Michael loves Ava Gardner.

Then Michael got a big inheritance. Louise has kept in touch with them all along but neither me or Padgett has had anything to do with them at all, even though I have to admit that Daddy has left me a long sweet message on my cell phone every week since he left. Now Daddy and Michael have bought this old completely run-down plantation out in the country between Hillsborough and Burlington, NC, and they are fixing it up into a very fancy bed and breakfast.

So I was surprised to get a message from Michael instead of Daddy on my cell phone right after my little marriage ended in a disaster which I will not go into.

"Tuscany," Michael said, "I know that you took that documentary studies class at the university and I wonder if you might be interested in looking at a young girl's diary from the 1870s which the carpenters have just found out here at Agate Hill. It was in a secret room up under the eaves. Let me know. We would love to have a visit from you too."

So I got in the car and drove up there, and the rest is history.

Or I hope you will think it is history.

There is a lot of other stuff in this box too including letters (some mailed and some not), poems, songs, and sheet music, a Bible, a catechism (I never saw one of these before, it is very depressing), old newspaper accounts, court records involving a possible murder, a hand-tooled leather case with a silver clasp, a little heart-shaped stirrup, marbles, rocks, and dolls, and a large collection of BONES, some human and some not. So I will just put some stick-it notes and stuff here and there as we go along and then tell you some more at the end.

Hopefully,
Tuscany Miller

Agate Hill

Dear Diary,

This book belongs to me Molly Petree age thirteen today May 20 in the year of our Lord 1872, Agate Hill, North Carolina. I am an orphan girl. This is my own book of my own self given to me by the preachers wife Nora Gwyn who said, This little diary is for you my dear unfortunate child, to be your friend and confident, to share all your thoughts and deepest secrets for I know how much you need a friend and also how much you love to read and write. I do believe you have a natural gift for it. Now it is my special hope that you will set down upon these pages your own memories of your lovely mother and your brave father, and of your three brothers as well, and of all that has befallen you. For I believe this endeavor might help you, Molly Petree. So I urge you to take pen in hand commencing your diary with these words, <u>Thy will be done O Lord on Earth as it is in Heaven, Amen.</u>

Well, I have not done this!

And I will not do it either no matter how much I love pretty Nora Gwyn who looks like a lady on a fancy plate and has taught me such few lessons as I have had since Aunt Fannie died. NO for I mean to write in secrecy and stelth the truth as I see it. I know I am a spitfire and a burden. I do not care. My family is a dead family, and this is not my home, for I am a refugee girl.

I am like the ruby-throated hummingbird that comes again and again to Fannies red rosebush but lights down never for good and all, always flying on. And it is true that often I feel so lonesome for all of them that are gone.

I live in a house of ghosts.

I was born before the Surrender and dragged from pillar to post as Mamma always said until we fetched up here in North Carolina after Columbia fell. Our sweet Willie was born there, into a world of war. He was real little all waxy and bloody, and Old Bess put him into a dresser drawer while the fires burned red outside the windows. Mamma used to tell it in that awful whisper which went on and on through the long hot nights when she could not sleep and it was my job to wet the cool cloths required for her forehead which I did faithfully. I loved my mamma. But I was GLAD when she died, I know this is a sin. I have not told it before. But I am writing it down anyway as Nora Gwyn said and I will write it all down every true thing in black and white upon the page, for evil or good it is my own true life and I WILL have it. I will.

I am the legal ward of my uncle Junius Jefferson Hall who is not really my uncle at all but my mothers first cousin a wise and mournful man who has done the best he could for us all I reckon. We arrived here during the last days of the War to a house running over all ready thus giving Uncle Junius more than thirty people on this place to feed, negro and white alike. Uncle Junius used to be a kind strong man but he is sick and seems so sad and lost in thought now since Fannie died.

This is his wife my dear aunt Fannie who is recently Deceased it has been seven months now, and the baby inside her born dead and backward.

I will NEVER have a baby myself!

I sat out in the passage all night long on a little stool and listened to Fannie scream then moan then watched them run in and out, the negros and old Doctor Lambeth who stayed here for three days all told. He is a skinny old man with a horse that looks just like him. He came riding in at a dead run with his long gray hair streaming out behind him under his high black hat. He has always been Uncle Junius best friend. At first I did not get to see the baby though Old Bess thrust him out the door past me wrapped in a bloody cloth then Liddy took him away and washed him and wrapped him again in a clean white sheet like a little bundle of laundry. They put him on the marble top table in the parlor.

What is his name? I ventured to ask Uncle Junius once when he came out of the bedroom but he cursed and said, He has no name Molly, he is dead.

But then Mister Gwyn the preacher arrived and said, Now Junius, you must give him a name, for I cannot baptize him without a name, and he cannot enter the Kingdom of Heaven without baptism.

So then they unwrapped him, and I got to see him finely, pale blue but perfect, he looked like a little baby doll.

Mister Gwyn dipped his hand in the special water in the rose china bowl and touched the babys little blue head and blessed him saying, Lewis Polk Hall, I baptize you in the name of the Father and of the Son and of the Holy Ghost, Amen.

Amen, Uncle Junius said, Amen, then gave a great sob and rushed over and knelt down and kissed the babys little cheek then went straight back into the bedroom.

Nora Gwyn held the baby for a long time while the servants and some of the neighbor people came in to see him, then they laid him out on the table again with dimes on his eyes and a little white lace dress that somebody had brought him. Uncle Junius had named him for his oldest boy Lewis that served in the Twenty-second North Carolina Regiment under Colonel Pettigrew. Now he is dead, and Uncle Junius is old, and Fannie was old too, she did not have any business with any more babys, Old Bess said. Babys are always dangerous but it is even more dangerous when you are old. But everybody except me wants them, it is hard to see why.

The things that people really want are the most like to kill them, it seems to me, such as war and babys.

More and more people came. They sat in the parlor and gathered outside on the piazza and all over the yard in the shade of the trees. Why do they keep coming? I asked Liddy in the kitchen but she just wiped her face and gave me some parched corn and said, Here, go on, take little Junius down to feed the chickens. Little Junius is a snively little boy who looks like he is about a hundred years old. I got his hand and took him out the door and down the hill to the henhouse where all the chickens came running. He threw out the corn like it was a job of work.

Then I heard hammering from inside the barn.

So after he finished feeding the chickens little Junius and I went into the big barn to find Virgil there making something, with Washington helping him. Washington is Liddys son and my best friend on this place, he is milk coffee color with gray eyes and a big smile. Virgil and Old Bess came all the way from South Carolina with Mamma. Old Bess is what they call a griffe negro but Virgils face is as round and shiny black as that globe our uncle Harrison brought back from the Cape of Good Hope, I believe you call it obsidian. Virgil is real old now, but he can still make anything.

By then it was late late afternoon and the sunlight fell through the golden dust to make a shining block in the air and a shining yellow square like a magic carpet on the old barn floor where Washington sat planing a long piece of wood. Yellow dust flew everywhere. A little wooden box sat on the straw beside him. Virgil was fitting two wide planks together up on the sawhorses.

What are you doing out here Missy? he said.

That is her coffin, isnt it? I asked him. Nobody told me, I said.

Dont nobody have to, Virgil said.

Junius held tight to my hand and looked all around the barn like he had never seen it before. He is four years old.

The time will come when it come, Virgil said. He reached into a deep pocket of his overalls. Here now Washington, see can you teach this here little white boy something.

Washington jumped up and Virgil gave him the leather bag full of marbles.

Washington whooped. Come on, he said, and got Junius other hand and led us both to a level spot just outside of the door in the shade of the big hickory tree. This ought to do us, Washington said, so we all sat down in the crackly leaves as it was November. Then he took a board and scraped off the leaves and made a round place in the dirt, then used the edge of the board to draw a big deep circle around it. All right now, Washington said. Then he put all the marbles down in the middle of the ring. They were mostly made from the agate and quartz on the hill, but one was sort of silver and one was greeny gold, and another blue as the sky.

Little Junius clapped his hands.

Now this how you do it, Washington told him. He picked up a white marble and held it cupped in his fingers with his thumb behind it. I picked up a clay marble and held it the same way. Junius reached over and got the blue one but he couldnt hold it in his little hand like we were doing so he started to cry.

Now thats all right, Washington said. You dont got to do that honey. Why looky here. You can just roll it. He showed little Junius how to roll it to hit the others and Junius got the hang of it right away.

As for me, I am just as good as a boy at everything.

So we sat there in the dirt playing marbles for the rest of the afternoon until the sun went down in a red ball of fire, and color spread across the whole big sky. I could smell leaves burning someplace. A little cold wind came up.

It got dark in the barn but Virgil kept on hammering. Its about time for supper now aint it? he called finely, and the minute he said it, I was just starving.

I pulled little Junius up by one hand and Washington pulled the other and like that we walked kicking leaves up the hill to the house where they were laying out little Junius mother in the bedroom and big Junius was beating his head bloody on the brick kitchen wall behind the house. We walked right past him into the kitchen.

I bet yall are hungry aint you? Liddy said. She set us all down at the table and gave us some chicken and dumplings out of the big black pot. We ate like wild animals as Fannie used to say. It was nice and warm in the kitchen with that big fire glowing. Here honey dont you want some more? Liddy asked and even little Junius ate another whole plateful. I dont know if he knew his mamma was dead or not.

That was seven months ago, and things around here have gone to hell in a handbasket ever since. Nora Gwyn and Mister Gwyn do not know the half of it. But they have come only to say good bye to Uncle Junius as they are moving to Tennessee where Mister Gwyn will be the headmaster at a new boys school, old sourpuss Presbyterian he has got a poker up his ass as Selena says.

Uncle Junius and Mister Gwyn and Nora Gwyn are sipping sherry wine in the parlor down below me as I write.

Now dont you want to know where I am? For you could never find me in a million years. This is my number one hiding place in all the world, a cubbyhole right in the heart of the house yet invisible and unknown to all. Come see. Nora Gwyn says you will be my friend and now you will be my guest, I have never had one before.

But first you will have to come out here to Agate Hill so you will be riding up from the Haw River on the road and then along our dusty lane with trees and fields on either side. The land will rise as you come up and up, yet so slowly that it will surprise you to turn and look back to see the countryside spread out like a dreamy quilt below you now, orchards and woods and overgrown fields with piled-up rock walls between them. White quartz rocks stand out in the fields. You can find agate and fools gold too at the very top of the rise behind the house where I often climb though I am not allowed to.

I love to sneak down the back stairs in the night time and run across the yard from tree to tree and up the rocky path to lie on the big flat rock which stays warm from the sun long into the night. I call it my Indian Rock. I love to lie there flat on my back and let the wind blow over me which is not like any other feeling ever felt by anybody else in the world I am sure of it, known only by me and now by you, my friend of this diary. Sometimes the moon is so bright it is nearly like day and casts shadows among the rocks. One time I fell asleep on my rock and slept there all night long until King Arthur started crowing in the dawn, THEN I had to skedaddle. Liddy and Old Bess both saw me from the kitchen door but they did not tell, they gave me a corn pone and sent me on my way.

I am like a ghost girl wafting through this ghost house seen by none. I truly think I would blow away save for this piece of fools gold I keep here in my pocket for good luck. Often I take it out and turn it this way and that in the sun just to see it shine. Mamma loved gold jewelry but I am not a thing like Mamma. I am NOT. I like rocks instead. All of her jewelry is gone to the

Yankees now except for a few pieces which Selena has wheedled out of Uncle Junius. I have to say, it kills me to see Mammas jade ring from the Orient on the little finger of Selenas fat hand and the coral bead necklace around her neck, I wish it would choke her dead.

Anyway you will come up the lane past the falling down sawmill and the gin and the two big barns one empty now, and then you will ride into the grove of cedar trees where it is always dark and the soft needles rustling. It smells good in there too. When you come out you will be here at Agate Hill plantation which was never a real plantation at all in Mammas opinion, not even before the War, not such as Perdido which she left behind in South Carolina.

This house was once white of course but now the paint has peeled off leaving the old brown wood which I like better anyway. The top piazza is held up by plain square posts while the floor of the one below is made from great flat stones brought in long ago from the fields. The top piazza is another place I love for it is there I often sit rocking and reading or dreaming or watching a thunderstorm roll across the land with its lightning that stands like a tree in the sky and its corn wagons rolling. This is what Virgil calls the thunder.

Myself I love a thunderstorm better than anything. Sometimes I will run to the top of the hill to whirl around and around on my Indian Rock in the wind, it is like a dance I can not stop. The smell of the lightning goes into your nose and down your whole body. Old Bess says if you get hit by lightning yet live you will have special powers, well I could use some of those. So I dont care if I get hit or not. Many times I have got wet clear through and been scolded for it though lately nobody cares.

All around this house you will see out buildings such as the corn crib, the red carriage barn with its two stables, the pigpen, and the old blacksmith house which has fallen in, you cant hardly see it for the honeysuckle which has run all over it now. And watch out, you will fall into the icehouse hole if you are not careful, so stay out of there! The brick kitchen is right behind the house, with the four-room tenant house on back.

Negros still live in that row of cabins, some of them work here and some do not, but Uncle Junius hates to send any of them packing for where would they go? Not a one has got what they were promised, that we know of. Besides Virgil and Old Bess and Liddy and Washington there is Daddy Rex the old root doctor who is dying now, I reckon he cant cure himself. In addition there is always negros coming and going or staying awhile, and often they have made off with our things such Aunt Fannies Mexican silver candle sticks won by her daddy in a poker game, and the worst, the curved saber my father carried in the War as he was Cavalry. I hate this for I would like to have it so much, I do not remember him anyway. But it is easy to steal from us as Uncle Junius leaves the house unlocked now since Fannie died, he says if anybody takes anything, why then they need it more than we do and they are welcome to it.

So the door is wide open.

Come on in.

This house is not really very big with only one parlor and a dining room and the middle room and Uncle Junius and Aunt Fannies bedroom down stairs, then a jumble of bedrooms up stairs fitted out with lots of feather beds and ticks that can be spread out on the floor for it was Uncle Junius and Aunt Fannies pride that they never turned any one away, such as Nora Gwyn and her poker ass husband who have stayed the night.

Come into the passage which goes clear through the house as you see. It is our sitting room in the summer, cool and breezy when they bring the chairs out, but freezing cold in the winter time. Then we must hurry through it. Take the narrow door to your left and climb up the wooden stairs.

Do not be afraid in this dark staircase for no one will bother you, no one is here.

But of ghosts we have these:

Alice Heart Petree, my mother, b. 1822, Charleston, South Carolina,
    d. New Years Eve, 1869, Agate Hill, North Carolina.

Charles William Petree, my little brother, b. 1865, Columbia, South
    Carolina, d. March 25, 1869, Agate Hill, North Carolina.

My baby sister never named so I know for sure she has not gone to Heaven if there is such a place, this breaks my heart. I see her sometimes in the high dim air up near the ceiling in the parlor before we light the lamps, and once I saw her fly through the trees in the woods among the rising fireflies, just at dusk. B. and d. summer 1866, Agate Hill, North Carolina.

Charles Pleasant Petree, my father, a soldier and a scholar. They say I take after him. If so it must be in spirit not flesh for see, here is his image made in camp on the eve of war. Does he not look dashing and daring with his long mustaches and this fancy hat? He looks like he is French, like he is going to a party. With him is Simon Black a friend of his youth then a scout attached to my fathers Company C, Sixth Regiment, South Carolina Cavalry. See how solemn they are staring into the camera as if into the awful future which has now come to pass. My father was b. Edgefield, South Carolina; 1823, d. March 20, 1865, at Bentonville, North Carolina, where he is buried in pieces.

Tennyson Polk Petree, my eldest brother, b. 1843, Perdido, South Carolina, named for a poet Alfred Lord Tennyson, d. May 5, 1863, at Chancellorsville, Virginia.

Henry Heart Petree, my other brother, not but seventeen upon his death, b. 1846, Perdido, South Carolina, d. July 1, 1863, Winchester, Virginia.

My beloved aunt Fannie Ogburn Hall, b. 1826, Four Oaks, North Carolina. d. October 30, 1871, Agate Hill, North Carolina.

Their son Lewis Polk Hall, b. 1838, Agate Hill, North Carolina. d. July 3, 1863, Gettysburg, Pennsylvania.

And their baby, Lewis Polk Hall, b. October 30, 1871, Agate Hill, North Carolina. d. October 30, 1871, Agate Hill, North Carolina.

And of the living we have these:

Uncle Junius

Spencer Wade Hall, Uncle Junius and Aunt Fannies son who walked home from the war Insane. He lives out at Four Oaks with Romulus.

But Spence is nice and not dangerous, he bothers no one, working in the field with Rom. His moon face is scarred by grapeshot.

Little Junius, that I told you about.

And me.

This is <u>all</u> of us here at the present time. Now you know why I say, I live in a house of ghosts. It was not always so. Alive yet gone from us now, we have these:

George Jefferson Hall, known as Georgie, gone West to seek his Fortune, estranged from Uncle Junius.

And finally my beloved Julia and Rachel, Aunt Fannie and Uncle Junius eldest daughters, far too old to be my playmates of course but my dear friends. Julia is so pretty with curly yellow hair and a face that turns pink when she laughs, which is often, while Rachel is dainty and tidy as a little mouse, with mouse-brown hair. They are both teachers now. Julia is a governess in Wilmington, North Carolina, while Rachel is at the Jackson Orphans Asylum in Norfolk, Virginia, where she is very important and earns twenty-five dollars a month, it is so much money. She tried to send some of it home when Aunt Fannie was sick but Uncle Junius would not have it. And when Rachel asked to stay here after Aunt Fannies funeral he said NO for this is a sad place of sorrow and death. <u>Live your life,</u> he told her. Uncle Junius gets all broke down.

I remember the summer before they left, Rachel and Julia used to sit out on the upper piazza all day long doing Baltimore work, feather stitching and herringboning until it came full dark and they could not hardly see to take those tiny stitches required for the white clothes worn by Northern babys and children and even brides. They earned ten dollars a batch. I loved to sit out on the piazza with them, me and my doll Margaret who used to be their doll when they were little. They were trying to teach me to sew, and that very day I had bit my lip until it bled trying to thread the needle. I was supposed to be making a skirt for Margaret out of a little piece of beautiful yellow silk they had saved just for me. But it was hard going, and I was sorry when they commenced again after supper, for I had had enough sewing by then to last me a life time. Now it was getting dark in earnest. Oh look! How beautiful! cried Julia as the moonflowers opened one by one on the vines which wrap the piazza railing.

Then here came Uncle Junius, filling up the doorway. He is very tall.

Now now girls, thats enough, come inside the house now, you will ruin your eyes and then where will you be? he said.

Just one more minute please Papa, Julia said. I am almost done with this christening dress.

Yes Papa if we can just finish these pieces we are working on, we can send the whole batch off tomorrow with Mister Littlejohn, wouldnt that be wonderful? Rachel tied a knot then prepared to thread her needle anew though she was squinting in the dark.

Damnation girls, I said get on in the house now. Have you gone deaf as well as blind? Uncle Junius grabbed the white cloth up from Julias lap and dashed it down, the embroidery hoop striking against the floor.

Oh Papa you will ruin it all, cried Julia, whereupon Uncle Junius came forward and stomped on the white cloth with his boot while Julia tried to grab it, screaming out when he stomped on her hand in all the uproar.

Oh Papa now look what you have done, what if you have broken my hand? she wailed and even I understood what that would mean, that she could never earn the money then to finish school nor play her piano again. Rachel set up a wail beside her, and I cried too for I copied them in everything.

Oh my God. Oh God, Uncle Junius said, I am so sorry, forgive me my little girls.

Julia sobbed holding her hand in the bunch of snowy cloth she had gathered up onto her lap.

Why what do you think you are doing Sir? Go on now, go lie down, you poor thing, it will be all right. Suddenly there was Aunt Fannie leading him away now meek as a baby, but soon she was back with a lighted candle she placed on the table.

Come here Molly, she said, and I came and climbed into her lap where

I loved to be most in the world. My own mamma did not have a lap. Aunt
Fannie reached over and took Julias hand and kissed it and worked all her
fingers back and forth.

Oh that hurts, Julia said.

But it will be fine, Fannie said. Nothing is broken. And we will wash
this little christening dress tomorrow, it will be good as new. Now listen to
me my darlings, she said, looking from one to the other including me with
her sweet plump face all solemn for once and tears in her big brown eyes.
You know that your father loves you, she said, and we all nodded, for you
had to believe whatever Aunt Fannie said. But he hates to see you work at
day labor. You may not understand that he is in dispair because he can not
provide for you in the way he feels he should have been able to provide for
his daughters—all three—she said, smiling down at me. This War has just
about killed him. Now come and give me a kiss, she said, so we drew closer
in the candles glow. She kissed us one by one then stroked our hair. Now lets
just sit out here awhile, she said. Its almost time for the moon to come up,
and it is such a pretty night. It was. We set out there on the piazza in our little
circle of light until the moon came up big and yellow over the Caney Creek
mountains beyond the river.

That is a gibbus moon Aunt Fannie said. Look, you can see the dark side.
Julia sang Beautiful Dreamer and Sweet By and By. We joined in on Good
Night Ladies and I do not remember when I went to sleep or who carried
me off to bed.

But now you are all most here. At the top of the steps you turn left and
enter the sisters room where I sleep with little Junius for company. Now you
must go into the long closet which is big enough for old trunks and dress
forms and even a chest of drawers. At the very back is a long row of hooks
for hanging dresses. If you push the green dress with the black ribbon trim
aside, you will find another door, that little low door which you must push
HARD and then WELCOME to my cubbyhole!

Ever since I found it three years ago I have been bringing things up here,
this is why it is furnished so nicely, and all by me! I found this little red chair

with the painted flowers on it by the side of the road, I imagine it had fell off of somebodys wagon. I carried it up here with my heart in my throat but no one said one thing about it. I call it my fairy tale chair. I stole the blue velvet cushion from Mama Marie, she has been looking for it ever since, and blaming her servant. I made my table from a plank and two ammunition boxes stood on end. This little white chair belonged to my little brother Willie.

Nora Gwyn gave me these pastel crayons, and Fannie the milk glass vase. These Aurora roses are from her garden all overgrown. She used to say, <u>There is nothing like flowers to dress up a house</u> and <u>Flowers soothe the soul.</u> So all together this is an elegant spot dont you think? As you see I have enough light coming through the cracks in the wall to read and write by, and here are my fairy lights that I use when its too dark to see, sweet gum balls that I float in lard in two of Fannies finger bowls, she thought the negros took them too but it was me. Here, see this really big chink next to the chimney, it is like a window giving out onto the back yard, so I can see everything that goes on out there. Everything! But nobody can see me.

And now look, there is Washington getting wood from the woodpile for Liddys kitchen while Liddy sits out on that bench Virgil made and snaps beans in the pan on her lap. Away over there is teenytiny Daddy Rex propped up in the door of his cabin like a little old doll, his white hair stands out all around his face like a dandylion gone to seed. Whose papa is he? I asked Old Bess once and she burst out laughing and said, Law child, he is nobodys daddy in particular that we know of, it is just his name. Liddy sings, <u>Going down in the water O Lord,</u> as she snaps the beans. I can just barely hear her.

But I can hear everything that happens in the parlor just fine, for sound travels right up here along the chimney space. I can hear them all calling me now.

Molly! It is Uncle Junius deep voice. Molly where are you?

Molly dear, Nora Gwyn calls, we have to leave, please come and tell us good bye. Where in the world do you imagine she has got to? she asks Uncle Junius, who says he does not know.

But I can tell you one thing, he says clear as a bell, he must be standing right by the mantel, she has gotten wild as a March hare since Fannie died, I swear I dont know what is to become of her.

She is not a pleasant child, Mister Gwyn says.

Oh I heard him perfectly.

Now dear that is not true at all, my lovely Nora says, but you must always remember that she has been through a great deal. In fact I have been thinking just this afternoon that perhaps we could send for her once we get settled in Tennessee, and she could come to stay with us for a time, Junius, and get a proper education, what do you think?

Oh yes! It is all I can do not to cry out. Oh yes! as I would love that. But then in the next moment my heart is pounding and I am terrified and thinking, No, No, No. I know I can not go. For I am the only one left in the world who remembers these ghosts, who thinks of them now, and if I go then they will be gone too. For ever and utterly gone, as Mamma used to say about Perdido. So I can not do it.

I can not leave them now.

But Mister Gwyn will not permit it anyhow. He says, Why this is completely out of the question Nora. You will have an entire school to run.

Ah but that is a woman for you, isnt it Robert? Uncle Junius says. The source of every good and generous and civilizing influence, we should be living in caves in the darkness without them. It is a lovely idea Nora, he says, but you must not fret about Molly. Molly and Junius both will be well taken care of I assure you.

But your health Junius, she says.

Nora I implore you! Mister Gwyn says.

Forgive me if I speak too bluntly, Nora goes on. I can imagine how she puts her lips together just so. She says, It is obvious that you can not possibly take care of Molly and little Junius and Spencer and this entire house hold, Junius, even with Liddy and the rest, it is just too much. Why no man could do it. You need someone to take care of you now.

Nora! Mister Gwyn says in a mean way.

You are a kind and compassionate woman Nora, Uncle Junius says. And you Sir are a lucky man, he tells Mister Gwyn. I can just picture how that gentleman paces before the fireplace all dark in the face and glowering. I know that Uncle Junius stands leaning over the back of the blue wing chair or against the mantel, a huge figure of a man whose frock coat hangs on him now as on a scarecrow. His breathing fills any room. Selena Vogell has been a great help to me, he says.

Well of course, but, Nora Gwyn says.

I can not say a thing.

However, I do have a bit of news which may set your mind at rest, at least for the time being. Uncle Junius stops to breathe.

I can not think what this news could possibly be.

Yesterdays post brought a letter from my sister Cecelia—

The one in Alabama, Nora Gwyn says.

Yes, Uncle Junius says. Her husband died recently, and she is determined to come here for a visit in about a month.

Nora Gwyn claps her hands. O that will be wonderful. Perhaps she can stay on awhile.

Well we shall see about that. Sissy always had very definite ideas about everything. Uncle Junius voice has a smile in it now. He says, I suppose it will be good for Molly, in any case. Of course Sissy knew Molly's mother, Alice, as a girl back in South Carolina.

Oh really? Nora Gwyn says.

Alice and I were cousins, Uncle Junius says, and Nora Gwyn says, Oh I had forgotten that.

Uncle Junius clears his throat. Well we were more than that, he says. In fact I would have married Alice if she would have had me, but she chose Charles Petree instead. He was the more dashing specimen, I suppose.

I am surprised that Alice chose to come here, then, Nora Gwyn says.

Alice knew that she could all ways come to me, Uncle Junius said. No one ever said no to Alice, as you may recall. I knew he was smiling.

But Fannie—

Fannie was a remarkable woman, Uncle Junius said. Her wisdom and compassion knew no end. She snatched me out of the darkness that had been my habitual mode, and I followed her in all things, as a beacon. Of course she knew all about Alice. But she pitied poor Alice, and it was at her urging that we took them in, though in all ways it was the correct thing to do. I relied upon Fannie utterly. And now that she is gone, I tell you plainly, I fear I am losing my way. Here he stands breathing and after a time continues, I have had such thoughts, I can not tell you.

O Junius, Nora says.

You must turn back to God, Mister Gwyn says.

Robert, I can not, says Uncle Junius. For any God who has done what he has done is not a God I care to associate with much less worship. Nor would any God worth his salt have anything to do with the likes of me.

Pray with me now, Junius, Mister Gwyn says.

I can not. Uncle Junius sounds like the end of the world.

I shall pray for you then, Mister Gwyn says like it is all up to him.

And I—for you know that Fannie would not want to see you so disconsolate, Junius. She would not want to see you suffering so.

And now we must leave, Nora, Mister Gwyn says in the voice people use when they really mean it.

Oh but where is Molly? she says. Molly! she calls, and then she says, But you must find a way for her to attend school eventually Junius, you do know she is very bright.

What Molly needs is discipline and a firm hand, says Mister Gwyn.

No one answers that.

Nora Ive told you I will do the best I can, but as you have correctly surmised it is all I can do to keep this place going, Uncle Junius says. In fact I am like to lose it. I will tell you frankly, were it not for the cash money Alice left, I should not have paid the tax on Agate Hill these past few years.

I remembered Fannie saying, Cash is as scarce as hens teeth.

And now we are at the end, Uncle Junius says in his dark voice.

Oh but surely, Nora Gwyn says, and then they move to where I can not hear them, until Noras musical voice floats up to me like a song. Good bye, good bye, and it is so stupid, I do not mean to cry, I am a big girl and too old to cry so please excuse me, but I know I will never see her again.

Every time somebody leaves here, we never see them again.

I do appreciate all that you have done for her Nora . . .

Why it has been a pleasure Junius . . .

Their voices fade as the front door opens and now I peep out the other side to see them climb up into the carriage. Washington stands holding the horses heads. Nora waves and Mister Gwyn whips up those nice gray horses harder than he has to as they trot off down the lane.

Dust hangs in the air a long time after they are gone.

Uncle Junius watches them out of sight. He puts out a hand to steady himself on one of the urns which sit on either side of the steps, two great urns where Fannies flowers used to grow but now they are full of weeds and ivy which is taking over everything. I think Uncle Junius does not see any of this. I think perhaps he goes back in his mind to see things as they used to be, this busy house where everyone had a place including me and all things turned around Aunt Fannie like the earth and the moon and the planets turn around the sun. I know Uncle Junius is sick but it is more than that. Look how he stands on the steps with his hands hanging down by his sides in that curious way he has now, like he does not know what to do with them.

Or perhaps the circle makes him think of that scary night that happened here before we came. Mamma told it to me, as she told me everything.

It was a summer evening and the house at Agate Hill was jam packed full of visitors as always, little children already asleep on a pallet upstairs while the others were finishing supper such as it was, Mamma always said when she told this story. For of course there was never enough to eat in those days but that night as there was company it was hopping john which Mamma herself always scorned as negro food. At the table there was Aunt Fannie and a big bunch of Ravenels from Charleston who were passing through and a funny little Quaker schoolteacher Elizabeth Lott who stayed for a while, Uncle Junius thought highly of Quakers, and the big girls,

Rachel and Julia, and Mamma Marie and Aunt Mitty who had come in from the country to see the Ravenels. Mamma Marie and Aunt Mitty never come in from the country now, we have to go out there to see them which I love to do. Uncle Junius was not present that evening having gone to Raleigh to the Legislature, or maybe to court, he was very important then. There was even dessert, a Confederate cake as Aunt Fannie called it because they had to use sorghum instead of sugar.

The big girls were excused to run outside while the grown ups lingered on to talk of the War and those that were dead and gone. The Ravenels told a terrible story of a widow smothered to death in her sleep by her slaves who left wearing her clothes and taking all her valuables.

But what else can we expect? asked Miss Olivia Ravenel the tall thin maiden aunt with frizzy black hair and a head shaped like an egg, according to Mamma.

But Miss Lott said, I beg to differ Olivia, there are criminals and killers among all people of every race, why look at what our very own home guard did to that boy who would not tell where his father was hid . . . Miss Lott was very insistent in manner, and without Uncle Junius there to guide it, the conversation would surely have taken a turn for the worse, but just then Julia and Rachel came running in from the piazza crying, Mamma! Mamma! Come quick!

Why who could it possibly be, at this time of night? Aunt Fannie wondered, but jumped up and ran out with the rest onto the piazza and into the warm windy night, a night in the dark of the moon. Olivia Ravenel said she felt funny out there immediately and did not like it. The wind jerked at her skirts and pulled at her hair, threatening to pull it loose from her ivory combs.

I am going back inside, she said but Fannie said, O stay Olivia, the air is good for you, you ate scarcely any supper, now this will brace you up. Here, take my shawl and stay just a moment longer.

So Miss Ravenel agreed.

I dont hear a thing silly girls, Aunt Mitty said. She is bossy and very severe.

We heard it, we heard it! Be quiet, the girls implored, for truly it is possible to hear someone coming from a long way off due to a <u>trick of geography</u>, as Uncle Junius has always said.

Hush then, Fannie said, and for a moment all was still save for the rushing wind.

Why I do believe I hear something, old Mister Ravenel said.

But just then a brand new wind, a cold wind, came blowing onto the piazza from a different direction altogether with such force as to knock the candle out leaving all of them there in the rushing darkness.

This is when they heard it, in the dark.

Oh listen, Olivia Ravenel cried.

What? Fannie said.

There! Miss Ravenel cried. Dont you hear it?

What is it Olivia? Aunt Mitty asked sharply. <u>What</u> do you hear?

Oh Lord please let it be my boys, Fannie begged, for of course they were still in the War. Lewis! Spencer! She called into the wind, and now all could hear the pounding of a horses hoofs in the dark at the bottom of the yard coming up the lane and getting louder and louder as the horse drew near.

Who is it? Ho there, Mister Ravenel called out.

Stop! cried Fannie.

Who is there? Mister Ravenel called again.

But no answer came.

The sound of the hoofs was deafening in front of the house. The wind blew Aunt Fannies shawl right off Miss Ravenels shoulders and off the piazza and into the Dutch iris bed. Mama had to hold her skirt down.

<u>Boys!</u> Fannie screamed and tried to run toward the sound. The Ravenels and Miss Lott held her back. <u>Please,</u> Fannie wept but by then the hoofbeats were going away, getting fainter and fainter down the lane until they were heard no more. The wind died down.

But though they all went inside and lit the lamps, Fannie could not stop crying. This was not like her at all of course. Something awful has happened, she said again and again, for she <u>knew</u> it. She could not be persuaded to the contrary though everybody said it was only someones horse that had gotten loose, just a runaway horse, probably it was a traveler staying the night out here in the country some place, and the horse was lost.

No. Fannie went over to stand right in front of Aunt Mitty and bent over so she could look into her eyes. You know that is not true Mitt. It is a sign of death, isnt it? Fannie said this just came to her.

Then all the ladies started crying and bunching together and Mister Ravenel had to pat them. Julia and Rachel clung to each other on the horsehair sofa and wailed as one.

Fools, Aunt Mitty said. This is all nonsense. You are over tired Fannie Hall, now see what you have done. Go to bed, all of you.

Pray for them, Fannie tried to say, but suddenly she was too tired to speak and did as she was told, putting the girls to bed first.

The letter came a week later, saying that Lewis Polk Hall had exhibited great valor but died crossing the open fields to the stone wall on Cemetery Ridge at Gettysburg July 3, 1863. Aunt Fannie read the letter and fainted dead away.

And this is my mammas story of the ghost horse that came in a storm on the very night of Lewis Polks death to tell us.

So how can Uncle Junius not remember this as he stands on the piazza steps to tell the Gwyns good bye? He stands there a good long while shading his eyes from the sun. Then he walks back across the piazza and into the house and shuts the door behind him and calls me one more time. Molly!

Then he calls, Selena!

Then I can hear his slow hollow tread through the passage and out the back door and now I can see him from my cubbyhole window, see the top of his white head and then his back as he passes the brick kitchen and pauses to take off his dark jacket and put it over his arm. He stands there to breathe for a while. Then slowly he crosses the yard and passes the well and walks down past the garden and the cabins to the tenant house.

I have never seen Uncle Junius do this before. I have never seen him walk over there.

It takes him the longest time to get across the yard for he breathes so bad now, and walking hurts him. He drags his leg as well. Why Uncle Junius has suddenly got to be an old, old man! I realize as I watch him. This scares me. In fact he looks like a man in a white shirt in a painting of a man in a white shirt walking across a green yard in the hot still part of the day, he has to stop from time to time to rest, it takes him forever to get there. And there is no one else in this picture at all no one present to help him, not Old Bess nor Virgil nor Liddy nor Rom, just nary a soul, as Virgil would say.

All of a sudden I realize that I am not in this picture either.

I am no where, a ghost girl.

Uncle Junius goes to stand at the gate of the low picket fence surrounding the tenant house. He puts his hand on the latch and then they must see him for the door of the house opens up like Aunt Mittys coo coo clock from Germany and out they all come tumbling, tough little Godfrey mean as a snake and her two girls Victoria and Blanche, dont you think these are fancy names for the tenant farmers children? as Rachel pointed out.

But Selena has got notions, in fact she is full to bursting with them.

Selena is the tenant farmers wife.

Now that would be Mister Vogell of German descent, but where is he? Up and vanished into thin air one hot day last summer while Selena and the rest of us were picking peaches and cutting them up and drying them out on the scaffold in the sun. Selena told Aunt Fannie that Mister Vogell went to the field and never came home, and has never been heard from since. He did not show a sign of leaving before he went, according to Selena. It is hard to imagine Mister Vogell doing a thing so out of the ordinary, for he was a thick glum man like a side of beef who never said anything at all. He had an extra big head like a melon with a straight shock of yellow hair that fell into his eyes and gave him a stupid appearance, like a window with the shade pulled down. He wore his pants hiked way up high to show his fat white ankles. He was considerable older than Selena.

I just can not see why she ever married him, why she is an attractive woman, Fannie used to say, and Uncle Junius said, Now Fannie, we will never know what kind of a situation she came from, nor what has happened to her along the way. And it is true that those two daughters look very different from Mister Vogell, being dark and curly headed like gypsy girls. Selena herself is dark complected and dark haired, a tall woman strong as an ox. She can work all day long in the field then split wood like a man, many is the time I have looked out my cubbyhole window here to see Selena out by the wood pile with her skirt hitched up and the ax upraised, and the ringing of the ax lasts all morning long. She is a good worker, and with those children, it is clear that Uncle Junius could never kick her out. It would not be in his nature. So Selena is still in the tenant house.

But little by little since Aunt Fannie died, Selena has been worming her way into this house too. Now Uncle Junius has took to calling her the housekeeper though Liddy will not do hardly a thing Selena says and Old Bess pays her no mind at all.

I look out my cubbyhole window.

There stands Uncle Junius at the gate to the tenant house. There stands Uncle Junius bareheaded in the sun with his jacket folded over his arm. It is like he is under a spell. He stands there until Selena herself comes busting out of the open door with her black hair just washed and hanging down almost to her waist in waves like some animals shiny coat. She is bare foot wearing a loose white blouse and a red skirt, she has got a big smile on her big red mouth and her black eyes flash in the sun like the fools gold I keep in my pocket. Uncle Junius says something and Selena says something and throws back her head and laughs. Her hair falls all down her back. Then she opens the gate and goes to Uncle Junius and wraps her arms around him like a vine.

Like poison ivy, is what I think.

All I can see of Uncle Junius is the back of his head but Selena lifts her head all of a sudden and stares straight up at this chimney. I know she can not see me really but it is like she is staring right at me. And then she smiles. She knows she can do anything, or have anything she wants. They stand like this in the hot sun awhile and then keeping one arm around his waist Selena walks Uncle Junius into the tenant house through the open door. Her girls head off down toward the creek dragging Godfrey who fights them all the way. They disappear from view. Now the yard is quiet once more with no one present except for Virgils old dog that dreams a running dream in the sun and Daddy Rex who sits outside his cabin but never saw a thing since he is blind. And as for me my heart is beating very hard in my chest and I feel like I can not breathe. I know for sure that everything will be diffrent from now on.

❧

June 5, 1872

Dear Diary,

Oh now we are having a time for Selena the housekeeper is bossing us all around, we must clean up the house to a fare thee well for the grand arrival of Uncle Junius sister Cecelia, or Sissy as he calls her. Aunt Cecelia to you, Selena says to me. Her daughters Victoria and Blanche will call her Mrs. Worthington. And now they are here too, in the house, helping to clean though they are lazy. Victoria is a big mean strapping girl like her mother, thirteen years old, but Blanche age eight is skinny with flyaway hair and knobby knees and elbows and a big grin. I like her better. They keep stopping to look at things, they touch everything. Old Bess does not like it. In any case Liddy must now boil out all the bed linens, and yesterday Washington and Spence had to carry all the bed ticks and pallets out to the yard where they beat them with sticks and allowed them to air in the sun while Selena and the rest of us scoured the bedrooms scrubbing the heart pine floors and rubbing the beds and dressers and chests with tallow to give a shine. Spence carried a whole mattress on his head with one hand. Selena was like a whirl-wind with her elbows flying. Then she pulled up her skirt and got down on her hands and knees to thrust the broom under the bedsteads and sweep up piles of dust and God knows what all. Her rump stuck way up in the air but she did not care. We were in the girls bedroom.

Just look at them dust devils, she said, for some of the piles of dust and hair held together like little tornados.

Ooh, ooh, screamed her girls, dead mouse, dead mouse. They danced all around the dust devils pointing.

Selena rocked back on her heels and wiped the sweat off her face with a rag she pulled out of her bosom. She stuck out her bottom lip and blew her black hair up out of her eyes. Lord God. Its a pig sty in here, Selena said, like it pleased her.

Old Bess stood in the door with her hands on her hips.

Well what are you looking at, Selena said.

Old Bess said not a word.

Selena had me sweeping out the closet making a great big cloud of dust that stuck to my face for it was hot in there. Horses sweat, men perspire, ladies glow, my mother always said, but that was back before ladies worked.

Selena got back down under the bed to take another swipe with her broom.

Victoria pushed me aside as she ran into the closet and started pulling out drawers in the bureau. Oh look oh looky here, she said holding up a long white ruffled petticoat.

That was my mothers, I said. It goes over a hoop skirt.

Well wheres the hoop then? Victoria said, and I said, Over there, and showed her where the hoops were leaning up against the closet wall. The cloth strips that held them together had gone for bandages. Victoria threw the petticoat down and pulled out a silk camisole and held it up to herself. It had lace around the neckline. Why look it is just my size, she said, though Mamma had been real little and dainty. There in the hot dusty gloom with the camisole glowing white and Victorias dark messy curls all down in her face I suddenly saw how pretty she will be one day.

I hate Victoria.

Take it then, I said, and pushed her real hard so she scrambled backward and fell in the corner with the camisole clutched to her chest.

Girls, girls what is going on in there? Selena called.

Nothing, I said.

Molly pushed me. Victoria set up a big fake wail like I was killing her.

Molly what is going on in there? Selena asked from the door.

She is just telling a stupid lie, I said.

Well get up from there now Victoria, Selena said, but Victoria lay on her back like a junebug and bawled like she was dying, and all could see her drawers.

I said get up. Selena went over and yanked at her shoulder.

That hurt, Mama, she cried harder.

Come on now we have got a lot of work to do, Selena said. Instead Victoria scrambled up to her feet and ran out the door past both of us and straight into Bess who said, You stop right there Miss and snatched at the camisole.

But Victoria held on to it for dear life.

You are not going to have that now Miss, it belong to Alice Heart. It belong to Miss Molly now, Bess said.

I dont want it, I said.

Let go now child, Old Bess said. But she is getting little now, she has got a misery in her back too.

Oh just give it to her Victoria, for Gods sake, Selena said.

I dont want it, I said again.

Miss Fannie done save these things for you by the hardest, Bess said, and I knew this was true, for almost everything else in this house has been torn up and made into clothes even the curtains, and then patched and patched again.

I dont care, I said.

Old Bess turned to look at me hard, and in that instant Victoria gave a big tug and the camisole tore right down the middle and she stumbled back against a bed. She clutched the shiny cloth to her chest and cried harder than ever. Bess smoothed the other piece of the camisole over her arm, over and over, looking at me from the doorway.

<u>What?</u> I said. I hated them all.

Selena stood still in the middle of the girls bedroom with her hands on her hips and her face on fire. Her black eyes darted everywhere. Her bosom went up and down. She seemed to get bigger and bigger while I watched, like the gods and goddesses of ancient Greece in Nora Gwyns book. I felt she would fling a thunderbolt. Blanche clung to her skirt. Go outside now girls, Selena said finally. She yanked Victoria up off the floor but before you could say spit, Victoria ran back in the closet and came out with one of the hoops. Ooh! I want one, Blanche said and ran in for another.

Molly? Selena looked at me.

I dont care, I said

Go on out then girls, you go too Molly, Selena said.

You are not the boss of me, I said. I did not bat an eye.

The girls ran whooping down the stairs.

Selena looked at me and nodded slightly, just once. Then she pushed back her hair and grabbed her broom. Bess, lets get this done, she yelled from under another bed. You go on down and get them to bring me some more water up here. I want it hot too. Go on now, Selena said, and then, <u>Bess?</u>

The doorway frame stood empty.

Bess was gone, and she has not come back yet to help with the big cleaning.

But Selena proceeded like a house afire.

I watched her daughters roll those hoops in the yard until I could not stand it any more. Finally I got one for myself and ran out in the yard with it. Like this, Molly! Like this, Victoria said, rolling her hoop toward me, while mine wobbled and fell over. But soon I got the hang of it, and before long I was better at it than they were.

<u>Look,</u> I called to Old Bess who came walking back from the garden with a mess of greens in her basket, but Bess did not speak. She set her face against me, and went into Liddys kitchen without a word.

June 8, 1872

Dear Diary,

Washington and me got to beat out the parlor carpet with sticks, it was a lot of fun. This was Fannies favorite, blue with a gold fleur-de-lee. Dust flew everywhere. You like that dont you Molly? Selena said as we whacked away and this was true but I would not give her the satisfaction of saying it.

What? I pretended I could not hear.

June 14, 1872

Real Hot

Dear Diary,

Today when we got done housecleaning Selena rared back and said, Well you all have done a good job. Now why dont you go down to the river and cool off some. So Washington and me took little Junius and Victoria and Blanche and Godfrey fishing. Spence came too.

I have not yet written of Spence, though I see him nearly every day and wonder, <u>What will happen to him?</u> What can I say about Spence. He is still young, not yet thirty-five but looks younger still for his face is as blank and fair as the moon. He is a great big man, almost as big as Uncle Junius but not thin, for he will eat anything and he will eat until you take the plate away. In fact once you get Spence to doing anything, he will do it until you get him to stop, and sometimes this is not easy. This is why he was so good at war. And this is also why he is such a good fieldworker and why Romulus is the best sharecropper around here with Spence helping him. Spence loves Rom, they were raised together. Spence loved his older brother Lewis too beyond all measure, they went to the war together and did all things as one until Lewis was killed as they ran across that rocky field to the stone wall together, Spence made it and fought on until Petersburg where he was a hero then presumed dead until some men that knew Uncle Junius found him wandering in the countryside near Raleigh in a confused state of mind and brought him back here to Agate Hill where all had mourned and had already got over mourning his death. Yet here he came smooth-faced as a stone, and like a stone he has not hardly spoken since, though as Aunt Fannie always said, His face is benevolent, like the sun. And Spence loves to fish, he has fished in the Haw ever since he was a little boy.

So here we set off walking down the dusty road under the bright blue sky with Washington in front and Godfrey running circles all around him, then Victoria and Blanche then me holding little Junius hand, then Spence behind us all, like a tree walking. He carried the cane poles over his shoulder.

It felt like a parade.

Then we went off the road on a little path and climbed down the weedy hill with Blanche and Victoria whining. We went through joe pie weed bigger than us and blackberry bushes that scratched at our legs. The berries were not ripe yet. Watch out for snakes now, Washington said, and the girls screamed. Little Junius held tight to my hand. Finally we reached the shady, grassy bank of the river where all of a sudden it was a lot cooler.

Spread out some now, Washington said.

One by one Spence put worms on the girls hooks and then on Godfreys hook while Washington and me did our own. Ooh ooh. Godfrey yelled and hopped on one foot when his worm bled.

Hush now, Washington said. You will scare the fish.

Fish aint got ears, Godfrey said.

Sure they do, Washington said. Everybody knows that. They just real little ears. Aint that right Molly.

Yes, I said.

Not, Godfrey said.

Shut up Godfrey, Victoria said.

Little Junius did not want to fish so we sat down on a mossy log where our feet could hang in the water and I trailed my line from there, watching the sun and shade and the little fish playing in the shallows beside us. It was a real nice day. The willows made a curtain where we were. Washington caught two fish, little ones, and put them in the bucket. Victoria got a bite but lost it, and Blanche lost her worm. Godfrey put worms on everybodys hooks because he liked to see them bleed. He is built like a bullet with blond hair like Mister Vogell his daddy. The breeze ruffled the willows like curtains at a window. I saw a shiny snake on a rock in the water near the opposite bank but before I could say a thing, it was gone as suddenly as if it had never been there. Finally Junius let go of my hand and sat down in the water to play. Blanche and Victoria each caught a fish and Blanche fell in the water and then Victoria and me got in too, just splashing. We got to building a dam. Washington went up a ways and caught another fish.

Why where is Spence? I asked all of a sudden, looking around. For he was gone.

Just you wait. Washington grinned at me.

And sure enough after a while we heard a lot of splashing and here came Spence walking around the bend hip deep in the middle of the river carrying a great big fish in his arms and grinning to beat the band.

Did he get that on this line? I asked Washington, for our hooks were little, made out of pins we had best not lose.

No, he been hand grabbing, Washington said. Thats how he always fish.

But what is it, I asked.

That is when you reach way down under a rock or a old log or a stump and grab the fish right up out of the water, Washington told me. A big old dead stump is the best. They like to hide down in there, they get real old and fat. Its like they house in there.

Spence waded over and laid his fish on the mossy bank so we could all get close and look at it. It was a huge slimy old catfish bigger than a baby with its head all bloody and smashed in though I could still see its whiskers. Its eyes were wide open.

Ooh ooh. What happened to its head? Godfrey screamed.

Well, he have to kill it some way or nother, Washington said. I reckon he kilt it with a rock, aint that right, Spence?

But Spence just grinned. He had blood on his shirt and his pants.

It was the King of the Catfish.

We all gathered round to admire it for a while.

Liddys going to want to cook this fish, I said.

But nobody moved. Nobody wanted to leave the river.

Then, Oh Lord, Mama is going to kill us, we have got to wash off some, Victoria said all of a sudden and we all set to splashing again and washing off in the river as good as we could except for Washington who had never got into the river at all.

Our pail held seven brim. We took turns carrying it, and after a while it wasn't too heavy since most of the water splashed out on the road. Spence carried little Junius who was too tired to walk, while Washington carried the fish, walking in front of us.

Lord God! Liddy said when she saw us coming. She stood in the doorway, shading her eyes with her hand.

⁂

June 18, 1872

Dear Diary,

Yesterday I left this cubbyhole in the late afternoon during a thunderstorm. I paused at the closet door to get my bearings. The girls bedroom was dark with rain beating hard as bullets on the roof.

But there in the gloom I spied Selena standing in front of the mirror, holding that white ruffled petticoat of Mammas up to her waist. While I watched she took a little step backward and bowed her head, like a curtsy. When the lightning flashed I could see her face which looked heartbroken to my surprise, sad and not mean for once though I know she is mean, she whipped Blanche and Victoria for going in the river, and would of whipped me too if she thought she could get away with it.

I hid in the closet until she left.

June 21, 1872

Dear Diary,

At last the day of Aunt Cecelias arrival has come. Virgil took the wagon out before dawn, headed to Hillsborough, he was gone when I got up. But oh what a hustle and bustle was still going on, for now all must be perfect. Uncle Junius hates an uproar. He had disappeared into the middle room where he hides from all, door closed. It was a foggy dewy morning with all the birds tuned up as I stepped out of Liddys kitchen, heading off to find Washington. But Selena grabbed me by the back of the skirt.

Not so fast there Miss, she said. I need you to go back in the house and help Victoria. Here, take this. She handed me a cloth and an Irish potato cut in half. I knew what that meant. Go on, she said giving me a boost in the direction of the house, away from my beloved woods which were calling out to me. The dewy wet grass tickled between my toes. But it was not the day to make a fuss so I went on into the passage and back to the dining room which is used almost never now since Fannie died.

This morning it was dim and gloomy as the light ventured but feebly in through the dark leaded panes to show the drop leaf table by the door and the huge old sideboard looming as big as a boat, filled with china and God knows what all, all the things ladies have which I will NEVER have, I swear it, and so much the better. For if you have things, why then you have to take care of them, I have noticed this all ready. On top of the sideboard stand the china statues of a lady and a gentleman plus the cranberry glass vase, some cut glass decanters, and the silver filigree cake basket which was buried in the garden when the Yankees came. The table itself is a huge dark mahogany thing that pulls out and out to accommodate a crowd. Victoria prissed around it placing the linen mats and the silver.

I hate Victoria. She is like some accident that has happened to me. I cant believe I have to see her all the time.

Those mats need ironing, I said, which was true. Aunt Fannie would have had a fit.

What do I care? she said. I aint going to eat here. Mama said for you to clean these—and she threw the ivory-handled table knives out on the table with a clanging noise.

I know, Miss Smartypants. I said this part under my breath. I pulled up a chair and spread out my cloth and rubbed the steel blades one by one with brick dust and the cut side of the Irish potato until they shone. Victoria grabbed them up so fast she nicked my hand with one of the blades. At first I didnt understand what had happened, it felt like a pin prick. But then I looked down to see the blood blooming like a flower from my thumb. Then it hurt. Without thinking I stood and flung the brick bat straight at her, it hit her shoulder and struck the floor.

Immediately I was seized from behind by Selena who shook me until my teeth rattled in my head and I could not see for crying.

I am such a baby.

There now Miss, she said, finally letting me go but I was too wobbly-legged to stand, sinking down to the floor while the two of them finished setting the table. I did not want to look at their hateful faces so I did not move. I rubbed my cheek back and forth on the bristly fleur-de-lee carpet until it hurt and somehow that helped me. I remembered beating that carpet out in the yard with Washington only a week before, in the sunshine, it seemed like ages ago.

Come on now Molly, we are done, Selena said, but I said nothing and stayed where I was. As you wish then, she said, and then she was gone, Victoria with her.

Suddenly I noticed the table foot right in front of me, a huge mahogany claw that had seized a mahogany ball. Its talons were big and sharp. They scared me oh I am such a baby. I stood up fast. In the little slit of the curtains I noted that the sun had broke through outside. I was dying to get out there. But first I looked back down at the table, thinking, It is like this house, it looks so fancy and fine but it is all ugly underneath, it is that mean cruel claw.

Then I had to start laughing for I noticed that Selena and Victoria had not even set the table right, they had put the water goblets on the wrong side. This is how much they know about ladies and good manners!

I ran outside to find Washington.

I didnt see any of them again until they rang the bell which meant, <u>She is coming.</u> Like the rest I ran to the front of the house and stood out on the piazza shading my eyes to catch the first glimpse of the wagon. All I could see was a dust cloud rising like the plume of a hat way down in the hazy hills. While I waited, here came Liddy pulling Little Junius along by the hand. She had cleaned him up for the grand arrival, with wet clean hair and a clean white shirt.

Selena and her girls stood all in a row, shading their eyes with their hands. Selena looked so different that I might not have known her if I had seen her in the street. She wore a gray O-bodice dress which had belonged to Aunt Fannie, with a white lace collar and black jet buttons running straight up the front. All that wild black hair had been pulled straight back and bound up in a big bun at the nape of her neck, exactly like a schoolteacher. She gnawed at the inside of her cheek, a habit she had, staring straight ahead. Victoria and Blanche wore shoes.

Liddy wore a white cap, and Old Bess wore her apron.

<u>Why, it is like the Queen is coming!</u> I thought. My Mother Goose book sprang to mind.

Even Uncle Junius troubled himself to come out on the piazza, wearing a jacket in spite of the heat. He did not join us but stood well back, smoking a cigarette cupped in his hand, shaking his head from time to time as if he carried on some pressing conversation in his mind.

The plume of dust came closer, trailing out like a horses tail, and we could see that it was not one but two wagons coming.

Had to hire anothern in town, Selena said to nobody.

The wagons came up the lane past the old sawmill and then were lost to view in the cedar grove, popping out directly so we could all see that it was Mister Potter from the livery stable in town driving the second wagon, wearing the stovepipe hat that was his trademark. Old Virgil clicked to the mules but made no sign as the big lady on the seat next to him waved grandly. Her face was hid by her hat and the traveling veil which wrapped all around her somehow, as if she was a great package being delivered to us. Whoa now. The wagons stopped in front of the house, the air was filled with dust. Washington ran out to grab the reins.

Then Uncle Junius was there too, his hand held out, saying, Cecelia welcome. She stepped down with the greatest of difficulty, Virgil holding her by the arm on one side and Uncle Junius on the other, her middle so big she could not hardly see over it to the steps or her feet—that was the problem. She grunted like a pig upon landing, then wheezed Aah! and put a hand to her heart. Liddy rushed forward and started unwinding the veil, running round and round Aunt Cecelia like a maypole until I got dizzy watching. First we saw the great wide waist, then the bosom like a huge shelf, then her puffy red face with its big red mouth, the arched eyebrows, the eyes bugging out, and the many chins that rippled like a waterfall disappearing into the wad of lace at her neck. She removed the hat from her piled up red hair and handed it over to Liddy along with the veil. Aunt Cecelias hands were little and fluttery, like the hands of another woman. They came up to pat here and there at her face and breast.

There now, she said to herself finally, then My dear Junius in a grand public voice, offering her cheek to be kissed. You look terrible. And My God, what a journey! What a journey I have had! Aunt Cecelia shook all over with distaste, so that the journey seemed to roll off her like water off a duck. But never mind! She went on, My comfort is not a consideration. The important thing is that I am here now, you poor, poor thing. Aunt Cecelia patted Uncle Junius arm then looked all about herself—at the unpainted house, at the outbuildings, at us all lined up for her inspection.

Behind her, Virgil and Spence lifted luggage and supplies down from the wagons. Selena watched them too and narrowed her eyes as trunk after trunk came down.

Rest assured, Aunt Cecelia announced, I shall take care of <u>everything</u> Junius! You may leave it all up to me!

Uncle Junius appeared embarrassed yet still supported her arm.

As for Selena, she looked like she could spit nails, and for once I did not blame her, the way we had all been working like dogs to get the house ready.

Then Aunt Cecelias roaming bug-eyed gaze settled hard on me. Molly! My dear, dear Molly, why you poor, poor little thing! She swooped me up and pressed me to her bosom which was like the horsehair sofa in the parlor, not soft like Aunt Fannies had been. Then she thrust me out at arms length. Well, she is certainly plainer than Alice, I must say, but that may be a good thing in the end. Too much beauty corrupts the character, dont you agree? she said to Uncle Junius who studied the ground.

Close up, I could see how the pink gums above her large teeth were exposed, while spittle formed in the corners of her mouth, to be sprayed when she spoke. I turned my head and wiggled to get free.

Aha! Not so fast, Aunt Cecelia said before setting me down. Let us make our manners first. I am happy to meet you, Molly.

I stood in the sun saying nothing.

Cat got your tongue? Aunt Cecelia advanced on me like an ironclad.

Now Molly, Uncle Junius said.

Nevermind, Junius. I see I shall have my work cut out for me, thats all, Aunt Cecelia said. But I like a challenge. Now where is young Junius? who was dragged forward crying by Liddy in order to make his manners which he would not do either. <u>My my,</u> Aunt Cecelia said. <u>What a pile of savages you are raising here Junius.</u>

Then Selena who could stand it no longer came forward to curtsy like a lady of the court. Well I for one am happy to welcome you here to Agate Hill, she said. Let me introduce my daughters Victoria and Blanche who bobbed forward to curtsy too.

Uncle Junius hid a smile.

But Aunt Cecelia arched her eyebrows. And who might you be? she asked, taking a long look.

Selena Vogell, Selena said.

Selena is the housekeeper, Uncle Junius said.

Aunt Cecelia stood looking from one of them to the other. <u>I see,</u> she said finally. She pressed her lips together, then shook her head slightly as if to clear it. Well, let me get inside before I have a heat stroke! I have a very delicate constitution, you know . . . She set off for the open door where Old Bess now stood.

Mary White! she called suddenly, turning back to the wagons. Mary White, come along now, this is ridiculous, you are trying my patience to a fare thee well—

And suddenly a little girl popped up like a puppet behind the drivers box! She was giggling and waving her hat with an arm that was thin as a stick. Surprise! She called. Virgil lifted her out of the wagon and set her down next to me.

<u>Oh dear. Peas in a pod.</u> Aunt Cecelia stood grimly looking at us. <u>Molly meet Mary White. Mary White this is Molly.</u>

But Cecelia, who is this? Uncle Junius asked.

Aunt Cecelia gave her pig snort. Why it is my granddaughter Junius, daughter of my daughter Susannah, of whom the less said the better!

Uncle Junius took Aunt Cecelias arm and drew her into the house. Selena rushed ahead while everyone else scurried about except for Mary White and me. We stood in the hot sun and looked at each other. All dressed up for the journey, Mary White wore a green plaid taffeta dress with a white lace collar and a green sash that tied in a lopsided bow straggling down. Lace pantalettes peeped out from under the hem of her skirt. She wore white stockings and black shoes like a princess in a fairy tale book.

I have never seen a little girl got up so. And she is pale as a princess too, not tan from the sun like me. In fact Mary White is so pale that I can see through her skin to the blue veins at her temples and her neck. I can watch them throbbing. She is very thin also, I can see her bones. It is like she is inside out—an inside-out girl! Her hair is frizzy as can be, escaping its center part and pigtails to stand out around her head like the light around angels heads in paintings.

Mary White! Aunt Cecelia called from the door. Come in this house this minute!

Why? I said.

I'm sick, Mary White said to me. I have to go lie down, I reckon.

Sick? I said. She looked fine to me.

They say I am living on borrowed time. I could go any minute. She snapped her fingers. Just like that.

An awful thrill shot through me.

But I dont care, Mary White said. I dont give a damn. I'm tired of it. Looky here, and while I watched, she rolled her eyes all the way back in her head until the blue was gone and naught but the white part remained.

I know we will be best friends.

❧

July 22, 1872

So the reason I have not written for so long Dear Diary is that now I am a real girl with a real friend who sits in the little white chair up here in my cubbyhole and does every thing with me unless she is sick, such as today she can scarcely breathe so must lie in the dark in Aunt Cecelias room with shades pulled and shutters drawn and the hissing spirit lamp in the corner. The camphor smell is so strong it fills up my head and flies into my bones whenever I sneak in there which I am not supposed to do. I am supposed to let Mary White rest. Aunt Cecelia bumbles around like a big bee driving Mary White just crazy.

Meanwhile I have been picking up interesting bones for Mary White's bone collection, now I am making one too. See? Here is a possum skull, here is a big cow leg bone, here is a turkey foot ripped off the barn wall where somebody had nailed it, I know this one is cheating.

Aunt Cecelia says Mary White will be up and about by the end of the week. I hope this is true for we have so many things to do and take care of. She has been here for over a month now, I can not believe it. The time flies along so fast. Now it is July with its hot thick yellow days. <u>Dog days,</u> Old Bess says, if you get a cut or a sore place now it will never heal. But we dont care, we slip off to the river where we have a Willow House right out in the running water just downstream from where Washington took us fishing that time with Spence.

It is cool and green in the Willow House. Long lacy branches fall down all around us making a screen for perfect privacy, so none can see where we sit on our three white rocks to read or eat a fancy lunch on magnolia leaf plates. Liddy lets us take whatever we want from the kitchen without a word. Time you have you some fun, girl, Liddy said to me. While we are in the Willow House, time stops still it seems, and all we can hear is the music of the river in our ears. But we are not alone for a whole big family of lizards live here too, the little ones so fast it breaks your heart to see them move like bright green streaks across the rocks. An old old granddaddy snake suns himself back on the bank then slides into the water so slow its like he is not even moving but then he is gone.

And the most exciting part—though we have not seen them yet—Mary White and I have reason to believe that a band of fairies comes here also, Mary White knows all about fairies and now I do too. They wear little green jackets and red caps with an owl feather sticking up at a jaunty angle. They come to ride the frogs and hunt the skittery waterbugs that play back there in the shallows. They live on fried waterbugs and flower pudding, Mary White says. One day we surprised these fairies and almost saw them—but they flew away fast on their gossamer wings leaving only a rainbow shimmer in the air and an owl feather floating in the little pool by the littlest rock where it went round and round in a magic way for as long as we watched, until Mary White plucked it up from the water to put in our collection of phenomena. Mary White says the fairies are coming back soon, she can feel it. She says we must go to the river in the light of the moon if we really mean to see them. So we are planning to do this on the next full moon, I can not wait.

Another thing we play is dolls, though my china doll Margaret is very old, having belonged first to Julia and Rachel when they were girls. Her painted hair was all gone on one side but now Mary White and I have made her some more with bootblack, so she looks fine, and her blue silk ballgown is especially elegant. Underneath she wears a chemise, a petticoat, and pantalettes, feather-stitched and herringboned, made by Julia. Mary White can not get over Margarets pantalettes!

And in truth I like Margaret old as she is far better than Mary Whites wax doll Fleur which is much larger, able to open and shut her eyes and say Mama and Papa quite plainly. But Fleur is too much of a baby doll for me. I like a doll who is old enough for romances and flirtations.

And guess what?

Margaret has had many romances and several marriages already because now Mary White and me have got a man doll too. I have never seen one before. He is not a store doll nor a rag doll either one but a knitted doll made by Aunt Cecelia who knits all the time, saying, <u>Idle hands are the devils workshop.</u> This man doll is the latest thing in knitting, with gray wool pants and jacket, stripes on his sleeve, and a soldiers cap on his head. As for a face, he doesnt have one. It is pure white knit, so I can imagine him any way I want. I can make him up. So sometimes he is gay and smiling while other times he is angry or scornful or curls his lip in a frown.

What is his name? I asked the day Aunt Cecelia finished him up and gave him to us.

Name? Aunt Cecelia looked at me. Why its just a doll Molly.

But he has to have a name, I said. Dolls are supposed to have names.

I know! Mary White cried out from the chair where she sat dressing Fleur. <u>What about Robert E. Lee?</u>

Now girls, I hardly think this is appropriate. Aunt Cecelia bunched all the parts of her face together. Why the General was too fine a man for such silly games as you girls make up, you must put your minds to higher things.

But Mary White and I stared at each other in perfect accord.

<u>Yes,</u> I said.

So he is still Robert E. Lee even though Aunt Cecelia made us put our dolls away that very minute and read the shorter catechism aloud followed by the Ten Commandments which we have to memorize now according to her. Hell looms wide for such frivolous girls as yourselves, she said, with spit bubbling up in the corners of her mouth, while Mary White rolled her eyes up in her head and I started coughing so as not to laugh. But just then a wagon drew up in the lane, and Aunt Cecelia went out to see who it was, so we escaped and ran out to the barn where we played for the rest of the morning.

It is easy to get away from Aunt Cecelia because she is so busy with Social Life. Other ladys are always coming to call now with their cartes de visite.

Who the hell are all these people? I'd like to know. Hell, I live here, says Uncle Junius who hates it.

But Aunt Cecelia does not care. She thinks she knows everything. I shall not let you fester away here as you have been doing Brother, she says. Nor must you lower your standards one iota. We shall make a new life in due course. Aunt Cecelia specializes in rising to the occasion and keeping up standards. This takes a lot of time so we are mostly free to do what we want if we will only stay out of her hair. This is easy. It is a big plantation, and we are all over it. No one ever knows where we are!

So Robert E. Lee has been married again and again, to Margaret and Fleur and the neighbor girls dolls when they come to visit with their mothers. He has even married Victoria and Blanches rag dolls, though they dont have fancy dresses. But Mary White insists that they should have weddings anyway, she makes up long love stories for them as well as for Margaret and Fleur. Mary White adores love stories.

She met him by the rushing stream where she was washing clothes, Mary White began one hot afternoon, walking Blanches sad little doll Sarah along the riverbank. It was so hot, and Sarah was so tired, but she was just a poor girl who had to work for her food. So Sarah was scrubbing and crying when here came a gentleman soldier, his jacket all covered with blood. He just about scared her to death! Hello my pretty Miss, he said, could I trouble you to wash the blood from my jacket? For I have been in a fearsome battle where I killed a lot of men.

Why yes Sir, Sarah said, and she did, and she bandaged up his arm too and gave him some pound cake and boiled custard for supper which he liked a great deal.

Are you married? He asked her then, and she hid her face and said, No Sir. Why then I hope you will do me the honor of becoming Mrs. Robert E. Lee, he said, and Sarah said Why yes Sir, and the wedding plans began.

I laid Sarah and Robert E. Lee down on the mossy bank while we were building the wedding bower out of sticks but Mary White said, No they can not lie down, they are not married yet! So I sat them up while we finished it and decorated it with flowers from the woods and along the riverbank. It was the prettiest thing you can ever imagine. Poor Sarah had only her calico dress but we put some of the flowers in her hair. Then Mary White began the wedding.

Is all in readiness? Robert E. Lee asked in his big voice and Sarah said, Yes Sir.

Do you Robert E. Lee take this poor, poor girl to be your lawful wedded wife, to honor and cherish till death do you part? the minister asked.

I do, said Robert E. Lee.

Do you Sarah take Robert E. Lee to be your lawful wedded husband, to honor and cherish, to love and obey until death do you part?

I do, said Sarah.

You may kiss the bride, said the minister, and Mary White put their two faces together. Then for the wedding feast we all ate some scotchbreads that Victoria and Blanche had stole from the press. I used to hate Victoria but now I dont so much since Aunt Cecelia hates her even more. Aunt Cecelia tells us repeatedly not to play with <u>those rough girls</u> as she calls Victoria and Blanche.

• • •

On Sundays we have to keep the Sabbath holy and go to whatever nearby church is holding service, and afterward we can neither play nor work, it is terrible. No games or toys allowed, not even for little Junius. We all have to rest or read tales from Aunt Cecelias special Sunday school books, awful stories about children who go out in boats on Sundays and drown.

We will go to Hell if we play dolls, I whispered to Mary White who lay in bed last Sunday with her eyes closed.

I dont care. She giggled and got right up.

I dont care either, I said as we grabbed up the dolls and ran down the stairs and into the parlor, shutting the door behind us.

It was my turn to tell the love story.

Robert E. Lee went off to War leaving Margaret with a diamond ring and a kiss, but soon he was declared dead in a fearsome battle in Virginia. Then oh how Margaret wept and flung herself face down beating her fists on the floor, oh how she mourned him. Margaret mourned Robert E. Lee for two years and then finally agreed to marry her ugly old neighbor man Mister Snow who just would not leave her alone.

We dressed Margaret up in her white wedding dress and her veil to marry Mister Snow, we stuck little rosebuds on her head. Now all was in readiness and the wedding began. Fleur was Mister Snow.

Mister Snow do you take Mary Margaret Petree to be your lawful wedded wife? the minister asked.

I sure do! Mister Snow said in his big voice.

But just then came the sound of approaching hoofbeats, I said—Mary White made a clicking hoofbeat sound with her tongue—and sure enough, here came Robert E. Lee on his gray horse Traveler to save the day, kicking Mister Snow face down on the floor so he could marry Margaret himself. He was not dead after all!

Then they were happily married for ever and ever amen. Mary White finished the story.

But I got another idea. Now lets do it again and have her marry Mister

Snow but be so unhappy crying all day long at her tasks and then Robert E. Lee will come in the night as her demon lover.

For I do not want a husband myself nor a big clawfoot chest full of silver, I want a demon lover and so does Margaret, this is her secret desire.

Mary Whites big blue eyes got bigger. Well, Robert E. Lee cant do that, Molly, she said. Either he is Robert E. Lee or he is a demon lover, one or the other, he cant be both.

Why not? I asked.

Because he just cant. Mary White shook her head so her pigtails flew all around. Robert E. Lee is a gentleman. He is supposed to marry them.

I was getting mad at Mary White who had suddenly got this expression just like Aunt Cecelia on her face.

He doesnt have to, I said. He doesnt have to marry them.

He does so! So they can have babys.

Maybe he doesnt want any babys, I said. All babys do is cry and get sick and die. Maybe Robert E. Lee hates babys.

<u>Oh!</u> Before I knew what was happening, Mary White jumped up and started kicking me hard in the side.

<u>You quit that.</u> I grabbed her legs and pulled her down on the fleur-de-lee carpet. I am a lot bigger and stronger than Mary White but she fought me as hard as she could, all pink in the face now and blubbering. Finally I grabbed her wrists and just lay down on top of her. Will you stop now? I said.

She shook her head back and forth and tried to twist out from under me, but it was not hard to hold her for she is so weak.

Now? I said.

No. Her eyes looked all red and puffy. The blue veins throbbed in her head.

Girls? Girls? Aunt Cecelia was coming down the hall.

My mother did not want a baby. She had me in sin and then went off with a Yankee, Mary White said, and she has never been heard from since.

Never?

<u>Never.</u> Now Mary White sounded like she couldnt breathe so I rolled off her. We lay side by side on our backs on the floor in that dim twilight which always fills the parlor.

Are you all right? I was worried that she might die. Then I would be a murderess.

But she said nothing.

Mary White? I said after a while.

I hate you, she said. Ignorant country girl.

I hate you too, I said.

Mary White lay silent, breathing.

Far away Aunt Cecelia was calling our names.

<u>I'm sorry.</u> I gritted my teeth and said it.

Then, finally, she said, Molly?

Yes?

What is a demon lover?

I dont know, I had to say.

But Dear Diary we are going to find out.

<u>Answer:</u> It is a lover who comes in the night to kiss you on the mouth! Mary White believes it may be an Assyrian.

July 27, 1872

Tiger Butter

We are always in trouble with Aunt Cecelia who makes us work to chasten our souls and improve our attitudes, but we dont care. We like it! Two of our jobs are claying the hearth and making lamplighters out of old letters, rolling the strips at the bottom together for a handle then curling the cut parts at the top with scissors.

We churn for Liddy out under the hackberry tree by the well, with a bunch of leaves tied to the dasher to keep off the flies, and sing at the top of our lungs:

Fee fi fo fum
I smell the blood of an Englishman
Be he alive or be he dead
I'll grind his bones to make my bread
Fee fi fo fum
Come butter come

And also:

Tiger tiger burning bright
In the forests of the night
What immortal hand or eye
Could frame thy fearful symmetry?
Come butter come
Come butter come

This is a poem from Mary Whites big book. The first time we used it, we had a fight over whether to say symmetree, which Mary White wanted, or symmetry, as in try, which rhymes, which I wanted. Finally we made Washington pick and I won. Liddy and them all get tickled when we do this one. But even Liddy has said, That tiger butter sure is good, girls, and Aunt Cecelia eats so much it is gone right away every time. Mary White and I are the Champion Butter Makers in the county!

August 5, 1872

The Yankee Hand

Several times we have walked down the road and through the woods to Mister Gaithers big field to pick the berries that grow all along the stone fence rows. Liddy makes pies and preserves with these but they are best ate right off the bush in our opinion. Washington gets to go with us then, to shoo off stray dogs and carry the basket, though usually Aunt Cecelia will not permit him to be in Mary Whites company saying, I dont care what you think Junius, he is a <u>servant boy.</u> This is just another example . . .

Yet when we came back from berry picking yesterday, even Aunt Cecelia said, Why upon my soul Mary White, I do believe you are better, this country air must agree with you. She pushed back Mary Whites sunbonnet and stared at her intently, stroking her face with a pudgy finger. Why look you have roses in your cheeks, she said in a different voice, then almost said something else, then turned away abruptly. Go on in the house now and clean yourselves up for supper, and you—to Washington—you run on now, theres a good boy.

Washington headed down to the barn. But first we took the berries to Liddy who gave us some clabber to eat and then we ran straight up the stairs to this cubbyhole where we keep all our collections.

<u>Now,</u> I said.

And Mary White said <u>Yes</u> and took it out of her bloomer pocket where we had wrapped it round and round in honeysuckle vines so no one could tell what it was. Careful, be careful, she said as I started slowly pulling the vines away. She jiggled up and down on one foot and held her breath the way she does when excited. Her pale blue eyes were huge. I took my time unwrapping it. But finally it lay revealed on the floor, the bones of a HUMAN HAND minus two fingers and the thumb.

I had almost stepped on it as we were walking home. Just in time I looked down to see two finger bones sticking up out of the ground like flower bulbs growing. It was like they were pointing at the sky. Oh my God, I cried, then, Stop!

They ran back.

<u>Look!</u> I pointed down.

Lord Jesus. Washingtons eyes got real big when he saw it. Less go on now please Molly. Less us go on home.

What! Mary White looked all excited. Then she stuck out her bottom lip. Why we will do no such thing. We are going to dig him up for our phenomena collection, arent we Molly? For this is a poor brave dead soldier.

Oh yes, I said. <u>You all just stay right here,</u> while I ran back to the creek and got two flat rocks for digging. I handed one to Washington. He wouldnt take it.

<u>All right then.</u> I gave it to Mary White. She got down on her knees immediately and started scraping the dirt away. Be careful, she said. We want to keep him all hooked together if we can. Remember that song? How does it go? Then she sang, <u>Headbone connected to the neckbone, neckbone connected to the backbone</u>—

<u>Now hear you the word of the Lord!</u> I sang at the top of my lungs.

But the hand was not connected to anything else, and we didnt find any more bones there either, though we dug for a pretty long time.

Washington refused to help us. Yall is crazy girls, he said from the shade of a tree.

We wrapped the bones in honeysuckle and washed off our hands good in the creek before we left. Now the bones are here in a fancy little box I have had forever, just waiting.

And sure enough, when we asked Uncle Junius about the creek, he said, YES there was indeed a skirmish there toward the end of the war, some of the county home guard surprised by Shermans bummers, and three men dead.

Mary White knows how to do very fancy handwriting with many curls and flourishes. On the shoe box she has written, YANKEE BONES, <u>Property of Mary White Worthington and Molly Petree.</u> This is the jewel of our phenomena collection so far.

August 11, 1872

Dear Diary,

Though Blanche still plays with us sometimes, we had not seen Victoria for days and days. Washington told us she had got in some trouble, but he would not say what kind. So it was a big surprise when she ran in the barn yesterday and threw herself down in the straw and smiled her wide crooked smile which works on Mary White every time.

Well where have you been? Mary White said. And where is Sarah? Dont you want to play dolls?

I am not playing dolls no more, Victoria said. She is all arms and legs now, she has grown up a lot this summer. Her eyes are that dark snapping black like her mothers.

What do you want then? I wanted to get on with our game, in which Margaret and Fleur were getting ready to take a trip to New York City.

I dont know. I just thought I would come over here and find you all. Victoria sighed, which was strange. Usually she is all sass, all get-up-and-go.

Victoria, what happened to your leg? Mary White shrieked, and then I saw it too, the blue imprint of a hand on her pale white thigh.

That was your mama, wasnt it? I said. She hit you.

That is nothing, Victoria said. Looky here. She leaned forward and hiked up her bottom turning slightly so we could see the welts and bruises on the backs of her legs.

Ooh. Thats awful. Mary White shivered.

What did you do? I asked.

I reckon I have got me a boyfriend, Victoria said, and Mama doesnt like it.

Mary White peered at her. A real boyfriend?

Oh yes. Victoria sat back down in the straw and smiled. <u>A real live man doll.</u>

But where did you get him? I asked, for there is nobody like that around here.

He is working with his uncle over at the Bledsoes, Victoria said. They got hired on when Mister Bledsoe got so sick. He's got red hair, she said.

How old is he? I asked.

Seventeen. She grinned at us.

What is his name? Mary White asked.

His name is Declan Moylan. Victoria said it slow like it was something important. He is Irish. I like the way they talk, it is kind of like music.

Mary White and I stared at her as though she had come from another world. Her black curls fell down all around her long face.

His uncle plays the fiddle for dances, she said. I snuck out and went to one.

You DID? Mary White said.

How do you know how to dance? I asked.

Victoria laughed like her mother. Anybody can dance, she said.

Is that why Selena hit you? I asked.

She doesnt even know about the dance, Victoria said. She never knows where I am anyway, she is over here all the time now. She hit me for something else. Her eyes got big and she leaned forward.

What? Mary White and I said together.

I reckon she caught us, Victoria said.

Caught you what?

Nothing. Victorias face was full of scorn. Just about nothing at all. He come over for a visit and I was showing him my boobies, that is all. That is the only thing that has happened so far. And after all Mama done, I dont know why she even cares. But she started crying and hit him on the shoulder and drove him from the house and said, Oh Victoria I am raising you for better things honey. And then she started in hitting on me. But I am going to get her back. Victoria said this in a way you would not doubt.

We sat very still looking at her.

What are you going to do? Though I hate Victoria, I humbled myself to ask. Never you mind, she said darkly.

It was hot and still in the barn. I was covered in sweat all over. We sat in silence in the straw.

Suddenly Mary White said, Can WE see your boobies? For our collection of phenomena, she added.

Sure. Victoria sat up straight. She pulled up her blouse and chemise and there they were, with pink pointy tips on them. Do you want to touch them? she asked.

No, Mary White said, but thank you very much anyway.

Victoria pulled her clothes down and tucked herself back in again. Ive got to go, she said.

<u>Good bye,</u> we said together as she got up and shook the straw off her skirt and ran out through the wide sunny door, in a big hurry like always.

Mary White and I looked at each other. I felt light headed, like I was excited about something and getting sick all at once.

You know, I believe there is something to all that, Mary White said after a while.

Both our chests are flat as pancakes, flat as boys, at this time.

August 16, 1872

Dear Diary,

Please excuse me for I have no time to write as we are going in to Hillsborough today. Aunt Cecelia is dragging us with her to have a fancy lunch with the widow Muriel Brown who keeps a great house overlooking the river and knows how to live in style. You girls are perfect bumpkins in spite of my efforts! Aunt Cecelia said. So Mary White and I have had many lessons about the lunch. I am sick to death of it all ready.

Aunt Cecelia is the <u>bane of our existence,</u> I have recently read this phrase which surely applies to her. She makes us sew and do sums and raps our knuckles with a ruler if we get them wrong. Personally, I prefer literature. I take after my father, a poet and a gentleman, I told her. She turned up her big nose and sniffed.

Well Molly I sincerely hope that will not be the case, she said. Nor should you wish to follow your mothers example, though luckily there is no one here to spoil you the way they all spoiled Alice. Its a good thing Alice is dead, in fact, she could not exist in this new world. And as for you, you had best get your feet on the ground and fast.

Mary White likes poetry too, I said. We are memorizing Wyncken, Blynken, and Nod right now. So does Uncle Junius, I said, not entirely for spite remembering all of a sudden how he used to stride up and down the parlor reading Robert Burns My love is like a red red rose thats newly sprung in June, and Tam O Shanter and My hearts in the highlands wherever I go. I cannot imagine him doing this now.

Aunt Cecelia looked at me and pushed her face together. Go change your shoes, she said. Virgil is down there with the wagon, we are leaving now!

August 17, 1872

Dear Diary,

Now we have seen a magic lantern! Which showed a running horse. And eaten snow pudding from cut glass bowls while a little negro boy waved a fan over the table to keep off the flies. Then walked through the streets with two sissy daughters while the big town clock struck three. Aunt Cecelia fell asleep in the wagon and snored all the way home while Mary White and I played Twenty Questions. I was Pandora and Annabelle Lee.

Once here we ran to the Willow House, we were so glad to be back. We would HATE to be town girls!

Oh yes. We have found another Fairy Ring in the Big Woods on the way to Mama Marie and Aunt Mittys house.

Do I want to be <u>taken off</u> by a demon lover, like Madeline gliding past the sleeping dragons with Porphyro to his home oer the southern moors across the fairy sea? Or do I want to BE one, like the snaky Lamia or La Belle Dame Sans Merci who walks by the withered sage where <u>no birds sing?</u>

This is a hard decision.

October 19, 1872

Dear Diary,

Fall is here with a chill in the air and Mary White lies very sick. I know why but can not tell it. Four nights ago was another full moon and so we went to see the fairies hunting as we had tried to do twice before. <u>You only get three tries,</u> Mary White said. She knows all the fairy rules.

The first time we went it was July, hot and stormy with more and more dark clouds sailing across the moon and sure enough it started thundering when we came to the path. We got back to Agate Hill just as the first fat drops started landing all around us in the lane. Luckily little Junius had not woke up as he sometimes does when it thunders, so we crept back to bed and watched the storm from our window up under the eaves. We love the lightning.

The second time, fairy conditions were perfect. A hot still August night, and we went early. We sat on our rocks like rocks ourselves while the silver light came down through the leaves and shone on the water.

But then I heard something back in the woods. Mary White do you hear that? I asked.

Hush, I see them, they are coming! she whispered.

I strained my eyes at the silver pool but saw nothing. Then the noise in the woods got louder, branches crackling and a dog barking furiously, until here came three deer pursued by a big black dog. They all jumped across the stream, their white tails flashing, to disappear as fast as they had come.

<u>Oh damn it!</u> Mary White said. <u>Now the fairies are gone too.</u>

So last night was our last try.

I had stayed awake watching a big yellow moon rise up over the river hills, then when it hung like a lantern in the sky and the whole house was deathly quiet I poked Mary White. <u>Mary White!</u> I said. She lay on her side in deep sleep clutching Robert E. Lee. <u>Mary White!</u>

She sat up like a jack in the box. Oh is it time? And I said it was, and we pulled on our shirts and jackets and bloomers and tiptoed past little Junius and headed out barefoot as always into the heavy dew.

Oh its cold, isnt it? Mary White said as our feet sank into the grass.

We better go back for our shoes, I said.

But she shook her head and said, Its too late. We had best not risk it. Mary White talks in an old fashioned way when ever she talks about the fairies, it is almost like a fairy language. So on we went down the lane holding hands with the moon so bright it cast shadows behind us three times taller than we are.

Look we are giants! she said, and I knew it right then. <u>This time we will see them.</u>

The moon was so bright, we walked down the path to the river and found our way to the willow house as if it was day. Our white rocks shone out to welcome us, but the water was cold on our feet as we waded out.

<u>Now.</u> Mary White climbed up to sit cross-legged like an Indian and I did the same. She says it is a spiritual pose.

A little wind blew across our faces and rippled the waves and all of a sudden Mary White grabbed my knee so hard it hurt and said, See? Oh Molly—see? And sure enough the air was suddenly full of fairies like a swarm of bees all around us. Their high voices filled the night. The air was bright with the beat of their wings, too fast to see. Swooping down to the shallows they rode the waterbugs like horses and gathered the foam for their babys to eat and laughed and sang in their high, high voices. Their little faces were pointed and dark, their little green suits were darling.

Look it is the queen of the fairies! Mary White whispered for it was Titania with a flower crown and red hair that falls to her feet. She landed on the rock just inches before us and stood there quivering. Her wings beat too fast to see, giving off light like a firefly.

The fairies stayed for I dont know how long, until Titanias prince flew down riding on a swallow and led them all away. Then swoosh! A round shimmering light rose up through the trees to be lost in the starry sky.

Silently Mary White and I grabbed hands and climbed down from our rocks and splashed back to the bank through the freezing shallows. She was already sniffling then. So now she is imprisoned in Aunt Cecelias room sick with a terrible cough and can not play and I miss her so, with no one for company except little Junius who sleeps like a log.

And now I have started to sleepwalk again which I used to do. I had not done it since Mary White came.

October 23, 1872

Dear Diary,

Last night I woke in the dark at the top of the stairs with no idea of how I had got there, my heart just pounding. It was pitch black and very scary. But having been a ghost girl, I can find my way in the dark, and so after a while I took heart and went on down the skinny stairs. It was like something was drawing me on. I opened the door and stepped out into the passage where moonlight fell in a shiny patch on the heart pine floor. I shivered for it had rained in the night. I walked through the moonlight then on down to Uncle Junius door which stood open too.

I went in. Children are not allowed. It is like his cave in there. One oil lamp burned low on the desk, giving light enough to see that he was gone. His rumpled couch held coverlets thrown about. The big desk overflowed with papers and more papers, books lay piled and tumbled to the floor. The walls are filled with bookcases floor to ceiling while other books and clothes lay strewn about as if a hurricane had hit here, coming straight in the door. It smelled like tobacco, like whisky, like Uncle Junius. The end of a fire glowed still in the hearth.

Picking my way along, I went over there and sat down in one of his big rockers, drawing up my feet and wrapping myself in an old soft musty-smelling blanket and settling in for a nap until heavy slow footsteps sounded in the passage. I peeked around my chairback to see Uncle Junius, his white shirt half unbuttoned and hanging out of his pants, his white hair sticking up like straw all over his head. His eyes looked sunk in his head.

Ah Molly. Uncle Junius did not seem at all surprised to see me. He lowered his big self down slow into the other rocker, making a face from pain.

He rolled a cigarette and lit it and reached down to take a drink from the bottle that stays on the floor beside him. So, Molly. Come to help me with the sunrise? he asked, and I said, Yes Sir. Well then, he said, and together we sat in silence while it came on. The window filled with light. Dogs barked someplace. King Arthur crowed. Uncle Junius took another long drink while I snuggled back into my blanket, hating for night to end.

Aha! Finally you are here. Aunt Cecelia pushed the door so hard it banged into the wall, then stood there snorting and breathing like a bull in her big green dressing gown.

I know exactly where you have been Junius, <u>I know,</u> and dont try to tell me anything different. Why this is typical of you isnt it, to be absent when we are threatened by these outlaws that come in the night—

What? What is this Sissy? Uncle Junius stood to face her, putting a hand on his desk.

Well might you ask Sir! Well might you ask! Though it is doubtless your fault that they choose to come here at all. Never would they do so had you been on the side of God in the first place, had you not voted against Secession and supported the Republicans, weak lily-livered son of the flesh as you have turned out to be.

Whoa Sissy. What happened? His voice was raspy and hoarse.

Those—those <u>ruffians</u> came after Romulus. There was some incident in town. I presume it is his manner which you have encouraged Junius, you know you have. And to let him take on the care of Spencer, why it is just not right for Spencer to live out there. I dont blame them for being scandalized. But I must say, I put the quietus on them Junius. I had scarcely gone to bed when I heard the horses and those tin pans and whatnot and went out to the piazza where I said, Well Sirs, Romulus is not here, so you can just turn around now. You will have to shoot me in order to pass this way, and I warn you, if you do so, if you DO shoot me, why I will welcome it! For then I shall go straight to Heaven.

And what did they say to that Cecelia? Uncle Junius sounded like he was laughing.

They rode away of course while you lay fast in the arms of your gypsy whore—

Sissy. Uncle Junius drew himself up tall, with rasping breath. <u>One more time Sissy,</u> he said in a voice like God.

I jumped up from the rocker, throwing my blanket down.

Oh good Lord! Aunt Cecelia jumped a mile. Child, child, what are you doing here?

I am helping Uncle Junius with the sunrise, I said.

Aunt Cecelia snorted then turned away.

Uncle Junius put his hand on my shoulder. And a damn fine job you have made of it too Molly, he said. I thank you. For here is the sun fully risen, and you are a good, good girl. Well done.

November 9, 1872

Dear Diary,

We have had a big fight here, and it is not clear what might happen next.

I learned all about it this morning when Liddy sent me down to the cellar to get more cream from the springwater trough that runs along the sidewall, a chore I hate because it is so dark and damp down there. It is like a dungeon. Several times I have almost stepped on a snake lying across the sill or coiled up like a rope on the dark dirt floor. Since Washington knows how scared I am of snakes, he comes down too if he is around, and it is here that we have had many talks, sitting on those wooden crates in the cool musty cellar while its blazing hot outside. So although I jumped, I was not really surprised when he said <u>Molly!</u> Right behind me yesterday.

Why where have <u>you</u> been? I asked, for I have not seen him for days.

I been working, I reckon. Off cutting wood with Rom and Spence. But what do you care anyway? You are too busy being a white girl now, you aint got time for me.

I grabbed the cream bottle up from the trough and whirled around. That is not true! I said, though it <u>was,</u> a little.

Thats all right Molly, Washington said. I know she dont like for me to associate with you all.

I didnt have to ask who he meant. Of course it is Aunt Cecelia who had a fit when she surprised the three of us out in the barn with Gullivers Travels and found out that Washington can read. Fannie gave him lessons, along with Victoria and Blanche and me.

I think it is the very height of irresponsibility! Aunt Cecelia had practically screamed at Uncle Junius when he came back from Raleigh that evening.

Uncle Junius sat down heavily in the wingback chair and opened a newspaper.

What in the world was she thinking? Aunt Cecelia went on. I'd just like to know.

Uncle Junius sighed and looked up from the paper. It is my great and lasting sorrow that <u>everyone</u> on this place does not know how to read Sissy. Now leave me in peace for Gods sake.

God has very little to do with the state of things on this plantation, I assure you! Aunt Cecelia had snorted.

Now I went over and pulled the cellar door shut behind me and Washington. I hate Aunt Cecelia, dont you? I said to him. Mary White hates her too, even if she is her own grandmother. So where have you been? I asked finally.

Mama been sending me out to Miss Marie and Miss Mitties to work with Rom and them. Keeping me out of trouble, she says. But I seen trouble enough anyway.

Like what? I went over to stand right in front of Washington though I could hardly see him in the dark.

Selena got into it with Miss Cecelia finally, it come right out in the open when they was all out there in the kitchen making sausage after we killed those hogs, he said.

I nodded in the dark. Mary White and me had been furious when Aunt Cecelia wouldnt let us go to the hog killing which I have always loved, the first part is bad but then it goes on all day like a party. I remembered how Aunt Fannie always directed this operation herself, saying, <u>We shall use everything but the squeal.</u>

Well, everybody was working, Washington said, that is, Selena and Mama and Bess and me, and in come Miss Cecelia, saying, We do this in Montgomery and We do that in Montgomery, but it was real clear she did not know what she was talking about as she is a city lady. She got them killing the hogs too early anyway, then she wants them to grind all that meat up again so it be real fine. Just when they think they ready to stuff it in the casings, she wants them to start over. Mama and Bess been making sausage all they life, but they not going to tell her. They not going to go against her. So they are not talking, while she is talking real hateful to all them. Finally Selena she just blow up.

What did she do? I asked.

She jump up and say, Miss Cecelia I am in charge of this job and I can tell you, we know what we are doing here, so why dont you just keep your nose out of it. Go on back to Agate Hill and leave it to us hired help.

I could just imagine how Selena would look when she said this, head flung back, eyes on fire.

But Miss Cecelia not give an inch. Liddy, Bess, she said. Run that meat through the grinder again.

Did yall do it? I asked in the dark.

Oh yes, Washington said.

What did Selena do then?

She stand right up and look her in the eye—you know Selena is ever bit as big as your auntie—and she say, You will be sorry for this Cecelia. No Miss Cecelia nor nothing. Then she say to us all, <u>Yall can go to hell.</u> Then she go running out the door, and none of us has seen her since.

But where is she?

She got Rom to drive her over to Greensboro, leaving them children to fend for their selves. Mama been feeding them. Mama said Selena probably out walking the streets.

Walking the streets? I said. Why would she want to do that?

Washington was laughing. Nevermind, he said. But Mama said we not going to get rid of her so easy. And now today, Mister Junius has done sent Virgil back over there to find her and fetch her back.

I bet Aunt Cecelia is mad about that, I said.

Mama said Miss Cecelia is fit to be tied. But she is treading on mighty thin ice now.

I knew that meant Aunt Cecelia might leave, taking Mary White with her. Mary White has never seen a hog killing and now she never will. All of a sudden I wished I could go back to the days before Aunt Cecelia and Mary White ever came here, when I was just a ghost girl running this place and playing in the woods with Washington. Come on Washington, I said. Lets go up on the hill and ride some saplings like we used to. For we used to ride them one after another all the way down Agate Hill.

I cant, Molly, Washington said. They are waiting for me now. They will be mad all ready. He reached back and opened the door and the sunlight poured in making Washington into a black silhouette like the silhouettes of those old dead people hanging on the wall in the parlor. All of a sudden I realized how tall he got last summer, though he is still as thin as a rail.

Well bye then, I said.

Bye, he said, then, Molly?

What, I said.

The sunlight shone out all around him but he was black in the center of it.

What happened at the end of Gullivers Travels?

He lived with the horses for a long time, I said. They were real nice, remember?

I remember, Washington said.

Then he made himself a canoe and sailed back home.

Thats good then. Washington grinned at me, then waved, and then was gone.

I took the cream up the steps and in the kitchen to Liddy who was mixing something up in the big blue bowl. She looked at me good when I set the bottle down on the table. What taken you so long? She asked.

I been talking to Washington, I said.

Liddy shook her head and turned her mouth down. Dont you be bothering Washington, she said. He got work to do.

Sometimes I think Liddy is just as bad as Aunt Cecelia, she doesnt want Washington and me to be friends either.

November 19, 1872

Dear Diary,

Now we have been to the Tableaux Vivants, the best and most beautiful thing I have ever witnessed though I did not want to go at first as Aunt Cecelia said they are edifying. Well she has edified me almost to death all ready but Mary White said, Oh do come, Molly, you will love it, you can wear my blue velvet dress! So we took the carriage with Virgil driving and even he was dressed up. Where did you get that hat? I asked him. But he just clicked to the horses and off we went. Mary White and Aunt Cecelia sat in the back under a lap robe but I got to sit up in the front with Virgil, like a scout. I waved to all. It was a real pretty day not even cold. I remembered that poem Aunt Fannie used to read about Octobers bright blue weather. I took off my hat for I love to feel the sun and the wind on my face.

Put that hat back on Molly, you little fool! Aunt Cecelia screamed up to me. You will get freckles.

I dont care, I called back. Two wagons passed by, loaded down with wood from Mister Grissoms sawmill. I grinned and waved to the Grissom boys who sat perched like blackbirds on top of the wood. I did not even bother to say, I dont care if I get freckles or not because I am not going to be a lady, I would rather die than be a lady like you. I remembered way back when Rachel and Julia were trying to get rid of freckles by slathering themselves every night with a potion they made up from cucumbers and milk, which did not work.

Diary, I have forgot to say that Julia and Rachel are coming for Christmas, both of them, and Julia is bringing a beau! I can not wait. Mary White and I hope for a big wedding though Uncle Junius says, Who in the hell will pay for it? You girls had better stick with Robert E. Lee.

Anyway, it took us two hours to get to Hillsborough. Mary White and I were too excited to eat our cold suppers—which consisted of a ham biscuit and a fried apple pie apiece—so Aunt Cecelia ate all of them. I waved to everybody. The sun had gone down in a blaze of fire by the time we got into town. Virgil drove the carriage around to the back of the widow Muriel Browns house.

Then we all went inside for tea cakes and lemonade. Aunt Cecelia and the widow had sherry wine. Show them your dolls, girls, the widow Brown said to her two mean daughters, so there we went up the long curving staircase with Adeline and Ida, who we hate.

There they are. Adeline pointed at a chaise longue covered with them, all kinds of dolls in all kinds of costumes, even a doll from Spain. But when Mary White bent down to pick one up, Adeline said, Please dont touch, its time to go now anyway.

Oh I'm so sorry, please excuse me! Mary White jumped back as if she had been shot and said in her nicey-nice way.

Going back down those long stairs, Mary White ran ahead of Adeline who somehow tripped and tumbled down the last five or six steps to land on her backside and come up sobbing. You—Adeline started to say, but there was Mary White helping her up, attended by the widow and Aunt Cecelia.

So then we were almost late, and off we went down the street toward the Masonic Lodge, falling in with a great raft of people all dressed up and talking gaily. Good evening, Miss Brown, Miss Worthington, good evening, girls. Gentlemen tipped their tall hats. It was already dark. Lanterns shone.

You forget how dark it is out in the country until you come to town. Adeline and Ida ran off with their friends, so Mary White and I were free to hold hands very tight and walk behind Aunt Cecelia and the widow.

What do you think . . . , Mary White started to say.

But I said <u>Sssh</u> for Aunt Cecelia was saying, The situation is rapidly becoming intolerable. Honestly I sometimes believe that my brother has lost his mind.

Then we arrived in front of the square two-story Masonic Lodge which was all lit up, every window blazing, luminaries placed at intervals from the road to the steps of the hall. Oh look! cried Mary White. For we were greeted at the door by a personage in a turban and a shimmering gold cloth wrap, whether man or woman I could not say. Kerosene lamps lined the wooden stage, and other huge lanterns hung on ropes, as dazzling as the sun. Beautiful music came down from the balcony where only a few candles glowed, so as not to take away from the tableaux. Every chair in town must have been gathered up for the audience, while we children sat on the floor at the front. Adeline and Ida complained.

<u>Laydees and gentlemen!</u> The velvet curtain parted and out came Doctor Lambeth dressed in a top hat and tails. Everyone cheered. The ladys of the Hillsborough Relief Association welcome you to their Tableaux. You may rest assured that all proceeds from this event will go toward the care of the neediest among us, especially widows and orphans of the Confederacy. <u>And now, on with the show!</u> Doctor Lambeth bowed low to the crowd which screamed when two birds flew out of his upraised hat and swooped around the hall, finally to disappear in the vast dark shadowy balcony where the hidden musicians were playing dramatic music.

And now—Doctor Lambeths gray hair streamed down to his shoulders—And now, allow me to take you back in time to ancient Greece where we shall present The Nine Muses!

Two little boys dressed in red suits appeared at the center of the stage then went running back on each side to pull the heavy curtains open revealing a classical scene like an engraving from a mythology book. Everyone in the audience gasped. Applause began and continued. The Muses did not respond to the cheers but held their poses perfectly, moving not a muscle. They looked like statues. White columns of varying heights stood at either side of this tableau, while the floor in front of the Muses was strewn with cunning cloth roses. Aunt Cecelia had edified us so much we all ready knew that the Muses were nine in number, daughters of Jupiter and the Goddess of Memory, Mnemosyne. We all ready knew their names too which were written out on placards in fancy printing.

Each white-gowned Muse had a placard propped up in front of her. Calliope, Muse of Epic Poetry and Rhetoric, wore a Grecian war helmet over her long golden curls. One pretty hand rested on the short sword stuck in the rope at her waist, while she glared off to the side at some oncoming enemy army. Red spots gleamed on her cheeks. But the one I most wanted to be was Tragedy, who knelt in an attitude of misery and dispair. Her head was bowed so low that we could not even see her features. She wore a crown of myrtle leaves over her smooth black hair.

Polyhymnia, the Muse of Religious Hymns, held a songbook aloft and appeared to be singing vigorously. This meant that she had to stand still with her mouth wide open which is very hard, Mary White and I have since tried it. Plain red-headed Clio sat at a little spindly-legged writing desk wearing gold-rimmed spectacles, looking down at a huge thick book which said HIS-TORY across its cover. Erato, the prettiest, held one hand to her heart for she was the Muse of Love Songs.

The Muse of Lyric Poetry, Euterpe, appeared to be begging someone for something, arms outstretched, her face in anguish. The great fat girl who wore a jesters hat was Thalia, the Muse of Comedy. She looked like a big puffy cloud in her billowing dress. I poked Mary White and pointed, for Thalia was the best, really. You had to laugh when you looked at her. Urania was a serious round-faced girl who carried the moon in one hand and a little globe of the earth in the other. She is the Muse of Astronomy. Terpischore wore full white trousers and held a difficult dance pose, to everyones amazement. Immediately I wanted to be her, instead of Tragedy.

Everyone in the hall clapped, some crying out, Bravo, bravo! But the Muses did not move, or acknowledge the applause in any way, holding their attitudes. We all jumped to our feet, still clapping. Some wags called out things such as Watch out there Lucinda, you are going to drop the moon! Or why so sad Betsy? while others said, Hush boys, hush! We were directly in front of Tragedy who looked up once and gave us a wink. The curtain was drawn back together by the two little boys who had opened it, one of them stumbling over his own feet to the crowds delight. Bravo, they called out to him.

I just do not think a married woman should participate in something like this. It is not right! Aunt Cecelia said severely to the widow Brown while a lot of bumping and scraping went on behind the curtain as the association prepared for the next Tableau, advertised as the death scene from Romeo and Juliet. Mary White and I could not wait for this one, as we had read the entire play in preparation, and it promised to be even more tragic than Tragedy. There was scattered applause here and there as the Muses came out to join the audience.

Then the descending hush, then Doctor Lambeth bowed low and announced, Romeo and Juliet, the Death Scene, in a deep and serious tone. The fiddle wailed down from the balcony. Mary White and I held hands. This time, Calliope and Urania opened the curtain. We had to crane our necks to see, for a lot of this scene took place on the floor.

Now the columns supported an arch, the entrance to the Capulet tomb. Flares burned in sconces. There lay Romeo dead on his back, the vial of poison still in his hand. Fair Juliet, also dead, lay in a pool of crimson created by the skirt of her silk dress. The jeweled hilt of the dagger jutted up from her chest, catching the torchlight—later, Mary White and I figured out that she had thrust it under her armpit. But it looked perfectly real, exactly like she had stabbed herself. Another young man lay dead beside her.

That must be Paris, Mary White whispered pointing at this body whose sword lay at his side.

Or maybe Tybalt? I couldnt remember.

Friar Lawrence, whose face was hid in the hood of his gown, a plain old rope tied around his waist, stood leaning on a twisted cane. A soldier in uniform stood outside the tomb, arms crossed, while a King and Queen in gold crowns knelt by the bodies. Dazzling sparks of light glinted off the crowns, the swords, the jewels. Sad music from the balcony floated down over all. This time, no applause, but a general intake of breath, a huge gasp. Sobs were heard around the room.

Then I caught on.

Though Romeo wore a cap, a blue silk vest, black tights, and fancy pantaloons tucked into his high black boots, clearly he was a girl, one of the members of the Hillsborough Relief Association, her features calm and classical in death, large nose, dark brow. Paris too was a girl, as was the Watchman, the King, and even Friar Lawrence!

Why, Romeo is one of those Walker girls! The widow Brown exclaimed aloud, causing titters throughout the hall.

The mood was broken. Excited conversation erupted everywhere, as the Muses raced across the stage dragging the heavy curtain shut.

Doctor Lambeth came back out. Laydees and gentlemen, it has been our great pleasure—, he began, but his voice was lost in the hubbub.

Who was responsible for the choice of this scene? A pig-faced man demanded angrily, while another man said that personally he had found Romeo and Juliet to be totally charming and elevating in the manner of all great tragedy.

Oh poppycock! A skinny lady with spectacles said to our right.

Adeline! Ida! shrilled the widow.

Stay right where you are, Aunt Cecelia said severely, pointing to us. She did not look a bit edified. She held her special-smelling handkerchief to her face while we waited for the widow to grab up Adeline and Ida. Then Aunt Cecelia set forth across the hall, followed by the widow Brown. Mary White and I came in their wake, straight out the big double doors into the dark chilly night. I had to hold up the skirt of the blue velvet dress, which was too long for me, as off we went down the street toward the widows house.

Well! Aunt Cecelia said. I must say I had misunderstood the nature of this spectacle. The Muses were all well and good, but Romeo and Juliet went beyond the pale, dont you agree, Muriel? And good heavens, those costumes—girls in pants, in public! What has become of modesty? of femininity? I would like to know. Young ladys should not appear in public at all if their judgment is shown to be this faulty, this rash. Especially not young married ladys, the very idea.

Oh come now, Sissy, the widow Brown said in her high voice. Certainly there can be no immodesty in a young lady doing something which the whole community approves. Why these Tableaux are performed everywhere now, they are quite the thing. And look at how much money they must have raised, and for a very good cause, I might add.

To say that a thing is done does not make it right, Muriel. Each of Aunt Cecelias words came out in a puff of white breath as we paused by the last streetlight on our way back.

You need not preach to me, my dear. The widow sounded mad. Perhaps you have been too long in the country.

Country has nothing to do with it, I assure you, Aunt Cecelia said. Those girls were not comporting themselves as ladys. Mark my words, this never would have happened before the War.

Then it is high time for a few changes, the widow said. No one thought I could take over for Aldred either and yet I have done so quite competently if I do say so myself. For the widow owns and operates the Brown Printing and Engraving Co. Inc.

It is a completely different issue. Aunt Cecelia bit off each word.

No, I dont think it is, the widow said, but then we were there and all the dogs ran out barking. The carriage stood in front of the widows house with Virgil ready to tuck us all under the robes. Then he clicked to the horses and off we went through the clear and starry night.

Molly? It was Mary White coming forward to sit on the bench with me and Virgil. Isnt it beautiful? Mary White said, and I said, Yes. It is beautiful. Soon she was asleep too, her head against my shoulder, her breathing as light as little Junius. Aunt Cecelia snored in the back. I made sure that Mary White was fully covered by the robes. As for me, I was much too excited to sleep. The dew fell all around us, turning fast to frost which had given the whole countryside a shine well before we reached Agate Hill. I pushed the robe down so I could feel the frost on my face, for I want to feel everything Dear Diary. I want to feel everything there is. I do not want to be a lady. Instead I want to be in a Tableaux Vivant myself, I want to be Tragedy, I want to be Juliet, I want to be Romeo. Thus with a kiss I die.

December 7, 1872

It was the worst thing I have ever seen Dear Diary or ever hope to see.

It all started yesterday when Aunt Mitty sent for some of Liddys boiled custard, for Mama Marie continues to fail, and wont eat, and this is the only thing that will tempt her. Law Law! Aunt Cecelia said. Today of all days, and of course Virgil is gone, well I suppose Liddy can make the custard, but I just dont know how I can get it out there to Four Oaks. Aunt Cecelia patted her special handkerchief all over her face.

Mary White and me can take it! I said, jumping right up for I love that walk better than anything.

Now Molly, you know you must say, Mary White and I, she corrected me.

Mary White and I would love to take it, I said.

Yes, please please please Grandmother, please let us go, we can take it, we know the way, and we will come right back, we promise. You know you like for us to do good deeds, oh please let us go. Mary White hugged Aunt Cecelias fat waist and wound herself into her big skirts.

Oh I suppose . . . let me just speak to Liddy then . . . but first you girls must finish your sums.

Oh yes mam. We sat back down, surprised as could be, while she went back to the kitchen. Mary White copied my numbers down fast, for I am always right.

So that is how we were excused from lessons and got to walk to Mama Maries on such a bright and frozen morning. Of course we have made this trip many times together in summer and in fall, yet never before in this biting cold when your feet crunch down the icy grass in the yard with every step. I could HEAR us walking! And when you breathe in, it goes straight to your brain like Uncle Junius liquor which we have tasted too. When you breathe out, your breath makes a cloud in the air. The sky was a bright deep blue, like the blue of Aunt Fannies Dutch plate which hangs on the wall in the dining room. We walked down the lane, through the whispering cedars, and set off on the path through the icy woods. Everything was sparkling.

Why look at this, it is a work of art. Mary White broke off a weed encased in ice and waved it shimmering in the sun. She danced along the path in front of me, light as a fairy in her red coat. I followed, feeling drunk. We passed through a dark stand of big pines whose sharp scent stuck in our throats. Oh look! Mary White was all ready back out in the sunlight ahead pointing up to where a hawk was making big lazy circles in the sky. When he swooped down low we could see the red on his wings.

Soon we came to the sandy spring, where we broke the ice with the gourd that lay on the rock just waiting for us. This is the best water in the universe, Mary White said solemnly.

On we went, her red coat flitting in and out of the trees ahead of me. Sometimes she seemed not even to touch the ground. We came into the clear and struck out along a fencerow surprising the little birds who flew up all around us. We passed that pile of rocks which used to be the chimney of an old homestead, we know because daffodils pop up there every spring. Fannie said, Daffodils remember when the people are all gone.

Finally we came to the bridge over the mill creek and crossed it carefully, holding hands with one hand while clutching our bottles of boiled custard tight with the other. The wild black river roared below us, edged in silver lace. Cold air rushed up under our skirts. The water wheel turned at the side with its dripping buckets, yet we saw no one. Shutters were drawn on the mill, like sleeping eyes. We saw no one at all, not even the crazy old man who so often sits smoking his pipe on the stone slab by the old red plank door, now closed and bolted tight.

I feel like we are the only people alive in the world, I told Mary White who said she felt exactly the very same way.

On we went speaking of this and that, I cant think what, for me and Mary White are such good friends it is like I am only thinking aloud when I talk to her. We passed by the fairy ring known only to us and then came to the biggest tree in the county, a tree so big that a man once lived in it, so they say, and we always go inside it where we can both stand up and walk around.

We can come here, I said, if we ever really run away.

We moved around in the woody dark.

I can still smell him, Mary White said, all of a sudden.

Who? I asked.

That man who lived here! she said, which scared us to death so we ran down the road as fast as we could go.

Now we walked between fences through the Big Field which is almost a hundred acres including the old orchard and the special meadow where Fannie used to have us gather sweet grass for the bureau drawers. Here the public road comes in from another direction, yet still we saw no one as we walked along to the privet hedge and Mama Maries stone gate which always stands wide open. Mama Maries house is very old and rambling, it has been added on to many times. Four huge oak trees in the front of the house have roots so high that all you have to do is lay some sticks across them for a roof, then make a carpet with moss, and then you will have a doll house. One time last summer when Mary White and me got to spend the night out there, we made five houses so our dolls could visit to and fro, and get married and die and go to church, and have a Social Life.

We climbed up the steps and stomped on the porch, hallooing so they would hear us.

Mama Marie is very sweet but Aunt Mitty is mean as a snake. She is not actually related to any of us, being merely Mama Maries old friend who came to visit one time about a million years ago and stayed on to help run the place after Big Papa died of a heart attack at the dinner table, falling forward into the gravy. Big Papa was a high roller. He raised trotting horses and made his own brandy and went to Congress and held parties that lasted for days. Mama Marie was just a young girl who got into a lot more than she had bargained for. But she got good at running things while he was off at Congress, and raised her children mostly by herself and with Aunt Mitty, and is beloved by all in the countryside.

Hello, we called, stamping our boots on the porch.

The door opened and there stood Susie, their only servant, a white woman from a good family in Raleigh which has cast her off. Mary White and I would love to know why.

Yall come on in. Susie smiled as she took the boiled custard from us. Oh she will like that, she said. Didnt you get cold on that long walk? Lets put your coats back here to warm up. We followed her back to the kitchen which is part of the house itself, and very old fashioned. Susie does all the cooking on the hearth, with cranes in the fireplace to hang pots and kettles on. She gave us a potato apiece, right out of the ashes. I ate mine all up plus most of Mary Whites, she eats like a little bird.

Well now you will want to visit them, Susie said, leading us up the stairs into Mama Maries big sunny room where she has been confined forever. Mama Marie lay propped up in her lacy cap on the four-poster bed, she looks like Blanches apple doll. She is smaller every time I see her.

You sweet girls, she said, Come sit right here and talk to me, which we did, both of us in the stuffed blue chair at the head of her bed. Her Bible sat on the table next to her knitting. Susie put a cup of boiled custard down on the table. Now what have you been doing? Mama Marie asked, and we told her all about Robert E. Lee and his weddings and the Tableaux Vivants and Uncle Junius bad health and the walk over there. Mama Marie laughed and laughed, her face all crinkled up. I swear, you girls are a tonic, she said.

Pictures of animals, fruit, flowers and old dead people hang all around the room including one I like particularly, actually it is an embroidered picture of Mama Marie and her six sisters grouped around a table in their parlor doing various things—needlepoint, reading, playing the harp. <u>Where are your sisters now?</u> I asked, and she said, <u>Gone, all gone, my darling, off into the world of light.</u>

She smiled peacefully, to my amazement, for my family is dead too and I am NOT peaceful. I <u>hate</u> it that my own family is a ghost family. I dont know if Mama Marie is too old to care, or if she has got a philosophy. I keep waiting for one to come to me.

Julia has a beau, I started telling Mama Marie, but she drifted off to sleep right then before our very eyes.

Come on now, Susie whispered.

We followed her out looking back from the door to see Mama Marie so slight in the bed it seemed that no one was even there, sunlight winking off the cut glass punch cup that held her boiled custard.

Yall better come on and get your coats now, Susie said, for Aunt Mitty lives on the ground floor and keeps her door open all the time even in the winter, she cant stand a closed room or a room without a door in it. We went inside.

Its about time. Where have you been? Her strong old ratchety voice sounds like a rusty hinge opening.

We stood looking all around the messy room. As always, her coffin rested on its low wooden stand in the corner.

Well? Cat got your tongues? she asked.

Mary White and I looked at each other, but we could not figure out where the voice was coming from. Aunt Mitty wasnt there.

<u>Good morning!</u> Suddenly she sat bolt upright in the coffin. Mary White screamed, backing out the open door, while I started laughing and couldnt stop.

What in the world are you doing Aunt Mitty? I asked. Trying to scare us to death?

Just practicing, she said. I find it keeps me focused.

Focused on what? We both drew nearer.

On what is important, she said. And I would advise you to do the same Molly Petree, for though I have always liked you, I see that you are a rebellious girl with a dangerous nature, headed into a lot of trouble. I advise you to turn to God my dear, for He is watching you every moment, always and everywhere. Forget all this makebelieve. Read your Bible.

I all ready read it once, I said. And now Aunt Cecelia is making us read it again. I would rather read something else. I would rather read poetry.

Aunt Mitty pointed her long skinny finger at me. You have an eternal soul Molly Petree, she said, whether you want it or not.

Well I dont want it, I said. This is true. I did not say that I dont want to go to Heaven either. I dont want to be an angel any more than I want to be a ghost girl. I want to be a real girl and live as hard as I can in this world, I dont want to lie in the bed like Mama or be sick like Mary White. Or be a lady. I would rather work my fingers to the bone and die like Fannie. I want to live so hard and love so much I will use myself all the way up like a candle, it seems to me like this is the point of it all, not Heaven. I want to have a demon lover and also a real boy who will be my husband and love me more than life itself. I want to live on my own land not somebody elses plantation. I dont give a damn about Heaven. But the horrible thing about Aunt Mitty is that she seems to know all this without me even telling her. Her little black eyes behind her spectacles are bright and sharp, like jet earrings. It is like she can see right down into my soul, like she knows how hard Mary White and I laughed after the camp meeting when old Mister Pink McCloud got saved, falling down on the ground in a fit of religion and hollering out, Boys he's done got me by the short hairs now. Mister Pink McCloud has this big old goiter. I dont care to go to Heaven if he is going to be there, or Aunt Cecelia, or Mister Gwyn either one. But I dont believe in Heaven anyway. I have seen too many die. I have seen their spirits leave their bodies as in the case of Mamma and Willie, and believe me, they are gone. They get cold and hard very fast. They do not fly up to Heaven on angel wings, if they are anything they are ghosts. I used to be a ghost girl myself but now I am a real girl, and I am not going back.

Molly, Molly. Aunt Mitty sat straight up in her coffin staring at me. Oh I know you Molly. I recognize you. For you are my own girl, the girl of my heart. But the time draws nigh. You must listen to me, as I dont have long to tell you the things you need to hear, the things you must take to heart.

Come on. I pulled Mary White out the open door onto the gallery.

What is the matter with her? Mary White asked.

She is just old and crazy, I reckon. She is old as the hills, I said.

Molly! Aunt Mitty shrieked after us like a witch.

I pulled Mary White down the gallery steps and we ran around the side of the house giggling and did not say good bye to anybody, not even Susie.

We started the long walk home. First through the Big Field and past the hollow tree where we encountered a black and white dog who was very friendly. I patted him while Mary White rested, she gets so tired. We had crossed the mill race on the bridge and were walking through the forest when all of a sudden Mary White, running ahead, began to scream. At first I thought she was playing a game. What is it? I called.

Molly come here quick, please come, oh Lord this is awful, she called, so I took off running and found her standing stock still in a clearing where an old wagon trail crosses the path. She pushed at her head with both hands like she was trying to hold it together. Her wispy bright curls made a halo in the sunlight. Oh Molly. She gulped to catch her breath and in the silence I heard birds chirping. A squirrel ran across the path.

What is it? I said.

Look. She pointed down the wagon trail and then I saw it too, a negro hanging by the neck from a rope attached to a big old oak tree. His body turned slowly in the air. He was a large negro, very black, with his swollen head drooped over to the side and his mouth open and his tongue out, eyes naught but bloody holes. He wore no shirt nor shoes, his back a bloody mess. From whipping. Or beating. I knew this. The day was as bright and sunny as before except that now the ice was melting and in the quiet we could hear trickles of water running everyplace, like a little song. Some clothes and trash lay at the negros feet where the mud was all trampled up. Mary White was crying and I started crying too.

We must have walked right past him on the way over here, she said.

We didnt even look down that road, I said.

But now we could not stop looking.

It was the KuKlux, I said. You know it was. I told Mary White how they had hanged another colored man down in Chatham County a while back, and drowned a colored woman in a mill pond because she was impudent to a white lady.

How do you know that? Mary White whirled around.

I read it in Uncle Junius newspaper, I said. And over in Moore County they killed a colored blacksmith and murdered his whole family and set the house on fire. They found everybodys bones the next morning.

Stop it, stop it! Mary White put her hands over her ears.

I'm sorry, I said. I dont know why I always have to know things like that, why I have to go on like that, but I do. It is the way I am. I always have to know everything.

The body turned round so slow. The red dirt road went on underneath and beyond it, into the dark piney woods.

Mary White took her hands down. She was paler than ever, with red spots on her cheeks like a doll. We have to go back to Agate Hill right now, she said.

And so we left then, walking fast, and the sun was low over the river when we got there. It was getting colder.

Aunt Cecelia flung open the door, hair falling out of her bun.

Grandmama! Mary White, who can be a real baby, hugged her skirts. Grandmama the most terrible thing happened—

But Aunt Cecelia pushed her out to arms length and said, For once, girls, none of your nonsense. Lets not dramatize. Junius is gravely ill, do you hear me? Gravely ill. I have sent Washington for Doctor Lambeth.

But we saw a dead man hanging from a tree, Grandmama, a negro, and he was all bloody, and his eyes were gone.

Aunt Cecelia shook Mary White like a rag doll.

You did not, she said. Listen to me. Girls you did not see that, do you hear me? I wont hear another word about it. Not another word. Now is that understood?

But Uncle Junius will want to report it to the magistrate, I was saying when she slapped me hard on the cheek. It felt like a burn.

Listen to me Molly, she said, eyes wide and nostrils flaring. This is none of our business. Just forget it. We have got enough trouble here, there is no sense borrowing more. Now do you understand?

Yes, I said, but I dont, and I am going to tell Uncle Junius anyway, and I am going to tell Doctor Lambeth when he gets here, which ought to be soon. I am looking out through the chink for him now.

December 8, 1872

Dear Diary,

I have done what I said. I sat on the heart pine floor of the passage just outside Uncle Junius door for an hour, waiting for Doctor Lambeth. Finally he came out shaking his head. He put on his coat.

Cant you do anything? Aunt Cecelia wailed. She popped her eyes and twisted her handkerchief up in her hands.

They didnt even see me.

No Cecelia, he said. I regret to say this. I have loved Junius Hall from the day we first met, when he and I were young men together fifty years ago, running these woods like bird dogs. I was just remembering the time we went down the Cape Fear River on a flatboat, all the way to Wilmington. Now that was a memorable trip. He smiled his wide sad smile. Ah, but that was a different time, he said. The wrinkles on his face looked like cobwebs. Keep him comfortable, he said. Give him the medicine.

Aunt Cecelia made a sound and turned away.

Doctor Lambeth put on his hat. He picked up his doctor bag.

I jumped up and darted in front to open the door.

Molly, he said. My goodness but you are growing up into a real young lady now. It has been some time since I've seen you.

I held the door and Doctor Lambeth came and we went outside into the cold gray day and stood on the stone piazza while Washington rode the horse up the lane.

<u>Listen.</u> I grabbed Doctor Lambeths bony arm and told him all about the negro hanging and where it was. I told him everything. Report it to the sheriff, I said. Tell the magistrate. Somebody has to do something. I did not say that whenever I close my eyes now I still see that bloody body turning around and around on the rope in the little breeze.

Yes, Doctor Lambeth said in his deep kind voice. I will do so Molly, I promise. I will do everything in my power. But I cannot promise what the outcome will be. I want you to know that. I cannot say what if anything will be done. He put down his bag and hugged me into his great black coat. <u>These are hard times, honey,</u> he said. His coat smelled like tobacco and traveling. Then he got on the horse and Washington stood beside me while we watched him ride away.

December 10, 1872

The middle of the night

Dear Diary,

Again as before I have been sleepwalking. Last night soon after we had laid down I awoke with a start to find myself in the hall with a light still burning below and angry voices floating up the stairs. Making no noise I tiptoed down them and along the passage. There stood Aunt Cecelia in her monstrous blue dressing gown just inside Uncle Junius room where he lay propped up on many pillows with his mouth open, breath rattling in his chest. Doctor Lambeth says it will not be long. Selena sat on the rumpled bed beside him. Her hairbrush lay on the counterpane, her clothes were thrown about the room. She stays there with him now.

Aunt Cecelia was saying, Junius, this is intolerable.

Let him be. Selena said. For Gods sake. Go to bed Cecelia. Her black hair fell to her waist. She was wearing one of his old shirts which she clutched together across her breasts.

Junius! I am speaking to you, Aunt Cecelia said.

Uncle Junius turned his head and looked at her but he was not himself, and will not be himself, as he is dying. <u>Drowning</u> is what he says. <u>I am drowning</u> in that awful voice. Before, he was thrashing around and yelling but now since Doctor Lambeth came he is quieter. He is dreamy and more content.

Selena gave him a spoonful of the medicine from the little blue bottle and then put it back on the table next to the lamp. Listen here Cecelia, she said. I have some news for you. Junius and I will be married within the fortnight. Her black eyes were flat and shiny.

Why this is preposterous! Junius is not a stupid man, I will wager that he sees what you are up to as plainly as the rest of us. My brother will never marry you, you hussy. You whore. You have just cooked this up while he lies here dying too weak to protest.

<u>Ce-ce-lia.</u> Uncle Junius pushed himself up from his pillows looking like Death itself. What does it matter? If I marry or if I do not marry? What does any of it matter? I am tired Cecelia. I am tired to death of this stupid life. He drew in a long gurgling breath and fell back exhausted against the pillows.

But Junius—<u>Agate Hill?</u> Aunt Cecelia could scarcely speak.

Frankly Cecelia Agate Hill is nothing but an encumbrance and a monument to the colossal vanity of men who enslaved other men. Let it go, I say, back to a pile of rubble, back to the rocky earth of this rocky hill. Let it all go. He closed his eyes.

You see? Selena smiled her big triumphant smile at Aunt Cecelia.

In that case, I shall be leaving immediately. Clearly Junius has lost his mind. Aunt Cecelia puffed herself up like one of Liddys pullet hens.

Selena rared back hooting with laughter. And where will you go? she asked. You didnt come here to <u>help</u> us—Selena spat out the word help—We didnt need any <u>help.</u> The truth is that you came here because you had no-where else to go. The truth is that you thought Junius was a rich man, didnt you? You thought you would take over. You thought you would take advan-tage of him, and see how it has worked out now. Junius doesnt want you here. Nobody wants you anywhere.

Insufferable bitch, Aunt Cecelia said all red-faced. Dont you worry. I have powerful friends and resources. I have innumerable connections. I will go back to Alabama where people were vying for my presence and aid. This was only one of my many choices. We will be just fine, I assure you.

Selena sat up straighter and composed herself. You do know that I will take good care of Junius, she said in a different voice.

I know nothing of the kind, Aunt Cecelia said. You will watch him die, thats all. He will never marry you. This is a dream my dear. He would never cheat his children out of their inheritance, this is ridiculous.

Selena laughed. What inheritance? There is no inheritance, you must know that by now. You would never leave, otherwise. If there was any money to be got, youd stay here and try to get it. Dont deny it Cecelia. I have never had the luxury of being good—but if I am bad, you are just as bad as me. We are exactly the same. If I am a bitch, you are a bitch too. We are two bitches from the same litter.

<u>Well said my dear,</u> came Uncle Junius voice.

Aunt Cecelia started violently, her hand flew up to her breast.

The carrion speaks, Uncle Junius said in his deep and gurgling voice, while the buzzards fight over him. His mouth turned up in a smile. Selena smiled too. As she leaned down on one elbow to kiss him, her shirt fell open to show one long breast.

<u>Good bye Cecelia,</u> Uncle Junius said, raising his bony hand a few inches above the counterpane.

Aunt Cecelia made a sound which was neither a sob nor a snort but something in between. She whirled and collided with me before I could understand her intentions and get myself out of the doorway. Her shriek would have woken the dead.

What is it? Selena jumped up and stared at me.

Oh Molly! Aunt Cecelia shook my shoulders hard. You bad girl, I thought you were a ghost.

I am, I said. I am.

December 12, 1872

Dear Diary,

Here I sit while the business of packing is heard throughout the house, a dragging scraping sound as the trunks are dragged out and then packed and then dragged away, it is like they are dragging them across my heart to leave a bloody scrape like you get when you fall down running in the road. It is the worst kind of bloody knee to get for it never heals.

I hate Aunt Cecelia.

December 16, 1872

Dear Diary,

Mary White has left in the dark of the morning with Aunt Cecelia, the horses breaths making clouds in the air, lanterns lit on either side of the carriage driven by Washington, Virgil following with the wagon. They started off so early due to the threat of more snow.

First there was the comickal scene of Aunt Cecelia getting up into the carriage, this required everybody pushing despite the stepstool they had brought out for her. The carriage bounced on its springs when she finally plopped down, I saw it. It would have been funny if it wasnt so sad, for there was Mary White too in her little red coat looking up here to this cubbyhole where she knew I would be watching, for I could not stand to go outside and say good bye.

She did not smile. Her face was round and white in the lantern light, it looked like a little moon. She kept on staring up here. It was all I could do not to run down there although we have already split up our collection of phenomena—I gave her the Yankee hand—and said good bye yesterday at the willow house in a special ceremony of Mary Whites devising.

❧

December 18, 1872

Dear Diary,

I feel like a top that someone is spinning faster and faster.

First Selena moved Blanche and Godfrey up here as soon as the carriage disappeared. Back and forth from the tenant house they trudged in the snow carrying all their possessions. Now Blanche is staying here in the girls room with me and actually I am glad of this, though she is a dim quiet little girl who is not much company. She sleeps in the other bed with a sighing noise all night long. But I will never show her this cubbyhole. I do not know where Victoria is, nor have I asked.

Selena tried to make little Junius move into the boys room with Godfrey but he is scared of Godfrey, and with good reason, so he refused, Selena insisted, and then little Junius had a fit where he shook all over and rolled his eyes back in his head and cried so hard that Selena had to give him some of Uncle Junius medicine. <u>All right then,</u> she finally said, <u>but I have never seen such a namby pamby lily livered little boy.</u>

So now little Junius is sleeping in the bed with me, I can hear him sucking his thumb whenever I wake up in the night. Sometimes I am so lonesome then that I scoot over behind him and put my arms around him so that we lie together like silver spoons stacked up in Aunt Fannies silver chest. I can count his ribs one by one in the dark. And I feel awful, like about a hundred people have left us, not just two.

December 21, 1872

The Wedding Day

The first we heard of it was yesterday morning when Selena lined us all up after breakfast in Liddys kitchen and told us that today was the day, and we should get washed up by afternoon and not go off anywhere because Uncle Junius would wish us to be present—You and little Junius in particular Molly, she said to me. So I am holding you responsible for him, is that understood?

I was looking down.

Molly. Is that understood?

Yes, I said looking up at her finally.

In the firelight from the hearth, Selena was like a handsome, fiery animal half wild, a horse or a dog maybe, with her hair springing out from her head. Play with him, she said, then bring him back in here for a bath.

All right, I said.

Behind her Liddy said nothing, mixing something up in a bowl. Water boiled in the big black pot on the stove behind her.

We are going to play marbles with Washington, little Junius said, and I winced for now Godfrey and Blanche would want to play too.

Selena sighed. Just dont get dirty again after you get washed up, she said, any of you. She turned to leave the kitchen.

Mama? Blanche was twisting her foot back and forth.

What?

Do you have a wedding dress, like Margaret?

Selena snorted, then grinned. Not hardly, she said. You all get on out of here now and let Liddy work. She gave us a little push and left, not seeing Liddy give her a look of purest hatred. Blanche and Godfrey ran ahead out the door while I walked out behind Selena with little Junius clinging to me.

I want the blue one, he said.

You can have it then, I said, almost stumbling over Selena who had suddenly stopped on the path ahead, leaning over to vomit in the snow.

I stopped and held little Junius close. We watched Selena gagging.

Well? She stood up straight and wiped off her mouth with the back of her hand. Its just the baby. You will see Molly. You will have one yourself sometime.

But I will not.

Selena went on into the house while little Junius peered at her vomit making a yellow stain in the hard old snow. The sky was low and gray all around us. Then here came Washington walking across the yard with the bag of marbles.

This was the longest day in the world Dear Diary, waiting for the magistrate to come. We played marbles out in the barn and Godfrey cheated, then lost anyway, then got mad and ran away. Blanche and little Junius and me had baths in the kitchen and helped Liddy and then got to play with the dominoes and checkers right there.

Once I came into the house and went upstairs to get my paper and pastels to draw with, and heard a big commotion in the hall when the widow Brown and two other ladys arrived by carriage to see Uncle Junius but were turned away by Selena now very demure in Fannies black and white checked taffeta dress with her hair pulled back in a bun. She slammed the door in their faces nevertheless, then opened Uncle Junius door and said, in answer to his deep gurgling voice, Oh it was nobody. Just nobody. A posse of busybodies from town, thats all, with nothing better to do than run around the county getting in somebody elses business.

Well my dear you made short work of them, Uncle Junius said.

Then Selena laughed, and went into his room, and shut the door behind her.

We ate cabbage and roast pork for dinner in the kitchen and you can be sure that Godfrey came back in time for that. He slurped his food and made a mess and kicked little Junius underneath the table.

You quit that, I told him.

Little Junius jumped and I knew that Godfrey had kicked him again. In a flash I turned over his chair and got him on the floor.

Molly, Molly, Liddy said.

Then Washington stood in the door and said, He is here. You all come on.

Liddy tucked my blouse in and pulled my hair back and clipped it with the mother of pearl barrette which she picked up from under the table where it had fallen in the fight. Then she led us out the door and into the house and along the brightly lit passage to Uncle Junius room where everybody was drunk, including Spence who loomed in the corner like a tree, grinning from ear to ear. The whisky bottle sat out on the bedside table. They crowded around the bed. There was wild-haired Doctor Lambeth, there was Selena, there was Uncle Junius sitting up in the bed looking like Death itself, attended by Virgil who sat to one side like a black carved statue staring straight ahead with his hands folded in his lap. The fat jolly redheaded man with the peg leg was evidently the magistrate, wearing a green silk vest and a gold cravat and a top hat, smoking a fine cigar which he kept jammed in the corner of his mouth throughout the service. A thin nervous young man with spectacles accompanied him, and a woman named Sadie who reminded me of Selena though she was blonde and not so pretty. Selena and the woman were drinking too, out of Fannies green liquer glasses from Portugal. They flung back their heads and upended the little glasses to toss the liquer down.

Aha! The arrival of the children! The magistrate said. He was not our regular magistrate from Hillsborough. We had never seen him before. Come, come now, come closer, he directed, lining us up at the foot of the bed.

A fire blazed in the hearth and candles flickered on the mantel and the writing table and the windowsill and every surface which was not completely covered by Uncle Junius papers and books. The room was hot and bright, smelling of liquor and smoke.

<u>By the authority vested in me</u> . . . , the magistrate began, putting an arm around the blonde woman who threw back her head and laughed. Then a roar began in my head which blocked out the rest of the words. But then I

thought of Fannie so kind and good, I could see her bright face in my mind as clearly as if she were sitting right there, smoothing my hair. It will be all right Molly, she said, but then her face faded away and the magistrate was saying, I now declare you man and wife, and everybody cheered except for Virgil who sat as if made of stone. Selena leaned over to kiss Uncle Junius glowing bony head. His eyes were almost closed.

Then Selena pointed at Spence who pulled out his harmonica and played Beautiful Dreamer as lovely as it can be played. His slow music wove in and out of the smoke and all the people who stood completely still, as if we were all in a Tableau Vivant. Beautiful dreamer, wake unto me, starlight and dew-drops are waiting for thee . . . I know the words because Julia used to sing it around the parlor fire when I was little. Then will all clouds of sorrow depart, beautiful dreamer, awake unto me. The last haunting note rose way up over our heads, higher and higher before it slowly died away quivering. A deep hush had fallen in the room.

Doctor Lambeth burst into loud tears and cried like a baby, wiping his long horse face with his handkerchief. Ah Junius! Ah Lord! That it could come to this! Ah Lord, Lord! He cried waving his handkerchief in the air.

The Lord has got nothing to do with it, Uncle Junius roused himself to say with a strange skeleton smile. Ladys and gentlemen, let us consider the act. Everyone looked at each other. And now, a toast to my lovely bride! All cheered, clinking their glasses together.

Spence started in fast on Shoo Fly, Don't Bother Me. The blond woman said something to Selena and poured the whisky all around. When Selena leaned back to drink hers, I saw the wide red hole of her mouth which seemed to go on and on forever. I clung to little Junius as hard as I could. Soon Romulus came to fetch Spence, he led him away staggering and grinning, still playing his harmonica. Well I had a real good time, Spence said from the doorway, which made them all laugh and cheer again. It is hard to tell if Spence knows what is happening or not. Virgil rose in silence and left with them.

The roar picked up in my head. Finally the blond woman whispered something to Selena who looked at us then came over and flung her arms around us in a hot fast hug and said, Go on then sweeties, go up to bed now. You take them Molly which made me feel big all of a sudden, and proud. It is not that Selena is so mean exactly, she is just too large and too much to deal with, like a lightning storm or a house afire.

Liddy stood waiting for us in the passage. She gave us some sweet bread and milk before we went upstairs where the last thing I heard before I fell asleep was that womans loud voice laughing down below.

December 23, 1872

Dear Diary,

As I write, it is early morning and I am so cold here in this cubbyhole, I can see my breath in the air. I have been up for hours.

Last night I awoke as I often do, yet this time still in my bed with one arm flung across little Junius chest. It was getting on toward morning. I can always tell by the feel of the house. Moonlight came in through the long window slanting in bars across the beds, across Blanche so slight I would never know she was even there except for the funny sound of her breathing, across little Junius whose white face shone in its light.

Victoria is not here but we know where she is now, Mrs. Bledsoe has taken her in out of pity and given her a chance to improve her lot in life by working in their kitchen. Ha! Selena said. That will not last long.

Anyway I stood tingling from head to toe in the moonlit room, I felt like screaming or running. I felt like everything was alive, even the furniture, from the big old Chinese chest to the spool beds where Blanche and Junius lay sleeping.

<u>Something is going to happen. It is happening now.</u> This thought came to me. I put on my shoes and a jacket and tiptoed across the room, grabbing up a coverlet from the end of our bed. I walked out into the hall and stood there, looking all around. Then slowly I was drawn to the door leading out onto the upper piazza, where no one has been in months.

I pushed the first bolt, leaning into it as hard as I could. At first I didnt think I could do it by myself but then it slid with a screeching sound loud enough to wake the whole house. But I listened, and no one stirred. I put my weight against the second bolt, I knew I could do it now. Nothing. Nothing. Then all at once it slid, fast. I pulled on the knob as hard as I could and at last the door gave inward toward me with a whooshing sound. Cold air poured into the hall.

I stepped out and pulled the door shut behind me. The wide porch lay bare except for piles of furniture stacked against the house and dead vines and drifts of snow over by the railings. The full moon shone like midday. Wind blew steadily across the fine new snow which had covered all tracks from yesterday so that the whole world beyond Agate Hill lay shining, changed and new.

Then all of a sudden I saw something I had not noticed before, a strange beast moving all humpbacked and slow down the lane. Or was it even moving? What was it? I held my breath and gripped the rail, peering. It was almost down to the first barn. Could it be a horse, with a pack on its back perhaps? Two horses? No, it was not moving. Fine crystals of snow blew into my eyes so that I had to shut them and then when I could open them again I saw that it <u>had</u> moved, it really had. It was moving so slow that you could not tell it. I stood and watched. I knew that something important was happening. And it was familiar, that figure, whatever it was. It was familiar to me. A faint glow of pink appeared on the horizon as I watched, above the line of hills.

The dark figure left no tracks as it passed down the long lane, picking up speed as the dawn came on. The wind blew across the snow. The figure moved faster and faster until I could scarcely see it. Snow blew off the railing and into my eyes. But a knowledge was growing in me, all along, blooming slowly in my mind like a flower. It was two people, walking together, carrying their belongings piled up on their backs. It was Virgil and Old Bess. The sky grew lighter and they moved faster, faster and faster, until they were flying over the snow like a great black bird, skimming the stand of cedars, flying over the river, heading over the hills. The sky turned silver and the snow turned pink. King Arthur was crowing. A horse neighed. My teeth knocked together like a baby rattle.

I opened the door and stepped back into the hall and closed it, screeching the bolts. It didnt matter. Sounds and voices were already coming up from below. But Blanche and little Junius slept on like angels as I passed back through the bedroom and the closet and entered this cubbyhole where I now write to you Dear Diary.

Virgil and Old Bess are gone. They were with me every day of my life, from South Carolina to Agate Hill. But I am glad they are gone, to think of it makes me feel good. There is a song Liddy sings sometimes,

> The little baby gone along,
> The little baby gone along,
> The little baby gone along,
> For to climb up Jacob's ladder.

So now they are gone along. But Liddy and Washington are in the kitchen, I see smoke coming up from the chimney. And all of a sudden I want some coffee the worst in the world. Its cold up here.

Christmas Eve 1872

The top that is myself continues to spin and spin, I dont know who is pulling the string, I go faster and faster. Too much has happened too fast Dear Diary. What I want is for nothing to happen at all. I dont even want good things any more, I just want nothing. As I write I look over at the box of phenomena in the corner of this cubbyhole, where Margaret and Robert E. Lee lie as if buried in a mass grave.

Victoria is back but we dont play dolls any more. Mrs. Bledsoe sent her packing, just like Selena predicted. Mrs. Bledsoe said that Victoria can not be trained to rise above her nature. Victoria and Selena fight all the time now, Victoria sticks out her bottom lip and will not obey. She sleeps here in the girls room with us but snuck out once to see the Irish boy down in the barn. Tis too cold for courting, he said, and has not come back. Victoria is downcast, as in a novel. She is only fifteen but she looks almost grown, it is not only her boobies. There is a faraway look in her eyes now. I am just biding my time, she says. She talks to me because there is no one else to talk to, and guess what? I am glad of it.

Uncle Junius is in mourning for Virgil. One of the finest men I have ever known, he said. But this was his home. Agate Hill was their home.

They were damn lucky to have a roof over their heads, Selena said.

I would also like to know how the hell they got out of here in such a hurry. Uncle Junius sounded more like himself for a minute.

You can ask HER about that. Selena tossed her head back in the direction of the kitchen. Or maybe Rom. But they wont tell you, of course. There is not a one of them that wouldnt stab you in the back if they got the chance.

Selena, Selena. Uncle Junius shook his head, falling back against his pillows. It smells bad in there now, like sickness and whisky and camphor and filth. I guess she keeps it as clean as she can.

Washington says that Virgil and Old Bess had not been paid for over a year, not since Fannie died and Uncle Junius turned all that over to Selena. Washington says Liddy is the only one getting paid on the place now and every time, Selena says it is the last time, there is no more money.

So Mama Marie is very sick and Uncle Junius is very sick but Christmas is coming anyway. You dont have to celebrate it but you can not stop it, Selena said, though she has stopped Julia and Rachel. She got me to write out the letter telling them not to come as Aunt Cecelia is gone and we are not receiving.

Social Life is over. People stay away from Agate Hill now as if from a plague house, except for old Doctor Lambeth who still comes out to see Uncle Junius then stays on drinking whisky with Selena. I think he brings it to her. Last time, she staggered out into the hall and then stood clutching the newel post for dear life when he left. I was trying to pass unobserved but she saw me, reaching out with her quick strong hand to grab my shoulder. Well? Well, Molly? I know what you are thinking. Her hair fell down in her face and she pushed it back and I saw to my surprise that her eyes were filled with tears.

I am not thinking anything, I said.

Its not what it is cracked up to be, Selena said, but not really to me, as if to herself. Its too hard. It is all of it too goddamn hard. Then she seemed to forget me and let go of my shoulder and set off wobbling down the passage toward the kitchen, leaving Uncle Junius door open behind her. I went over to close it so as not to lose the heat. The spirit lamp hissed in the corner. The wood was getting low. He raised his head. Selena? he said.

I closed the door.

All he ever says now is Selena, its like she has bewitched him.

<u>Christmas is coming, you can not stop it,</u> she said. But does Uncle Junius not remember how it used to be? Am I always the only one who must remember everything? Does he not remember how it smelled for instance, when Rom and Spence brought big armfuls of red holly and cedar boughs and pine branches in from the woods to tie along the staircase railing, to line the mantels and stick in the big Chinese vases on either side of the front door and in the parlor? That sharp smell still prickles my nose as I think of it. It meant Christmas along with the smell of the oranges that came from faraway in a wooden box and were much prized for we never saw them at any other time of year.

Fannies fruitcakes were lined up in the cold corner of the kitchen for weeks on end, drenched with whisky. Julia and Rachel made divinity fudge, and Liddy made fried apple pies. Sometimes we had ham for Christmas dinner but more often it was a big wild turkey which Spence had shot in the woods. It was roasted all day then served on the ironstone platter surrounded by parsnips and sweet potatoes dug up from the cellar. Fannie and Liddy scrimped and worked for weeks on that dinner, and Uncle Junius said the blessing.

Mama Marie sat smiling at everybody, while Aunt Mitty glowered and ate each helping of food on her plate up separately before she began on the next one.

Now the passage is empty and cold and dirty where we have been tromping in mud with the snow. Selena does not appear to notice. She says it is all she can do to keep wood in the house and food on the table. She says anybody who wants Christmas dinner this year can damn well get it off the stove in the kitchen. Squirrel stew. No gifts. Liddy is cooking the stew right now in the big black pot on the tripod over the fire outside. Tomorrow morning Washington and me will take some of it over to Mama Marie and Aunt Mitty along with some roasted quail and a pound cake. Arent we having carols then? Blanche asked, for she loved to sing as Fannie taught us, but Selena said, <u>Not hardly.</u> Victoria grinned. She is not so bad after all. I hope Selena will let her go over there with us tomorrow.

December 26, 1872

Dear Diary,

Washington came to wake me and Victoria at first light. Liddy gave us some coffee and johnnycake to eat in the kitchen, ham biscuits to put in our pockets for the long walk to Mamma Maries. Victoria was sleepy and sullen but I was excited, after all it is always an adventure, like Gullivers Travels and Robinson Crusoe and the Odyssey. All the books are about somebody going someplace. Liddy wrapped us up in all the old clothes she could lay her hands on. It is real cold right now. We set off across the yard and through the woods under a low gray sky, it was like walking under a blanket. There was only a couple inches of snow. Washington carried the pot of stew. I went last. Ahead of me Washington and Victoria looked like snowmen, their arms stuck out from their bodies because they were so bundled up.

We walked through the big pine forest and came to the sandy spring now covered by solid ice. I imagined it gurgling underneath, <u>biding its time,</u> as Victoria said. We walked along the stone fencerow past the old homestead. Animal tracks were everywhere. When we came to the place where the negro had hung, there was no way to tell it, just a big tree with a long limb and the old road passing underneath in a stretch of unbroken snow, as if nothing had ever happened there at all. But it DID happen, I thought. It did, I remember, I remember everything. I said nothing.

We went on but the sun never did come out. Victoria kept complaining. I kept thinking I saw Mary Whites red coat ahead of us through the trees. I knew this was not true, but it made me happy to think so. By the time we got to the mill, we could hear distant pops in the air as people shot off their guns the way you do on Christmas. The sky stayed dull and low. Morning never came.

At the big tree Victoria said Frankly I cannot go one more goddamn foot. We sat down on a rock to eat our biscuits. I gave her my second one. So Victoria ate three biscuits and I ate one and Washington ate two. The dim gray woods were very peaceful.

Its nice out here, isnt it? I said.

No it is not Miss Fancypants, Victoria said. What is the matter with you? Its too dark out here. You cant see anything. I want to SEE what I am doing. I am sick of snow. I am sick of mud. I am sick of being poor and everybody dying. I want a city, she said, with streetlights and paving stones. I am tired of working my fingers to the bone. Work work work. Thats all they know around here. It was even worse at the Bledsoes. They prayed all the time too. Well there is a lot more to life than this. I want some pretty clothes and a pretty boy like Declan Moylan and there aint no reason in the world why I cant have it.

Washington and me sat looking at her. I bet you gets it then, he said.

She looked over at me. What do YOU want, Molly? she asked in a different voice.

I dont know, I said. But I'll know it when I see it, and I'll want it the worst in the world. What about you Washington?

He looked away. I aint saying. He stood up. Less get on then, he said.

We saw lots more tracks, wagon and horse and foot, when we got to the public road. They continued under the big stone arch and into the Four Oaks lane.

Something going on, Washington said.

We walked faster. The huge trees spread their black arms out across the snowy yard where three or four wagons were parked helter skelter, mules and horses stamping their feet in the snow. People stood on the porch. A man drank from a bottle then put it back in his pocket and stared at us. Spencer stood out in the sideyard all wild-haired and wild-eyed smoking a cigarette. We went over there.

Spence, I said. Whats wrong? What is happening? Wheres Rom?

Spence grinned his big grin at us. Miss Marie up and died in the night, he said, and now Miss Mitty gone too.

What? Victoria and I looked at each other.

You going to eat that? Spence was looking at the food we carried.

Come on, I said. We went over to the porch and climbed up the steps and walked through the people. Two rough looking men in black coats and hats were trying to talk to Susie through a crack in the door. One of them waved a sheet of paper.

Yankees, Victoria said into my ear.

You will have to speak to Mister Junius Hall, he owns this place now Susie was saying. She had big dark circles under her eyes.

I am telling you, I now own this property! said the fat one with the mustache.

You will have to leave now, Susie said.

Madam, if you will allow us to come inside for a moment—

At that point Spencer picked the man up like he was a stick of firewood and threw him off the porch into the yard where he landed all spraddled out like a child playing angels in the snow.

I am hurt! I am hurt! he cried, then cut loose in a string of language such as I have never heard. Everybody moved over to the edge of the porch to get a look at him. The other man walked down into the yard.

Why good Lord, looky here at you children, where did you come from? Get on in the house, Susie said. We went in with Spence following us all the way back to the big warm kitchen where Susie put the pot on the stove and we sat down and Spence started eating the quail one after the other.

What he had said was true, all of it. Mama Marie had died in her sleep with her Bible in her hand and a smile on her face. Nobody could have gone more peacefully, Susie said, adding that somehow Aunt Mitty had known it, that she had got up in the night and gone upstairs and got on the bed beside Mama Marie to keep her warm as she was passing. When Susie came into the bedroom in the morning, Aunt Mitty got up, straightened her nightdress, then kissed Mama Marie on the mouth. <u>Good bye Marie,</u> Aunt Mitty said. Then she went back downstairs and took a little sponge bath and dressed herself in her good black bombazine dress, calling Susie in to put up her hair. By then, Susie said, Mrs. Goodnight and two other women had already arrived to start laying out Mama Marie.

Susie gave Spence a bowl of the squirrel stew.

Now Mrs. Goodnight appeared in the kitchen door. Miss Marie is ready, she said. Mrs. Goodnight is a thin sour looking woman with moles on her face.

I did not want to see Mama Marie. I have already seen enough dead people to last me the rest of my life. But it was clear that we had to. So we all got up and followed Susie straight back into the hall and up the stairs and into Mama Maries bedroom where she lay with her hands folded together as if in prayer. Now Mama Marie herself had gone off to the world of light. Susie started crying.

Dont she look nice? Mrs. Goodnight said.

Susie put her hand over her mouth and turned away stumbling, Spence caught her before she fell. We went back downstairs where Mrs. Goodnight set Victoria and me to lighting lamps in the parlor. Then Spence and Rom carried Mama Marie down there on a board and placed her between two straightback chairs.

And how is your dear uncle? A woman who used to be Fannies friend was pinching my arm.

Come on, I told Victoria.

Aunt Mittys door stood open as always. A big fat woman named Maude Lear was telling the tale—how Miss Mitty had got all dressed up, how she had said, <u>Ashes to ashes, dust to dust,</u> then climbed into her coffin. Well I knowed better than to try and stop her, Maude Lear said. She laid herself down in that coffin and said Maude, come over here and fix my dress, and so I fixed it, and then I got up my nerve and I ast her, Miss Mitty do you expect to see God?

<u>I expect to see Marie,</u> she said, <u>but we shall see what we shall see.</u>

She closed her eyes and died within a hour, bless God. Maude Lears voice and her chins were quivering. We went over to the coffin to look at Aunt Mitty whose mouth turned down like a shovel as in life. She wore the black dress and her accustomed lace cap which looked sillier than ever above her stern dead face.

All of a sudden I got tickled. <u>Lets go.</u> I jabbed Victoria. We did not go back into the parlor, but grabbed our coats from the kitchen where we found Washington. The three of us set off fairly running through the woods.

Selena met us at the door. Before we could say a word, she told us that we had just missed Julia who had arrived after all with her fiancé, an older man very stuck up and wearing a bowler hat which he never even took off his head. They had not received my letter. Julia was real mean about everything that had happened at Agate Hill, and did not have any appreciation at all for what good care Selena was taking of her father. Harsh words were exchanged. Julia and her fiancé had left within an hour of their arrival, taking little Junius with them.

<u>What?</u> Everything went black for a minute as I sank down upon the cold stone steps of the piazza. Did she say anything about me? I asked. I did not say, Didnt she ask for me too?

She brought you all some oranges, Selena said. But that so-called fiancé of hers was egging her on, I swear I would rather be horsewhipped than marry that one. You get up from there now Molly. It is cold as a witches tit out here. Get on in the house.

So I did, and then Victoria and me told her everything else.

She stared at us open-mouthed. Well honey, she said, there is not a god-damn thing I can do about any of it. You better go in there and tell Junius, which I did, though the medication keeps him so dreamy now it is hard to tell if he takes things in or not.

I was feeling light headed myself by the time I finally got back to the kitchen. Liddy had left the stew still warm on the stove. The wooden box of oranges sat beside it. I got some stew and ate it all alone at the big pine table which used to hold ten or twelve of us, negro and white alike. A low fire burned in the hearth so that points of light gleamed from the hanging pots, and shadows flickered on the old brick walls. I finished the stew and got an orange from the box.

Suddenly I remembered it was Christmas. And now it was almost time for all the animals to kneel in prayer as they did in the stable so long ago, Fannie used to tell us the story. If I got up and went down to the barn right now, would I find Buck and Bill on their knobby old knees in prayer? I did not think so. I thought of the baby Jesus born in the stable and then I remem-bered Mamma telling about some family back in South Carolina who had so many children to die that they didnt even name them when they were born, they waited to see if they would live until their first birthday. They called all of them Captain, Mama said. But the baby Jesus was Jesus right from the beginning and everybody knew it. I started peeling the orange. The white stuff makes my nose wrinkle.

Actually I like the baby Jesus better than I like the grownup Jesus whose eye is on the sparrow and I know he watcheth me. Aunt Mitty said, <u>You have an eternal soul, Molly, whether you want it or not.</u> I hate that. This makes Jesus seem to me like a sharpshooter in Wade Hamptons army, moving from tree to tree with his rifle aimed at me.

The orange exploded with sweetness in my mouth.

☙

January 13, 1873

Dear Diary,

We did not go back to Four Oaks. There will be a funeral later for Mama Marie and Aunt Mitty when it thaws and the minister can come. As for now they are froze in their caskets out there in the little tobacco barn with Rom and Spence to watch over them. Susie disappeared from the house leaving a note which I had to read aloud to Uncle Junius. She said that she had been well provided for thanks to Aunt Mitty, and that she would pray for us all. Selena sniffed. I am certainly glad SOMEBODY has been provided for, she said. Selenas baby is starting to show now. I put the note into Uncle Junius hand but he dropped it onto the counterpane. His eyes are like old milkglass when he opens them, but mostly he sleeps. Liddy boils chicken to make him a hearty broth though he has nearly quit eating. He sleeps, and Selena sleeps, or else she paces, I can hear her in the night. Sometimes she takes Uncle Junius medicine herself, to help her rest. Sometimes she talks to herself. Those men in the black coats have come here twice now. Victoria is planning to run away with Declan Moylan whenever he gets a horse. Victoria and me work like dogs and sometimes we play games but whenever I look in her eyes I can tell, she is already gone. In the interests of phenomena she has showed me her breasts which have gotten bigger. But guess what Dear Diary? Now I am getting some too.

January 18, 1873

Dear Diary,

It is nothing but snow and work here now. This is the coldest winter that anybody can remember. Since Godfrey lies sick it is my job to go to the well for water and when I drop the bucket down, it breaks the ice every time. So I must go often in order to keep it broke up, Washington does this at night. Let me go for Molly, he said this morning, but Selena made him chop more wood instead as there is no one else to do it. The springhouse trough has already froze and quit running down in the cellar.

At least I get to wear Julias old green boots now, I found them up here in the closet. Victoria tried to take them but Selena gave them to me since Victoria refuses to work outside. Selena slapped her yesterday.

January 21, 1873

Dear Diary,

Selena doses Godfrey up with whisky and honey which does not help, you can hear him coughing all over the house. For years I have wished he would die but now I am not so sure as it seems he might. He will burn in Hell for sure if there is one. But I am so cold right now as I sit here writing that Hell sounds pretty good.

I put socks on my hands for gloves but they are cracked and bleeding anyhow. Liddy rubs them with lard. My face is as red and rough as a cob   I can not write my hands are too cold   This is my blood on this page

It is snowing again

January 25, 1873

Snowing and Snowing

Dear Diary,

Washington and me played checkers in front of the hearth in the kitchen while Liddy baked sweet potatoes in the coals. Selena did not mind, she came in and smiled and touched my head. Her face is very thin now but all of a sudden I see that she is beautiful, in the way of La Belle Dame Sans Merci in Mary Whites book which is gone. This is a poem which I am forgetting already. But it is hard for me to read now anyway, for some reason I can not keep my mind on the page. I dont know what is wrong with me.

January 30, 1873

Dear Diary,

For once I have some good news! Spence and Rom came with a load of wood and some food stuffs from Four Oaks, so Liddy fried pork chops and eggs before they left and we all ate so much we could not move and Spence played Liza Jane on his harmonica for Uncle Junius who never opened his eyes. I wonder if Spence even knows Uncle Junius is his father. Cant he remember riding his pony Silver Shoes and learning his lessons with Fannie? Cant he remember anything? Sometimes I think, which is worse? To remember nothing or to remember too much, like me? Rom is a skinny mean looking negro man with scars on his cheeks, he used to be the slave driver. But he is devoted to Spencer and sometimes he plays the banjo along with him.

I hated to see them go, watching from the parlor window as they drove their wagon off into a landscape so gray that you couldnt tell the land from the sky. My breath made ice on the inside of the pane.

February 3, 1873

Where is he? Selena stood in the kitchen drinking coffee, her hands shook so bad that the coffee splashed onto the floor.

She means Doctor Lambeth, who has not come for days.

Nevermind. Here now. You have got to eat, Liddy said. She dished up a plate of fried potatoes and bacon and put it on the table. Sit down. Liddy is small and quiet but she will boss anybody, even Selena, if she takes a mind to.

Selena sat down and picked up the fork then looked away. Oh Liddy I cant do it, she said.

Liddy said, How you think that baby is going to eat?

I dont care. I cant understand where he is, Selena said. Junius will die without his medicine.

Liddy looked at her. Mister Junius going to die anyway, she said.

Then Selena twisted around to grab Liddys skirt. Send Washington, she said.

But Liddy shook her head. Its too bad out. Look how dark it is out that window.

Washington has got to go right now, Selena said.

Finally even Liddy could tell it was no use talking to her about it.

So Selena ate her breakfast and Washington left for Hillsborough in a sleeting rain and now it is night and he has not got back yet.

February 4, 1873

Dear Diary,

The worst has happened, the well has froze. Now I must go to the spring in the woods and break the ice to get the water. Yesterday I got so tired on my last trip out there that I sat down to rest for a minute before starting back. The buckets get so heavy when they are full. I lay back in the snow underneath that big pine tree which makes the nicest sound, like it is sighing or singing a lullaby just for me. It was so quiet and peaceful in the snow that I might have gone to sleep for a while but woke to see a fairy sitting on the bough just above my head. His face was dark and pointed, his little cap was red. <u>Wake up Molly Petree,</u> he said in his high chirping voice. <u>Go home.</u> He pointed his green gloved finger straight at me. Then he lifted off. His wings beat the air to a silvery blur. It was almost dark but he shone like a star as he disappeared into the tree. I got up from the snow and hoisted my buckets and headed home.

Washington has not returned, may be he never will.

February 5, 1873

Dear Diary,

I can scarce write this, it is not that I am cold but exited!

I was coming down the little stairs this morning when someone pulled the doorbell, giving me a terrible fright, for who could it be? Our bell has not rung in months.

<u>Molly stop. Dont open it.</u> Selena stuck her head out of Uncle Junius room.

My heart bumped in my chest as I disobeyed and ran to throw the latch. I thought it must be something terrible, something about Washington. The hanging negro turned on the rope in my mind.

A tall man dressed all in black stood on the wide stone step of the piazza. His big black hat and his mustache were frosted with crystals of ice, his breath made a cloud in the air. Beyond him through the chilly fog I could barely see—thank God!—Washington out there hitching up a huge gray horse to the post.

The mans eyes were deepset and dark, his brow jet black though his beard was shot through with gray. He did not smile, but stared at me intently.

I am looking for Miss Molly Petree, he said.

I am Molly Petree. I took a deep breath and stood up tall.

Of course you are. You look just like your mother.

I do not, I said.

You do. He looked me up and down as if to memorize me. Allow me to introduce myself. I am—

<u>I know who you are.</u> A deep thrill passed through me.

For Diary dont you remember this photograph of my daddy with Simon Black, the boy he went to war with? See, here he is, this rough looking dark-haired boy with the stern face and the piercing black eyes, he is the very opposite of my fair and handsome father. Here he is. He too was born and grew up on the place at Perdido where his father was the blacksmith and farrier, a trade Simon Black took into the war and followed until they made him a scout, for he could out ride anybody. I knew all these things.

I knew him too. Immediately.

Selena stood in the door. For once she appeared speechless.

Selena this is Simon Black, I said. My fathers best friend from childhood.

Selena inclined her head with her wrapper clutched at her throat, she scarcely even bothers to dress these days.

Pleased to meet you, said Simon Black. I bring you news from town.

First, I am sorry to say that Doctor Lambeth is ill. But after a fortunate encounter with young Washington, I have taken the liberty of delivering this medication to Mister Hall myself. He produced the vial from a pocket deep in his long dark coat and handed it to Selena.

<u>Ah.</u> A change came over her face. Well hello there, she said, as if she knew him. Please come in, Mister Black.

Thank you. He came inside the house and closed the door behind him. I stepped back. I was wearing some old woolen trousers that had belonged to one of the dead boys.

Welcome to Agate Hill. Selena had recovered her manners.

Thank you, he said, taking off his hat. Actually I had the pleasure of visiting here twice previously during the last year of the War, with Mollys father. He looked around. Suddenly I was aware of all the mud and mess in the hall. But Simon Black went on, Now I find Agate Hill . . . diminished. But you must pardon me. I am not a civilized man, and I have been out of this country for many years now. He cleared his throat. Well. I should like to see Junius, he said.

He is so ill. We are not—, Selena said.

<u>It is very important.</u>

To my surprise, Selena stood aside.

Simon Black entered the smelly room with me trailing behind though Selena grabbed my arm and pinched it. Stay, she said, but I would not have stayed if my life depended on it. A low lamp burned, and the spirit lamp hissed in the corner. Simon Black dumped a pile of clothes off a ladderback chair and pulled it over next to the bed where Uncle Junius lay twisted to the side breathing open-mouthed while his arm hung down to the floor. May be he has already died, I thought, but then Simon Black got up close to his face and said, <u>Junius.</u>

Uncle Junius dark eyelids fluttered.

Selena came closer.

<u>Junius,</u> Simon Black said.

Uncle Junius opened his milky eyes.

You know who I am, Simon Black said.

Uncle Junius eyes seemed to change somehow though still he did not speak.

Good. I am sorry to find you like this Junius. And I am sorry it has taken me all these years to get here despite the promise I made to Charlie so long ago, after the battle at Bentonville. I should have come to you sooner. I should have come to you then. I should have done many other things as well. But the fact is that I was sick, sick unto death of this poor bloody and broken land. I needed more room. I had to get out of this sad old history. So I did not look back, and I swore I would never come back either. But recently I had a—tragedy—and I have undergone a change, and I am here to fulfill my obligation to Charles Petree, for in fact I owe him this life which I do not much want yet can not get rid of either.

This strange speech sounded like something in a play, like something Simon Black had been planning to say for a long time. After delivering it, he fell silent.

They thought you was dead too, Selena said after a while.

He gave a short laugh. Perhaps I was dead, he said. Perhaps I am dead still. But the fact is that I never surrendered with the others at the Bennett farm house, I rode off from there headed for points south where I have remained ever since. And now I am too late. She is gone.

Who? Selena asked.

<u>Why, Alice. Alice, of course.</u>

The way he said my mothers name gave me a chill.

<u>I am too late for Alice, yet not for Molly.</u> He turned to look at me, then addressed Selena. Clearly you are all in some distress here. Perhaps I could lighten your burden by taking charge of Molly and—

Dear Diary I can not say how I felt at this moment, so furious and scared to death with my heart beating hard in my chest. I could scarcely breathe.

But Uncle Junius hand flapped back and forth against the bed like a chicken with its head cut off. Get out of here Simon, he said finally. By God I am not dead yet.

You heard my husband, Selena said. He is Mollys guardian.

Simon Black turned to look at her. I always respected Junius Hall, he said. Yet I gave Charlie my word as well. He stood up and put his hat back on. He seemed to fill the room. He inclined his head to Selena then strode across the floor, silver spurs clanking, to pause before me. Molly I am pleased to make your acquaintance at last, he said.

I said nothing, for I was terrified.

Good bye then, he said from the door before he closed it.

Well I never, Selena said.

Uncle Junius made a terrible gurgling sound from the bed as a dark liquid flowed down the corner of his mouth. Selena rushed forward. Get Liddy, she said.

April 16, 1873

Dear Diary,

I am so sorry I have not written for so long, my mind goes around and around so fast now that all is a blur I can not slow it down long enough to put pen to paper.

But I will try. I will try.

Uncle Junius died.

Uncle Junius died, and the next thing I remember, we were all riding out to Four Oaks. We had got dressed up as best we could, it was Godfrey and Blanche, Victoria and me and Selena and Liddy all jammed into the carriage, Washington driving. Selena wore Fannies black hat with a veil and Fannies black velvet evening cloak to hide the baby. Victorias dress was too small while Blanches was too large. I wore one of Fannies dresses too, I am big enough now for ladys clothes though I hate to wear them.

I rode with Godfreys knee jabbed into my back but did not say a word. I felt that if I spoke, I might explode and blow away in dust along the roadside, never to be seen again.

It felt so odd to be going to Four Oaks by road instead of through the woods, it was like a journey to a strange new place. It was sunny and cold. We bounced in the deep muddy ruts, Selena gritting her teeth. The casket bounced in the wagon ahead while Rom drove and Spence waved at everybody.

Look. Victoria punched me and pointed and I turned back to see the Bledsoes coming in a carriage behind us and somebody else in a wagon behind them. By the time we got to the big public road there were others behind us too, and people lining the road all along the privet hedge and the old stone arch and the lane, holding their hats in their hands. It was the whole countryside negro and white turned out for Uncle Junius. But I couldnt tell who they were because we were driving straight into the sun and now I was crying so their faces were all a blur to me, as blank as the face of Robert E. Lee my man doll.

We got out and went up onto the porch. To my surprise there were Julia and Rachel, crying and hugging and kissing everybody including me, but not Selena. No one spoke to Selena. She stood apart holding Blanches and Godfreys hands, chewing the inside of her cheek.

A new minister Mister Ricketts spoke the words but I did not listen, instead looking out at Uncle Junius coffin which lay on a bier in the yard and remembering how Mary White and me played dolls in the roots of those oaks only last summer which seems like another lifetime or like it was some other girl who did that, who laughed and played so free.

Amen, Mister Ricketts said. Then all sang Amazing Grace led by Julias pure piercing voice.

> Amazing grace, how sweet the sound
> That saved a wretch like me!
> I once was lost, but now am found
> Was blind but now I see.

I do not believe that Uncle Junius is now found, and I do not think he believed it either.

The pallbearers were Spence and Rom and some of Uncle Junius and Aunt Fannies former slaves including Big John who used to lead us around on Spencers old pony. They took up the bier and walked down the old farm road and across the Big Field and up the rise where all are buried, my entire ghost family, with Mama Marie and Aunt Mitty lying close together beneath their pile of new red dirt. A marble spire points up to the blue sky on top of the rise just beyond them, that is Big Papas marker. Old Ben stood leaning on his shovel by the open grave which was next to Fannies. I looked at Selena but she stared straight ahead with her face working. Now the Masons took over, Mister Ogilvie and Mister Short from town in their outfits saying words which were very strange. They threw shovels full of dirt on Uncle Junius coffin. Then Spence grabbed the shovel digging with a fury while ladys wept and a chilly breeze swept over us, blowing my hair.

Look, Godfrey said, pointing up. Buzzards.

They are coming for you! I said to scare him, but actually I think it is me. Then all of a sudden I looked down and noticed that I cast no shadow Dear Diary <u>none.</u> So may be I really am a ghost girl all ready.

I ran ahead, I couldnt wait to get out of there.

Molly, Molly! Rachel called me from the yard, but I acted like I didnt hear her. I got back into the carriage. Giddy up, Washington said. Selena cried all the way back to Agate Hill, turning once to me to say, <u>Well you know I loved him.</u> I did not know what to say. I had loved him too.

Then at Agate Hill there was an uproar for while we had been gone to the funeral, Julias fiance had come with some men and a wagon and taken the silver and lots of other things as reported by Selenas blond friend Sadie who ran out to tell us. She had been there but unable to stop them.

What do I care? Selena threw back her head. I swear I dont give a damn, lets go have a drink then. They went on in the house.

That left me to stand by myself in the full sun blinking and looking down at the new green grass in the yard. For the life of me, I could not think what to do next.

Finally I went in the house too where all was a wreck and Selenas friend the magistrate gave me and Victoria some little glasses of whisky and laughed when it made us cry. You will have to do better than that, girls, he said giving us more.

April 25, 1873

Dear Diary,

Victoria has left with Declan Moylan, they did not even sneak off. Instead he came straight to the house with an old horse and wagon he got from someplace. Victoria came out with her things in a poke and he boosted her up, then sprang up himself. Bye Sissy, Blanche called out in a little voice. Declan Moylans hair shone red as a candle flame. Selena stood behind me watching with her belly pushing against my back and her fingers digging into my shoulder, then said Shit shit shit and went into the house with Doctor Lambeth who lives here now drunk as a Lord.

May 8, 1873

Godfrey was the one who told me first, he loves to bring bad news. Liddy and Washington are going away, he said this morning when I got up and went down into the passage. Mama gave them a cart and a mule.

That is not true, you are lying. I flew through the passage out the door and into the kitchen where the coffee pot sat on the stove as it does every day and biscuits were in the old pan under the red checkered cloth same as always. Liar liar pants on fire! I grabbed two biscuits and ran out the door to their cabin the dew was all cold on my feet.

But sure enough there was Washington loading up the old cart, Buck tied to the hackberry tree.

See stupid? Godfrey was panting along right behind me and I whirled to hit him but missed and he ran off laughing.

Washington stood in the door with his arms full. I was just coming over there to find you, he said.

But all of a sudden I was hitting him hard as I could. Damn you damn you damn you, I said like Selena. I knew he had known for days.

Washington dropped his bundles which fell all over the place, one quilt rolled out on the grass. He stood there and let me hit him until I got tired of it. Oh Molly he said. He gripped my arms at the elbow. I was crying. Come here, he said. Come on in. He held the indigo cloth aside for me to go into their cabin where I had not been since long ago with Fannie when someone was sick. Though it was dark inside with no window it did not have a negro smell as people always said but smelled sweet and fresh. Liddy had cleaned it for leaving even though no one would care, no one but me would ever know it. That is how she was.

Liddy was over in the corner doing something. She did not turn when we came in. Elijah, she said. Bring me a light over here.

Washington let go of me. He stuck a little piece of kindling into the fireplace coals, then blew on it till it flared up and I could see his gray eyes. He took it over to his mother and lit the tallow candle she gave him.

What did she call you? I asked.

Elijah, he said. It is my real name, Washington my slave name, give to me by your Uncle Junius.

But its a good name, isnt it? I said. Dont you like it? Its the president of our country after all.

Not my country, Washington said.

I could not have been more surprised if the heavens had opened up and the angel Gabriel appeared as in that song that Liddy sings.

I tell you what, she said to Washington, you let me hold the light, and you dig in the wall. Dig right here. She had already chipped a hole in it.

What are you all doing? I went over to the corner and watched while Washington dug into the wall.

All of a sudden I had an idea. What if I hold that door cloth up so we can get some more light in here? I said.

Liddy said, Just go ahead and rip it down Molly, we taking it with us anyway. After I did this, things went along better.

Washington was scooping out old stuff that looked like dirt.

What is that? I asked.

Thats the old mortar, Liddy said. They made it right here on the place, out of sand and water and hogs hair, thats what keeps it together.

I stepped back so as not to touch it piling up on the floor. Uncle Junius always had floors put in the cabins because he thought it kept the negros from getting malaria. He <u>was</u> good, I thought, he <u>was.</u> But I knew it was awful anyway. Uncle Junius always said so himself.

Here, Washington said, pulling out a small wooden box that rattled when he shook it.

Liddy snatched it away.

What is it? I came closer to see.

Liddy opened the top and emptied the box out onto her palm while Washington held the candle right there. It was a pile of shiny little shells—six or seven of them. Liddy sucked in her breath and said something I could not understand. The shells glowed like pearls in her hand. Their tops were rounded like snail shells or like the dinner rolls that Liddy used to make for company so long ago. The bottom of each shell had two rows of teeth, almost like a little open mouth.

From Africa, Liddy said.

I grabbed one. It felt solid and warm and good in my hand, like a little rock. Can I have it? I asked, for suddenly I wanted it the most in the world.

No. Liddy did not look at me. She took the shell from me then one by one she put them all back in the box and closed the top.

I was too upset to say anything.

Mama. Come on, we got to go before she change her mind. You know how Miss Selena is, Washington said from the door.

Wait. Where are you going? What will you live on? I followed him out.

<u>Looky here.</u> Washington held up a solid gold piece which shone in the sun.

I couldnt believe it. Where did you get that?

He grinned. Mister Simon Black done give it to me for bringing him out here that day. He say I am going to need it sometime. Now Mama come on!

Selena came out of the big house shading her eyes from the sun. Get a move on then, she called. Get out of here. Molly you come on.

Washington helped his mother into the cart where she sat on top of their piled up things with all the dignity of a born lady. She still didnt look at me. He made that clicking noise and moved the reins and Buck pricked his ears up. Then <u>Oh Molly I almost forgot!</u> Washington bent over and grabbed something up and threw it at me. <u>Catch!</u>

It was the bag of marbles. I caught it with both hands. <u>Good bye Liddy, good bye Elijah,</u> I called.

What? What did you say? What did he give you? Selena asked.

But they had already gone off into the sunny day leaving me stuck here as in a Tableau Vivant forever.

June 4, 1873

Dear Diary,

The big news is, Doctor Lambeths two sons have come out here with a servant and rough language and taken him away. They put Doctor Lambeth into a wagon and hauled him off to a sanitarium. Well that is all right, Selena said, though he had his uses. The problem with a man is, you think you want one but then you get him and then you dont. Remember that Molly.

But now she has already got another one.

June 11, 1873

Dear Diary,

We have lost Four Oaks.

So Spence and Rom are back on this place now which is good for they are a big help but Selenas new friend came to visit and has not left, I do not like him, no one likes him, his name is Nicky Eck.

June 13, 1873

More about Nicky Eck

He is a smooth-talking smooth-haired traveling man who showed up at the door, Selena knows him from someplace. He has white-white teeth and a rosy mouth like a bow, like a girl. He wears checkered shirts and red suspenders and two-tone shoes. I do not like him. His eyelids seem always to shade his eyes, you cant tell what he is thinking, nor will he give a straight answer to anything. When I asked him where he is from, he said <u>Not from around here thats for sure</u> and when I asked him what he does he said he <u>represents a line of notions</u> but he would not say what kind, nor any more about it. He said, What is this Missy, the Inquisition?

What is that? Selena asked, but I knew. I know about the Inquisition and the French Revolution and the Leaning Tower of Pisa and many more things which mean nothing now though once I thought they did once I thought oh nevermind   I do not like Nicky Eck I do not like the way he calls me Missy and follows me around with those hooded eyes it makes me feel funny. But Selena likes him. She has cheered up considerable in his company.

It is getting hot already. I cooked up some greens from the garden Spencer planted, I am not a bad cook either. You would be surprised! I am helping Selena in the kitchen, she is so big now. I reckon I learned a lot from watching Liddy without even knowing it. Everybody eats in the kitchen whenever they want to, whatever they can find. Meals are gone now. Many things are gone from the house too and more are disappearing all the time it seems to me. I think Nicky Eck takes them when he goes off for a day or so though I can not keep track, I am so tired. Nor do I care. He brings presents back for Selena such as sweet-smelling soap, a silver barrette, and stockings. Nothing for us and nothing for the baby. He follows me with his eyes. I do not know if Nicky Eck is a Yankee or not which seems likely but some of them are nice anyway and Nicky Eck is not nice, he is something much worse than a Yankee it seems to me. Agate Hill looks like the Yankees have been here but it was not even the Yankees, it was us.

June 21, 1873

Oh Diary,

Something else is happening now   I can not stop it nor do I want to, it is Nicky Eck touching me up under my clothes first my breasts when he came upon me in the passage last night with no one present then again in the kitchen this morning where I worked at the stove he came up from behind and pushed himself against me I could feel him through my skirt   I dropped an egg   I can not tell you how I feel   I can tell no one but it is the opposite of ghosts, that is for sure! He breathed in my ear, it sent shivers all down my body, I have thought about it all day long. He said, <u>You like that dont you darling.</u> No one has ever called me darling before as in a poem but I hate it, I hate Nicky Eck. Stop it! I am going to tell Selena, I said, but he said, <u>No you wont, you wont tell Selena or anybody else.</u> And he is right. I will not.

Now he is gone again. I took Blanche and Godfrey down to the river today where we made a dam in the shallows by the Willow House and I showed them how to sail magnolia leaf boats. It was a lot of fun but I didnt tell them anything not about the Willow House itself nor the people who live there nor the fairy ring which is gone from the woods now nor anything else that me and Mary White used to do. And all the time my mind was spinning above my head as it is doing right now. Nicky Eck has three moles on his cheek. He says, <u>You like that dont you darling? You are a bad girl.</u> He stood on the upper piazza watching us walk back up the lane from the river, I knew my shirt was sticking to my chest. Nicky Eck smoked a cigarette saying nothing.

June 25, 1873

Dear Diary,

I am hiding up here from Nicky Eck, it is the only place in the world he can not find me. It is real hot. I have been in here for a long time. But I dont care how hot it gets I will not come out. I am considering the items in my collection of phenomena one by one, I love to do this, but most of all I am remembering. I am remembering everything.

Today I turned back to read the beginning of this Diary in which Nora Gwyn urged me to <u>set down upon these pages your own memories of your lovely mother and your brave father, and of your three brothers as well, and of all that has befallen you.</u> Well I see that I have not done this exactly, I have not written about them so much, but now I will do so, for they are stuck in time as I am stuck in here so I will write some Tableaux Vivants for my family too.

Mamma

Mamma sits on a rock by a campfire deep in the swamp holding me. I am very little. It is nearly midnight. She left Perdido the night before under cover of darkness ahead of the Yankees, rumors were flying, slaves turning on their masters. Mamma is trying to get to Columbia, to cousin Sudies house in town. Everything she has is in the wagon pulled up into the oak grove hidden by bushes and hanging moss. It is dangerous to have even this little fire built by Virgil. Mamma is <u>on the very verge of starvation!</u> as she will tell me again and again but then Virgil catches three fish which twist flashing silver in the moonlight and Bess fries them up in the skillet right there over the open fire. Nothing has ever tasted so good, it was the most delicious supper I have ever eaten in my entire life, why that was the sweetest fish, she will say, telling me how she picked out the bones and mashed up little bites for me, how much I loved it too. As we eat we can hear the bullfrogs and the peepers and now and then a splash out in the lagoon which gives us all a start and then later, toward morning, the hoot owls way back in the trees.

Bess brushes Mammas hair with my grandmothers silver brush. It has fancy initials engraved on it ELH for Eleanor Logan Heart, I used to trace them over and over with my finger. Mama was determined to bring that brush and the French pier glass mirror with her at all costs. Bess brushes Mammas hair which is long and honey colored, stroke after stroke. Mammas curls spring up from the brush. It has all come down during the journey. <u>My hair is just a rats nest!</u> Mamma says. <u>There now honey,</u> Bess says brushing and brushing to calm Mamma down. Mamma has always been <u>kindly nervous.</u> She has never brushed her own hair. The moonlight shines on the silver brush and on Mammas hair, it makes a shining path straight to us across the still water of the lagoon.

This is the most beautiful night Mamma has ever seen. She does not sleep a wink, <u>not a wink!</u> her heart is too full of fear and a strange excitement, she can not describe it. For so long she has been <u>confined by the duties of her station and an indescribable longing for something</u> she knew not what. But now, anything could happen to her. Anything. My mamma will remember this night forever, the sweet sweet taste of that fish and the moonlight on the water, she will tell it again and again.

Papa

Papa is Captain of Company C the Edgefield Hussars who form up in front of the Planters Hotel on the public square the glorious morning of June 6, 1861, before they ride off to join Hamptons Legion. Papa wears a red jacket and a white plume, he rides his great black stallion Beau who will be shot out from under him at Brandy Station. Papas long yellow hair falls down past his ears. <u>He is a vain and quick-tempered man with a certain lack of judgment, yet great charm,</u> in the words of Aunt Mitty who had no use for glory or charm either one. Papa has a handsome reckless face. He sits his horse like a cavalier. He has lived here all his life, man and boy, he has scarcely been out of this state. Everyone in town is there to see them off including a <u>lovely array of beautiful women,</u> as it says right here in this clipping. There is food and music and flags waving.

Captain M. C. Butler says Ladys and Fellow Countrymen. In these ranks many of you have sweethearts, brothers, and husbands, and we go to the tented fields in the defense of our homes and fireside against the invasion of the hireling foe. We will go to the front remembering that we are all Carolinians, and we will return as honored soldiers or fill a soldiers grave. It is ours to act and not to speak. You will hear from us! Farewell!

Papas heart is swelling. It is the moment he has longed for all his life, for he is a famous horseman and the best shot in the county. He would not miss this war for anything. Later in camp he will write a poem named The Tented Field which will be printed in newspapers all over the country including the

Edgefield Examiner then clipped and folded and carefully saved in Mammas lavender silk purse along with all these other clippings I have here now in my collection of phenomena. Papa will be shot through the ear at Pocataligo, wounded in the leg by a minié ball at Hawes Shop, and finally killed at Bentonville where he will be <u>blown to smithereens</u> by a bursting shell then gathered up in pieces and buried beneath a green willow tree as in a ballad. He would have liked that, Uncle Junius said. <u>Bloody symbolic fool.</u>

Willie

Willie sits up on a pillow at the table for Sunday dinner at Agate Hill. He is small for his age but very grown up in other ways, he cocks his head to listen like a little bird. Uncle Junius calls him <u>the Judge.</u> Willie has a high solemn forehead and round blue eyes and long yellow curls, no one can bear to cut them. This is as old as he will get. He looks like an angel already.

Spencer brought him a little black puppy found on the side of the road. Why how in the world will we feed it? Fannie said. We cant even feed the people on this place! But then she relented of course and now the puppy follows him everywhere. Willie has named him John.

I just never heard of a dog named John, Julia said. Why dont you name him Midnight or Blacky or something like that?

<u>His name is John,</u> Willie said. <u>He was BORN John</u> which tickled everybody.

Now Willie has been sick and he is very thin while John grows bigger and bigger. I am the only one who knows that Willie is feeding John his own food under the table.

. . .

June 27, 1873

Dear Diary,

I just realized that May 20 my birthday has come and gone so I will not have it this year of our Lord nor ever again no one knows it but me anyway, no one will ever remember it. So I will be like a slave, they have no birthdays either, all their birthdays are January first, that was market day too. It will be my birthday from now on.

July 2, 1873

Dear Diary,

This is the last time I will ever be here in my cubbyhole the last time I will gaze at the world through my chink in the wall or sit in this little chair or consider my collection of phenomena or write in this book given to me by nice Nora Gwyn who would die to know what has become of me, so would Fannie. They seem like ladys in a story to me now.

Here is what happened.

Selena sent me to the barn to look for eggs yesterday morning. I am the best at finding them but while I was in there Nicky Eck came I guess he followed me and pushed me down in the straw and did the things he does to me but do not worry Dear Diary for I was not really there anyway I was up in the hayloft looking down and thinking <u>Why look at that!</u> When in came Spence with a pitchfork he stuck it into Nicky Eck making a row of bloody little holes all up and down his back which has moles on it too. It was comickal but horrible at the same time. Nicky Eck did not die of course but screamed like a pig and ran out of the barn then Spence was carrying me like he used to do when I was little and we played Take a Trip and then we were back up at Agate Hill where, guess what?

Surprise! Simon Black had arrived in a carriage with a brown-haired young lady wearing spectacles. He helped her down then stood in the lane with his black hat in his hands and the sun beating down on us all and said very formal-like, Good morning Molly Petree, allow me to introduce Miss Agnes Rutherford, a teacher at Gatewood Academy which you will be attending immediately, as ordered by Judge Draper, for you are now a ward of the court. I have the papers right here. It is all arranged.

But the young lady rushed forward and said, <u>Why good heavens Mister Black, something is terribly the matter here,</u> just as Nicky Eck burst out of the woods and Selena began to scream.

So I will be going away now Dear Diary.

I will be going to the Gatewood Academy.

I do not care that the fairy ring is gone from the woods now   I do not care that I am leaving my ghosts   I am such a bad girl   I do not care about anything

Notes from Tuscany

INFANT CATECHISM
[*Is this depressing or what? —TM*]

Q. Who made you?
A. God

Q. Of what did he make you?
A. Dust

Q. For what were you made?
A. To be good

Q. Where do good children go?
A. They go to heaven when they die.

Q. Where do bad children go?
A. They go to hell.

Q. Who loves good children?
A. God, and all good people

Q. Who loves bad children?
A. The Devil

Q. Who died to redeem you?
A. Jesus Christ

Q. Should you not love Jesus?
A. Yes, with all my heart

WYNKEN, BLYNKEN, AND NOD
Eugene Field

Wynken, Blynken, and Nod one night
    Sailed off in a wooden shoe,—
Sailed on a river of crystal light
    Into a sea of dew.
"Where are you going, and what do you wish?"
    The old moon asked the three.
"We have come to fish for the herring fish
    That live in this beautiful sea;
Nets of silver and gold have we!"
            Said Wynken,
            Blynken,
            And Nod.

The old moon laughed and sang a song,
    As they rocked in the wooden shoe;
And the wind that sped them all night long
    Ruffled the waves of dew.
The little stars were the herring fish
    That lived in that beautiful sea—
"Now cast your nets wherever you wish,—
    Never afeard are we!"
So cried the stars to the fisherman three,
            Wynken,
            Blynken,
            And Nod.

All night long their nets they threw
    To the stars in the twinkling foam,—
Then down from the skies came the wooden shoe,
    Bringing the fishermen home:
'Twas all so pretty a sail, it seemed
    As if it could not be;
And some folk thought 'twas a dream they'd dreamed
    Of sailing that beautiful sea;
But I shall name you the fishermen three:
            Wynken,
            Blynken,
            And Nod.

Wynken and Blynken are two little eyes,
    And Nod is a little head,
And the wooden shoe that sailed the skies
    Is a wee one's trundle-bed;
So shut your eyes while Mother sings
    Of wonderful sights that be,
And you shall see the beautiful things
    As you rock in the misty sea
Where the old shoe rocked the fishermen three:—
            Wynken,
            Blynken,
            And Nod.

THE FAIRIES
William Allingham

Up the airy mountain,
   Down the rushy glen,
We daren't go a-hunting,
   For fear of little men;
Wee folk, good folk,
   Trooping all together;
Green jacket, red cap,
   And white owl's feather!

Down along the rocky shore
   Some make their home,
They live on crispy pancakes
   Of yellow tide-foam;
Some in the reeds
   Of the black mountain-lake,
With frogs for their watch-dogs,
   All night awake.

TUSCANY MILLER

30-B Peachtree Court Apts.

1900 Court Blvd.

Atlanta, GA 30039

Hi Dr. F.,

What do you think so far?

Those poems are from Molly's big Treasury of Children's Verse which is just falling apart now. And as a matter of fact I think it is pretty depressing too with such scary poems as The Raven and that really sad one about the little toy soldier covered in dust but sturdy and staunch he stands. I would not even read that to a child, I will stick with Dora the Explorer myself if I have any.

Now this section was not even in the box at all. Michael, Ava (Daddy,) and me found it when we went on a field trip up to Lynchburg, Va. looking for Gatewood Academy which is now a part of Liberty University, that is Jerry Falwell's outfit, you know they are all right-wingers! We took a picnic and drove up there in Michael's convertible. It was not far at all. Michael wore a sports jacket with his blue jeans while Daddy (Ava) and I wore a nice suit. This was Daddy's idea because he said they are all big Christians up there. But they were real nice to us and they have saved everything, right down to the household records. Their Library has an entire Gatewood Collection including all of Mariah Snow's papers which follow. (She was so weird.) On the way back, we stopped for the best picnic on a riverbank, brie cheese and French bread and cherries and champagne. Michael drinks only Dom Perignon.

I have named the next section Paradise Lost, you will soon see why. Keep going, it gets weird now.

Best Wishes from me,
Tuscany

Paradise Lost

"First Impressions"
As duly recorded by Agnes Rutherford
To the attention of Mrs. Mariah Snow,
Headmistress, Gatewood Academy

July 2, 1873

My Dear Sister,

I scarcely know how to start this record, so agitated am I by the events which transpired this morning when I accompanied Mister Simon Black to Agate Hill Plantation. O Mariah! I fear I am unworthy of this task! Better you had sent Olive Reid, as she is a strong practical soul who might better know what to do in such a situation. You said that Mister Black had requested a "tender-hearted chaperone for Molly Petree, as she will be in need of kindness," and I do appreciate the compliment which you and Doctor Snow have paid me in entrusting her to my care; you know that I would do anything for you, Mariah; I hope I shall not fail you. But I cannot help wondering: Is Doctor Snow fully cognizant of the situation? And did you yourself understand the circumstances of this child's life? If so, I find it hard to believe that Molly Petree has been accepted sight unseen. But pray do not misunderstand me; I should like for her to be admitted, as even in her present state of dejection and withdrawal I sense a sturdy spirit which may indeed resurrect itself with the best of care in benign circumstances. I shall do my best to befriend her. In fact I shall take her over as my special project thus saving you if possible from further worry in your already overburdened state.

But you must forgive me, my dear sister. As ever, my heart runs away with my pen. Let me go back a bit. I trust you can read this report and have already pardoned my uneven penmanship. The carriage jounces from rut to rut as I attempt to write, yet I do have a measure of privacy here, as Mister Black, ever solicitous of my own welfare and the delicate condition of my charge, rides outside upon the seat beside his servant Henry (who at first sight appears to be Negro yet upon closer inspection proves to be some sort of aboriginal Indian, with filed teeth and a grossly distended lower lip). This Henry is remarkable in many other ways as well, including his apparent level of education. He is extremely well spoken and converses with Mister Black upon virtually equal terms. I hear their voices now though I cannot make out the import of their conversation. I shall miss my guess if they are not discussing the strange and disturbing scene which occurred this morning upon our arrival at Agate Hill Plantation.

But first a word as to the place itself. Here I found an old home of great distinction and dilapidation in the loveliest of settings, upon a high prospect of sweeping vistas and incomparable charm, yet surrounded by an air of loneliness and—how shall I put it? Defeat. Failure. Loss. Decay. And beyond that: wrongdoing, malfeasance. For something is wrong there, Mariah, dreadfully wrong. I know that you consider me fanciful and often chide me for having my "head in the clouds" and my "nose in a novel," yet do not doubt me on this, dear sister.

First, no one awaited us. Nor appeared to expect our arrival, though eventually Mrs. Hall came out to stand silently upon the piazza, babe in arms, as we progressed up the long lane during which time she neither waved nor smiled nor openly acknowledged us in any way. It was all very disconcerting, and I became increasingly nervous as we approached. Weeds grew high along the road and about the outbuildings, many of these now fallen to ruin. Disheveled is too kind a word to describe Mrs. Hall's appearance, Mariah, with her steely black stare, that messy hair, and blouse untucked.

Yet she walked forward with no embarrassment. "Simon," she said clearly, to my surprise.

"Selena." Mister Black went over to her and bowed in as gentlemanly a fashion as if he were at court and she were a lady. "I bring you greetings and condolences as well as congratulations upon the birth of your child."

I have noticed, Mariah, that Mister Black speaks the English language as if he has just learned it, in a most formal and stilted manner.

Mrs. Hall bent her head in reply then straightened back up, perhaps unconsciously, carrying herself now with greater dignity, as if she had just remembered who she was. She loosened the child's wrapping and thrust him forward toward Mister Black. "This is Solomon Junius Hall," she said, "my own little Junius."

"That is a very large name for such a small child," Mister Black said.

"Yes, actually he is too small, as you see. I fear for his health."

"I am sorry to hear that. But I am pleased to make his acquaintance nevertheless, and to see you again, as there are now some matters which we must discuss together."

Mrs. Hall glanced up at him sharply as if to assess the situation. Her face changed before my very eyes; a certain (how shall I put it?) appraising friendliness appeared. For the first time, she smiled. She put her hand upon Mister Black's arm. "Ah, is that so?" she asked.

I could not hear his reply, but he moved closer to her, appearing to have forgotten me altogether. Since I had not yet been introduced, I was forced to remain in the sweltering carriage in an awkward state of misgiving while the two of them stood at a distance talking together earnestly.

Thus was the state of affairs when from the corner of my eye I chanced to glimpse a sight so astonishing, so alarming, that I was struck dumb and could not say a single word of warning. Up the aforementioned lane at great speed appeared a giant, a huge straw-thatched farmer type of giant, taking long strides as if in a fairy tale, carrying a child in his arms and making a loud noise all the while, moaning and babbling, though his meaning remained obscure. At length he came close enough for me to see that his burden was not a child at all, but a girl, a young lady, albeit a pretty poor specimen at the time, being filthy dirty and most inappropriately dressed.

Simon Black had turned at the sound of this person's approach; now he made his way back toward him with slow deliberate steps, hand held up in greeting, as if such an apparition were the most ordinary thing in the world. "Hello, Spencer," he said. "I am Simon Black, your father's old friend, perhaps you remember me."

Then with no warning Mister Black suddenly crossed to the carriage and yanked the door open. I almost tumbled into the road, for I'd been leaning out the window, literally hanging on every word. Mister Black put out a hand to catch me, then helped me down the steps, a gentleman as always.

The giant stood holding the girl aloft in the sunshine. Beneath the tangled honey-colored hair, her eyes were as blue and as blank as the July sky above us. They gazed at me with no interest whatsoever; they chilled me to the bone.

With that exaggerated formality I alluded to earlier, Mister Black said, "Good morning, Molly Petree, allow me to introduce Miss Agnes Rutherford, a teacher at the Gatewood Academy which you will be attending immediately, as ordered by Judge Draper, for you are now a ward of the Court. I have the papers right here. It is all arranged."

Not a trace of understanding or even awareness flickered in those eyes. Nevertheless I was determined to try, of course. I had just opened my mouth to greet her when (as if all that had transpired were not enough) out of the woods ran a yellow-haired, red-faced man (I shall not say "gentleman") naked from the waist up. He ran right past us toward the house without a word; when he had passed, I saw that his entire bare back was covered in dripping blood. It was a horrid sight. At his approach, Mrs. Hall showed no sympathy for his evident plight but began to scream at him in the vilest language imaginable, dropping all pretense of ladylike behavior. She followed him toward the house screaming. Her poor baby began to wail. The gentle giant now set the girl down upon her feet before us with great care and tenderness. This accomplished, he stood up to his full height, took a huge breath and bellowed at the top of his lungs, taking out after the yellow-haired man who continued running past the big house then headed off into the woods. We watched until the green wall of trees had closed behind the two of them and even their cries could be heard no more. I felt as though they were strange animals that had disappeared into the forest.

I turned back to Molly Petree who opened her mouth as if to speak but did not, instead crumpling down onto the lane where she simply sat, head bowed, until Mister Black himself picked her up and carried her inside the house, myself and Henry following. He placed her upon a settee in the wide hallway where she half-lay, half-sat while he engaged in an intense whispered conference with Mrs. Hall who had now reappeared sans baby at the far end of the hall. Once my eyes had adjusted to the dimness, I gazed about in astonishment. The interior of the house was so unkept as to appear ransacked. I did not attempt to speak to Molly Petree during this time, yet remained near her.

At length Simon Black and Mrs. Hall approached us, apparently united. Some sort of bargain appeared to have been struck. Mister Black spoke directly to Molly, telling her once again that she would be returning to Gatewood Academy with me, that everyone feels she is a brilliant girl who will benefit from further schooling and enjoy the company of other girls.

"No." This was the first word Molly said.

"Now Molly," said Mrs. Hall.

"No, no no." Now Molly fully comprehended; now she was crying. She said she would not leave Agate Hill, that she would never leave Agate Hill, that she could not leave her "ghosts," whatever that means. She made scarcely more sense than the blubbering giant had done. At this point, Mrs. Hall stepped forward suddenly, jerked the poor girl to her feet, and shook her until her eyes rolled back in her head and I feared she would fall apart. But just as Mister Black stepped forward to intervene, Mrs. Hall gave it up and enveloped her in a close embrace. "Go, Molly," she said, sobbing hoarsely. "Go, go."

In return Molly herself hugged Mrs. Hall tightly, crying all the while. "You want me to go?" she asked in a whisper, the first coherent words I had heard her speak. "You want me to leave, Selena?"

Mrs. Hall inclined her head and shut her eyes. "Go, honey," she said fiercely. "Go now."

Molly held her tight, then nodded.

I watched this exchange in astonishment. It was impossible for me to judge the true nature of the intense relationship between the two of them (as, indeed, it was impossible for me to judge the true nature of anything at Agate Hill). I can only report these events to you, Mariah—not interpret!

But clearly it was decided. I went upstairs with Molly and helped her pack up such few things as she has brought with her, but I must tell you, Mariah, she will have to be completely outfitted and clothed once we have got her at the Academy. Never have I seen such filth and disarray as in that house so stately on the outside, so chaotic within. I shall spare you the most disturbing details. At length two more children appeared like apparitions in the gloom of the second story. They refused to speak to me, indeed appearing wary of strangers altogether. I imagine there have not been too many visitors at Agate Hill of late. I wondered: Could these be the "ghosts" Molly spoke of? They are solemn and pale enough. But she would not say. She would not speak at all now. She had almost no clothing and no personal effects. Her pitiful belongings fit into an old haversack we found in the closet. I left her to clean herself up as best she could with washbowl and cloth while I carried the haversack downstairs to Henry who took it out to the carriage, past Mister Black who paced back and forth on the piazza waiting.

"Where is Molly?" he whirled to address me.

"Why, she is bathing off," I said, "in preparation for our journey."

His face went dark as a thundercloud. "Go back to her at once," he said. "Don't let her out of your sight again, Agnes." It was the first time he had called me by my given name.

Off I went, but to my horror, I could not find her. I ran all through the tumbled bedrooms upstairs, looking, I ran into a dark parlor and a dusty dining room downstairs, I went out the back and into the kitchen, I grabbed one of the children, the boy, who was surly and said he knew nothing. I then reported to Mister Black on the front piazza, who said simply, "Find her." He joined in the search.

"Mrs. Hall!" I knocked on what I believed to be the nursery door, off the downstairs hall.

"Come on in," she said, yet when I did so, I found her nursing the baby, and quickly averted my eyes as I blurted out my business. Mrs. Hall was not at all embarrassed.

"Molly does this often," she said simply. "She has got a way of disappearing. I reckon she'll be on back, bye and bye."

This was not good enough for Mister Black, in a towering rage by this time, though not at me. "Of course it is not your fault, Agnes," he said kindly, though I felt it *was* my fault and was suffering bitterly for it. He dispatched Henry to search the barns, and went through the cabins out back himself. I confess that I sat down upon the doorsill in the front hall and engaged in a good cry, Mariah. It was all so strange; but at least neither the giant nor the yellow-haired man with the bleeding back ever reappeared. Henry came back with no good news to report, and Mister Black the same. He paced back and forth on the piazza, hat in hand. I sat in dejection upon the sill. The sun climbed higher in the sky.

"All right, then. I'm ready." Suddenly a little voice was heard from the top of the stairs.

"Mister Black!" I called.

He sprang to the door, shading his eyes with his hat. Together we watched Molly Petree descend the stairs as if she were making her entrance to a fancy dress ball. She was like a different girl, head held high, back straight. She did not smile. She will be a handful, Mariah.

Mister Black took her arm and escorted her straight to the carriage, handing me up after her. The carriage rocked as he and Henry mounted, then shuddered as the horses pulled away. As the urns by the gate gave no shade, I judged it to be noon, merely noon, though I felt we had been there for an eternity, so much had transpired.

Now that we were under way, I felt sorry for Molly, remembering how she had cried at the thought of this departure. "You can always come back," I said. "You can come back for visits." I attempted to reassure her, but she shook her head, no. I think she has a great deal of natural composure and determination, Mariah. You shall see. She sat staring straight ahead, never once looking back at the home of her childhood though I myself could not resist doing so. Immense and indecipherable, it stood upon its hill, no person in sight, in its surround of mystery and decay. I confess, my heart rose precipitously in proportion to our distance from it.

Now what can I do to encourage this girl, leaving all she has known? I wondered. What would Mariah do? I asked myself. Then it came to me. On impulse, I leaned forward and began: "I will lift up mine eyes unto the hills, from whence cometh my help. My help cometh from the Lord, which made heaven and earth," etcetera.

For the first time, I had a genuine response from Molly Petree. Her eye gladdened, her expression lifted. "The Lord shall preserve thy going out, and thy coming in, from this time forth, and even forevermore," she quoted.

I was much encouraged. "Do you like that Psalm?" I asked her.

"Not so much," she said surprisingly. "On the whole, I prefer a poem, like 'Annabelle Lee' or 'The Lady of Shallott.'"

So, more is here than meets the eye, Mariah.

Then she yawned, a huge wide child's yawn.

"Why don't you see if you can sleep?" I asked her. "You must be exhausted," for *I* too was exhausted, suddenly and profoundly, and both of us then slept until afternoon when we woke up at an inn where we could use the necessary. Mister Black ordered up a fine big meal of roast chicken and a peach pie which we ate outside on a wooden table under an apple tree, the cook and her sister serving us. We were all ravenous, Molly Petree included. Mister Black has a way of making things happen, I notice. His is an elaborately polite form of coercion and commandeering, yet his manner is such that no one could term it so. Everyone loves to do his bidding, it seems. Even I am not immune to his charm, yet find it impossible to divine the import of the only request he has made of me. This occurred at the end of our dinner, as we prepared for the next leg of our journey.

Mister Black pulled me aside. "Agnes," he said, "perhaps it will not be necessary for you to tell your sister and her husband all that you have seen here today."

"Why, what do you mean?" I asked. "I always tell her everything" (which is true, Mariah), and in fact I still do not know what he meant. I am puzzling over it as we clip along, now through the purple twilight. Already Agate Hill seems to exist in the past, as if in another country.

Molly Petree sleeps quietly on the carriage seat across from me now, and it is possible to tell that she is even pretty, though small, with a long straight nose and a somewhat wide mouth. I believe she will clean up nicely. Mister Black has said that we will drive all night, as we did coming. Neither he nor Henry ever sleeps, I suppose. This seems in keeping with Mister Black's other somewhat mythical qualities. He appears larger than life in every respect. I find him both terrifying and reassuring, in equal proportion. I am anxious to hear what you have to say of him, Mariah, and of Molly Petree.

It is almost full dark now. Fireflies arise from the woods all along the road. Henry is lighting the lamps.

> Sincerely Yours,
> Agnes

• • •

The Gatewood Academy

Hopewell, Virginia
Founded 1848

THE SITUATION OF THIS SCHOOL combines the advantages of town and country and, in its healthfulness and purity of moral atmosphere, is thought to be peculiarly eligible.

The primary object of our course of instruction is to qualify young ladies for the discharge of the duties of subsequent life. We seek to cultivate in every pupil a sense of her responsibility for time and for eternity. Our instruction in every branch is thorough and rigorous. "Not how much, but how well" is our motto.

The Gatewood Academy offers guidance, instruction, and nourishment for the mind, the body, and most particularly, the soul of each young lady entrusted to our care.

Boarding students shall number 15–20; the number of day students shall be the same.

Each boarding pupil is required to furnish raincoat and rubbers, her own towels and table napkins, 1 pair sheets, 1 bolster case or 2 pillow cases, a counterpane, and a drinking vessel.

Pupils are recommended to bring: a large dictionary, atlas, slate, dictionaries of Latin or French, and sheet music.

Tuition and board, $250 per annum, exclusive of lights, washing, and pew rent, $20 additional fee. Use of instrument for practice, $20. Tuition payable one half in advance, cash. Firm, no exceptions.

The Reverend Cincinnatus Snow
Headmaster, Gatewood Academy

GATEWOOD ACADEMY FACULTY
Under the Direction of Mrs. Mariah Rutherford Snow,
Headmistress and Director of Curriculum

Miss Agnes Rutherford—Grammar and Composition
Miss Olive Reid—English Studies and Composition
Miss Lovinia Newberry—Art
Miss Bessie Barwick—History
Miss Laura Vest—Languages and Singing
Mrs. Frances Tuttle—Natural Studies, Deportment
Professor Jacques Bienvenu—Music
Professor Clyde Fogle—Mathematics
Mrs. Mariah Snow—Elocution, Bible Studies, Domestic Arts
The Reverend Cincinnatus Snow—Advanced Bible Studies and Philosophy

THE PROGRAM OF INSTRUCTION
Gatewood Academy
(Shall vary in accordance with age and need of students)

Elementary subjects to include:
  Reading
  Spelling and Grammar
  Composition
  Geography
  History
  Mathematics
  Bible Study
  Natural Sciences

Advanced Studies to include:

    Composition and Literature

    Algebra and Geometry

    Ancient or Modern Languages

    Tuition in Piano, Guitar, or Melodian

    Tuition in Vocal Music

    Tuition in Pencil Drawing, Crayon Drawing, or Watercolor Painting

    Advanced Bible Studies

    Evidences of Christianity

    Intellectual and Moral Philosophy

    Compulsory participation in Gymnasium, Elocution, Deportment, and
the Domestic Arts

Exquisite neatness, decorum, and silence shall be required of all students
during each school day.

DAILY SCHEDULE
The Gatewood Academy

6:30 A.M. Rising bell. Dressing and tidying rooms.

7:30 A.M. Breakfast bell. Breakfast followed by morning prayers,
led by Mrs. Snow

        20-minute period of exercise, outdoors whenever possible

9:00 A.M. School opens. Opening prayers and announcements

9:00 A.M.–12:00 P.M. Classes and study times

12:00 P.M. Dinnertime

1:00–3:00 P.M. Classes and study times

3:00 P.M. Roll call. "Perfect" or "imperfect" behavior noted

3:00–4:00 P.M. Study hour, sewing, or music practice times

4:00–5:00 P.M. Exercising and dressing

6:30 P.M. Supper

8:00–9:00 P.M. Gymnasium on Monday, Tuesday, and Thursday
WEDNESDAY EVENING: Prayer meeting
FRIDAY EVENING: Parlor games and music
Occasional visiting lecturers upon worthy topics, when available

---

SATURDAY SCHEDULE
The Gatewood Academy

7:00 A.M. Breakfast bell.
8:00 A.M. Breakfast, followed by morning prayers, led by Mrs. Snow
9:00 A.M. Exercise time
9:30 A.M. Study hour
10:30 A.M. "Pie Letter" writing hour, at conclusion of which letters
    must be presented for mailing in order to have dessert at
    tomorrow's Sunday dinner
12:00 P.M. Dinner followed by personal time
            Shampoos
6:30 P.M. Supper
8:00 P.M. Evening preparation for Sabbath including Bible reading,
    Bible lessons, and hymn singing

SUNDAY SCHEDULE
The Gatewood Academy

8:00 A.M. Breakfast bell
8:30 A.M. Breakfast and morning prayers
10:00 A.M. Dress review
10:15 A.M. Procession to church services, Hopewell

11 A.M. Church services

1:00 P.M. Sunday dinner (with dessert)

> Afternoon time for reflection and reading of Bible or appropriate Sunday school books (Family and family friends permitted to visit.)

6:30 P.M. Cold supper

7:15 P.M. Procession to evening church services, Hopewell

ROLL OF BOARDING STUDENTS, 1873
Gatewood Academy

Abigail Baird	Lynchburg, Virginia
Emily Lunsford Berry	Greensboro, North Carolina
Constance Adeline Brown	Hillsborough, North Carolina
Ida Louise Brown	Hillsborough, North Carolina
Margaret Clark	Oxford, North Carolina
Josie Covington	Araby Farm, Bertie County, North Carolina
Daisy Mae Dupree	Beaulieu Plantation, Warrenton, North Carolina
Lily Coit Dupree	Beaulieu Plantation, Warrenton, North Carolina
Ruth Ann Fuller	Danville, Virginia
Lucy Lenoir	Yanceyville, North Carolina
Courtney Leigh Lutz	Chinquapin Plantation, Reidsville, North Carolina
Emma Belle Page	Goldsboro, North Carolina

Jemima Jane "Mime" Peeler	Roanoke, Virginia
Molly Margaret Petree	Agate Hill, North Carolina
Mayme Snead Ragsdale	Silk Hope, North Carolina
Susannah Rankin	Statesboro, North Carolina
Hattie Cane Stokes	Raleigh, North Carolina
Phoebe Rowena Taylor	Salisbury, North Carolina
Eliza Valiant	Charleston, South Carolina
Georgia Strudwick Vance	Durham, North Carolina
Fern Whittaker	Raleigh, North Carolina

• • •

Selections from the Journal of
Mariah Rutherford Snow
Headmistress, Gatewood Academy

July 1, 1873

Today I commence this journal with:

1. The Desire to cleanse & purify my own black soul, so oft beset by demons & thoughts too Dark to tell.
2. The Hope of greater Resignation to my lot, for what woman was ever more fortunate in being given such an opportunity to be of service? I struggle to be worthy of my Role.
3. The Intention of Living so that Death may never pay an unexpected Call, as I have awful fears of Death, deriving I know not whence, yet tormenting me to distraction though all the while I must put on a cheerful face for the sake of my children, my students, & for Dr. Snow who requires it, & rightly so.
4. The Determination to curb my Temper, Impatience, & Nervousness. Ah, why was I not blessed with a sunny disposition, like my sister Agnes? Why must I worry a thing to death?

✝ ✝ ✝

For No One's Eyes

July 8, 1873

And yet no sooner am I under way with this program than I am sorely tested, presented with a scholar so unlikely as to try me in every respect, she having come to the Academy late & under most peculiar Circumstances. I cannot help but blame Dr. Snow for this, as it is he who arranged her admission entirely, telling me virtually NOTHING about it in advance save that

Agnes should travel along with the girl's guardian to fetch her. "Who is this girl?" I asked. "Who is this guardian?" but to no avail. Dr. Snow was writing a sermon as usual, & could not be disturbed. Now it appears that Simon Black, the aforementioned Guardian, served as one of the Iron Scouts in Wade Hampton's army; hence he can do no wrong in the eyes of Dr. Snow, who apparently made his acquaintance during the War. Never mind that I ran this entire Academy perfectly well during Dr. Snow's absence, with the school overflowing & showing a profit at the bank. But now—NOW, how dare he call me the Headmistress yet refuse to allow me the right of participation in even such a basic decision as this one? Truly I am his Servant, NOT his Partner, whether he owns it or not. Basically Dr. Snow does nothing but read, while I work my fingers to the bone, yet have Nothing to say on any topic, him determining all according to his whim though he understands nothing, I repeat NOTHING about the administration of this Academy or anything else.

Good Lord, forgive me. Forgive me. Help me gain greater Understanding & Acceptance, oh Lord. Help me keep these thoughts to myself, & to this Journal.

But as for the girl:

I could smell her hair the minute Agnes brought her before me. I must say I have never seen a more unkempt specimen within the walls of this Academy. I attempted to converse with her but she would not speak, hanging her bedraggled curly head all the while, rubbing her dirty bare feet on our nice carpet. She would not even look at me.

What Manner of child can this be? I was wondering when in came Dr. Snow with the man he introduced as Simon Black, Molly Petree's Guardian & Benefactor. Immediately my attention was riveted by this unusual individual, dressed all in black, yet with white beard & mustaches. He swept his hat off his head & bowed low to the floor, startling me. Indeed, I was entirely unnerved by these exaggerated manners. It was almost like a performance; I suspect he is not a true gentleman.

"Ah!" he said, catching me off my guard. Then "Mrs. Snow," as if he had been searching for me all my life. He looked straight into my eyes, on a level with his own, as I am a Tall Woman. "I sense already that you will be just the one to take Molly Petree in hand. With the least bit of encouragement and structure, I feel that she will prosper, for she is a very bright girl."

I looked askance at that tangle of hair & those bare scuffed feet. "Well, we shall see," I heard myself saying, though I had intended to reject her out of hand by suggesting, albeit delicately, that her obvious lack of Social Skills might make her uncomfortable at this Academy.

As Mr. Black smiled, which almost seemed to pain him, I became conscious of Dr. Snow hopping about below us as if he were a dog leaping up for a bone. He can be so annoying at times. He yapped about "business" & "terms." I felt myself flushing, a problem I have had of late; it is very embarrassing.

"Take her on, then, Agnes," I said. "Tell Delia to run a bath."

But Agnes colored up herself, thrusting a fat envelope into my hands. "Here is my report, Sister," she flung back over her shoulder as she dragged Molly Petree from the room. "You had better read it."

"Wait!" Simon Black crossed the room in an instant, blocking the door. "Molly," he said in a low, urgent voice. "Listen to me. You are safe here, & I believe you will prosper. Mrs. Snow will keep me informed as to your needs & your progress. She will know how to contact me at all times. Now I urge you to work hard, & make the most of your Opportunities. Look at me, Molly"—which she would not do, Ungrateful Girl! Mr. Black touched her chin, tilting it up. There was something shocking in this gesture. From my angle of vision, I could not see her face, only his, which wore an expression of strange intensity. "Ah yes," he said, as if to someone not there, not in the room with us at all, "How she favors Alice." I do not believe he meant to speak these words, which I found both incomprehensible & bizarre. "You will be fine, Molly," he said to the girl. "Now you will be just fine."

But Molly jerked her head away from his hand & bolted through the door, poor Agnes at her heels.

I sat down to read the "report" while Simon Black & Dr. Snow retired to his little outdoor study to "talk Business." But you had better believe I was there in no time, knocking on the door!

There they sat drinking Whisky. I might have known. Simon Black jumped up at my entrance.

"It will not do," I said straight out. "No sir, it will not do. I refuse to have this girl come here, she will sully the other girls. Poor Sister Agnes may be too dim-witted & naïve to understand what she witnessed at Agate Hill, but I understand it all too well. Whatever her degree of complicity may have been, it is clear that Molly Petree has undergone experiences of a Compromising Nature. We do not run a home for Wayward Girls, sir."

"But what about damaged girls? I was led to believe that this is a Christian establishment of charity, of love . . . Am I mistaken then?" Simon Black asked respectfully in his deep voice.

Of course I was taken Aback. "Yes, but—" I began.

Then Dr. Snow stood up with that red face I know all too well. "This will be entirely enough, Mariah," he said. "Miss Petree has been admitted to Gatewood Academy today, & she must be outfitted immediately. You & Agnes will see to this. Mr. Black wishes that no outward distinction can possibly be made between Molly Petree & the others. Have I made myself clear?"

I thought of the shoes & hats to buy, the bolster, the pillows, the trunk— the sheets & linens to make, not to mention her clothes! The gymnasium outfit would have to be fitted & made from scratch, for instance, as we have no more made up & available at this time. I sent the last one by post to a girl from Wilmington yesterday. "It is impossible," I said firmly. "The girls will arrive in only four weeks. There is no time. And there is nowhere to put her, in any case."

Simon Black bowed over my hand which he took in both of his. "You will find a way. I trust you implicitly, Mrs. Snow," he said. I found him quite Presumptuous.

I looked at Dr. Snow, who narrowed his eyes at me with an Expression I recognized.

"You had better get busy, Mariah," he said. Then to Simon Black, "Do you remember Kemp? from Spartanburg? A very good man—"

So it is done! And I am left with a wayward, sullen girl on my hands, a girl who could be the ruination of all my hard work in establishing this Academy. I shall take her, then, but I shall keep an eye on her, for well I know: one Bad Apple can spoil the entire Barrel.

Mariah Rutherford Snow
Headmistress, Gatewood Academy
Hopewell, Virginia

✝ ✝ ✝

For No One's Eyes

July 18, 1873

Dr. Snow will not discuss his foolhardy decision with me at all, closeting himself in his little house then riding off to preach at country churches hither and yon. Meanwhile Agnes & I struggle to deal with our recalcitrant student who does nothing but sigh & stare blankly into space, answering all attempts at conversation in monosyllables. She shows no interest in anything except our books; yesterday, she grabbed up a collection of Fairy Tales from the parlor table & hid it in the folds of her skirt (actually Agnes's skirt, I should add.)

"You do not need to do that," I told her, retrieving the book & handing it back to her properly. "We are happy for you to borrow this book, or any book we have here at Gatewood Academy."

She clutched the book to her chest & stared at me.

"You may say, 'Thank you, Mrs. Snow,'" I told her.

"Thank you, Mrs. Snow," she whispered, eyes filled with Anger & Ingratitude. Though I have prayed without ceasing for Forbearance in this matter, I cannot, I simply cannot find it in my heart to be sorry for her.

I shall speak to Dr. Snow promptly upon his return.

> Mariah Rutherford Snow
> Headmistress, Gatewood Academy
> Hopewell, Virginia

† † †

FOR NO ONE'S EYES

July 20, 1873

My attempt having ended in terrible Argument, I excused myself from the breakfast table & went out to water the plants on the porch. Not five minutes had passed before I sensed the silent presence of Dr. Snow behind me. I continued my work, every nerve on edge. "What is it?" I finally whirled about to ask, whereupon he told me frankly that Simon Black is paying so much money to Gatewood Academy that we shall be able to meet our note after all, plus send our own boys off to their respective Boarding Schools as planned, AND have adequate funds left over for repairs to the Academy!

"So you see we have no Choice," he said, following me along the row of pots. "Simon Black has made a substantial investment in this Academy."

"But Dr. Snow, that is Bribery!" I said, though I dared not turn to see his face.

"On the contrary, Mariah, it is Business. Do I make myself clear?" He gripped my elbow so tightly that I cried out in pain, dropping my bucket which rolled off the porch spilling water. "Furthermore, I consider it our Christian duty to save this girl. And frankly I am surprised that you, of all people, do not see it this way, Mariah, given your own circumstances." (He WOULD have to bring this up, of course!) "Nothing happens without God's Knowledge; remember that, Mariah. Molly Petree has been sent to us for a reason. The Lord works in mysterious ways, & it is not up to us to question Him. I know you will do your best with her."

"Dr. Snow," I said, "you are hurting my arm."

But he did not release it, pulling me toward him & into the house where to my surprise he exercised his Conjugal Rights upon the hall bench in broad daylight. He seems to be quite worked up, in general, by all that has transpired. I occupied myself by reciting the beginning of Paradise Lost all the while, finishing about the same time he did.

Today I took my cold bath a bit earlier than usual.

Of course Dr. Snow is right, & I am wrong, & ungrateful & evil & low-minded, imagining only the worst for reasons he understands all too well. Yet I shall endeavor to rise above myself, & be worthy of Simon Black's trust, & live up to Dr. Snow's opinion of my capabilities, & understand that in all matters of Business, he knows best. (Yet WHY does he know best? Oh stop it, Mariah.) Better I should remember the words of John Milton:

> The mind is its own place, and in itself
> Can make a Heaven of Hell, a Hell of Heaven.

Yet I confess I do not like her, this girl, this Molly Petree. I can not like her, pure & simple, though she looks presentable enough now, bathed & clothed, albeit Sullen & Quiet as ever. There is something about her I do not trust, some dormant spirit I sense within her—though she looks so meek & mild, I have the distinct feeling that she could do anything. Anything.

And there is something else I must confess as well. When I have closed my eyes to Pray these past two nights, I have seen—unaccountably—His face. I mean Mr. Simon Black's face: that heavy brow, those steady dark eyes looking into mine when he said, "I trust you implicitly, Mrs. Snow." Oh why is this new Trial visited upon me? And who is this Mrs. Snow? I sometimes ask myself. And who are all these Children, Mrs. Snow's Children? Eight of them! & another on the way. I am locked in a golden chest, I am bound round & round by a silken rope. Simon Black should not trust me. Nobody should trust me! For I am filled with the most base & contradictory impulses, no matter how I struggle to be worthy of God's love, & do His bidding in this world, & live up to my Responsibilities.

> Mariah Rutherford Snow
> Headmistress, Gatewood Academy
> Hopewell, Virginia

† † †

FOR NO ONE'S EYES

August 10, 1873

All students have now arrived save Lily & Daisy Dupree, our beautiful little twins from Warrenton, so good & sweet. Their mother is severely ill, I fear the worst! Therefore I have issued acceptances to Adeline & Ida Brown of Hillsborough accordingly, who arrived with a great deal more Luggage than allowed. I was forced to send quite a lot of it straight on back with their Servant, causing bad feelings all around. Indeed there has been no end of trouble with these two, as nothing will do, nothing is suitable, nothing is up to their standards. This bed is too close to the window, this bed has lumps, etc. "My goodness, Hillsborough must be a very grand place indeed!" Miss Barwick teased them finally in gentle Remonstrance, whereupon they nodded earnestly saying, "Yes ma'am, it is!" Their clothing is unsuitably Lavish. They are quite Spoiled; I shall have to knock them down a peg or two.

> Mariah Rutherford Snow
> Headmistress, Gatewood Academy
> Hopewell, Virginia

✝ ✝ ✝

FOR NO ONE'S EYES

August 28, 1873

Classes now in progress.

I have my doubts about Prof. Bienvenu, who turns out to be quite a case, he wears a purple ascot & carries a palmetto fan.

As I feared, Molly Petree does not mix well with the others, though this may be a blessing, in my view, as it prevents her from spreading any of her sexual poison among the rest of the girls. As of now, she spends a great deal of time alone, often reading. Now a certain amount of reading is a fine thing in my opinion, but too much is a bad idea for a girl, leading to fancies, whims, & nervousness. I have given her a chore or two accordingly. And I told Dr. Snow again this morning that I did not know if his little experiment would work out or not.

"It had better work out," he said grimly.

My husband's coldness of manner toward me is my sorest earthly Trial— oh for the Grace to bear it aright!

Mariah Rutherford Snow
Headmistress, Gatewood Academy
Hopewell, Virginia

✝ ✝ ✝

FOR NO ONE'S EYES

September 10, 1873

As re. Molly Petree: This girl will be the death of me! having now occasioned yet another tremendous Disagreement between Dr. Snow & myself, & the term scarcely yet begun.

At issue being Molly Petree's living quarters.

I had found a perfectly nice little space for her to sleep under the stair, where she could enjoy both Privacy & Peace as she adjusts to the rigors of this Academy. She did not complain, nor did she say anything at all (not even thank you!) when I showed it to her. There is adequate room to stand and dress, though that is all, but what else does one do in one's room? I aim to keep them busy all the time anyway, this is my Philosophy, tried & true. I saw no reason to burden Dr. Snow with this decision, nor indeed with any such decision. Yet he has taken an inordinate interest in the girl, & chanced to overhear Sister Agnes complaining to me in my classroom during the lunch period.

"She cannot get to know the other girls, living in that closet," said the poor simple-hearted soul.

Exactly my intention! I did not say.

"I have been observing her, Mariah," Sister Agnes prattled on, "& I have felt so sorry for her during the morning Exercise Period, as she is always alone." After breakfast it is the girls' routine to go out in couples promenading along the paths in a sweet embrace, sitting on the joggling board, or whirling up & down on the flying jenny, which the more adventuresome never seem to tire of. The girls make these engagements well ahead of time, with the popular girls such as Mayme Ragsdale & Eliza Valiant always engaged days in advance. "But Molly hides during the Exercise Period, Mariah, I have seen her, she asks to go to the privy, or back upstairs to her closet for something she has forgotten, or sits alone on a bench affecting to study the vegetation with great care."

"This is perfectly acceptable," I pointed out. "Reflection builds Character. She has plenty of opportunities to get to know the others during the rest of the day."

"Ah, but they cannot speak except in class," Sister Agnes pointed out. "And imagine how she must feel at night, listening to them tramp up the stairs above her head as they go to their rooms, imagine how their voices float back down . . ."

"What? What's this?" Dr. Snow stuck his head in the classroom door, & the jig was up.

Thus I have yielded, deferred to him as in all things, yet it is a bitter blow, undermining my Authority with Sister Agnes & with my Staff now containing four new teachers who must know not what to think. Am I the Director of this Academy, or am I not? Molly Petree has been moved into a dormitory room with Emma Belle Page, a minister's daughter from Goldsboro; Courtney Leigh Lutz, a reliable girl who has been with us for years; Jemima Jane Peeler, the most musical of all my girls; Eliza Valiant, the friendliest & gayest; & Phoebe Taylor, who ought to be a good influence at least! We shall see how Miss Petree likes to have so much companionship! And we shall see how the girls like her—a development I await with great trepidation though I must say, so far her Deportment has been restrained & exemplary as far as I can tell. I have had no bad reports. Her marks are excellent. Indeed, Olive Reid has switched her from Composition to Advanced English Studies. She seems neat in her habits and assiduous in her daily chore of trimming the lamps. So far, so good. I believe in giving credit where credit is due. Yet there is something hidden, something sly and held back about her. I shall keep watching her closely.

But now to the bath, at last.

Mariah Rutherford Snow
Headmistress, Gatewood Academy
Hopewell, Virginia

† † †

For No One's Eyes

September 19, 1873

Found Washing & Ironing unfinished & badly done, found Mahala tipsy again, do not know where she gets it. She was laughing! Surely negroes are a lower order of being altogether, this is readily apparent, though one cannot say it, of course. There were Slaves in the Bible, after all. I shall dismiss her as soon as a suitable Replacement can be found. I was forced to have Claude & Parker help out though they did a poor job being inexperienced, I am at my wit's end! Dear God, I am sorely tried. Violent headache, fear I shall miss Church.

> Mariah Rutherford Snow
> Headmistress, Gatewood Academy
> Hopewell, Virginia

"Impressions"
As duly recorded by Agnes Rutherford
To the attention of Mrs. Mariah Snow,
Headmistress, Gatewood Academy

September 22, 1873

My Dear Sister,

I have a very interesting story to tell you as regards Molly Petree.

Today as you know was the younger girls' picnic to Onaluskee Mountain, accompanied by myself, the new Miss Vest, and Olive Reid. We took the omnibus with Claude at the reins, plus a hack from the livery stable, as usual. The girls sang all the way; I thought we should all go deaf (though they were ably led and encouraged by Laura Vest who is scarcely more than a girl herself).

We traveled up the gentle incline of the mountain road beneath the arch of trees, at length reaching the overlook where we spread our cloths and cushions upon the flat gray rocks quite warm from the sun, and looked out upon the countryside. "See, there is the Academy," said Olive Reid, who pointed out the sights and passed her telescope around. The girls fell upon their fried chicken and gingerbread, eating ravenously, and I did not have the heart to comment upon their manners or slow them down. There is something about a meal taken en plein air which always activates the appetite, I have noticed. But Molly Petree took her food and repaired to a spot beside a great pine tree a bit distant from the others, though she had sung as lustily as the rest . . . at length I joined her, surprised to find that she had left half her food upon her plate, and seemed pensive.

"What is it, dear? Is anything the matter?" I asked.

She sighed mightily. "No . . . ," she said. "Only this makes me think of Agate Hill, this view. I miss Spencer," she added. Spencer is the giant's name. This was the first time I had ever heard her mention "home," though the others speak constantly of their families, their pets, their brothers and sisters, etcetera.

I squeezed her hand. "A bit of homesickness is to be expected," I said. "Come, let's join the others. Look, they are making daisy chains."

"Molly! Where have you been?" Mime Peeler scooted over to make room for Molly, showing her how to split the stems and intertwine the daisies. Soon all the girls were wearing daisy crowns.

"Now let's make a really long chain," somebody said, and they started in on that, each one creating a section.

Olive Reid, never one to miss an educational opportunity, began to tell the girls that the word flora, which designates flowers and plants, comes from Flora, the goddess of flowers; while fauna, meaning animal life, comes from the fauns of classical mythology.

I drew back, struck by the beauty of this scene, very like a French painting, with the girls' bright skirts and beribboned straw hats set vividly against the green grass and flat gray "table rocks" of the mountainside, the blue sky above, and back at the edge of the clearing, the thick old forest. *How sweet this is!* I thought. And yet I could see what they could not see, dark stacked clouds rising rapidly over the brow of the mountain behind them. I was reminded of how fast youth flies, how soon these girls—including the young Laura Vest—shall be ladies with pressing duties and girls of their own, ladies who cannot while away long afternoons in an alpine meadow. This thought brought tears to my eyes, Mariah. I thought of you who never had such a carefree girlhood yet have fashioned it for so many others. And I confess I cried a tear for myself as well, the little shepherdess of the alpine meadow, who will remain at the Academy long after these girls and other girls have come and gone, for it came to me in that instant that I shall be neither wife nor mother, that I shall grow old here, like Bessie Barwick, and become a character. Olive Reid began to tell the story of how the ancient Greek gods became supreme, led by Jupiter. "He lived with his daughters, the Muses, and their famous winged horse Pegasus, upon Mount Olympus, which might have looked something like *this* mountain," she added.

"Oh, we already know all about the Muses!" Ida, the younger of the Brown girls, announced scornfully. "We went to a tableau vivant about them last year in Hillsborough, didn't we, Adeline?"

"What is a tableau vivant?" Courtney Leigh Lutz comes from an old plantation outside Reidsville; she is one of our loveliest and least worldly students.

"You don't know what a tableau vivant is?" Ida Brown turned to see who could possibly be so backward.

But this question was not answered, for just then Molly Petree looked up from the daisy chain on her lap. "Why, I went to that too!" she exclaimed as if involuntarily, then turned rueful and red-faced, and bit her lip, and looked down.

It was too late.

"Why, we know you, don't we?" cried Adeline, standing up. "Look, Ida, it's that poor girl, that bad girl from out in the country—"

"You mean the one who pushed you down the stairs?" Ida cried.

"Yes—she's the orphan girl, don't you remember? The one whose daddy married the whore."

Needless to say, these words produced a sensation, with all the girls craning their necks to look at Molly. Before any of us faculty members could think what to do or say, Adeline and Ida Brown were prancing around the outside of the daisy circle chanting, "Orphan! Orphan! We know you're an orphan!"

Molly turned brick red; she kept looking down.

"Bad girl! Orphan!" the Brown girls sang.

"Well, what if she is an orphan?" cried Eliza Valiant, leaping to her feet. "What's wrong with that? Aren't we supposed to be kind to orphans?"

"That's right," said the exemplary Phoebe Taylor, "and it's wrong to make fun of people. It's not Christian, is it, Sister Agnes?"

"Absolutely not," I said. "You Brown girls sit back down."

"Come on, Molly," said Emma Page. "Race you to the bridge and back!"

Molly jumped up and they all took off in a flash, hats and links of daisy chain scattered about on the grass. The Brown girls linked arms, pouting, while Olive, Laura, and I hid our pleased giggles as best we could. The girls had just reached the old swinging bridge when thunder began to roll; big raindrops spattered the rocks as they ran back, squealing. We all rushed round packing up the picnic things and got thoroughly drenched in the process though no one minded. All were in a great good humor singing "The Old Gray Mare" on the way back to the Academy, wet curls plastered to their foreheads. Finally, even Ida and Adeline Brown joined in.

The result of this escapade is: never has a moral lesson been better taught, Mariah, charity and kindness to one's neighbor having ruled the day thanks to the aptly named Miss Valiant. I do not believe this issue need be addressed any further with any of these girls, even Ida and Adeline. For their revelation has had the opposite effect from their intentions. Now everybody vies for Molly Petree's friendship. Both Emma and Phoebe insisted upon helping her trim the lamps this morning before church. At exercise time, Eliza Valiant and Molly strolled arm in arm then whirled round and round upon the flying jenny until I feared they should both lose their sense of balance permanently (which they did not).

Indeed, our orphan Molly Petree is become the pet and darling of them all.

And I remain

Your Devoted,
Agnes

✝ ✝ ✝

For No One's Eyes

September 26, 1873

Ah, it is like those Chinese Boxes within boxes—for dear Sister Agnes's report has had quite the opposite effect upon me from what SHE intended. I DO NOT want Molly Petree to thrive, there, it is out! I know not why. Overnight she has gone from being sullen to obstreperous. She does not know her Place; she does not appreciate her Good Fortune. Now—now, her True Nature comes out. As does mine.

> Mariah Rutherford Snow
> Headmistress, Gatewood Academy
> Hopewell, Virginia

✝ ✝ ✝

For No One's Eyes

November 13, 1873

If I could sleep, if I could but sleep instead of awakening so early assailed by such troublesome thoughts and dreams as I shall not attempt to write here lest I legitimize them, evil Phantoms of the Night. Oh I am Vile, to think such thoughts as these. Yet they will not leave me though I pray to God for Deliverance. Why, why will He not come to me, and bring me His Peace? Patience, Mariah, I counsel myself, yet I have no Patience. I know I do not deserve Him. I am ungrateful, I am impatient, I am full of temper and evil thoughts, I do not deserve His intervention, to ask for it at all is doubtless a sin of Pride.

If Strength comes through Suffering, why then I should be the strongest of all women, yet I am the weakest, God help me. Help me.

> Mariah Rutherford Snow
> Headmistress, Gatewood Academy
> Hopewell, Virginia

✝✝✝

FOR NO ONE'S EYES

February 9, 1874

Today I attended to the Housekeeping as usual, went in school & heard three classes, but by that time the Pork came. I changed my dress, went out & with my own hands trimmed seventy-four pieces of meat, then came in, washed & dressed up in my best & walked up the Cedar Walk to call upon Mrs. Joseph Devereaux in the Village, Miss Pleasants that was. Then I went to Dr. Barney's, to Dr. Greene's, to Mr. Vogelsong's Pharmacy, & thence home, thank goodness at least Dr. Greene is sympathetic to a lady's Plight, for a lady must finally sleep, must she not? Rather than lying awake with awful thoughts in her head that even her old friend John Milton cannot keep at bay.

I presided at supper & the day was finished with a lecture on Eastern Religions by Professor Theodore Grumly retired from the University of Virginia, during which some of our girls Dozed Off, unfortunately. I have made a list, I shall speak to them. I am rethinking my rule of not allowing them to do handwork during lectures, at least it might keep them awake. And in the end they shall all have more to do with mending & tatting than with Philosophy. I noticed Molly Petree listening quite intently, however; who knows what she is thinking, the little Heathen.

Mariah Rutherford Snow
Headmistress, Gatewood Academy
Hopewell, Virginia

✝✝✝

FOR NO ONE'S EYES

April 25, 1874

Gave birth.

Mariah Rutherford Snow
Headmistress, Gatewood Academy
Hopewell, Virginia

† † †

For No One's Eyes

April 27, 1874

Dear Lord, I shall try to love this Child as I try to love all my Children, yet I confess my Sorrow at having a girl, for I know how she will struggle in this world. The burdens of our sex are heavy. Yet I believe I will name her Susannah in hopes that she will have a happier Spirit & a Lighter Heart than her mother.

> Mariah Rutherford Snow
> Headmistress, Gatewood Academy
> Hopewell, Virginia

† † †

For No One's Eyes

May 3, 1874

At last Dr. Snow has come in to see the child, he has named her Frances Theodosia, for his Mother, whom I Hated with all my being. Yet I suppose it does not matter, after all. For what's in a name? as the Bard asks. We lose our names as we lose our Youth, our Beauty, & our Lives.

> Mariah Rutherford Snow
> Headmistress, Gatewood Academy
> Hopewell, Virginia

† † †

For No One's Eyes

August 11, 1874

Have visited Dr. Greene, with no good results.

"Abstinence, Mariah," he counseled. Which is not possible, as all depends upon the whim of Dr. Snow who is a perfect Demon. Of course I could not tell Dr. Greene this—nor can I tell any one. Once I heard of negro girls using marbles for the purpose. Since I am entirely at my Wit's End, perhaps I shall give this dire remedy a try if necessary.

Mariah Rutherford Snow
Headmistress, Gatewood Academy
Hopewell, Virginia

THE RUSKIN HOSPITAL
10 Mimosa Street
Montgomery, Alabama

October 23, 1875

Dear Molly,

It is me your old true friend Mary White Worthington writing to you after so long a time. Here is how it happened. The Brown girls, Adeline and Ida, complained to their mother that you are at school with them, and Mrs. Brown eventually mentioned this in a letter to Grandmother who has forbade me to get in touch with you but could not resist telling me anyway. You know she never quits talking. So Jane Joyner, the nurse, will sneak out to mail this letter for me, and watch for your reply. Can you read this, Molly? And will you write back to me? For now I am forced to lie with my back on a board and weights on my shoulders to straighten out my spine. It is the newest treatment for my illness which is more severe now though I believe I am finally getting better, I hope so. Doctor Ruskin a famous doctor has recommended the board. I am his favorite patient! Now I am in his special clinic where he sees me every day and I do breathing exercises with Jane, and many other exercises as well. They have rigged up a kind of wooden frame and a board for me so I can write and draw though not much as it tires me so, I hope you can even read this. You know how I love to draw. See, this is me, in my bed with the frame and the board and my little writing desk above my special bed, and here is Jane with her long pigtail, and here is Grandmother who has gotten a job now running the Confederate Widows Home. She dearly loves this for now she can boss everybody around! They all hate her too. See how fat she has gotten, swelled up like a tick! See out the window there is my own private maple tree all aflame, and the busy street, and the square. But Montgomery is the opposite of Agate Hill which I think of so often, how we played dolls and collected our phenomena and ran through the woods like the wind. I can not do this now, nor even walk. (Nor write, it looks like!) So Molly if you get this letter, write me back quick, tell me everything. Write me a love story.

Your best friend forever, signed in blood,
Mary White Worthington

Molly Petree
Gatewood Academy
Hopewell, Virginia

November 12, 1875

Dear Mary White,

Your letter has thrown me into fits for I am so happy to hear from you, it <u>almost</u> makes me forgive the Brown girls who are my sworn enemies forever. But Mary White I cannot stand it that you have to stay in that bed, it makes me want to run and swing and do everything even harder, for you. I want you to think of this letter as another window so you can look out of your room.

Peep in here, through the French doors with the little wavy panes, into the big classroom. This is me on the very first day of school a year ago, walking down the long aisle with all eyes fastened upon me, wishing myself back in my cubbyhole at Agate Hill where none could see me, or even know where I was.

Though I am dressed like the others in my Normandy apron and my new blue calico dress, I am sure they all know that I am a bad girl, and an impostor among them. In fact, I can not really see the other girls at all. My eyes blur, I stumble and almost fall. Sister Agnes is holding my hand. But then there is a desk of my <u>own!</u> with a space for a row of books in front of me, and a red dictionary already placed there, and an ink bottle on its tiny shelf, and below the sloping top, a drawer where I find a brand new slate and pencil and a little notebook with my name written in Sister Agnes's beautiful penmanship on the front of it, <u>Mary Margaret Petree, Gatewood Academy.</u>

I take my seat.

"Good morning, girls," says Mrs. Frances Tuttle, skinny as a rail, with her great bun of black hair held up on top of her head by a knitting needle. Or it looks like a knitting needle, Mary White, you ought to see it. And she looks like a stick doll!

"Good morning," say the girls.

"Cat got your tongue, Mary Petree?" She smiles straight at me.

"Good morning," I say, though I still want to die.

But I did not die.

I have not died yet.

I will write more to you later.

Now look in here. These little circular dormer windows seem to me like the portholes on a ship, and our attic bedroom is like the ship itself with its pointy peak in the roof, its wooden walls and low eaves—we go sailing along through the trees. Remember that poem we used to love,

> Wynken, Blynken, and Nod one night
> Sailed off in a wooden shoe,—
> Sailed on a river of crystal light
> Into a sea of dew.

Our attic bedroom is like that.

There are five girls' bedrooms here at the Gatewood Academy and this is considered the worst because it is so cold, but we consider it the best because it is farthest away from all. No one minds the climb!

My room mates are these:

Emma Page. Her father is a Presbyterian minister in Goldsboro, but she is tired of being good all the time. She has curly brown hair and lots of freckles which she hates.

Eliza Valiant, tall and blond, she comes from a family of seven boys who all adore her, in fact she can run and ride a horse like a boy, hell for leather, as she says. She brought her horse Galahad to school, and boards him at a farm down the road, and rides in the country with Miss Vest and sometimes the Snow boys when they are here. She is fearless too, she will say or do anything she thinks is right. Even Mrs. Snow has been known to defer to Eliza.

Courtney Leigh Lutz from Chinquapin Plantation who is merry and funny, she has shiny black hair and jet bracelets like I would love to have. Her mother jumped into a river and killed herself.

Mime Peeler from Roanoke, Virginia, her mother made her practice the piano for three hours a day with weights on her wrists for years so she is better than anyone here except Monsieur Bienvenu. She has round blue eyes like my doll Fleur (don't you remember Fleur?) and smooth white skin like china, she looks like a figurine.

Phoebe Taylor who is plump and very shy and stutters but giggles and giggles when she gets going, she cannot stop. "Oh you d-d-d-d-don't mean it!" she says. Mrs. Snow thinks Phoebe is a good influence but she is not. Phoebe is so sweet that she cries in class whenever we read a sad poem such as "The little toy dog is covered with dust, / But sturdy and staunch he stands" which brought her to tears yesterday.

In our attic bedroom we have six old spool beds and dressers, six frilled dressing tables with basins and pitchers of water which we must carry up here ourselves from the well which is about a hundred miles away, not to mention the slop jars! But we do not care. For here we can do whatever we please, such as pillow fights and wrestling matches galore, why we have even had levitations and séances led by Courtney whose Aunt Delores is a famous spiritualist. Courtney has a Ouija board hidden under her bed.

On Saturday nights we are supposed to be getting ready for the Sabbath, so we can sing only hymns and read only serious books such as <u>Stepping Heavenward</u> which Mrs. Snow read aloud to us in the parlor last week until we thought we would die. At last we were released to our attic where we soon got into a serious pillow fight which ended with everyone piled on the floor in giggles.

"Listen!" Courtney raised her head just as Eliza pummeled her.

"No, really," Courtney said again when she could get her breath. "Listen, it's the Old Hoot Owl." And sure enough, it was. Even I, on the bottom of the pile, heard the dreaded sound of heavy steps—punctuated by a little groan between each one—coming up our steep attic stairs.

"Girls," Miss Barwick rasped. "All right now, girls, I hear you."

"Quick!" Eliza said. "Let's pray."

"Oh, let's!" said Emma, and we all scrambled over to kneel demurely beside our beds, hands folded, heads bowed and eyes closed, just as Miss Barwick flung open the door to stand there huffing and puffing. Miss Barwick has a big old square body and square-rimmed spectacles behind which her gray eyes look enormous, which is why everyone calls her the "Old Hoot Owl."

"Amen," Eliza sang out, and we all jumped to our feet.

Then, "Good evening. Miss Barwick," we said as one, though I could scarcely speak from trying not to laugh.

Miss Barwick stood there huffing and puffing. "Don't imagine that I have been fooled by this display. Everyone else has gone to bed. We could hear you girls all over the house."

"It was a bat, Miss Barwick," I said. This just came to me.

"A h-h-horrible bat," Phoebe Taylor said. "It flew right at me."

"Well, where is this famous bat now?" asked Miss Barwick.

We all looked at each other. Nellie raised her pretty hands in a questioning gesture. "We don't know. It was the strangest thing . . . ," she said in a wondering voice.

Courtney was taken by a coughing fit at that moment, she covered her face with her hands.

Old Hoot Owl smiled in spite of herself. "Well, you are very imaginative girls," she said finally. "Let us hope that you will put the same degree of creativity and effort into your studies as you have put into this little performance here tonight. But remember, this is the Sabbath eve. Now I expect to see you lining up for dress inspection tomorrow morning in the proper frame of mind. And if I break my neck going back down these steps, girls, you will have it on your consciences forever."

We held our breaths as she made her slow groaning way down the creaking stairs. Then we all went to bed but I read to the end of <u>Macaria</u> by the light of my own little lantern. The others do not care if I stay up reading all night long. Have you read this book, Mary White? It is all about sacrifice.

I do not see why sacrifice is so good for people, do you?

But Mrs. Snow says, "How sublime a thing it is to suffer and be strong," for she loves suffering, Mary White, she takes an icy cold bath in the closet off the kitchen every day of her life, even in the dead of winter. She shrieks when she gets into it, you can hear her from the hall. We all gather round to listen. And Mrs. Snow prays out loud in the coat closet, too, Emma Page swears she is taking literally the Bible verse which says "Enter into Thy closet and when Thou hast shut the door, pray to Thy Father which is in secret." Emma can quote the whole Bible from memory, it seems like. But Mrs. Snow can recite "Paradise Lost" by heart, she is famous for it. And for saying, "Young ladies, the best perfume is no perfume at all," and for this advice

> Have communion with <u>few,</u>
> Be intimate with <u>one,</u>
> Deal justly by <u>all,</u>
> Speak evil of <u>none.</u>

She made us write this in our copybooks. But we are horrified at the thought of Mrs. Snow and Doctor Snow being intimate! It is too funny.

Mrs. Snow has headaches all the time and about a million children, she just had another one last spring. She is a foot taller than Doctor Snow who reminds me of a little banty rooster with his red face and upswept red hair. On Sunday afternoons we have to talk to him individually about the state of our souls and then we have to kiss him, it is awful, his breath smells bad, like liquour, and his yellow whiskers are wet and brown with tobacco. His teeth are brown too. I will write you more, I will tell you everything. I am out of time. They are taking up the pie letters now. Oh Mary White, I am so sorry you are suffering, I guess you are the most sublime person that there is in the world. I remain

Your <u>best friend forever,</u> signed in blood,
Molly Petree

† † †
FOR NO ONE'S EYES

November 13, 1875

So. My intuition was, as usual, correct; all my suspicions are vindicated. Words fail me when I consider Molly Petree's evil Chicanery. (How stupid these girls are anyway, to think their "pie letters" will not be read!) I have made a fair copy of Molly Petree's poisonous missive; I shall keep it as evidence until the time is right, which surely is not now, as Dr. Snow remains wholly enamored of her & her entire Situation. He has recently received another letter & a check from the mysterious Simon Black who holds us in thrall; we can never repay this debt. I cannot imagine what Dr. Snow thinks he is doing.

Sister Agnes is clearly on Molly Petree's side as well, & I regret to add that Molly has just yesterday won the schoolwide Spelling Bee (with "catarrh," though it appeared to me that Olive showed a certain favoritism in her word choices for the contestants). Never mind. Never mind. Vengeance is mine, saith the Lord. Patience is bitter but its fruits are sweet.

And as for that Mime Peeler, she has been severely Chastised, & Professor Bienvenu dismissed. Him & his palmetto fan, indeed! How he cried & groveled & begged me to reconsider, as if that were even a possibility. I had to stick my fingers in both ears. "No matter how much you attempt to explain yourself & your Billets Doux, or try to tell me the details of your activities, I SHALL NOT LISTEN!" I told him. "God may forgive you if He chooses, but not I. Au revoir." I ended our interview with a Flourish.

I pray there will be no repercussions from this regrettable Incident.

I have now engaged Mr. Lucius Bonnard, who comes to us highly recommended from Saint Mary's Institute where he has been an Assistant Instructor for the past two years. Whatever his musical abilities turn out to be, I trust that his standards of Morality will exceed those of Professor Bienvenu. (This should not be difficult.)

Mariah Rutherford Snow
Headmistress, Gatewood Academy
Hopewell, Virginia

† † †

FOR NO ONE'S EYES

December 4, 1875

Rain & more rain, the streets are a sea of mud, the girls tromp along to church like oxen. Tis really enough to give anyone the Blues to live in such a provincial Mud Hole where you see nothing & hear nothing & no one says a thing worth listening to. I think of Simon Black, whose last letter was postmarked St. Louis, his life is unimaginable to me. But what am I saying.

Mariah Rutherford Snow
Headmistress, Gatewood Academy
Hopewell, Virginia

† † †
FOR NO ONE'S EYES

January 28, 1876

Today is gloomy, it snowed . . . you know Hopewell is not an interesting place anyhow.

Mariah Rutherford Snow
Headmistress, Gatewood Academy
Hopewell, Virginia

† † †
FOR NO ONE'S EYES

February 16, 1876

Two days down with Headache, I can neither See nor Hear. Yet sometimes I wonder if this affliction is not God's judgment upon me for

(REST OF PAGE TORN OUT)

• • •

✝✝✝

FOR NO ONE'S EYES

February 20, 1876

Frances is such a frail, annoying child, she whines and whines until I think I shall lose my mind, frankly. None of the boys were like this. I am fortunate to have had the services of Miss Beere's Kitty as wet nurse, she is the only one who can quiet her. Oh I know I am too much the Teacher. But I really do not like them at all until they can speak & learn, I know this is a horrible Sin and Failing on my part.

> Mariah Rutherford Snow
> Headmistress, Gatewood Academy
> Hopewell, Virginia

✝✝✝

FOR NO ONE'S EYES

February 29, 1876

Tonight I have suffered the attentions of Dr. Snow, followed by a delightful and shockingly cold Bath, then awake all night long with Palpitations of the Heart. I am not at all well.

> Mariah Rutherford Snow
> Headmistress, Gatewood Academy
> Hopewell, Virginia

✝✝✝

FOR NO ONE'S EYES

March 3, 1876

Oh dear God I did not mean to complain, I did not want her to Die, certainly, God knows I did not want that above all things. As she lay like a little wax doll in my arms, I was struck by her Beauty: too late, too late. I am a vile, unnatural Mother, deserving Nothing. He must Punish me as He sees fit.

> Mariah Rutherford Snow
> Headmistress, Gatewood Academy
> Hopewell, Virginia

† † †
FOR NO ONE'S EYES

May 11, 1876

I am more & more convinced that Molly Petree is a judgment upon me, no doubt well deserved. She continues to thrive, a big, healthy girl now, she attempts to please me by begging to work in the greenhouse, and the garden, affecting a real interest, knowing I am partial to my plants. But I shall not be swayed so easily, nor fooled by her wiles.

> Mariah Rutherford Snow
> Headmistress, Gatewood Academy
> Hopewell, Virginia

"Impressions"
As duly recorded by Agnes Rutherford
To the attention of Mrs. Mariah Snow,
Headmistress, Gatewood Academy

November 5, 1876

Dear Mariah,

As you are currently incapacitated by headache, I will take a moment to describe for you in detail an incident which just happened, while it is still fresh in my mind. I know you would wish to be apprized of it immediately.

No sooner had I convened the first Study Hour this morning than I was summoned by old Primus who appeared right at the classroom door, much to my surprise.

"What is it?" I asked him in the corridor, having left the girls under Mayme Ragsdale's jurisdiction. I closed the door behind me.

"They is a boy out front wanting to see Miss Molly Petree," Primus said in his raspy voice. "He has been there nearabout all night long, far as anybody can tell, and he say he won't go away till he see her."

"Well, what sort of a boy is he?" I asked, quite amazed, for as far as I know, Molly Petree has never had a visitor in all her time at this Academy.

This, then, was a mystery.

"He is a boy that don't have no business around here," Primus said unequivocally.

"I suppose I'd best talk to him myself then." I sighed and grabbed my jacket off the hook and headed for the front door, my steps dogged by Primus who was utterly determined to come too.

Upon the porch, I found an ill-dressed country boy, sixteen years old perhaps, leaning against a post smoking a cigarette. "Good morning," I said crisply. "I am Agnes Rutherford, a teacher here at Gatewood Academy, where, I have to tell you, we do not allow smoking."

Without a word he took another long pull on the cigarette before tossing it right out into the wet flower bed, staring at me insolently all the while. He exhaled smoke into the chill misty air. This was a thick-set, unattractive boy, Mariah, with not one shred of manners. No wonder he had alarmed Primus.

"And you are—" I began.

He stared at me uncomprehending.

"What is your name?"

He shook his head, causing his long thick yellow hair to flop upon his low forehead. "That don't matter. I need to see Molly Petree just for a minute," he said.

"Miss Petree is in class," I said. "Perhaps you can tell me what business you have with her?"

"No ma'am," he said, obstinate as a post.

I was still attempting to get to the bottom of it when classes changed and of all things, here came Molly herself walking around the side of the building. I was never so dismayed to see anyone.

"Godfrey!" she shrieked, dropping her books. "Godfrey, what are you doing here?"

Too late I recognized him as one of the "ghost children" at Agate Hill Plantation—to which Molly has never returned, following Mr. Black's express instructions—nor has she ever, to my knowledge, asked to do so.

"Spence is dead," the boy said bluntly. "We come over here to tell you, then we going on."

Molly sank down upon the wooden steps, her cloak slipping off her head and shoulders, her face upturned to the thin cold rain which now began in earnest. "Dead?" she said slowly, wonderingly. "Why what happened? Was he sick? Did he get sick, Godfrey?"

"Shot," Godfrey said with no expression on his flat pasty face. "What happened was, Rom went in that country store out by Big Pine to buy some hoop cheese and crackers"—Molly nodded, she seemed to know the place—"and there was some men in there that didn't like the way Rom spoke to the girl behind the counter, this was a white girl, married to the son of one of them, and they said something to Rom and he said something back to them"—Molly nodded, biting her fist, apparently she understood this recital better than I did—"and so when he went back outside with the hoop cheese, they was three of them that follered him and jumped on him and started beating him upside the head with a ax handle because they didn't like the way he had spoke to that white girl—" Here Molly waved her hand impatiently, but the boy went on: "Spence was out there waiting to get some hoop cheese for lunch, and when he saw what they were doing, he gave that kind of yell he does, and waded right in among them, and was laying them all out right and left when another man from the store come up with a shotgun and shot him in the back of the head. Four or five times," he added unnecessarily. "They wasn't much left by the end of it."

Toward the end of this horrible recital, I attempted to hug Molly, but by then she had covered her ears with her hands, sobbing.

The boy, on the other hand, betrayed no emotion at all. "He said for me to tell you," he said, looking out toward the gate where for the first time I saw the Negro on the horse there waiting. I don't know if he had been there all along or not, Mariah. It was like he had just taken shape from the rain and the icy fog. Something about the way he sat his horse frightened me, though I could not even see his face for the weather and the hat he wore. I elected to ask no further questions. Moving closer to Molly, I said, "Thank you very much for coming by to tell her. And now I know you will want to be on your way."

Without a word he stepped off the porch and crossed the yard.

Molly looked up. "Rom!" she cried.

The Negro touched his hat as the boy jumped up behind him. For an instant then I saw his face, as hard and scary as any face I have ever seen, Negro or white.

"Rom!" Molly screamed, running through the mud across the yard. The horse reared up and whinnied and blew out breath like clouds and they were gone.

Primus and I reached Molly at the same time. She would not get up out of the mud, nor would she stop screaming, so that soon a little crowd had gathered there around her in the yard, all of them getting soaking wet and more alarmed by the minute.

It was only with the aid of Lucius Bonnard and Primus that I was able to get Molly to my house where I have deposited her in my own room, as I did not wish to disturb the other girls more than they shall be disturbed in any case. Clearly I cannot return to classes this day. Molly cries intermittently and talks without cease, words tumbling out one over the other so fast it is hard to follow her thought, or to tell what is real and not real. I fear that this incident has brought back sad memories from her childhood which might have best been forgotten, I fear too that she is growing feverish. I have given her a sage infusion, with a little lemon juice and sugar, to no effect.

Sincerely Yours,
Agnes

†††

FOR NO ONE'S EYES

November 9, 1876

This entire Academy has revolved around Molly Petree for days, absolutely Nothing can be accomplished. All one hears is "Molly this" & "Molly that" as one walks down the halls. In truth I did not know the extent of this obsession until it had already gotten truly out of hand, when I was finally forced to rise from my own Bed of Pain by the goodness of my heart, & Attend to her.

I made my way to Agnes's little house where I found an astonishing scene. There lay Molly upon the bed like a carving upon a catafalque, surrounded by her worshippers who come tiptoeing in & out endlessly weeping and bearing little gifts: a poem, a bracelet, a pretty picture, a bit of holly from the woods, a piece of old lace, an owl feather. I have never seen anything like it. And Agnes was clearly in charge of it all, of course, finally in her true element at last, grim yet rosy-cheeked, on fire with Helpfulness & Sacrifice. But whoever thought that my own Sister would be sleeping on a pallet on the floor while a student of low degree lay in her bed? Education is all but suspended as everyone must come, students & faculty alike, to worship at this unlikely Shrine. The girls in particular have taken a terrible Fancy to it.

I asked Dr. Snow right out, I said, "What is the good of forbidding them to read terrible penny dreadful Novels when one has such a Novel going on under one's very roof? I told you this girl would be Trouble," I said as I stood there observing her so pale and still. "It would be just like her to die on us."

In reply he grabbed my elbow sharply. "Woman, if you value this Academy & your position in this world," he hissed at me, "you had better exert all your skills & cure her."

Which I did, beginning with my famous cure for Ague which was quite difficult to administer, for she dribbled it out the corner of her slack mouth upon the bolster, to my Frustration.

"Here, Mrs. Snow," said that sweet Emma Page, "let me hold her mouth like this, like so, & then you may try again . . . ," forming up Molly's thick red lips into a little cup, & then our Mission was accomplished, morning & night for two days, yet still she sleeps on.

Dr. Snow had already sent for the famous Dr. Grossbeck from Danville, our own Drs. Barney & Greene being not good enough for Molly Petree, though we can ill afford the expense. "But I shall not communicate with Simon Black yet," he said to me, frowning. "For therein disaster lies. Woman, do your work."

Thus I have also tried Catnip Tea & Tansy, forcing her to take a bit of broth and water as well. Nothing. No result. The girls have formed a Prayer Chain, so there is someone praying for Molly Petree constantly, round the clock, as if God has time for this.

> Mariah Rutherford Snow
> Headmistress, Gatewood Academy
> Hopewell, Virginia

† † †

For No One's Eyes

November 11, 1876

The famous Dr. Grossbeck arrived by coach this morning. I must say he did not make a favorable initial Impression upon me, nor indeed any Impression upon me, being quite thin, small, & poorly dressed, with stains upon his shirt front & very rheumy, weak appearing Eyes. He looked like he would blow away in a good stiff Wind. He performed his Examination with myself, Agnes, Dr. Snow, & Frances Tuttle present. I had sent all the girls to their own rooms though they wept annoyingly.

Dr. Grossbeck lifted her eyelids, first one then the other, & peered into her sightless blue eyes with a glass like a little telescope, muttering under his breath all the while. Then asking for Agnes's aid, he pulled Molly around on the bed so that her white knobby knees hung over the edge, & to our surprise, rapped them both smartly with a little hammer which he produced from his bag. "Oh!" cried poor silly Agnes as Molly's thin white legs flew up into the air. Dr. Snow frowned mightily, then helped the doctor place her aright again. Dr. Grossbeck said something inaudible.

And though Molly Petree has tried me sorely, I must say that I felt a wave of shock & pity when he motioned for Agnes to take down her shift, & placed his ear with its little horn against her sunken chest where all her ribs and clavicle stood out sharply. Agnes burst into tears.

"This girl has suffered Shock," the little doctor almost whispered, so that we all had to bunch up & strain to hear him, "which has produced a sort of Nervous Catatonia, a reaction which though frightening to us, may be actually beneficial to her, as it allows a deep rest which will either repair and refresh her—"

"Oh, thank goodness," murmured Agnes.

"Or kill her," Dr. Grossbeck continued.

Dr. Snow swore under his breath.

"But I see some positive signs. Look at the eyelids."

We all bent forward to do so, & sure enough, there was a fluttery movement beneath the shadowy lids. "You may continue the excellent care you have given her thus far—" here he nodded at Agnes, ignoring me altogether— "and let the Body do its Work. She has a young healthy body; she should come round directly."

For this he charged us eight dollars, the equivalent of a hog! While here am I, wearing last year's Blouse, walking around in last year's Shoes.

"I shall return on Wednesday," he said, which is two days time.

It was all I could do to contain my anger at that moment, but nevertheless it slipped out later this evening when I was sitting with Molly myself, having cleared the room & sent even Agnes over to Supper. God alone knows where Dr. Snow had disappeared to. It was only Molly & myself in that little chamber with its green ivy wallpaper & low eaves, the wintry gray afternoon fading beyond the little diamond-shaped panes of the window. Her breath came & went, her chest rose & fell shallowly in the oil lamp's flickering light. Her eyelids moved again & she murmured something.

My heart leapt up, in the words of the poet. Immediately I crossed over to her. "What?" I asked sharply, so that she could hear me. "Molly, what is it?"

But she refused to answer, Sullen Girl.

Before I knew it, I had slapped her. The sound cracked out in the room. No One could have been more surprised than I.

"Oh!" It was Agnes, prematurely returned from Supper, bearing a dish of Corn Pudding which she spilled all over the floor. "Mariah, how could you?" she wailed, rushing to Molly's bedside where she knelt to kiss her cheek & smooth her brow.

But Lo! At that instant Molly opened her eyes, thus vindicating me entirely, as if anyone cared.

And as of today she remains well though somewhat Listless & Lackluster, thus making sure that she will remain the Center of Attention after all, as always, Forever & Ever, Amen.

> Mariah Rutherford Snow
> Headmistress, Gatewood Academy
> Hopewell, Virginia

• • •

THE RUSKIN HOSPITAL
10 Mimosa Street
Montgomery, Alabama

November 17, 1876

Dear Molly,

This will be short for I am sick now. First I am so sorry that Spencer died and that you have been sick too but you do not sound like yourself and as for what you write about giving up and going to join your ghost family, Molly, I say this. Do you not remember how we wandered the woods at Agate Hill, how the river ran so cold on our feet and the sun gave us freckles out in the fields where we picked all those berries? Do you not remember how the clouds came in from the west and the thunder rolled and the lightning came down like a fork and hit the sycamore tree on the hill and we fell down and rolled over and over in the wet grass laughing? Or how we ran through the woods to Mama Marie and Aunt Mitty's and drank from the spring and how the fairies came? I think about Agate Hill every day. So live for me, Molly. Get up from there and live for me. You are my best friend joined in blood and you have to do what I say.

Mary White Worthington

† † †

FOR NO ONE'S EYES

December 23, 1876

So now thanks entirely to myself Molly Petree is recovered with a vengeance, she has resumed all school activities & is again the World's Darling. She does not seem to realize her pitiable situation in the least — & why should she — as for instance she is the guest of Eliza Valiant this Christmas time riding off in a coach with a Servant and two of Eliza's brothers down from their Virginia schools & no chaperone. I argued but had to let them go as per the Valiants' instructions. They disappeared through the gate with laughter floating back on the chilly air & bells jingling, while here we have positively no money to buy candy or toys for our own boys, according to Dr. Snow. Of course Dr. Snow is like an errant wind blowing first hot then cold, I never know what to think or expect from him, nor do the boys, who have gone skating on the pond just now, at least there is that, & hunting deer, & shooting down mistletoe. Perhaps they will shoot their father by mistake. Oh I am vile, vile, I do not deserve them, any of them, I shall put gravel in my boots as a constant reminder of my Blessings this Christmas O Lord, my Strength & my Redeemer, Amen.

Mariah Rutherford Snow
Headmistress, Gatewood Academy
Hopewell, Virginia

Molly Petree
Gatewood Academy
Hopewell, Virginia

January 8, 1877

Oh Mary White,

Why don't you write me back? I will hold on to this letter until I hear from you. When I think of you, I feel like a flame is running through my body like a fire across a field and I wonder if this is what it is like to be purified by suffering? And do you feel this way all the time, Mary White? But now I have been to the Valiants' house in Charleston with Eliza for Christmas, a very long journey, I will tell you all about it.

First imagine a huge white house with columns across the front all hung in greenery and Spanish moss, then a grand Christmas tree which reaches to the ceiling hung with wax lights and all manner of gilt things and presents underneath for the little children, and a midnight supper on Christmas Eve with crab cakes and candles and mistletoe under which Eliza's brother Ben snuck up behind me and kissed me or that is, he kissed the air near my head, he is so shy. I liked it too. Eliza says he is sweet on me, and she is sweet on her cousin Daniel Butterworth. They will become engaged after her commencement. Danny is a dark haired boy with a big grin, he is very good looking.

"But Eliza," I said, "don't you want to do anything else, before you marry?" For Eliza is very good at art, she has won all the prizes. You should see her pen sketch, "Vine Gatherer's Daughter."

"Why, heavens no," she said. "What would I do? All I want is Danny," which seems to be true. All the girls want to get married except me. Oh Mary White, I want <u>so much</u>, this has always been the trouble with me, and it is still true. I don't even know what I want. But I will not fall in love yet for then it is all over. Sometimes I think of it as a big lake, like Moon Lake, that I might fall into, and you know I cannot swim. So I will not give all my heart to anybody.

Early on Christmas morning we were awakened by a negro fiddler named Prince who went upstairs and all through the house playing and singing, soon followed by the little boys who ran outside with their negro playmates and shot off firecrackers. We dressed as fast as we could and went down to find Eliza's father in an apron making the eggnog in the pantry, great bowls of it, which we all drank for breakfast! We had hot coffee and raisin cake too. I got tipsy, I swear it, I started laughing and could not stop. Then there was the opening of the presents with a wild commotion throughout the house. The children rode tricycles over the carpets. I received a beautiful moonstone necklace from Eliza and a silver letter opener from her parents and a cunning little glass globe with a snow scene in it from her brother Ben. If you turn the globe upside down then right it, snow falls softly upon an entire tiny village.

Ben is tall and fair like Eliza, he could be her twin though he is not, being three years older. His eyes in their gold spectacles follow me everywhere and I have to say, I like this. It gives me a pins and needles feeling throughout my body, like when your foot has gone to sleep and is waking back up. Ben has finished school but still lives at home and works at the Cotton Exchange. He has asked if he can write to me and I have said <u>Yes.</u> He has also said he will see me at our commencement!

I am trying to tell you, Mary White. I am trying to do what you said.

The negros danced upon the piazza all day long. There were two fiddlers and a man who played the sticks and another who played the bones, and then the following day, <u>horse-racing</u>! Which all the Valiants are passionately devoted to. I sat with Eliza's mother and her grandmother wearing hats and veils to keep out the dust. Ben won a third place ribbon and rode by our bench and tossed it to me, I shall keep it forever.

Eliza won the next race, riding like a man, beating Ben and her father too. "When I am married," she told me later, "I can not do this any more." Though frankly it seems to me Mary White that when you are very rich like the Valiants, you can do anything. Finally there was a dance at their cousins' house on the Battery and I was so thankful for all those times we had whirled about the room at Gymnasium doing the Andalusian in a huge circle, and the schottische, and the polka. Mrs. Tuttle used to call out, "Heel, toe, and away we go!" Professor Fogle was induced to waltz with us, though usually we waltzed with each other. But dancing with boys is different, especially the waltz, when they have to touch you and are embarrassed. Eliza's cousin Martha says to each one, "Can I tell you a secret?" and whispers something, she says it does not matter what, in his ear. All the boys are in love with her, they rush to sign up on her dance card. She says it is the breath in their ears that does it! Eliza thinks this is terrible but I think it is funny. It is fun to flirt and feel powerful. I thought of Victoria, and wondered where she is now, and wished I could see her or even <u>be</u> her, just for a minute. Remember when we wanted a demon lover, Mary White? But Ben Valiant will never be one.

"Oh, I hate to go back to school, don't you?" Eliza said once we were in the coach, but though I said "Yes," it was not really true. I am glad to get back here to our busy attic room and the echoing halls and the class-rooms with their long wavy windows and Mrs. Snow's greenhouse where

I love to work and the big hall with its lemony early light when I go in to neaten up and wipe the slate before the school day commences. Everything happens at a certain time here, it is the very opposite of Agate Hill. I love this school in spite of Mrs. Snow who does not like me, I have never known why. Even Agnes admits it but says she does not know why either. I don't care.

In fact, I dread commencement as much as I anticipate it, in part because Mister Simon Black is coming. It has been four years, I can scarcely remember him, and yet I owe him everything, Mrs. Snow tells me this constantly. It makes me feel <u>very odd.</u> Please write me back if you can but I will write to you anyway.

Your <u>best friend forever,</u> sealed in blood,
Molly

January 9, 1877

A Love Story for Mary White

Now before the others arrive I will tell you the story of Mime Peeler. For we are all convinced that she loved our former music teacher, M. Bienvenu, though she swears there was nothing between them. His first name was Jacques (you do not pronounce the "s"). He had a high wide forehead with very pale skin and huge dark liquid eyes that were always glistening, and went everywhere carrying a palmetto fan. We all thought he was so silly, but Mime liked him. He told her that she could be a concert pianist (he said "peeyaneest") if she would "practeece, practeece, practeece," which she did, faithfully, and went around with her head in the clouds and a look of purest exaltation on her face. As for him, he seemed always as if he would burst into tears, fanning himself with his fan, which we made terrible fun of, but Mime would not laugh at him, ever. She <u>practeeced</u> and <u>practeeced.</u>

Once I came into a practice room bringing a freshly trimmed lamp to find her practeecing and M. Bienvenu very close behind her shoulder turning the pages. Red spots flamed on Mime's china cheeks. They were both so solemn and intent that I came and went without either one of them even noticing I was there. Mime was sixteen then, I know he was thirty-five at least. They had a special tutorial session together three afternoons a week, to prepare her for the concert stage.

That term, Mime was a prefect of the second study hall. M. Bienvenu used to pop in often, tiptoeing down the aisle in an exaggerated fashion which made all the girls laugh behind their hands, bringing Mime's sheet music so she could look it over and be ready for their sessions together.

But one morning Mrs. Snow chanced to appear in the doorway just after M. Bienvenu made his grand entrance, crossed over to Mime's high desk, and deposited his folder. Mrs. Snow followed him right down the aisle and pounced like a cat upon the sheaf of papers, startling M. Bienvenu so much that he had to grasp the prefects' desk for support. Deathly pale, Mime looked as if she wished she could sink through the floor.

"Aha! Mendelssohn! 'The Songs without Words'!" she announced in a loud hissing stage whisper. "Just what I was looking for! I shall return this to you in a second, Mime dear—"

She swept the folder up, causing five or six thin pieces of paper ("French paper!" Eliza would later claim) to flutter down upon the floor. M. Bienvenu bowed from the waist and quickly raced away. Poor Mime ran around the desk and attempted to grab up the papers, but she was too late, all of this drama being enacted in front of the entire study hall.

Mime is such a shy and private girl, she has never been quite the same since. M. Bienvenu was dismissed of course but she was forced to stay on at Gatewood by her parents who wished her to live down this scandal.

Though Mime has repeatedly claimed it was nothing, and said she doesn't care, sometimes she still gets up in the middle of the night and goes down into the great hall and plays the grand piano softly while we are all asleep, I have heard her, and once recently I snuck down to find her playing "Spring Song" with the moonlight from the tall windows falling across the keys. I am sure she was thinking of M. Bienvenu and his silly palmetto fan.

But here comes the hack from town, I see it out our attic window, it is filled with girls, waving.

I think of you all the time.

Your friend,
Molly

† † †

For No One's Eyes

February 27, 1877

Today I have been out all day in the cold, seeing to putting up three tremendous Hogs. The three weighed nearly eight hundred & I had no one to help Primus cut them up but little Billy Strudwick & he had only one hand he could use—then when I went into the wash-house to see about the Lard I found Mahala so tipsy that she was too foolish for me to put up with so I ordered her to her own kitchen or out of my sight & as Delia was here washing, I got her to help & now at nine o'clock have just washed off the grease & put on my dressing gown—

Mariah Rutherford Snow
Headmistress, Gatewood Academy
Hopewell, Virginia

† † †

For No One's Eyes

March 23, 1877

Gave birth.

Mariah Rutherford Snow
Headmistress, Gatewood Academy
Hopewell, Virginia

Molly Petree
Gatewood Academy
Hopewell, Virginia

May 4, 1877

Dear Mary White,

Here is <u>another</u> love story for you, with a sad ending. Last night was our final talent program of the year, and to our surprise a group of cadets from the military academy appeared, including that Calhoun Sparks who is sweet on Courtney. Since she was last on the program, he talked her into slipping out and running up the Cedar Walk with him to the drugstore for a soda.

"Don't do it," Eliza whispered furiously. "There's not time."

We were all in the back closet behind the great hall while Calhoun stood in the yard just below us.

"Oh, come on," he said with his long slow smile, "no one will ever know. We'll be back in a minute." He held out a white-gloved hand through the open door.

Courtney could not stand it. "Oh, all right," she said finally. Her black eyes shone as much as her jet bracelets which I so much admire. She tossed her curls once, grinned her pixie grin, and jumped down off the sill and was gone, running up the Cedar Walk between the ancient sighing trees, holding her pale blue satin skirt up with one hand. So that was the last we saw of them: Calhoun Sparks's white sash and gloves disappearing into the dark tunnel formed by the double row of trees.

Inside the great hall, Emily Barry led off by singing "Kathleen Mavoureen" in her thin, quavery voice. Eliza covered her mouth and squeezed my hand. The program continued. Lucy Lenoir recited "Abou Ben Adhem" followed by two of the little girls with a Schubert Serenade duet on piano and then poor Miranda Unsworth who played a terrible sort of polka over and over again until finally she turned crimson and burst into tears, exclaiming, "I'm so sorry, Mister Bonnard, I just cannot remember how to end it!" She jumped up and ran off the stage to general applause and laughter.

Mrs. Snow poked her lacquered head back into the closet. "Girls, where is Courtney?" she asked in her sharp voice, over the noise.

Eliza and I looked at each other.

"We don't know," I said, at exactly the same time Eliza said, "She has gone to the necessary."

Mrs. Snow's sharp face darkened. "I see," she said ominously, disappearing backstage as Ruth Ann Fuller started in on "The Dying Poet."

"I'm going to get her," I decided, since I was not on the program. Eliza was next with "Listen to the Mockingbird."

"O, Molly, don't, you will get into lots of trouble," she said, but I said, "I am in trouble with Mrs. Snow all the time anyway," which is true. I ran into the long tunnel of the Cedar Walk, my feet slipping on the cedar straw that lay everywhere like a fragrant quilt covering the earth, half expecting to come upon Courtney and Calhoun at any moment. A streetlight shone at the end of the Cedar Walk ahead, where it opens out into Main Street. Running as fast as I could, I was soon on the cobbled street outside the little store. Through the window, beyond the many-hued glow of the apothecary jars, I spied their backs as they sat on those high red stools facing the counter. Mister Vogelsong was drying glasses and talking to them. I ran right in. Courtney pulled her hand back from Calhoun's as if she'd been stung by a bee.

"You'd better come back right now," I said to her. I was all out of breath. "Mrs. Snow is looking for you."

"Oh Molly, sit down and have some soda." Calhoun Sparks is a big boy with drooping eyelids that give him a lazy, sneaky look. None of us can understand what Courtney sees in him.

"Calhoun, I am serious," I said. "Courtney has not got much time."

Courtney looked back and forth between the two of us, draining her soda through its straw. She wiped at her pouty red lips with a napkin.

Mister Vogelsong stood behind the counter in his accustomed striped shirt and red tie and suspenders with his arms folded, watching all this. "Best to get on back, then, girls," he said. "Let's not have no trouble with the missus now," for everybody in town is afraid of Mrs. Snow.

Calhoun said something under his breath, still seated. Courtney was looking at him. "Well, all right then," he said finally and stood up, but slowly, stretching like a cat.

Suddenly I could not be bothered with him another minute.

"Come on." I grabbed Courtney's hand and pulled her outside over the cobblestone street. We heard horse hoofs in the distance. Then we were running down the dark corridor of the Cedar Walk emerging into the back yard as Mime played "The Banjo" by Louis Moreau Gottschalk. It is <u>very hard.</u> The music poured out the open closet door. We paused by the Rose of Sharon bush to get our breath.

"See, now, there is plenty of time, look what you did, Molly," Courtney said, for she was to play after Mime.

"Wrong!" It was Mrs. Snow who appeared to pluck Courtney right up from the grass. Sometimes when she is angry it seems she has supernatural strength. "You will go straight up to bed right now, young lady. Whatever would your poor dead mother have thought of this behavior?" she said. This was <u>so cruel,</u> she can be like a witch sometimes. "Go on. I shall deal with you tomorrow."

"Please don't tell my father," Courtney cried, but Mrs. Snow had already turned to leave. "Come along now, Molly," she flung back over her shoulder.

Courtney ran up the back stairs sobbing into her balled-up fist while Mrs. Snow went back inside where everyone was applauding. I looked down the Cedar Walk where all that could be seen of Calhoun Sparks now was a shadow in the shadow of the trees. Of course he was too much of a coward to show himself or to see Courtney properly home. Perhaps he will never be an honorable man. I followed Courtney up the stairs to our attic room where her dress already lay in a puddle of shining silk on the wooden floor and poor Courtney herself lay still as a stone in her bed with the covers pulled over her head.

<u>Your friend forever,</u>
Molly

Molly Petree
Gatewood Academy
Hopewell, Virginia

May 25, 1877

Dear Mary White,

Why have you never written again? I am afraid to know, yet I shall keep on waiting in hopes of a response for I am doing what you said, I am living for you, and I want you to know everything, and be a part of it.

Commencement comes closer and closer. Our school days are almost over. But now I am in a strange position for unlike the others I will not be leaving. Dr. Snow has asked me to stay on as a teacher. He has told me in no uncertain terms that this is the wish of my benefactor, Mister Simon Black, since I am still so young. Dr. Snow reminds me that I owe everything to Mister Simon Black and Gatewood Academy. Well I know this is true, but I am <u>sick and tired</u> of hearing about it! For there is something awful about being beholden, I am just figuring it out. It makes me mad to be beholden! Though I am glad to stay on here where all is known and bells ring upon the hour. I bet I will be a pretty good teacher too!

I am not like Eliza who cannot wait to fling herself into her engagement to that wild cousin I do not trust, or Emma Page who will go to Boston to work in a settlement home with her aunt, or Courtney who will take a grand tour of Europe, though I would love to do that myself someday, or even Mime Peeler who returns to Virginia with a secret locked in her heart forever. I am keeping my heart to myself! I can not see why all these other girls are just dying to be married. For it is the end of everything. Fern Whittaker and Mayme Ragsdale will both do it immediately after commencement, Eliza and Margaret Clark will both become engaged, the list goes on.

I will be <u>very happy</u> to share Agnes's little stone fairy house where I will have a room of my own for the first time ever in my life, a room so small it is like my cubbyhole at Agate Hill but nevertheless my own, it is a start. It has pink wallpaper with darker pink roses on it in a repeating lattice print, they are so beautiful. And a little window with a lace curtain and a view of the side yard and the giant elm with its great limbs making a leafy room where the day students gather around the old stump to eat their lunches in fair weather—and beyond that, the orchard, then the woods. And Agnes says we will have a cat too, I cannot wait! For Primus and Delia's cat will be having kittens any day now.

But here is a secret: Last Sunday evening when we were all walking home from church in the dark, following Agnes's swaying lantern at the head of the line, with me bringing up the rear, suddenly I felt hot breath on my cheek and a hot whisper in my ear. "Don't be scared, Miss Petree! You remember me, Louis Tutwiler—" He is a young teacher from the military institute. The cadets are always jumping in line to scare us as we march home from church. "I am wondering if I can come to call upon you next Saturday afternoon. Please don't say no," he added all in a rush, "for I've made a considerable wager on it." Which got me so tickled I said, "Oh, <u>perhaps</u> . . . ," drawing it out just to tease him, then finally "yes" in spite of myself, though I'm sure I don't know what we will talk about as he seems a perfect dunce like all those boys. But in any case, I shall have a gentleman caller! And now Ben Valiant has written me a letter enclosing a four-leaf clover from South Carolina, he is coming for our commencement. The thought of seeing him again fills me with dread and also a sense of sweetness, it is very odd. I cannot describe it.

I will win the composition award if there is any justice in the world, we are all writing our graduation compositions now. My subject is "There is society where none intrudes" as suggested by Sister Agnes and taken from <u>Childe Harold,</u> it will be about our Willow House. Agate Hill has been sold now, Mary White, according to the awful Brown sisters. I do not know what has happened to Selena or Godfrey or Victoria or Blanche. It all seems as long ago and far away to me now as that cunning little town inside the globe which Ben gave me for Christmas.

I am always your
Molly

Molly Petree
Gatewood Academy
Hopewell, Virginia

June 10, 1877

Dear Mary White,

I did not get an honor at the commencement, not one, not even the composition award which I surely deserved hands down. Instead it went to Josie Covington who is much too flowery and quivering in her sentiments. "<u>Oh!</u>" she cried, covering her face which has those awful bumps all over it, you ought to see it, so perhaps it is a good thing she has received this honor, but I do not think so. Agnes also seemed very surprised and stared a hole into Mrs. Snow who looked straight ahead at the audience when she announced it. I think prizes should go to the people who deserve them, don't you? But Mrs. Snow is partial to Josie Covington, and she does not like me. I do not like her either. But no one could really like her, she is so strange and changeable, a wind blowing hot then cold. Oh I don't really care, for at least Ida Brown got nothing either. Perhaps her little sister Adeline will be in my classroom next year, I can assure you that her mark will be only a <u>passable.</u> I know we are supposed to forgive our enemies Mary White, but I don't. I can't forgive. This is why I will never go to heaven and be an angel, for angels have no memories, unlike me, for I remember everything.

And now, the commencement.

I will start at the beginning.

We had all been working for days, so that everything looked lovely that night, our old school transformed into a brilliant fairyland, for candles and sconces stood every place—at the gate, on the porch, in the entrance hall. The wrought iron porch rails were roped with running cedar. Garlands of flowers ringed the stone posts, while all of Mrs. Snow's precious plants bloomed profusely in their pots as if they too knew it was commencement. The perfume of jasmine and honeysuckle filled the night air. (Now, you see how fine this description is, you know I deserved that composition prize!)

Six large chandeliers hung from hooks in the great hall, making a blaze of light that reflected off all the little gleaming window panes (which I had polished and polished, my arms are still sore from it) and off the rich gilt frames of the paintings that covered the walls, all of them created by our faculty or students. There hung Eliza's "Madonna and Child," along with her conception of Daphne turning into a tree, and a pastel portrait of Mrs. Valiant gathering roses in her walled garden in Charleston, her mother's sweet face and those old pink bricks as true to life as the finest photograph. I knew, for I had been there. There was her pencil drawing of me sitting out in the orchard with apples in my lap, and a sketch of Eliza's horse galloping along a road beside a swamp with black stumps and feathery trees in the background. I could tell it was South Carolina.

Promptly at seven they started arriving, all the families and friends grandly dressed for the occasion, even dowdy Miss Newberry, even the Old Hoot Owl herself in a huge black satin dress with a kind of bustle, Eliza's three smallest brothers adorable in their matching blue suits, fathers and mothers and suitors and grandparents all alike, but none for me. I did not care! For many of these were my friends too and I peeped out of our upstairs window as excited as any to see them arrive. "Oh, look, there he is!" Eliza squeezed my hand when Danny Butterworth walked through the gate.

Once the crowd was assembled in the great hall (with a good number forced to stand at the back and on the sides!) we all gathered silently in the front yard while Laura Vest sang "Whispering Hope" accompanied by Mister Lucius Bonnard on the piano and Professor Fogle on the violin. How beautifully they sounded together as a great hush filled the hall. Out in the front yard, Eliza and Emma and I held hands. I started to cry though I knew not why, for commencement ought to be a happy occasion, should it not? When I looked at the school through the blur of my tears, it appeared as a blaze of light, the porch and every window aglow in the soft sweet air. Mime was sobbing openly. I could not help but wonder if she was thinking of M. Bienvenu. But then the song was over, the last quivering notes died into silence, and Lucius Bonnard pounded out the opening bars of "God Bless the Southern Land." It was our cue. Led by Phoebe, the class marshal, in the door we came, through the entryway and into the grand hall, marching down the center aisle between all the people who rose as one, clapping and cheering until we had attained the platform where we stood before our chairs on the rostrum in front of the faculty. When the march was over, we all took our seats.

We wore plain white swiss dresses with natural flowers in our hair, Mrs. Snow permitting no other adornment. Anyone who had received a token of jewelry as a commencement gift had to wait for another day to display it. For this grand occasion, Agnes had fastened my hair up with a white rose and her own mother-of-pearl barrette. I felt very grown up—I am very grown up now, I suppose. It was the strangest sensation to look out upon that sea of upturned faces, many of them familiar but all utterly transformed by the light and the dark and the drama of the evening. Though I craned my neck, I did not see anyone who resembled my long-ago image of Mister Black.

Then began the exercises, the music, reading the winning composition (which was perfectly stupid, it being "The Influence of the Bible," and Josie stumbled over her own words, maybe she didn't even write it!), conferring other honors, after which each one of us advanced in turn to receive our diplomas, printed in fancy script featuring Dr. Snow's indecipherable signature. We had all practiced crossing the rostrum to take the diploma in our left hand, shaking Dr. Snow's hand with our right, then curtsying—as low as possible! Luckily I was among the first to receive my diploma. Dr. Snow gave my hand an extra squeeze which made me furious because I could neither acknowledge nor protest it, under the circumstances. He pressed his sweaty fingers into my palm. But then it was done, leaving me free to watch the others and look out over the hall.

When Harriet Stokes went down in her curtsy, we all held our breaths to see if she would come back up, for she has gotten so heavy. But she did. And did I say that Mime Peeler took the music prize of course, and Eliza the art award which she does not give a fig for now that she is engaged to be married? Eliza could not stop smiling for even one minute during Dr. Snow's closing prayer, for there sat Danny right at the front of the hall, his long legs stretched out on the floor in a way that I found insolent, feet crossed at the ankles, hair tousled as usual, staring up at Eliza. He is very handsome, open and sweet, yet there is something in his bearing which I do not trust. It is like he owns the world. Certainly he owns Eliza. Four rows behind sat her parents and with them, her brother Ben, whose pale yellow hair was plastered down unnaturally on his head, making him look so funny I had to smile. He saw me and smiled back, all toothy and shy. I dared not glance at him again. Louis Tutwiler had not come, nor had Mister Black.

I stared straight ahead as we sang the parting song, and did not cry though Eliza and Emma Page were sobbing on either side of me. Dr. Snow gave the closing prayer, followed by the benediction. Commencement had ended. Then what a roar of voices, what a great confusion as friend rushed to friend and families overran the rostrum.

Suddenly I felt I could not breathe. I pushed through the crowd though I heard several people calling my name behind me. But I did not care who was calling for me, as I <u>had</u> to be out of doors! I ran through the closet back of the hall into the back yard past the Rose of Sharon bush and through the garden on the damp slippery stones and out into the orchard where the fireflies were rising up from the wet grass like stars. It had rained earlier that afternoon. Far away I could hear the happy hubbub of the commencement, though all I could see of the school itself was a gentle glow at the end of the orchard through the increasing mist. It looked like a fairy tale school, or like an imaginary city, or like Camelot. I threw myself face down in the grass, suddenly I did not care who was looking for me or what happened to my white swiss dress or anything.

A whippoorwill was singing in my ear. The wet grass was scratchy and cold on my face. I dug my hands into it, squeezing great wet clumps as hard as I could. I felt like a fool, or like a person just awakening from a long, long dream. No one had come to commencement for me, no one was missing me now. All the girls and all their families, all the life that I have known here at Gatewood Academy will be gone in the twinkling of an eye, as in the Bible. No matter how much I have tried to fool myself, in that instant I knew the truth. I am still an orphan girl, loose in the world, and do you know what, Mary White? I <u>like</u> it that way!

It seemed to me then like a terrible mistake to stay on here when they will all be gone—all, that is, save Agnes, whom I love . . . yet still it seems like a dreadful mistake, and when they rang the old bell to signal the end of commencement, it was like the end of everything, ringing in my head.

I lay in the grass until its last vibrating tone had gone entirely from the cool night air and then I got up finally and walked back through the dark gardens to the yard, furious to find the back doors already locked. I would have to go around to the front where I would undoubtedly be seen. There was no other way. I crept round the corner. People tarried here and there in the spacious front yard still conversing, though the candles guttered, all but gone. Louis Tutwiler stood by the gate with his hat in his hands. He raised it in a kind of wave when he saw me and opened his mouth to speak. But a slight dark form detached itself from the stone steps and jumped up to hug me. "Oh, thank goodness! At last!" It was Agnes, of course. "Why Molly, whatever has happened to you?" She pulled back to stare up at me just as Mrs. Snow appeared as a silhouette in the doorway. Then there was Dr. Snow himself advancing from the far corner of the porch holding a lantern so that all his features were lit from below, making him look monstrous, especially the huge red nose with its black hairs protruding. "Aha! The lady of the hour, at last," he said in a voice of strained humor. Another man followed close behind, but I could not see his face.

You know who it was.

I will write more later. And I will always be

Your friend forever,
Molly

† † †

For No One's Eyes

June 11, 1877

Five a.m. It is still dark outside, no one is stirring, & no birds sing. I have left Dr. Snow lying like a lump in the bed, & the little boys fast in their trundles.

I rise to write after a Night of Torment.

First, the Exigencies of Commencement, always such a Deal of Work, yet always unappreciated, as the girls & their families have eyes & thoughts only for one another . . . Alas, the poor Puppet-Mistress behind the scenes is all but ignored, totally unappreciated, & by Dr. Snow as well as the rest. What would it cost him to say, for instance, "Mariah, the flowers in the hall looked lovely?" Yet I shall never hear such praise from him. After all this time I should be resigned to it, & yet am Not.

Second, the late arrival of Simon Black, followed closely by the disappearance of Molly Petree, which did not surprise me in the least as she has been the bane of my existence for years. Small wonder I could not sleep, then suffered such Dreams . . . but in the words of Eve, "God is also in sleep, & dreams advise" (Book XII, line 615).

I have awakened trembling yet filled with Resolve.

It has been far too easy for me to get caught up in the duty & detail of life, the minutiae, the dross (the laundry, the hogs, the children, the marital duties, the money, the mud). Here I have been Praying Without Cease for acceptance of my Lot, yet to no avail, my headaches grown worse & worse, my Vision all but gone, my Sufferings immense. Yet as they say, it is never Too Late; for now it has come to me in a dream what I must do.

I must kick over the traces altogether.

I must follow wherever He leads, & damn the consequences!

For there is a scale, an empyrean Grandeur, which has been lost to Human Life. I was meant to dwell always upon such a scale; indeed if I may say so, I was born for it, & am particularly suited to it in terms both of Person (including Stature and physical characteristics, I dare not go further here), Intellect, Ability, Sensitivity, & Cast of Mind.

Imagine, then, my reaction upon being presented with an Entity so far above the rabble of average life on earth, & yet "from what height fallen" (Book I), & through "what dire event?" (Book I, line 155) The War, I suppose, & Circumstance, or Fate.

I refer, of course, to Simon Black. There, it is out!

Yet I must say, I recognized Him immediately, in my deep heart's core, & I tremble to say that He recognized me (Yes! upon his very first visit to Gatewood Academy) though He wisely chose to make no sign at the time, instead securing the means (Molly Petree) by which He might remain in contact & continue to see me.

I see Him now.

I know Him.

I simply cannot resist Him.

After all these years of effort, God hath sent me finally his Arch-Fiend . . . "So stretched out huge in length the Arch-Fiend lay chained on the burning lake . . . " He tempts me. Lord, yes, He tempts me.

Indeed, this morning I am prepared to say "Farewell, happy fields, where joy forever dwells! Hail horrors! Hail, infernal world!"

> I am ready to go with Him,
> What matter where, if I still be the same,
> And what should I be, all but less than He.
> Whom thunder hath made greater? Here at last
> We shall be free . . .
> Here we may reign secure, and in my choice,
> To reign is worth ambition, though in Hell:
> Better to reign in Hell than serve in Heaven.

Especially if one must serve the cruel & demanding Cincinnatus Snow, as cold as his name implies. Nothing can justify the ways of Cincinnatus Snow to me!

If I succumb to sin again (as once I did, famously) I shall lose Eden—all these plants & flowers which I have so carefully tended, both actual & metaphorical—yet what is that? What loss is that, to me?

I am prepared to look Him in the eye & swear that

… Thou to me
Art all things under Heaven, all places thou,
Who for my wilful crime art banished hence.

Better to Fall, to say with Eve ". . . but now lead on; In me is no delay; with thee to go is to stay . . . in Paradise" (Book XII, line 615) For Gatewood Academy is not Paradise, but rather Hell for me, despite my Hard Work, Prayers, & Good Intentions. It seems that these qualities should be enough, does it not? Yet it is not so. They are not enough. They have never been enough. There is in my soul an immense Hunger which gnaws at the edges of my mind like a ravenous wolf.

I shall see Him again in a mere seven hours, as He has arranged to take Sunday dinner with us after Church (which He will not attend). Dear God, can I contain myself? Can I bear to pass this time? I am both overtired & overstimulated. Perhaps I should go back to Bed, feigning sleep, claiming headache, though for once I have none! & it seems quite possible that I shall never sleep again, as I have a Fire running through my veins like a precursor of Hell itself.

> Mariah Rutherford Snow
> Headmistress, Gatewood Academy
> Hopewell, Virginia

Perhaps it is the last time I shall ever pen these words!

. . .

† † †

FOR NO ONE'S EYES

June 12, 1877

Dear Lord,

Thus am I tested, thus have I fallen, thus am I debased, yet now See. Though I have walked through the Valley of Evil, Thou hast set my feet upon Thy righteous Path again, Thou hast restored my Soul. Thus I say with renewed fervor, Thy Will be done, on Earth as it is in Heaven, Amen.

Under the clear blue sky of this Sabbath day that Thou hast made, oh Lord, I cannot even imagine what I was thinking of.

The cold fact is that Simon Black never cared for me. He used me. He continues to use us, & our Academy. Simon Black has no thought for anyone save Molly Petree, this was made manifest in our conversation with him yesterday following Sunday lunch which was excellent if I do say so myself, including a Charlotte Russe prepared by our new Mrs. Matney. But Mr. Black did not mention the dessert, nor the lunch, nor the beauty of the Commencement ceremony itself. He ate his food methodically, one serving after another without comment, until he was done. It was quite strange. He is quite strange. I have been quite deluded. It is as if Mr. Black has no time nor thought for the niceties. He is a driven man. Yet undeniably he does have charm of a sort, a kind of gravitas . . .

Dr. Snow had placed Molly across the table from him, along with Agnes, who blushed & made the silliest Remarks throughout the meal, she seemed quite lacking in Social Skills herself. Yet of course Simon Black ignored her as well, reserving all his attention for Molly Petree who appeared almost to scorn it, answering his questions as briefly as possible, fidgeting in her chair, flipping her hair back out of her eyes in that way she has, casting a beseeching eye toward Eliza Valiant when her family left their table.

At length Dr. Snow placed his napkin upon the tablecloth. "Girls, you may be Excused, though I daresay, Molly, that Mr. Black will wish to speak to you again before his departure."

"Yes Sir." Molly bobbed a curtsy, edging toward the door. "I shall be in the yard with Eliza & the little boys, Sir," she said, & he nodded.

Simon Black's eyes followed her out of the doorframe into the sunshine. He turned to me. "What relationship does Molly have with that young man, the brother?"

His question surprised me. "Why, none at all, that I know of," I said. "She visited the family at Christmastime, as you know."

He continued to stare out the door at her, now kneeling to talk to one of Eliza's little brothers. "And who was that student, that cadet, waiting for her last night after commencement?"

I did not know what he was talking about, & said so.

"You had better find out then," he said to me darkly, "for I am paying a good deal of money to have this girl chaperoned."

Here I took Umbrage. "I can assure you, Sir," I said, "that the utmost attention has been paid to the whereabouts & occupations of Molly Petree. Many of our girls have beaus, & some are engaged to be married, but despite her proclivities, Molly has shown no interest in any young man to date, isn't that right?" I queried Agnes who nodded, blushing.

"You may go now, Agnes," I said to her, & she scuttled out.

"What do you mean by Molly's proclivities, Mrs. Snow?" Simon Black turned to look at me. "What proclivities might those be?"

Now it was my turn to redden; I found myself biting my lip. "I suppose that her—er—History has made me particularly watchful concerning her Virtue," I admitted, after a pause.

"Though there has been absolutely no cause for concern," Dr. Snow said, stepping upon my foot so hard as to crush the bones, I was wearing my peau de soie slippers, no doubt I deserved it. "Molly has done extremely well here at Gatewood Academy."

"Indeed," Simon Black said, watching her now out the window as she held hands & danced round & round in a circle with two of the little boys. "She is not to be courted. She is too young for boys," he announced abruptly. "I shall appreciate your keeping them away from her in general. Keep her busy. I should like for her to continue her studies as well as teach. When she is old enough for courting, we shall discuss these matters further."

I could tell that the turn of the conversation surprised Dr. Snow. It did not surprise me. I know Him, as I said. I recognize Him. For me, it was as though a heavy iron door had swung to with a resounding clang that will echo in my mind forever. Of course, I realized.

My instincts are Infallible.

For Simon Black really is the Devil, I have known it all along. I have a sense of these things. Now I see that He wanted me only as a caretaker, a teacher, a nursemaid. For He has marked Molly Petree as His Own, & He will come back to claim her. I know it absolutely. Thank God that I myself have been spared his dark Attentions.

And now to the Bath.

> Mariah Rutherford Snow
> Headmistress, Gatewood Academy
> Hopewell, Virginia

On a final note, I wonder how much one should punish oneself for a sin committed only in the Mind, as opposed to Actuality? In other words, what part intentionality and what part actuality go to make up a Sin? For I feel as guilty as if I had committed the Act. I must Atone.

• • •

❧

Molly Petree
Gatewood Academy
Hopewell, Virginia

August 26, 1878

Dear Mary White,

We are leaving here, Agnes and myself, I write while she flits around this little stone house like a moth in the wavy light of all our candles and lamps burning at once, for it is late and we have not much time. I still cannot believe we are leaving. For I have been happy here in this quiet life, we have tea and read books, and take the girls on walks and expeditions, and give drama productions written by me, every other Friday evening. But now Agnes is packing up all she owns, which I have already done. Mine did not take long. Primus will drive us up to Danville at first light, then Agnes has hired a hack to take us on from there. It is all arranged. Chloe our cat will come too in her wicker basket.

I do not expect to sleep a wink all night. This is due to excitement not pain, for my eye does not even hurt now.

Agnes is a heroine.

You might not think it to look at her, for she is so slight and almost wispy somehow, as if she might blow away, she looks like this especially right now for her fine wavy hair escapes its bun to form a gentle halo around her head as she marches past in her night gown, arms full, red spots on her cheeks and her little mouth set in a line of determination. She looks like an avenging angel which she is.

Agnes and I and Bessie Barwick and Frances Tuttle (who are old, who have nowhere else to go) have been the only teachers left at Gatewood Academy for the past two weeks, save for the Snows, of course. The students were just arriving for start of term when word came of smallpox at the Military Institute, one cadet dead and two more fallen ill. We had to meet our girls at the gate and turn them back, Mrs. Snow beside herself with frustration. Then her own little Harry, not two, took sick and died. We buried him this morning in the old Gatewood family plot across the road, in a wooden box which looked so small to me as Primus shoveled the dirt on top of it, and so sad, for children <u>are</u> sad, they have no say in anything, anything at all. Mrs. Snow was not present at the service, being <u>prostrate with grief.</u> Dr. Snow said the words. We all stood out in the weedy grass under a heavy sky, with lightning off in the distance. Raindrops as big as quarters began to splash on the stone walk just as we came back through the wrought iron gate into the yard.

"Let's run," Agnes said, pulling my hand, but I stood still in the yard and turned my face up to the rain which I have always loved to do, remember how you and I used to dance around up on Indian Rock when it thundered. Those days are long gone, and I am a young lady now and a teacher, but I still want to run and scream when it storms. Agnes would not understand this, though she loves me. I guess I am sort of crazy! But I don't care.

I stood out there until it quit raining and I was thoroughly wet and then the sun came out shining off the drops on all the old-fashioned white musk roses and the bridal wreath and the sweet shrubs. It is like all the flowers are blooming as hard and as fast as they can right now because they know fall is coming soon, and they will die. A steady stream of water ran down off the roof from the high gable where I lived in the attic room for so long with my girlfriends, it seems like ages ago. Steam rose from the black earth around the sundial, it was like the whole garden was breathing. I closed my eyes and took in the thick sweet scent of the roses until a shiver ran over my entire body and I opened my eyes suddenly to find Dr. Snow, still in his heavy black suit, standing right in front of me, quite close.

He looked like a scarecrow in the garden.

"Ah, Molly," he said.

I jumped back stepping on some of Mrs. Snow's petunias. I knew I looked a sight with my hair falling down and my dress all wet and sticking to me. "I was just going in to change clothes," I said.

"No, wait—," he moved closer, awkwardly. "You are such a pretty girl," he said in a strange voice which I would not have recognized. He reached out to touch my breast, then began to stroke me. For a moment I stood quite still, looking out across his shoulder at the school. I remember thinking how empty and golden the garden seemed at that moment, as if it were a stage set. I felt like I was under a spell. "Come along now, Molly," he said, "just for a moment." He cleared his throat. "Since Mrs. Snow is incapacitated and we have so few of our faculty here now, I shall need to ask you to perform a few additional duties." He sounded very formal, though his blue eyes popped and his face was brick red. "Especially as your handwriting is so fine," he added. "Can you come with me now?" He pulled me roughly in the direction of his office, almost a twin of the fairy house I share with Agnes.

But the spell was broken.

"No Sir," I said, hitting him as hard as I could in his ugly red nose and pushing him backward at the same time so that he fell against the sundial, and me with him, into the wet black dirt. "No Sir," I said again as suddenly Nicky Eck came into my mind, and that little girl who lay on the floor of the barn, and how Spencer came to pick her up, up, and up, and I felt suddenly like I was flying, full of power, and I <u>kicked</u> him, Mary White, I cannot remember it really but I know I kicked him for Harry, and for Spencer, for Spencer is dead and I had loved him with all my heart. I <u>do not like</u> Dr. Snow, nor Mrs. Snow, nor even Simon Black who is my benefactor, for there is something awful about having a benefactor. I kicked Dr. Snow again, I kept remembering how it felt when Spencer lifted me up but how he is dead now like they all are, all my ghosts. <u>But I do not want to die yet.</u> I ran across the garden to our own little house with Dr. Snow calling out after me, and suddenly I looked up and saw that there was a rainbow in the sky. A rainbow! It started out over in the direction of town and ended up in the orchard.

I ran into our house and told Agnes everything.

"Oh Molly," she said, dropping her embroidery onto the floor. "Come on now, we must get you cleaned up, and then we must go to Mariah immediately. We have to tell her. She will know what to do."

"I think that is a terrible idea," I said immediately.

"Oh no, you underestimate my sister, she will fix everything, you'll see. Why just look at your poor face," for I had hit my cheek somehow on the sundial.

Agnes rinsed it off with a cool wet towel, and dragged me out the door.

They were waiting for us in the parlor, seated in the red velvet chairs on either side of the fireplace, as still as those figurines on the sideboard at Agate Hill. Mrs. Snow's skin had gone dead white. Her black hair swooped back in great stiff wings on each side of her face. Dark circles smudged her pale gray eyes. Her long thin fingers plucked at the folds in her skirt.

"Oh Mariah," Agnes began all breathless, but Mrs. Snow held up her hand, palm outward, in that way she has. "Do not even attempt to talk to me about the particularities of this incident, Agnes," she said. "Dr. Snow and I are in total accord."

For the first time I looked directly at Dr. Snow, who sat holding a white handkerchief to his nose. He had put on another jacket, but his pants and his shoes still bore traces of mud from the garden. I wondered if his rib cage still hurt where I had kicked him. I hoped so. He stared back at me, eyes narrowed, drumming his fingers on the arm of his chair. A Monarch butterfly fluttered in the butterfly bush outside the parlor window.

"I wonder if you <u>really do know</u> what the particularities of this incident are," Agnes said, to my surprise. Red dots of color had appeared on her cheeks.

"I know more than enough, thank you, my dear sister. I know all I need to know."

"And what is that, Mariah?" Agnes kept right after her, like a dog on a bone, as Selena would have said. "What is it that you think you know?"

Mrs. Snow took a deep breath and clutched the arms of her chair. "I know that your little friend Molly Petree is not what you think. Molly the beautiful, Molly the brilliant, Molly the poor orphan girl! Well, poor Molly may have pulled the wool over everyone else's eyes, but not over mine, I can assure you. I know that she attempted to seduce my husband, as if he would ever want the likes of her!" Mrs. Snow's sunken eyes bored straight into mine. "I know that when he attempted to reason with her, she attacked him, which is no surprise to anyone. Indeed, none of this comes as any surprise to me, I regret to say. It merely confirms the opinion I have held of Molly ever since her arrival at Gatewood Academy. For I am quite a judge of character, I pride myself upon it as you know."

"But Molly did nothing." Agnes interrupted her. "Nothing at all. Dr. Snow . . . made advances to her. He touched her, Mariah."

"Enough!" Mrs. Snow stood up, an immense black figure seeming to grow while we watched. "I will not listen to any more of this filth. Dr. Snow has told me all about her behavior in the garden. I know and have always known what you are, Molly Petree, do you hear me?" And the horrible thing was that I did hear her, and I feared that she was right, in spite of myself. "I cannot run the risk of having you at Gatewood Academy any longer," she concluded.

Suddenly the blue veins stood out in Dr. Snow's wide white forehead. "Now wait a second, Mariah—" He stood up. "Just hold your horses," he said. "A stern admonition will suffice here, as we discussed."

"No." Mrs. Snow held out her hand again in that palm-up gesture she has. "We cannot have her here, poisoning our girls. Corrupting them. You know that we cannot, Dr. Snow." She stared at him wildly. "Whatever are you thinking of? This girl must leave Gatewood immediately."

"Good," I said, turning to go.

"Wait," Agnes whispered.

I had reached the door when Dr. Snow recovered himself. "Molly, I'm sure you do not wish to jeopardize your entire future," he said sharply. "Agnes, stay right there. Keep Molly right there. Mariah, let us counsel together a bit, my darling. Let us think upon our Christian obligations as well as our practical considerations. Let us remember that we are in part a charitable organization, Mariah, and in particular let us recall that you were once a girl such as Molly, in need of kindness and guidance yourself—" He hissed these words at her as he took her elbow and urged her toward the door.

"I was? I was?" Mrs. Snow was screaming. She tore at her face and hair with her fingernails. "I was nothing like her. Nothing. I was an educated girl, a governess. I? I was tricked, then used, then vilified, then abandoned, then left in the most terrible circumstances with my little child, forced into the most degrading sorts of employment—I was <u>nothing</u> like <u>her</u>."

"Mariah, this is not necessary." Dr. Snow attempted to put his arms around her, but she batted him off as if he were an annoying child. Her face was bleeding, her black hair stood out all around her head like Medusa.

"Who did this to you, Mariah? Dr. Snow?" Agnes's voice was calm and clear. She stepped forward, placing herself between them and the door.

"Him? Lord, no." Mrs. Snow rolled her eyes. "Not him, oh no, are you serious? He would not have been worth it, why he could not hold a candle to—" She bit her lip. "No, I met Dr. Snow somewhat later, in Baltimore, a preacher who had lost his church. Doctor! He is no doctor. Let me tell you, I made him. <u>I made him up!</u> As well as this school which he seems determined to lose through his ridiculous decisions. Accepting the devil's spawn—" She gave Dr. Snow a final push and swept out the door, brushing Agnes aside.

Dr. Snow turned to face us. "Girls, as you can see, Mariah is not herself. In fact, you must ignore this outburst altogether, as it is nothing but the product of a fanciful, overtaxed, diseased mind. She is quite insane with grief. I must get her to bed somehow, I must send for Dr. Greene . . ." He paused, thinking. Suddenly he looked very old. "Agnes, will you help me?" he asked.

"No Sir, I will not," Agnes said firmly, to my surprise, as she is generally the most helpful person in the world.

Dr. Snow stumbled into the hall, calling for Primus.

I stood there staring at Agnes. "I don't understand," I said.

"Nevermind," she said briskly. "Come along now, Molly, we have things to do."

And we have been doing them ever since! The first thing Agnes did was to cut the string which held the asafetida bag around my neck. "Quarantine is over," she announced. "For we are leaving here as soon as possible." And we are! But I will write to you always, Mary White, I will find out where you are, and send these letters, for I remain your true friend,

Molly Petree

"Adieu"
As duly recorded by Agnes Rutherford
To the attention of Mrs. Mariah Snow,
Headmistress, Gatewood Academy

August 27, 1878

Farewell, Sister Mariah,

For this is how I shall always think of you, unspoken, secret Mother, though I do understand that perhaps you did the best you could for the two of us, given your circumstances as you describe them. Who can ever understand the anguish of another human soul? Not I, and far be it from me to judge.

I was going to recommend Rowena Drabble for a post that has come to my attention, but now I have recommended myself. I am taking Molly with me, to remove her from harm's way. Your secrets will remain safe with me only so long as you and Dr. Snow do not attempt to follow us, or contact us in any way.

God Bless You,
Agnes

✝✝✝

FOR NO ONE'S EYES

August 30, 1878

So now they are gone, while I remain here trapped in this cold stone school. Good riddance! I shall not miss them. Though I confess that I envy them, with all my heart.

> The world was all before them, where to choose
> Their place of rest, and Providence their guide;
> They, hand in hand, with wandering steps and slow,
> Through Eden took their solitary way.

Mariah Rutherford Snow
Headmistress, Gatewood Academy
Hopewell, Virginia

✝✝✝

FOR NO ONE'S EYES

September 8, 1878

Gave birth.

Mariah Rutherford Snow
Headmistress, Gatewood Academy
Hopewell, Virginia

Further Notes from Tuscany (FYI)

GATEWOOD ACADEMY SONG

Months of pleasure, months of joy,
    We together here have spent.
Freely, and without alloy
    Many mercies God has sent.
Hoping soon to meet again,
    Fare you well.

Gentle teachers, good and kind,
    Thank you for your tender care,
We shall ever bear in mind
    All the blessings each now share.
Hoping soon to meet again,
    Fare you well.

Loved companions, schoolmates dear
    We must bid you all adieu.
You we love with hearts sincere,
    We will still remember you.
Hoping soon to meet again,
    Fare you well.

REMEDIES

1.   CURE FOR AGUE: use 1 ounce best powdered Rhubarb and piece of Pearl Ash size of a large nutmeg; pour on 1 pt. boiling water stirring well. When cool, bottle it. Dose: 1 tablespoon before breakfast and the same an hour before dinner. Shake bottle before taking it.

2.   TREATMENT OF DEPRESSION AND SLEEP DISTURBANCES: Pour one cup boiling water over 1 to 2 teaspoons Saint-John's-wort flowers or leaves. Steep.

TUSCANY MILLER

30-B Peachtree Court Apts.

1900 Court Blvd.

Atlanta, GA 30039

Hi Dr. F.,

The Gatewood Academy closed its doors in *1880, apparently they could not keep on going after Simon Black withdrew his financial aid. Mrs. Snow was put into the state insane asylum at Staunton, VA. Dr. Snow disappeared. (I don't have a clue whatever happened to all those children, Dr. Ferrell!) The school itself is still standing but has now become a home for unwed mothers affiliated with the Reverend Jerry Falwell's ministry as I said. Girls can go there and have a baby and get their GEDs at the same time, and be ministered unto.*

Now here is what happened to some of Gatewood girls:

Emma Bell Page became a famous missionary to China.

Phoebe Taylor married a Boston minister and had eight children, one of them was a Senator.

Harriet Stokes (the one who was "heavy" at graduation) had a baby soon afterward, to her surprise, claiming virgin birth.

Eliza Valiant married her boyfriend Danny Butterworth, had several children immediately, then died at thirty of something that sounds like an ectopic pregnancy, though I don't know for sure, of course.

Mime Peeler never married at all, but lived with her parents in Roanoke, Virginia, where she taught piano lessons and played the organ at the First Methodist Church for the rest of her life.

Courtney Leigh Lutz killed herself at thirty-four by jumping off an ocean liner bound for France.

And if you want to know what happened to Molly and Agnes, just keep reading! The next part is by Agnes, it is on file in the Historical Society Reading Room at the Ashe County Public Library in West Jefferson, NC, you will soon see why.

Hopefully yours,
Tuscany Miller

Up on Bobcat

"Final Impressions"
As duly recorded by Agnes Rutherford

This piece of mica was given to me by Molly Petree when she married. I shall never forget it—the blast of freezing air when the door opened, a sort of whooshing sound as she swept across the floor in that blue hooded cloak I knew so well, though in fact it was pitch black, the middle of the night; the feel of her hair on my cheek and her sweet breath in my ear as she said, "Goodbye, Agnes, I love you. Here, keep this, I want you to have it to remember me by," pressing the mica into my hand. She had carried it in her pocket since I had first known her. "No, I cannot—," I began, struggling beneath the heavy bedclothes but to no avail, for she was already gone, leaving only a heady space of cold air to mark her presence. The little Badger girls on either side of me sat up and began to cry. I soothed them as best I could, saying, "There now, go back to sleep, it was nothing, nothing at all," which was not true, but even then I could never have foreseen the tragic consequences which were to spring from this event.

Now I hold the mica up to the sunlight streaming in the kitchen window, turning it this way and that, watching as it throws off rays like little bolts of lightning. I can never decide. Was I, in any way, to blame for what was to come? I have always worried about this, I have always felt guilty. For in actual fact I was responsible for both journeys: that is, first, removing Molly Petree from Agate Hill; and second, removing her from Gatewood Academy and taking her away so precipitously to these mountains.

See how this mica sparkles in the sun. I wonder if I could have done anything different, if I could perhaps have waited and chosen a less drastic course, and what would have happened then . . . but it is impossible to wrest a decision out of its time and place, and even now I cannot think what I should have done.

In fact, old age has been something of a disappointment in that I fully expected wisdom to come to me sometime, certainly by now, perching like a robin on my shoulder. This has not happened. I understand nothing. Yet I shall attempt to set the record straight nevertheless, aware of the all-too-swift passage of time in its flight, how it cloaks even our most important moments like the fog which hides Laurel Knob from view as I look out my kitchen window now.

Our journey here took days in a public coach, traveling first down to Winston Salem thence to Wilkesboro where we passed the night in a rowdy hotel, its lobby piled high with luggage and boxes and parcels of every sort. Wilkesboro was like a Western town in those days, a "jumping off place" full of men heading out to make their fortunes. As I sat in the bustling lobby on the morning of our departure, I thought that many of them had said goodbye forever to all, mothers and fathers and kin; they might never pass this way again. Then a thrill shot through me as I realized that this was our own situation exactly, though who would have guessed it, of course, a little old-maid schoolteacher and a pretty girl?

The next day we went in a line of wagons up the turnpike from Wilkesboro toward Jefferson, with teams of extra horses trotting along behind us. Straw hat on her lap, Molly dozed through the hot afternoon while I sat up ramrod straight as if electrified, watching the great blue shapes of the mountains gather around us. Yes, I said to myself. *Yes.* I thought of the peak in Darien in "On First Reading Chapman's Homer," by Mariah's beloved Milton. I felt that I was truly entering the "realms of gold."

At dusk the drivers stopped at the Reddies River in order to rest the horses for the morrow, setting up tents where we passengers might lie down on little cots to sleep, to the chagrin of a pair of thin lady sisters, raven-haired Miss Reedy and gray-haired Miss Reedy, traveling along with us. Necessary functions were performed in the pinewoods while an old wagoneer named Joe kept watch. Molly giggled, cheeks aflame, running back out. After the confines of Gatewood Academy, this was an exotic journey indeed.

The wagoneers cooked a "pinebark stew" in a big pot over a great fire, ladling it out into enamel bowls for us to eat with tin spoons. It was delicious. The Misses Reedys' snores did not bother Molly, but I couldn't sleep a wink all night long, watching the flickering campfire, listening to the men's indistinct laughter and voices, and now and then, the plaintive strain of a fiddle.

After bitter morning coffee, streaky bacon, and corn cakes fried over the fire—they call these "hush puppies," and throw them to the dogs too—we set off again, up the mountain which was arduous indeed, the horses straining and foaming with sweat, the men cursing and yelling at them. "I want to walk!" Molly announced at one point, pitying the horses, but as it was muddy along the bank, the men would not allow it, a good thing since the road grew narrower the higher we went, so that each lurching turn sent our hearts leaping into our throats. Below us, off the roadside, the mountains lay spread like the sea, peak after peak like waves disappearing into the misty blue distance.

"That there's Grandfather Mountain," one of the men rode back to report, "see, there's his nose," pointing across the airy miles to the biggest mountain of all, with a huge bump halfway down it. Then we passed around a bend, then it was lost from view. We went on, and on, and on, up through the Deep Gap and past Nettle Knob and the great somber Nigger Mountain and thus into Jefferson, a rough but pretty little town with its busy unpaved streets lined by beautiful cherry trees.

Thoroughly dusty and hot and worn out by then, we disembarked at a kind of depot, handed down by a strapping young man onto a wooden platform. I was so exhausted, my knees nearly buckled under me. All was hustle and bustle and barking dogs. The Reedys were met by three dapper little men half their size. Husbands? Brothers? They all drove off in a big green buggy. Molly and I stood next to our pile of baggage in the full hot rays of the sun. Suddenly the platform was entirely empty, as if all the activity of a half hour before had never occurred.

"Well, Agnes?" Molly squinted into the sun to smile at me.

"Ah, ah, Miss Rutherford?"

We turned around to find a plump red-faced young man in a light blue suit and a straw hat, mopping at his forehead. He was accompanied by a pale long-faced woman in a brown silk dress and hat who held on to his arm with one hand as tightly as she grasped her enormous purse with the other.

"I am, ah, ah, ah, Augustus Worth." His speech was a kind of chortle, bubbling up like a spring.

"I am Agnes Rutherford, and this is Molly Petree, the young teacher I mentioned to you in my letter."

"I am so, ah, happy," he began, but here the woman cut in sharply.

"And I am Drusilla Worth. Welcome." She turned abruptly to her husband. "Gus, these girls will not do at all. But there's nothing to be done for it now, so come along"—to us—"let's get you out of the sun. Miss Fickling's boardinghouse is just down the street. Careful now, it's Court Day." She turned him around and pushed him off the platform into the dusty road.

"But what about our luggage?" I called after them.

"I'll have it there directly, mam," said the young stationmaster who had reappeared and stood pointing out the sights, such as they were, to Molly.

"Come along, then." I pulled at Molly's sleeve. She put her hat back on and there we went across the dusty street behind this unlikely couple: her, stiff and narrow as a poker; him, round as a snowman.

"Look at his feet," Molly whispered, giggling.

They turned out almost at right angles to the side, giving him a waddling duck gait.

Suddenly I couldn't control myself either, I am ashamed to say. Laughing helplessly, Molly and I clung to each other for support as we progressed in our odd foursome across the main street of Jefferson, dodging wagons and carriages and attracting a great deal of notice. We attained the shade of the cherry trees along the line of stores.

"Hello, ladies." Two gentlemen stopped to bow, removing their hats. I took them for lawyers, as I knew Jefferson to be the county seat. A solemn storekeeper in an apron came to his door to welcome us, followed by his smiling frizzy-haired wife. "Come back and see us!" she said. "If we ain't got it, you don't need it!" Indeed it seemed as if they had every possible thing in their window or sitting out along the front. We stepped aside to make way for two men carrying a sack of flour to a waiting wagon. A country woman came by holding two flapping chickens by the neck. Children darted everywhere. A crazy man was preaching on the street corner though nobody paid him the slightest attention. "Hell is a-waiting!" he yelled. "It's a-waiting for you!" His shirt was filthy. We passed a bank, a pharmacy, a crippled shoemaker sitting on a chair outside his shop, and several nice frame houses where girls came out on the porches to stare at us, pointing. "It is rude to point." I heard Mariah's voice in my head. But of course it was entirely possible that no one had ever told these girls that. A little restaurant named Gracie's was packed with people; several of them came to the window to watch us pass by, napkins tucked into their shirt fronts. I realized how hungry I was. Two men stood outside playing fiddle and banjo; the tune followed us down the street. On we went through this little town nestled deep in the bowl of the mountains, bright blue sky above.

I was relieved when the Worths opened a gate and stepped up on a friendly porch lined with rocking chairs and blooming flowers in pots. A hanging swing moved slightly in the breeze. Two cats slept on a blue hooked rug before the screen door, which opened immediately. "Scat!" cried the fat red-headed woman who emerged smiling broadly with one gold tooth in front. "Well, Lord, look-a-here what the cat drug in! I'm Martha Fickling, and you all are the new schoolteachers, ain't you a sight, Lord, Lord! You must be all wore out. Come on in here and get yourselves some lemonade and pound cake, I've been a-waiting on you. Gussie, you and the missus can come on in and help yourselves to some pound cake too, iffen you want, but one way or another you'll have to move outen the door," she said severely to Mr. Worth, who was rolling his eyes and blubbering something to his wife. "You know he wants some of my cake," she said to the wife. "Why, I'm famous for it!" To him she said, "Gussie, I swear to God. Get in or out, one! These girls is starving. Can't you move him?" she asked Mrs. Worth.

"That's enough now, come along," Mrs. Worth said to Mr. Worth as one would speak to a dog, and off he went with her reluctantly, out the gate and up the busy street, having promised to meet us on the morrow to show us the school and further explain our positions.

"Lord, Lord!" Martha Fickling drew us inside through the cozy parlor where she evidently slept as well, for a big brass bed stood in the far corner next to an enormous parrot in a wooden cage.

A round oak table in the dining room held a sweating blue pitcher of lemonade and a large pound cake, the most luscious thing at that moment that I had ever seen. "Now get yourselves a piece, that's right, honey," to Molly who had thrown her hat on the floor and grabbed the knife. "Well, sure, I'll have one too. Now you all just make yourselves comfortable. Take them old shoes off. Shoes makes a person hot, in my opinion."

We did so, and she was right. Furthermore, it was the best cake I had ever tasted, bar none. I had two pieces, Molly three. The bird in the cage called, "Hi-ho! Hi-ho!" The luggage arrived and the young stationmaster got a big chunk of cake for his trouble, but Martha Fickling wouldn't let him come in. "You be on your way now, Johnny," she said. "She ain't going noplace, and Lord knows, neither are you. Go on, now." He went. I relaxed, beginning to like Martha Fickling very much. I had worried most about our accommodations, yet these seemed ideal. And Martha knew "the dirt," as she called it, on everybody.

Of Augustus Worth she said, "Why, he's right from around here, son of the old Judge and that flighty young wife of hisn that run off with the peddler. So everbody has knowed him all along, and knowed what he was like, full of book smarts but no common sense, the kind of kid that couldn't park a bike. Old Judge sent him down to the University at Chapel Hill and he never got over it, in my opinion. That's where he picked up his bossy woman, she's a lot oldern him, can you tell? He's blinded by pussy, I say." Of course, Molly was enchanted by this inappropriate information about our "boss," for Dr. Worth was the newly appointed superintendent of schools.

We slept like the dead in our cheerful bedroom overlooking the street, waking to the smell of coffee and the sound of conversation. Several lumbermen—"speculators"—had arrived in the night. Wearing an enormous red-flowered dressing gown, Martha Fickling served up pancakes and sausage and fried apples, joking with everybody. "Go to hell, fare thee well!" sang the bird.

Dr. and Mrs. Worth arrived promptly and walked us to a fine two-story establishment at the end of Main Street. I was delighted, having expected much more primitive conditions. There were eight classrooms here, four up and four down. As the term was soon to begin, several men were putting the finishing touches on a sparkling new coat of whitewash. Inside we met a jolly bald man who introduced himself as Felix Boykin, botanist and principal. "I want to show you something," he said to Dr. Worth, demonstrating a clever sliding wooden door he had put between two classrooms on the ground floor. "Now we can open it up for assemblies," he said, "or use it like a curtain for plays and performances. See, the audience can sit here, and this can be the stage."

"Oh, excellent, excellent," burbled Dr. Worth while his wife frowned, running her finger along a sawdust-topped desk.

"I just love to put on plays," Molly said suddenly. "Did Agnes tell you that?"

Felix Boykin raised his eyebrows to look at her, then at me, then at Dr. Worth.

Mrs. Worth poked him in the side.

Dr. Worth cleared his throat. "Ac-ac-actually, you will not be teaching at this school, ladies."

"What?" Molly said immediately.

"If you teach in this county at all," Mrs. Worth threw in darkly.

"Now, Drusilla," Mr. Worth said.

I sat down in one of the children's desks, for I could not stand, motioning Molly to do the same. A pleasant morning breeze blew through the double classroom. "Now," I said, looking at them, "perhaps you had best begin at the beginning, and tell me everything."

"Let me do the honors." Felix Boykin faced us solemnly, straddling the desk in front of us. "And let me apologize for this misunderstanding." (Though I was sure it was not *his* fault, since by now I was convinced that I had never met more of a nitwit than Dr. Worth, who took this chance to flee.) Felix Boykin explained that Jefferson Academy was attended not only by children from Jefferson but also by boarding students from the surrounding communities who wanted more education than could be got in their own one-room schools. "Which are quite good," he emphasized. "Some of them, especially in the Old Fields and Helton Creek area, are very old, with fine reputations. I am a strong proponent of the one-room schools in general."

"You are a stranger here yourself, aren't you?" I realized suddenly, for there was only the slightest trace of a mountain accent in his speech.

"Yes." He smiled. "To make a long story short, I fell into a bit of trouble as a young man, then decided to make a new start, mend my ways, and preach. I came to Ashe County fresh out of seminary, as a circuit rider, intending to return for further schooling at Harvard University the next year, but as you see, I'm still here."

"But you are no longer a minister . . . ," I said.

"No. I lost my faith, such as it was, I lost my ambition and my family, such as they were, but I fell in love with a local girl, one of the Colvards, and took up teaching, and have stayed on here to raise eight children—one of them, ironically, is studying at Harvard University right now."

"Really!" I could not help exclaiming.

"This country suits me," he said. "It does not suit everyone. Mrs. Worth will not last long, for instance. But it has gotten into my blood. This is a big, rugged county, ladies, and there are, to this day, many unmapped and even impenetrable areas. Maybe you don't know that we were once part of the State of Franklin, an area formed from western North Carolina and eastern Tennessee which seceded from the Union right after the Revolutionary War." I certainly did not know this. I stared at him, amazed. He went on. "Well, the great State of Franklin did not last long. But you will find the people here fiercely individualistic, not to say cantankerous, and so removed from the mainstream that to this day we are called the Lost Province. Some of us, such as myself, like to be lost. This is a different world, as you will see if you choose to stay."

"But if there is no position for us here . . ."

"The post in question is a one-room schoolhouse up in the Grassy Creek area near Hidden Valley and Chestnut Hill, on the South Fork of the New River. Of course these names mean nothing to you now. But I shall tell you about it. The Bobcat School has long since fallen into disuse. Recently, however, due to timber interests in the area, there are more jobs and more children, and six months ago, I had a visit from an old man—ninety if he is a day—named Memorable Jones. He had walked all the way out of the holler and halfway down the road to Jefferson before someone picked him up and brought him here. He had come looking for a teacher, he said, to 'open up the Bobcat School and teach the younguns,' for he has a smart little grandson and he doesn't want him to 'grow up like me,' as he said, 'can't read a lick and ain't got a pot to piss in'—ladies, pardon my French. So it is a remote school, but you would find enthusiastic parents, willing scholars, and you would certainly have a powerful advocate in Memorable Jones."

"But what did Mrs. Worth mean," I asked, "when she said we wouldn't do?"

"She has absolutely no authority; the board has already acted," Felix Boykin assured us. "Customarily they try to hire men for these remote schools, as the older boys come in the winter term when there is no work in the fields, and it is generally felt that a man can handle them better. Or perhaps a more experienced schoolteacher."

"Why, what they want is the Old Hoot Owl!" Molly broke in. "She's this old lady at Gatewood," she explained to Professor Boykin.

We all laughed. A bee flew in the window. Then Felix Boykin smiled, holding out his open hands. Clearly he still had a touch of the preacher in him, after all these years. "Agnes and Molly, it is entirely up to you. Certainly you cannot be expected to keep a contract whose terms were never disclosed. But if you choose to take on this school, I want you to know what you are getting into."

I liked him immensely.

"We'll do it!" I said, standing up. "We like a challenge, don't we, Molly?" Of course I did not tell him that we had only nine dollars between us and nowhere else in the world to live.

"I can't wait," Molly said immediately. Her eyes were as blue and clear as the Ashe County sky outside the academy windows.

It took a few days more to prepare for the trip. Felix sent out a call for books and supplies; the townspeople responded generously. Though I found these items quite worn and used, I knew I could not complain, as we would have nothing there, and these were all that could be got on such short notice.

Meanwhile, Martha Fickling fattened us up as if for the kill, giving us the lowdown all the while. Even at night she could not stop, sitting on the end of our bed smoking cigarettes and drinking glassfuls of her own peach brandy, telling stories until I thought I should expire from sheer exhaustion. We learned that the entire county had been split during the War, brother turned against brother, and many awful deeds done by the "bushwhackers." We learned that Nigger Mountain got its name because its caves had hidden escaping slaves headed north. We heard about the man who had looked into a spring up on Bluff Mountain and saw something so terrifying that he "had not spoke since," to this day.

"I like you girls," Martha told us that last night, "and Lord knows, I wish you well, but it's a hard row you've got to hoe up there, as a schoolteacher."

"Why?" Molly sat up straight in the bed.

"Well, they'll all be trying to marry you off, or marry you, like young Johnny there"—she winked at Molly, referring to the young stationmaster who had been driving us crazy for the last two days—"or else they will turn agin you, for something they think you've done, or how they think you look, or who knows what all, and then they'll gang up against you, and church you, and they might even turn you out. Why students has been known to turn a schoolteacher out theirselves if they didn't like them. They smoked one out up on Rip Shin."

"Well, they most certainly will not!" I had never heard of such a thing.

"Hell, they was a bunch that churched me," Martha announced, tossing back her brandy. "It was years ago, right here in this town, when the old man died. But I didn't care then, and don't care now. And you know what? I have outlived them all, goddamnit, ever one that did that. So it don't mean a thing to me." We proceeded to learn entirely more than I wanted Molly to hear about Martha's earlier life, how her daddy had "run off" and her mama had "got shot" and her granny had "died of her lungs" and Martha herself had "got a job cooking at the lumber camp up on Buffalo" when she was "naught but a girl," and how the owner, an old man, had "took up with me," as she put it, tossing her brassy curls, "and it don't matter what you think about that, either one of you, and whether you like it or not. Sometimes there can come an attraction between two people, even people as unlikely as we was, that is going to last though all hell breaks loose and longer than death, which is why I have got this nice house here that you all are a-sitting in right now, he heired it to me, and there was not a damn thing that old wife of his nor anybody else could do about it! So there!" She laughed and slapped her dimpled knee. "I swear, I'm going to miss you girls! Maybe I'll ride up on Bobcat before long and see how you are making out."

"Please come," Molly said immediately. Molly was fascinated by Martha Fickling, and why not? For this story was the exact opposite of all those dreary moral tales we had had them read on Sundays at Gatewood Academy.

The next morning we were up and ready before full light, tiptoeing down the stairs and through the dining room and the shadowy sitting room where I saw not one but two heads poking above the covers in Martha Fickling's big brass bed as we passed by. I didn't say a word, hoping that Molly wouldn't notice. "Hi-ho! Hi-ho!" the parrot sang. "Damn your eyes!"

Our fully packed wagon stood in the street, with two new additions.

A rough-looking boy in a brown slouch hat slumped on the seat smoking a cigarette, a huge shaggy black dog beside him. He jumped down, ducked his head, and mumbled something, grabbing our bags and tossing them up into the back as if they were weightless. Even in the pale early light, we could tell that he was blushing furiously.

"I am Miss Rutherford," I said, "and this is Molly Petree."

"Yes'm." He ducked his head.

"What is your name?"

"Cicero Todd, ma'am. They have sent me down here to get you, and I aim to get you there safe." He appeared mortified. Yet he handed me up with the greatest delicacy, though his hand was rough as a cob—but Molly jumped up herself, and we were off, down Jefferson's main street in the early light, Cicero clicking to his horses. On either side of us the great dark mountains loomed, while above them the sky turned pearl, then pink. "Oh Agnes, look," Molly said, clutching my hand.

I felt my soul expand to meet the country as we traveled those bumpy roads which were to become as familiar to me as the back of my hand. Ashe County remains the most beautiful part of the earth I have ever seen, with its great rounded mountains swooping up beyond green pastures and white farm houses and log cabins and the occasional tiny church, all under God's blue arch of sky. Under duress, Cicero pointed out Bluff Mountain, Paddy Mountain, and the immense Three Top Mountain, with its pointed peaks. "He hates us," Molly whispered, but I assured her—though privately I was not so sure—that he was "just shy." We forded creeks, passed through dense pine forests as black as night, and once crossed a windy bald with long blue views in every direction. Twice Molly and I got down and walked with Cicero to lighten the load as we went up a long steep grade, though he protested. Now we could see the sparkle of the New River off to our right whenever the trees parted.

"Hit ain't far now," Cicero announced suddenly as we rode along the spiny top of a ridge he identified as Pisgah. We soon turned off on a trace to the right—it was scarcely a road—passing several little cabins almost invisible back in the trees, and wound up the last long bend to the top of a sunny rise where stood the Bobcat School with old Memorable Jones himself standing out in front of it, his entire body bent into an S-shape, leaning on his cane, waiting for us. His gray hair streamed down his back. As Cicero drew the wagon to a stop, people began pouring out of the schoolhouse, brandishing homemade brooms and cloths. Children ran everywhere like chickens.

"What in the devil taken you so long?" Memorable Jones said to Cicero, not smiling. Then "Ladies," he said, "you have come a fur piece. Get down and let us take a look at you." Now it was our turn to blush. "Well," he concluded, "you are younger than expected, though you look right smart, and healthy enough, I reckon, though *you*"—he poked his stick at me—"might be a little stouter. Well, you'll have to do, I reckon. Come on, come on. We have got a great deal of work to do here, and time's a-wasting!"

"Don't pay no attention to Papaw, he is just awful sometimes!" A freckle-faced woman in a red kerchief ran over to us. "I'm Chattie Badger, and you-uns is going to stay with me. We live right over the mountain there"—she flung out her arm—"at Chestnut Hill, and it's as pretty a place as can be. You'll like it."

The rest of that day was a blur, as we joined in the cleanup of the Bobcat School. We met so many people at once that I was sure I could never put their faces with their names—Vannoy, Barker, Shoemaker, Roop, Sizemore, Hamby, Sprinkle, Bray. They had come with buckets, scrub brooms, rakes, scythes, and mattocks. Men had been chopping weeds all morning, so that a schoolyard already existed, ready for games. It was bordered on one side by the most beautiful bank of wild white roses you can possibly imagine, and by the thick green forest on the other. Behind the school, they had gathered rocks to hold two washtubs over fires to heat water brought from the spring nearby, and were busily cleaning all the desks. The windows had already been washed. The empty floors had been swept and were now being scrubbed by the men. Windows and doors stood open to let in the hot August sun and to air out the two classrooms. Memorable Jones sat to the side on a large "table rock," scowling and smoking his pipe. I dared not approach him—I could not have done so then if my life depended upon it!

The last thing they did was hang the bell on a post in front of the school. We finished up and left just as the sun set red and gold over the distant river—our subsequent view from the Badgers' long porch. I had never been so tired, but Molly appeared inexhaustible, playing Graces in the bare broom-swept yard with the girls, Tildy and Caro and Jane, while the boys—I couldn't tell how many boys there were—tended to the animals and did their other chores. Chattie was a "widder woman," her young husband having been killed in a sawmill accident. Cicero Todd carried in our bags and tipped his hat, scowling. He would not look at me as he waved away my offer of a dollar (to my immense relief).

The following morning, Molly and I went back over to the Bobcat School. We arranged the desks, putting chalk, erasers, slates, a water pail and a dipper and a new broom (brought in and apparently made by Cicero) in place. We put all the books which we had brought—blueback spellers, Mc-Guffey's Readers, Holmes' Readers, arithmetics and grammars, *Elementary Geography* by Matthew Fontaine Maury, a few storybooks, a dog-eared *Webster's Dictionary* and a couple of Bibles—behind the glass doors of a beautiful old handcarved wooden secretary which had been left in the building.

The next day we took up school.

I have the clearest image of Molly in her plain brown dress (for we had taken Martha Fickling's advice to heart) ringing the bell as hard as she could while barefooted children straggled up the red hill, giggling and shy, swinging their little lunch buckets. A few carried hornbooks as well. The old bell, donated by the Methodist Church in Jefferson, was neither tinny nor mournful but had a lovely clear tone. It sounded like an invitation pealing out over the mountains. And here they all came, little boys and girls ranging in age from six to twelve or thirteen, so many more than we expected. I counted ten, twelve, fifteen, twenty, more. They would have to sit two to a desk. I stood at the door to welcome them. "Girls on the right, boys on the left," I said, forming them into two lines. Oh how hopeful and sweet and scared they seemed, gap-toothed and grinning, holding hands, wiggling and wriggling, some of their clothes ill-fitting and threadbare but clean as could be for the opening of the Bobcat School.

The days took us over then, one after another after another, week after week through that first long golden fall and into the winter, each day filled with its lovely moments and its trials.

We divided the children into groups—Molly took the younger ones, who came forward first every morning to recite, toeing the chalk line we drew on the floor at the front of the room, while older students worked on their assignments in the back, reading or memorizing—much of this aloud, no wonder everybody started calling us the "blab school." But repetition was necessary, as we didn't have enough books to go round nor take home. At midmorning we turned them out for the privy, first girls, then boys, and then recess—they could not wait, running and jumping like rabbits. Next came arithmetic, then writing lessons, where we passed out the precious copybooks in which the older students copied out Bible lessons written on the board while the younger ones wrote their names and single words with only a quill at first—we could not spare the ink, while Molly moved among them to guide their hands.

And finally, lunch. We cleared the desks and they sat at attention while each row went in turn for their lunchpails. In warm weather, we all went outside. In rain or cold, they ate at their desks, sandwiches or biscuits with apple butter, jelly, sometimes egg or ham. Several children of one family always brought "crumbly," corn bread broken up in milk, carried in a tin syrup bucket with a lid. They gathered around the bucket to eat.

Chores came after lunch: carrying firewood, fetching pails of water, followed by yet more games—oh, those games! Snap-the-whip, andy-over, mumbly peg. Girls played jump rope, chanting,

> Oh Dan Tucker was a fine old man,
> Washed his face in a frying pan.
> Combed his hair with a wagon wheel,
> And died of a toothache in his heel.

We always began the afternoon session by reading them a story, for there is nothing like a story to calm even the most fractious child. Even little Shadrack Sturgill, who twitched all the time and had fits, did not move a muscle during story time. Being Mariah's disciple, I often took this opportunity to impart a little lesson, for you could not imagine the living situations of some of our children, how impoverished their lives in terms of moral guidance and even conversation.

I remember we had quite a discussion about "The Young Frog" from the Holmes' Reader, for instance. This is a fable wherein a vain frog complains about her "dull, out of the way life"; against all advice, she leaves home and moves to town to make her fortune. But once in the city, she is soon devoured by a hungry duck. "Boys and girls, we should be satisfied," decreed the Holmes' Readers, for "it is a bad thing to think of ourselves more highly than we ought to think." I closed the book. "Now, how do you like this story?" I asked them. It seemed like good advice to me, for these little lives proscribed by poverty and place.

But instantly a hand was waving—Jesse Badger, of course, old Memorable Jones's grandson, the smartest child in school. "Why, if a feller was to foller that, Miss Rutherford, he wouldn't get noplace atall in the world, now would he?"

I was taken aback. "Jesse is entirely right," I said, changing my mind in an instant, for I hope I never grow too old to learn from a child. The next story I read to them was "The Emperor's Clothes."

And so it went, grammar, geography, and history, then, at last, everybody's favorite, spelling! And every Friday the beloved spelling bee, attended by many a parent, standing at the back. At the end of each school day, the children helped us clean the slates, put away the books, sweep the floor, and gather up the dippers. Then row by row they retrieved their jackets and lunch pails and stood by their desks until dismissed. I was very strict about all this, for I have found that children love order, and that it is good for them. It is good for us all—alas, poor Molly!

But let us return to the days, the lovely ordered days, the hot sweet breeze in summer, bringing in the scent of the wild roses at the edge of the woods; or the smell of wet wool clothing in winter, when it was so hard to control the heat from our potbellied stove. Sometimes the classroom got so stuffy that we had to throw open the windows—ah, but then the icy wind came in. We either froze or roasted. Our woodstove was kept well supplied by Cicero Todd, glum and scowling as ever, his arrival every few days occasioning great excitement among the children, who were allowed to ride his huge dog Roy, fearful looking but endlessly patient with them. In fact, Roy seemed to enjoy this game as much as they did. Cicero Todd lived nearby in a little cabin he had built when he was practically a child, according to Chattie Badger. "Nobody knows where he came from, nor who his people was, nor how come him to fetch up here." He was a skilled carpenter, though, making chairs and tables and beds, poplar dough boards, rolling pins, barrels, and buckets, as well as more desks for us. "There's no harm in him," Chattie decreed, so eventually I paid no attention as Cicero came and went, part of the endless weave of our days, like the coverlets Chattie wove rain or shine on her loom by the fire.

That first year, only two incidents made a break in this pattern.

The first happened early on, when Molly had gone up to the blackboard to write out the day's Bible verse for copying. Unbeknown to us, several of the boys had caught a blacksnake in a slip noose and put it in my desk drawer, coiled to look like it was still alive. There it lay when Molly opened the drawer to get the chalk. She did not cry out nor even mention it, just calmly picked up the end of the noose and dangled the snake in front of the class, causing several girls to scream and the children in the front to scramble backward, overturning one of the desks. Then she let the snake down on top of the desk in its loose coil, turned her back, and said, "Ready, boys and girls?" and turned to write the Bible verse on the board. Her color was high, her eyes practically gave off blue sparks, and I was so proud of her at that moment. Molly thrived at the Bobcat School, she really did. I have to believe this now.

"For God so loved the world, that whosoever believeth in him shall not perish, but have Eternal Life," she wrote in her lovely slanted hand, a credit to Gatewood Academy. The children had all begun to copy when suddenly the "dead" snake, being only stunned, slithered to life. It slid off the desk and went straight for Molly. The children screamed—myself, I am ashamed to say, among them. Molly turned around, calmly put down the chalk and grabbed up the end of the slip noose again, lifting the snake high above her head where it twisted gleaming in the sunlight until it went limp again. Then she walked straight down the middle of the aisle with it. You could have heard a pin drop until she came back inside and resumed the lesson, never once mentioning the snake.

The second incident was more serious. Christmas had come and gone; it was the winter term. Many of the smaller children had been kept at home due to the severity of the weather, others because they did not have shoes or adequate clothing, and the "big boys" showed up, as promised. We had quite a time with three of them—Ira Lineback, Arthur Church, and Jemmy Vestal, who chewed tobacco in the schoolyard and spit it at the younger children's feet, terrorizing them. Then they took a fat boy's shoes and coat away—this was poor little Red Layless—and forced him to lie in the mushy snow and "make angels" all recess until he was freezing and sobbing. When he tried to get up, Ira kicked him in the nose, making it bleed, and he went back to making angels. The rest of the children were too afraid to tell us, so we knew nothing of it until they all came trooping in without him.

Molly looked up. "Why, where is Red?"

Busily taking off their coats, they did not answer.

"Where is he?" Molly darted to the door and soon returned with poor Red, sobbing and shaking, his nose bleeding copiously, his feet blue. Molly took him over to the stove where she wrapped him in her own coat.

I have seldom felt such anger. "All right," I said, standing before them. "Who is responsible for this outrage?"

The silent children looked down, studying their desks. At the back of the room, Arthur stared out the window at the darkening day, while Jemmy Vestal pretended to fall asleep.

"Who did this cruel thing to Red?" I asked them again, my voice shaking.

Now Jemmy began to snore loudly, which caught the fancy of the other two. When they put their heads down on their desks and began snoring loudly too, all three, the whole room erupted in laughter. It was like an epidemic—even my "good girls," such as Betsy Ray and Virginia Kershaw, caught it. I'm afraid I began screaming at them, but I could not even make myself heard above the uproar.

At that moment a blast of freezing air came into the schoolroom along with Cicero Todd, wearing his huge black overcoat and hat, followed by Roy. Cicero's dark hair lay on his shoulders unkempt, his coat had leaves and twigs and snow on it. Up the aisle he came, walking hard, leaving a trail of snow and dirt behind him. The laughter subsided into only a few titters, then silence, as he got to the front of the schoolroom. Automatically I stepped aside. I was hysterical, anyway. He crossed with heavy steps to my desk, where he took his time seating himself, scraping my chair across the floor loudly, then grunting as he sat down on it, facing the class. Roy lay down beside him, panting, ears up and hair on end, as if waiting for a command. Cicero stared at the students, his black eyes narrowed beneath his bristling brow, a formidable figure. Then reaching deep into his coat, he produced an enormous black pistol with a gleaming wooden handle, and laid it on the desk.

A general intake of breath was audible in the room. Nobody moved.

"All right then," Cicero Todd said after a while. "Let's let these ladies get on with school."

The next day, our three "big boys" were absent. They never returned, and we never had any more trouble with discipline at the Bobcat School.

Winter turned to spring, then summer again, then fall. There was no question that Molly had come into her own, fully self-possessed and capable, though the second part of Martha Fickling's prediction came true as well: everybody tried to court her, including poor Augustus Worth himself when his wife left him. Molly wouldn't have it for a minute, though she spared his feelings as best she could, poor thing, laughing away his intentions as if it were all a capital joke.

Likewise she sent away Eliza Valiant's brother Ben who would not take "no" for an answer to his letters, but insisted upon a visit to Jefferson to see for himself and press his suit in person. He stayed at Martha Fickling's for three full weeks, once arriving up at the Bobcat School with an armful of roadside flowers, to everyone's delight and consternation, for she wouldn't have him either, or encourage him at all, though our "big girls" were all swooning over him. The entire community took a shine to it: such a fine young man, so handsome, so interested in everything about Jefferson and Ashe County.

What was wrong with Miss Petree?

I wondered myself, finally determining to ask her on a misty May morning as we walked the familiar old Indian trail, a shortcut around the mountain from the Badgers' farm to the Bobcat School. On that particular day, Felix Boykin was taking Ben on a botanical tour up to the bog on the top of Bluff Mountain.

"Oh, Agnes, I don't know!" Molly said. "It's just . . . not . . . right." She kicked a rock along the trail ahead of her, like a boy.

"What's not right? He seems like a fine young man to me."

"He is a fine young man." Here Molly gave a great sigh. "But I don't love him, and I never have, and I don't know why I don't, but I don't, and so I just—can't—marry him! He's too nice." She hauled back to give the stone a big kick into the trees.

I had to smile at her childishness. "But Molly, what is all this folderol about love? You like Ben, don't you?"

She nodded, red-faced.

"And as far as you know, he is a perfectly fine and upstanding and morally unobjectionable young man, even an admirable young man, is that not so?"

"Yes, Agnes."

"Well, then, let me suggest to you that love will grow between you naturally in marriage, that commitment fosters love, as does intimacy; this is what marriage is all about. True love is not necessarily cataclysmic, or whatever it is that you imagine. Marriage provides a safe place, a garden, for true love to grow and flourish." There now. I was proud of myself.

"No." She shook her head vehemently.

"But Molly, when I think of what Ben could offer you . . ." I had to say this, though I'd hate to see her go, for we had truly become like sisters. "A life in Charleston, a fine house and a position in society, why you could see Eliza and her children every day—your future would be *made,* dear. You would have the kind of security you have never had." (*And probably never will have the chance to have again, you little nitwit!* I did not say.) "You should do it, Molly, you should say yes, you should go. I would be so happy for you."

"Would you? And what about *you,* Agnes?" Molly stopped walking and looked at me curiously.

"Why, I will be here, I suppose," I said lightly.

"Well, I will be here too." Molly stuck out her lip in a way that reminded me of how stubborn she had been when she first arrived at Gatewood Academy, and I knew I could not budge her.

Sure enough, she had convinced Ben of the futility of his suit by the end of the month, and it was with a sad heart that I told him goodbye on the platform in Jefferson. Molly had stayed at the farm, pleading headache. "Promise me, Agnes, that you will let me know if you and Molly ever need anything, if I can help you in any way," Ben said, his eyes huge and earnest behind his glasses. I promised. He leaped on board and the hack pulled away.

"Too bad," Felix Boykin said.

"Oh, hell, I don't know!" Martha Fickling snorted. "If it ain't there, it ain't there, ain't that right?"

"What's that?" Felix turned back to ask her.

"Chemistry," Martha Fickling said. "Dynamite. Ain't that right, Professor? You put two things together and the whole damn thing blows up, blows you clean out of the water. Just like they dynamite a mine."

Felix Boykin shook his head. "Sounds like a dangerous theory, Martha," he said, winking at me.

I agreed, waving as the hack drove away.

But Ben Valiant proved to be as generous as he was disappointed, for not a month had passed when in came a box from South Carolina containing a beautiful globe of the world, the latest thing, and a stand to put it on, as well as eight pairs of little eyeglasses and a note which read, "For the children of the Bobcat School, with gratitude and very best wishes from your good friend, Benjamin Valiant."

This romance concluded, our lives fast became fuller than ever, as that summer we began our "moonlight school" for grown men and women who wanted to learn to read and write, and it was surprising how many of these there were, and how badly they wanted to learn, walking the long roads home at all hours, often sleeping on the schoolhouse floor. We also dealt with outbreaks of both ringworm and head lice—I came to depend upon trusty old kerosene as a primary medication for "doctoring"—and, in late fall, we mourned the tragic death of little Eunice Ward who fell into a vat of boiling molasses at a stir-off.

The winter proved long and hard. Molly and I were separated by necessity, as the Badgers needed a place for their old granny, finally forced by a stroke to leave her lonely cabin on the top of Misty Mountain. Paralyzed and furious, she took over the girls' bed closest to the fire, sending two of them in to me, as Molly volunteered for a cot in the lean-to, a space which she professed to find quite suitable, though there were many mornings when she awoke to find her bed covered by a fine layer of snow that had sifted down through the cracks. She wore long linsey underwear and woolen socks to bed, keeping her school clothes under the covers at the end of her bed tick so that they would be warm in the mornings.

At school, ink froze in the inkwells overnight, attendance was very low, and once, two boys heading home with their pony and sled went down the steep bank, through the ice, and partly into the river—fortunately, a shallow spot very near their home. We had to close school several times. I enjoyed those long days of staying home, reading Dickens aloud to the Badger children while Chattie worked at her loom and the old granny spit tobacco juice into a little tin cup, squinching her eyes shut tight as she listened. We roasted chestnuts, made snow cream and popcorn.

It was this same snowy February when Simon Black appeared, all unannounced, and I shall never forget it, though Molly refused to discuss it with me then, or ever.

Since the sun had come out at last, Chattie and the children had walked over the mountain carrying food to her father, old Memorable Jones. The children were "stir-crazy," as Chattie put it, from days of being housebound. As soon as they left, Molly announced her own intention of "walking in the woods a little" and was off like a shot. She was still a child in many ways. I watched her run across the snow, wearing her old hooded blue cloak, with Chattie's red scarf flying out behind her. The sunlight was dazzling. "Agnes! Agnes!" croaked old Granny Took. Reluctantly I went back inside, closing the door behind me. I put more wood on the fire.

About a half hour later I was reading—old Took having fallen asleep—when suddenly I felt the oddest sensation, compounded of both alarm and anticipation. There was no reason for it. We were alone in the house. Bright sunlight fell through the window to make a block of light on the heart pine floor. The fire crackled merrily. Yet the hair on my forearms rose, and my scalp prickled. My heart was in my throat as I put aside my book and rose. Quietly and swiftly I crossed to the door and opened it—but here I stopped, with the door cracked about six inches.

Down at the gate by the road stood Molly talking to Simon Black. His horse breathed plumes of smoke into the clear freezing air. Of course I would have known Simon Black anywhere. The long black coat, the boots, the spurs, that unmistakable mustache and beard, now dead white. Though he faced me, I could not really see his features beneath the wide black hat, its brim lowered as he spoke earnestly to Molly. Head cocked, she appeared to listen, then said something, then made an emphatic gesture with her hand. He spoke again. Their breaths, like the horse's, made clouds in the air, eventually drifting together as one. They talked for some time. All the world was brightest white or starkest black—snow, trees, figures—with only the red scarf for color. The great snowy mountains rose into the blue sky beyond. Finally Molly stamped her foot, then surprised me by turning suddenly to run back up the long hill toward the house.

In an instant, I had pulled the door to and resumed my seat by the fire, heart pounding. I don't know why I didn't step forward, out onto the porch, and speak to Simon Black myself. It was an instinct I had, as strong as the instinct which had pulled me over to the door in the first place. I simply felt that their conversation had nothing to do with me, this conviction producing a sense of devastating loss as well as relief. How to put it? I felt *saved* from something.

Everything else happened quickly. Molly ran in, getting snow on the floor, followed by Chattie and the children, who had just arrived, full of questions. "Who was that? What did he want?"

"It was a stranger," Molly said evenly, unwinding the scarf from her neck. Her blue eyes stared directly into mine. "He had lost his way."

At last came spring, and with it a box supper held at the school to raise money for a piano—for now that we had the globe, we had all grown very ambitious. The date was set. The children lettered signs which were posted at the Jefferson Academy as well as churches and stores throughout the community. As the date drew near, everybody began preparing. There was stiff competition, especially among the single girls, for the most beautiful box and the best food. A number of women felt that they had reputations to uphold. Steady beaux were expected to buy their girlfriends' boxes even though other young men always "bid them up" out of devilment, so the fellow might have to pay a stiff price for his lady love's box. Husbands had to buy their wives' boxes too, with the same kind of friendly competition. The boxes themselves were works of art. Girls spent days trimming them with lace, feathers, scraps of cloth, ribbon, and even little pictures cut out of catalogs.

Molly decorated ours, much to the delight of the little Badger girls who were sent again and again to the woods for pine straw and robins' eggs which we stuck with a pin and blew out carefully for little "nests" on top. I crocheted a white froth of lace—this being my only domestic skill—to glue around the edges. Chattie put fried chicken, potato salad, pickled peaches, and fried apple pies in each. Biting her lip in concentration, Molly drew a freehand fairy for each box coloring them in with pastels from the school: pointed red caps, green suits, black boots, red hair. Caro cut the fairies out carefully while Molly folded layers of tissue paper for their wings. How in the world Molly ever came up with those fairies, I will never know. I always felt that she could have been an artist or a writer, either one—she could have done anything, really. Fresh violets from the creek provided a final touch on the boxes as we all sailed out the door.

Sure enough, our boxes were among the prettiest—and certainly the most unusual—with our fairies and birds' nests. But I was getting nervous by the time they came up for bid, since it seemed to me that there were more boxes and women than men, though the schoolhouse was packed, with many people standing out in the schoolyard.

"Miss Agnes Rutherford!" the auctioneer, Harold Stump, called out, and Felix Boykin gallantly bid a dollar.

"One fifty," another voice called out, then "Two dollars!" bid the newly widowed minister from Warrensville, Lester Ham. People turned to look; Molly elbowed me. I could feel myself blushing. "Sold!" cried Harold Stump, banging his gavel down. This being a decent price, I was not embarrassed at all, and was pleased to share Chattie's good food and keep Lester Ham company out on the table rock. He was a serious and shy but determined man, much older than I, with an emphatic way of speaking.

After we had exhausted the topic of teaching school (Lester Ham did not believe in too much education for women), I cast about for another subject. "Now, does your church believe in infant baptism?" I asked.

"Believe in it!" he said, sitting back. "Why, I have did it many times myself."

I got so tickled I almost choked, but Reverend Ham did not even smile, chewing steadily. *You will not do,* I thought.

Meanwhile Molly's box had been hotly contested then sold to the young lawyer Reuben Kirk, one of her admirers, for the maximum cash allowed. Harold Stump took the stage again. "Now wasn't that some of the best food you ever ate?" he demanded. "Yessir! Let's give all these ladies a round of applause. All right! Now it's time for dessert, and this here cake is for the prettiest girl in the county, and if you win the bid, you get to name her, and take the cake and her too. Yessir! All right! Let's go!"

"Rosalie Yates, one dollar!"

"Susan Trivette, one fifty!"

Men started calling out names, mine not among them, though Molly was bid for twice.

"Martha Fickling, five dollars!" someone called out, and everybody laughed. She had made the cake, as usual.

Then "Molly Petree!" an unfamiliar voice rang out from the schoolyard. "Ten dollars!" Heads swiveled and people leapt up to see who it was, bidding such a sum.

There stood a young man I had not seen before, a good-looking stranger wearing a three-piece tan suit and a green tie, all of which made him stand out like a sore thumb. His black hair was parted carefully, slicked back with brilliantine.

"What am I bid? What am I bid?" Harold Stump called. "Going, going, *gone!*" slamming down his gavel, on my desk.

Molly went forward through the crowd.

The young man said something in her ear.

Molly tossed her head, her color high. Then she cut the cake into little pieces, passing it out to everybody, apparently determined not to pay him too much attention, a thing he had not seen before, as this was a young man used to a great deal of attention.

Henderson Hanes was the black sheep in his family. But now he had come up from Salisbury to run the woolen factory for his father, its absentee owner, who was ill, and he was neither brilliant nor nice, and Molly did not even like him, but from the beginning, there was "chemistry." Even I observed it. "He is a slick customer," Felix said, while Martha Fickling only smiled when I asked her opinion. Chattie was worried, saying, "He will never marry her," though agreeing that Molly certainly had him "wrapped around her little finger."

Molly was furious when I repeated this opinion to her. "Well, who says I want to *marry* him? Maybe I don't want to marry anybody! What's wrong with that?"

Though Molly made endless fun of his affectations—especially those three-piece suits, which he was devoted to—by summer she was riding with him every Saturday and Sunday in his wire-wheeled buggy, unchaperoned. Tongues wagged. The Misses Reedy came to talk to me about it. "It's not right," they said. "What kind of a model does she make for these young girls?" When I told Molly about their visit, she bit her lip and burst out laughing. "Well, *I* don't care!" she said. That "contrary streak" which Mariah had complained about was emerging again. "What's wrong with having some *fun*, for a change? Those old biddies are just being silly."

Jealous is more like it, I thought, but I held my tongue and looked the other way until that Sunday in early September when a circumstance arose which I discovered by accident but could not then ignore.

I was wading in the creek with the little Badger girls when Molly ran down the path to join us.

"Lord, it's hot!" She peeled off her good ruffled blouse and tossed it onto the laurel, then gathered up her petticoat and waded in to join us, delighting Caro and Jane who were building a "dam" out of rocks.

"Look, Molly! Look, Molly," they chanted. "We've got a gang of minnows."

"Say 'a school of minnows,'" I instructed them almost automatically, for just then I noticed that Molly was very pink—back and shoulders and arms and legs as well as her glowing face. "Oh, Molly." I couldn't help saying it. "Just look at you. What have you done?"

"Well, I went swimming, Agnes," she announced defiantly, "over at Elk Creek Shoals with Henderson. So what? Don't sound so tragic. You wouldn't want me to ruin my Sunday clothes now, would you?" She tossed her head, eyes flashing.

"Oh no." I decided to make light of the situation in view of the little girls, who had stopped their play and were looking back and forth between us curiously, surprised by Molly's tone.

I was surprised too and found myself filled with conflicting strong emotions as she continued to spend more and more time with young Mr. Hanes whose high-handed manners and imperious bearing endeared him to no one. He never even bothered to speak to me these days, for instance, since I was apparently so uninteresting and he clearly felt he no longer "needed to." Was this, then, what I had rescued Molly for, at such great cost to both of us? Molly was moody and absentminded even in school, staring out the window, starting violently when a child asked her a question. Was this her idea of love, then, I wondered, to be miserable? And what had really happened—or had not happened—to her so long ago, back at Agate Hill? I was consumed by questions I dared not ask, for I had never once spoken to Molly about "country matters"—nor did I have any advice to give on the subject. Though I feared for her virtue, my more practical concern was that she would finally shock the community so much that she would get us both "turned out," and then what would we do? Where would we go?

There came that October morning—a Sunday—which told the tale. It had been a glorious fall, the leaves more colorful than any I can ever remember, even now—the dark red dogwood, the flaming maples, the yellow hickorys and orange sassafras. The gusting wind was filled with leaves as I stood out on the Badgers' porch in an old dressing gown drinking my coffee. The horseshoe bend of the New River shone below. The sky was a fierce bright blue. I sighed, wanting to stay right there, not wanting to go back inside to dress for church. But we were all running late. One of the Boykins' daughters had married at the stone Methodist Church down in Jefferson the evening before, followed by a party at the Academy where even I had danced. I had just turned back toward the door when Chattie emerged to whisper in my ear that Molly had not come home.

"What?" I dropped my cup on the porch.

"Hush," Chattie said. "She's not in the lean-to," cutting her eyes at the little boys, who sat on the porch steps making Jacob's ladders. Chattie went back inside.

I stood there gripping the rail and looking into the long blue distance, shading my eyes from the sun. The wind came up from the gorge with a moaning sound while hawks made big slow circles in the air. I had finally resolved to speak to Molly once and for all when she emerged suddenly from the forest like a forest sprite herself, on the old Indian trail from the Bobcat School. Henderson must have let her out there to save time. The air all about her was thick with whirling leaves; the wind whipped her hair around. She wore only her thin yellow dress from the evening before—no wrap, where was the blue cloak?—and carried only a handful of black-eyed Susans.

"Molly." I stumbled, coming down the steps.

"Agnes," she said simply, "these are for you," handing me the flowers, then hugging me. "And I have something to tell you." She pushed me back and held me out at arm's length. "I am engaged to be married."

Though I have been an English teacher all my life, I have never found the words to describe Molly's expression as we stood out in the steep swept yard that morning. Her face was so odd—so dire, so intense, yet in a strange way wiped completely clean of all emotion at the same time. She appeared calm, even stricken, yet fully, terribly alive. A blowing red leaf stuck to her cheek momentarily; she laughed as it blew away.

"I don't know what to say," I declared honestly.

"Then don't say anything." She wound her arm around my waist as we walked back to the house where Chattie waited nervously on the porch steps, her apron gathered up in her hands.

"Oh, Lord, I knowed it!" she declared when Molly told her. "Ain't it just wonderful?"

To my surprise, the whole community shared this reaction, even Vina and Ocie Reedy who pinched their lips together and merely said they were glad that Molly had "made a good thing of it at last." All was forgiven, all impropriety overlooked. Gone were the snide remarks, all the objections to Henderson's imperious personality. Even Henderson himself seemed determined to do his part, actually attending church with us all, for instance, and visiting once to bring old Granny Took a brand new red blanket with a white stripe down the middle of it, from the blanket factory. (Chattie grabbed it up to examine and strongly criticize, the moment he had left.)

Molly was driven down to Salisbury in the buggy for a visit to his family; she reappeared wearing a magnificent engagement ring which all approved, a round, fiery opal surrounded by little diamonds. It had belonged to Henderson's grandmother.

Only once did I dare ask Molly about her true feelings for Henderson Hanes. We were cleaning up the schoolroom at the end of the day. "Do you actually love him? *Can* you love him?" This just burst out of me.

Molly stopped wiping off the desks and stood stock still before the globe. She reached out to whirl it on its axis, round and round, biting her lip. The opal flashed in the light. "Listen, Agnes, Henderson is a lot of fun. And I want . . . I want . . ." She hesitated. Suddenly she stopped the globe's turning and pointed to the continent of Europe. "Look," she said. "This is Paris. This is where Henderson's grandfather bought this ring for his grandmother, fifty years ago. I want to go there too, Agnes. I want to go there—and there"—she jabbed at the globe—"and I don't see why I can't. Oh Agnes, I want a lot of things." Abruptly she ran out of the schoolhouse.

Later I watched Molly hold out her pretty hand again and again, showing off her ring, as she walked down the main street of Jefferson, while Henderson stood just behind her, showing them both off, just as if Molly were a prize horse, or so I felt, observing this spectacle.

I simply could not bring myself to like him.

Here I was in the minority.

Everybody was on their side now, endlessly hungry for details of the wedding which was to take place down in Salisbury, not here, to their dismay—but also, in a strange way, I think, their approval, as Molly appeared poised to ascend into another realm altogether. Even Martha Fickling refused to criticize the engagement, handing me a glass of her peach brandy, which I had become quite fond of, and saying only, "Hell, marriage is always good experience for a girl," with a wink of her eye and a flash of her gold tooth. "It ain't going to hurt her none, and it just might teach her something."

So I resolved to quit worrying, for I was also relieved, in a way. Truth to tell, by then I had a little secret of my own.

Now I give this piece of mica one last turn in the rays of the setting sun, then place it on the windowsill.

Reader, can you guess?

I married Cicero Todd within the year, despite the difference in our ages and what was to happen to Molly. I married him anyway. And we are still married thirty years later living here on the side of Pisgah Mountain which remains as beautiful to me as Heaven, in the fine house he built for me after our third child, John, was born. Whoever imagined that I should find such happiness? See, here he comes now, walking up the holler. Cicero has never learned to read nor write, nor needed to, staying at home with our children to make his furniture and such while I kept the Bobcat School, and he still calls me Miss Rutherford, and he treats me like a queen.

December 14, 1882

Dear Mary White,

This is the biggest news yet and it is about ME. But it is not a love story.

I am engaged to be married to Henderson Hanes from Salisbury, a rich boy who says he will give me the world. And guess what, Mary White? I want it. I want the world. He is a bad boy, like I am a bad girl, so I don't mind to take it from him. Henderson likes bad girls, he says, though he does not believe me when I say I am one. He thinks I am kidding. He thinks I am just a poor girl, like Cinderella, and he likes this too, for he is also marrying me to spite his mother. He hates his mother. Henderson has had everything he has ever wanted, and now he wants me, and do you know what, Mary White? I am enjoying it. We ride around and drink whisky and kiss and do other things too. Oh Mary White do you think I am awful? I can tell no one else. Henderson is very conceited—Chattie says he is "like something on a stick"—but he is fun too. It would have been wrong of me to marry Ben Valiant, who is a nice man, but it is not wrong of me to marry Henderson Hanes, who is not.

For I will never give all my heart away, as I told you so long ago. I know all about that.

But I have always wanted something, so bad I could taste it, and Henderson has a lot of things. His family house at Salisbury even has a name, Willowsmere, as in an English novel, and leaded windows with little diamond-shaped panes of glass, and a library with book after book which Henderson has not read. He is not a scholar, having left several universities. I don't care, Mary White. I am going to do this. I want to have fine sheets with HH embroidered on them like the sheets at Willowsmere. I want to go to Paris France Europe which is where we are going on our honeymoon. Henderson says we will stay in a hotel on the Île de la Cité in the middle of the Seine, he says we will eat rabbit, and drink fine wine, and go to the racetrack, and I will wear a hat with a feather in it. Why shouldn't I go, Mary White? Why shouldn't I have these things?

For I will never go to my benefactor, Simon Black, who has had the nerve to come up here, after all this time. He is crazy, Mary White, and he scares me, saying those things about destiny, and stars, and speaking wildly of battle, and Brazil, and my mother, years ago. He swears he does not mean to scare me, but to help me.

"I do not want your help," I said, "now or ever." I said, "Please go away."

But in truth I don't want to sleep in a leanto with sifting snow on my face for the rest of my life until I look like Granny Took Badger, spitting tobacco juice into a cup. She scares me as much as he does. Simon Black is a crazy old man. I have told him that I do not wish to be benefacted, or benefited, or helped in any way, that I am going to marry Henderson Hanes no matter what. So I will be happy, and rich, and that will be the end of it. Perhaps I am La Belle Dame Sans Merci after all.

But I remain your
Molly

January 26, 1883
Dear Mary White,

A lot has happened since last I wrote.

Henderson's father died and he took me home with him for the funeral, we drove it straight in the freezing rain stopping only for the horses. He is not very good to his horses. I sat close to him all the way while he drove and drank from his silver flask and the land flowed past in a foggy gray blur. "Don't you think you had better quit drinking that now?" I said once when we were nearing Salisbury, but he got mad and squeezed my leg so hard it hurt and said, "Leave it alone, honey," giving a sort of sob. I believe he loved his father, a hard man, after all.

We arrived just in time for the funeral which was immense, held in a huge cold Episcopal Church which his family has attended for over a hundred years and even built, I think. Everybody had long black coats and long white faces. Instead of preaching you read the service out of a book which I liked very much, the words were beautiful. I am determined to get the hang of this, Mary White! I even liked Henderson's mother, at least I liked her better than he does. She is fierce but frail, falling asleep in the middle of her sentences. I had to stay in a room off her room which was her idea of chaperoning. Agnes would have been very pleased.

Coming back we did not stop at his aunt's house as planned but drove on through the dark, Henderson did not say where we were going. It was still raining. I waited in the carriage while he got out and knocked on the door of a fair-sized house set back from the road in a grove of trees. He had said it was an inn but it was a bootlegger's, I knew it immediately. The door cracked slightly, a messy head poked out. Henderson leaned down close and spoke, gesturing to the carriage. The door opened more widely, throwing light out onto the muddy yard. The bootlegger's wife was a merry soul who showed us up to a large bedroom overlooking the front door then told us to come right on down for supper if we wanted any. Henderson dropped our bags on the floor and threw his overcoat across the bed but I moved it so it wouldn't get the bed wet and then we looked at each other and then he kissed me, hard. He is a good kisser. I had never been to any place like this before, though clearly Henderson was no stranger here.

We went down to a long messy table in a smoky room with a big fire in the hearth at one end. Five men were present drinking and smoking including the bootlegger. All talk stopped when I appeared. The men stared at me as if I were a ghost.

"Can a lady get a drink around here or not?" I said, and then they laughed, and toasted me. Henderson was grinning from ear to ear. I have noticed that in general he prefers the company of his inferiors, what do you make of this? Anyway our dinner was brought in by the innkeeper's daughter who was plainly furious, flouncing around, cutting her eyes at Henderson who would not look at her. She is a big pretty black-haired girl with a rough manner and a ready laugh. Damn him, I thought. I determined to have a better time than anybody.

We drank and joked with the rest—though I couldn't eat the greasy mutton stew—while all the while I thought of the big bed in the room upstairs, for Henderson has his strong points. He can be a lot of fun, but he was not fun that night, stumbling by the time we finally climbed the stairs, too drunk to take off his own clothes much less mine. He fell across me in a dead stupor like a tree going down in the forest. Though I had had a fair amount of

whisky myself, I was wide awake. I pushed him off me and went over to the
window, pulling back the curtains and pushing it up to let the cold air flow
over me. It was long past the middle of the night. The rain was gone. I saw
the Big Dipper and Orion's belt. The Milky Way stretched down the sky. A
bright half moon sailed in and out of the dark fast-moving clouds, reminding
me of that verse we used to love so much

> Wynken, Blynken, and Nod one night
>   Sailed off in a wooden shoe, —
> Sailed on a river of crystal light
>   Into a sea of dew.

It made me feel so strange to remember this as I stood in my shift in the
open window of the bootlegger's house with Henderson snoring on the bed
behind me. I never went to sleep at all that night but lay as if electrified, and
I am electrified still.

The next morning I got him up and going as best I could though he
was sick as a dog, hanging his head out the door to vomit as I drove the
carriage away from the house where the bootlegger's daughter had come to
stand outside with her arms crossed, to watch us go. To my surprise she put
her hand up suddenly, not exactly a wave, but something else, almost as if
she would stop us—would stop <u>me.</u> She had the strangest look on her face.
She opened her mouth as if she had something to say, then closed it, then
turned away.

So now I am back up on Bobcat, and Henderson is back in Salisbury,
and our wedding trip to Paris must be postponed indefinitely while he takes
over his father's business. But the wedding will be in the spring as planned
though I will not see Henderson beforehand, suddenly he is very serious and
says he has to work all the time.

Our wedding will be very simple as his mother says it does not pay to
advertise it.

I feel like I am about to jump out of my skin. I am going crazy here waiting, you know I have never been good at waiting for anything.

Oh my God how are you? Are you dead? I wish you could write me back and tell me what you think. For I am still your

Molly

Saturday, April 12, 1883

Dear Mary White,

Last night I rode up to Red Hill with Martha Fickling because her niece's husband was clearing a new ground and they were having a house party afterward. "It'll do you good," Martha said. "Get you out some." Also, I have always liked Roxy, Martha's "niece"—just one of the girls she has hired and taken in and raised over the years.

Martha rode out ahead on her big gray horse Valentine with me following on Chattie's little white mare. You would be surprised how well Martha sits a horse, even at her age, upright and light as a girl, skirts thrown up, riding astride. "None of this sidesaddle shit for me!" she said, and I had to laugh, for I feel the same way about it. I thought of Eliza Valiant as we rode along through the dripping woods, remembering how she looked in that race, up out of her saddle leaning forward as she came around the turn with pink cheeks and hair flying out behind her. I wondered what her life is like now, and what mine will be like from now on. I wonder if Ben is happy.

"Molly!" Martha was saying as our horses picked their way through the old wet leaves.

"What?"

"You heard me."

"I'm sorry, Martha, I didn't hear you."

"I said, You know you don't have to do nothing you don't want to, Molly. Nothing is wrote in stone."

"I know that." I am sick of people telling me what I ought to do or not do.

"Well, just as long as you do," Martha said, and we rode along in silence as the sun came out, changing everything. Now the woods went from being a dark woodcut landscape in a Grimms fairy tale to the fairy tale itself. Suddenly the black trees stood swathed in a pale green mist made up of their own tiny new leaves and the rising ground fog, with here and there a cluster of purple judas or white dogwood or red sarvis blooming like a giant corsage. Freshets of water had burst out everywhere—running along the ditch beside us, spurting down the rocky cliff on our right, coursing across the road to run down the mountain on our left. The whole earth seemed to be stretching and yawning, waking up. A robin, back early, sat perched in the crook of a tree ahead, then flew away at our approach. I gulped in the cool moist air like I was drinking the Spring.

Roxy and Merle have a nice big two-room cabin with a plowed garden beside it, and beyond that we could see the new ground already cleared too, with men still gathered around a pile of burning brush.

They had hauled all the furniture out into the yard, filled with darting children and standing groups of people talking. Dance music poured out of the house, with every window and door wide open. It looked to me like the house itself was moving, literally shaking on its cornerstones.

"Why you don't mean it's them old Jarvises, down from Plain View!" Martha said.

"Who is that?" I asked, but she did not answer for then we were surrounded by people glad to see her. "Light and hitch," they said, and helped to unpack the peach brandy and ginger cakes we had brought in our saddlebags. Roxy ran up and hugged us, big again, dragging a tiny little boy by the hand. "Say hello to Martha now, Troy," she said, but he would not, hiding behind his mother's skirts. <u>Oh Lord,</u> I thought. <u>In three weeks I will be married.</u> Martha carried Troy into the house where cornmeal had been thrown down on the wooden floors and both rooms were full of people dancing in the old style, stiff and mannerly above the waist but stomping and shuffling their feet too fast to see, flat-footing they call it up here.

An old hunchback fiddler crouched on a chair in the wide doorway between the two rooms, grinning fiercely as he thumped his foot on the floor and sawed away on "Rock about My Saro Jane." The words to this song are

> Rock about my Saro Jane
> Rock about my Saro Jane
> We'll lay around the shack
> Till the mail train comes back
> And rock about my Saro Jane.

I had to laugh—Agnes would NOT have approved! And Chattie doesn't hold with dancing in any form. Martha Fickling set Troy down and jumped right into it, wagging one foot way up in the air while those around applauded, for she was a famous dancer. The old fiddler nodded and winked at her. A fair-haired young boy stood behind the old man, shy but obviously determined, singing right out. Now the floor was full.

"Come on in, Molly," Martha yelled, and I joined them, for I have loved to dance ever since I was at Gatewood. I am good at it. They did "Goodbye Girls, I'm Going to Boston." They did "Shady Grove" which I love even though it has such a mournful sound to it, like all the music does if you really listen to it.

> Shady Grove, my little love,
> Shady Grove I know
> Shady Grove, my little love,
> I'm bound for Shady Grove
>
> Cheeks as red as a blooming rose
> Eyes of the deepest brown
> You are the darling of my heart
> Stay till the sun goes down.

The sun was already down by that time, and they were building a great big fire out front when all of a sudden there was a commotion out in the yard and then in walked a man in a wide hat with a banjo slung across his shoulder. "Hey, Jack! Yellowjack! Hey Jack! Jacky-O!" Everybody called out and fell back to make way as he crossed the dance floor. "Where the hell have you been?" the old man grumbled, but the man just grinned as he flung his buckskin coat down on the floor and started right in picking his banjo, jumping all around. He appeared to have no bones at all in his body. He was tall and skinny with yellow-red hair that fell forward into his eyes and a big nose and a wide crooked reckless grin, the kind of a face that you couldn't quit looking at. He played that old knockdown two-finger way, and had a loud clear singing voice. He was the kind of man that made everybody feel better just because he had walked into the room. The dancing picked up, with several people whooping out now. The music went faster and faster. Martha had long since stopped, and stood fanning herself, but I wouldn't have quit for anything.

I don't know what got into me, Mary White, but it has <u>still</u> got into me!

After a while I noticed he was looking at me, I mean Jacky Jarvis, and he was still looking at me when he sang

> I'll tune up my fiddle and rosin my bow
> And make myself welcome wherever I go.

> I'll buy my own whisky and make my own stew
> If it does make me drunk it is nothing to you.

> I'll eat when I'm hungry and drink when I'm dry
> If a tree don't fall on me, I'll live till I die.

They set lanterns in the windows and stirred up the fire in the hearth while I danced on, now with one, then another. Up there on Red Hill, there was nobody that knew I was engaged, nobody to whisper to each other that I should not be dancing. The old man called out the dances in a high sing-song voice. "All hands up and go to the left. Corners turn and sash-i-ate. First couple cage the bird with three arms around. Bird hop out and hoot owl in, three arms around and hooting again!" I didn't know what I was doing but it was all right and it was the most fun I have had since Henderson went back to Salisbury.

Finally they quit playing, and I was dying for air. I pushed my way outside where the cold night was filled with the smell of smoke and coffee. The big fire blazed. "Here, honey." Somebody handed me a tin cup with coffee and whisky in it. Now they had put a table of food out there too, but I couldn't eat for the stitch in my side from dancing. I stood back in the trees away from the fire and sipped at the cup. My hair was falling all down my back and my blouse was wet clear through from dancing.

"My name is Jacky Jarvis," he said into my ear, "and I've been looking for you all my life."

I whirled around. "That's a lie," I cried. "You never even heard of me before." His breath on my neck gave me the shivers.

"But I been dreaming about you every night," he said. "So I knowed you right off. Maybe I just dreamed you up." His face was real close to mine, he was grinning such a wide devil-may-care grin that he made me dizzy.

"Oh, is that a fact?" I said, stepping back from him. "Well, too bad, you're too late." I held up my hand and my ring caught the firelight, winking at him.

He gave a long low whistle through his teeth. "Mighty fine ring," he said. "Who is the lucky feller?"

"Nobody you know."

"Maybe, maybe not," he said, looking at me. He kept on looking at me until I couldn't breathe.

"Molly!" Martha called, peering across the fire. "Come on, honey, we've got to go." I knew she couldn't see me back there in the dark.

He touched my elbow. "Listen, I'm coming to see you tomorrow."

"You are not," I said. "You haven't been invited. You don't know where I live. You don't even know who I am."

He smiled out from under the brim of his hat. "I'll find out. I'll give you your own private music show."

"Molly," Martha was calling.

I turned to go, then turned back. "Don't come tomorrow," I said. "Come Sunday."

Then I ran around the circle and grabbed Martha and said, "Here I am," and we set off through the night on our horses with a burning pine knot to light our way. Martha rode ahead with it flickering. "That Jacky Jarvis is a natural antic, ain't he?" she said over her shoulder. "But them Jarvises are purely no good. They never have been any good, the whole lot of them. They run a store up there on the Tennessee line, there is a whole bunch of them up there. It's a sight. Folks come from all around for dances. Why I used to go up there myself, time was . . ." and then she was off and running, giving me the lowdown on everybody else who had been at the dance but I didn't even listen after she quit on the Jarvises. "Oh, is that right?" I said, riding, or, "I'll swear," whenever she slowed down. I was humming under my breath all the way, my whole head full of music. It was real late when we got in.

Oh Mary White, he is insolent. I like him and I don't, I feel like running down the mountain drooping trees the way we used to at Agate Hill but you know I am always still your

Molly

Monday, April 14, 1883

Dear Mary White,

On Sunday I lay in the girls' bed and watched them all pack up to go to the annual Association meeting. This would take place down on the river at the Pine Swamp Church near Windfall, with dinner on the ground and singing afterward. They would take the wagon, and Cicero Todd was to come with his wagon too, as they were carrying food, and quilts, and all the children, and picking up old Memorable Jones on the way. "Oh, I hate for you to miss it!" Chattie cried, for it was the highlight of her year. She had been cooking for days.

"Are you sure you don't want me to stay here with you?" Agnes asked, though she had already put on her hat.

"Oh no, I will be fine," I told her. I was claiming female troubles. But in all truth, by then I couldn't decide if I really was sick, or just acting sick, I felt so "strange-like," as Hattie would have put it. "Don't worry," I told them as they went out the door. "I'll make sure Granny Took gets something to eat while you're gone."

The minute they left, I jumped up and heated some water on the stove and washed my hair and sat down to let it dry over a chairback near the fire.

"Good morning, Granny," I said to Granny Took, who was watching me out from under her pile of coverlets. She has not spoken for months now.

I knew he wouldn't come but I was nervous as a cat anyway, watching out the window. I could hear the grandfather clock ticking, and the crackle of the fire. Pale sun slanted across Chattie's bright rag rugs.

"Hidy." Suddenly he was behind me, putting his hands on my shoulders. I had not seen him come out of the woods, nor heard him open the door.

I jumped up and screamed bloody murder.

"Lord God, you'll raise the dead," he said, which was exactly what I wanted to do suddenly, scream and holler and raise the dead. I felt like I was tingling from head to toe.

"Where'd they all go?" he asked. "I passed them on the road coming."

"To the protracted meeting," I said. "It will last all day." Then I could have bit off my tongue.

"It will, huh?" He ran his fingers down my damp hair. "Well, that's good, then. How come you didn't go to church with the rest of them? What are you, a heathen girl?"

"I'm sick," I said.

"That's too bad. I reckon I'll just have to hold church for you right here then." He nodded at Granny Took. "Who is that? She can come to my church too." He was still touching my hair.

"I don't know if you'll let me into your church," I said. "I'm a bad girl."

"There ain't no such of a thing in my church," he said.

"What's the name of your church?" I asked.

"It's the Jacky Jarvis Church of Love and Light and Redemption for All," he said. "I'll preach to you, sing to you, and save you too. Everybody gets saved in my church. You're welcome any time." Now he pulled up another chair and straddled it and sat facing me. "That ain't such a joke. I'm supposed to be playing gospel music right now, over in Bee Gum with the rest of them. We've got a little gospel group, well actually it's the same one as you heard up at Merle's place, me and granddaddy and Biddle, that's my nephew. We're the Rag Mountain Ramblers on Saturday night, the Angel Band on Sundays."

"Don't you get confused?" I asked.

"Not hardly." He grinned. "Matter of fact, I just quit playing a while ago, up on Rip Shin. Ain't even been to bed yet."

"Aren't you sleepy, then?"

"I figure I'll sleep when I'm dead," he said. "The way I'm going, it won't be long neither. But that's all right, I never figured on getting old, anyway. I ain't got a plan for it." Close up, he has these sort of hazel eyes with shiny gold circles inside them, around the pupil. I have never seen anything like them. "I wouldn't mind some of that coffee, though." He gestured to the stove where it was still hot.

I got up and got him some. "So when does your church start?"

"Right now." He took a big drink of coffee and leaned his head back and closed his eyes and started right in singing "There's Going to Be a Meeting in the Air" at the top of his lungs, startling me. "How did you like that, Granny?" he said when he was done.

To my surprise the tears were running down her knotted old apple face. When he sang "I'll Fly Away" she beat out the time on the side of the bed with her little claw hand.

"She's having a big time, ain't she?" Jacky said when he was through.

She was, but I was not, thinking what would happen if somebody came. And anybody might—Chattie leaves the door open all the time, with friends and neighbors always welcome.

"It's too pretty of a day to stay in the house," Jacky said, like he could read my mind. "Let's go someplace. Don't never stay inside if you can stay outside, that's my motto."

I was relieved. "Let me just get her some food, then," I said.

Jacky whipped out a harmonica and played "Amazing Grace" on it for Granny Took while I cut up some johnnycake into little bitty pieces and put them on her blue plate and poured some buttermilk over it. I have not heard anybody play a harmonica like that since Spencer at Uncle Junius's bedside, and all of a sudden I was crying because that time came flooding back to me, and the music was so beautiful, and because I missed Spence so much. I guess I always will.

Jacky Jarvis put the harmonica back in his pocket and came over to touch my wet cheek with his finger. He has real long fingers.

"I'm sorry," I said, grabbing up my cloak.

"Don't be sorry," he said, "and don't never apologize for a thing, that's my motto too. Hit's a lot to cry about in this world, a vale of tears as the feller said. Come on now. Bye-bye, honey," he said to Granny Took, who stared at us with her dark button eyes all the way out the door.

Outside, it was a windy, changeable morning. I hoped it would stay dry for the Association meeting and then I didn't think about the Association meeting anymore as Jacky took my arm and escorted me down off the porch real formal, like we were sashiating in a square dance. His brown horse Betty was tied to a tree in the woods, pack and banjo slung on behind. "Can you ride behind me?" he asked. "Can you jump up?"

"Bring her over here by the fence," I said, and I jumped up easy as pie and then we were off, I never thought to ask where we were going. Jacky Jarvis was skinny as could be, underneath that buckskin jacket. My arms went all the way around him. "Oh do you remember sweet Betsy from Pike?" he sang as we trotted back down the road to Jefferson. The wind blew my hair dry. A pair of bluebirds flew in and out of the fencerow ahead of us. Suddenly I didn't even care who heard him singing, or who saw us riding along, because by then it had become perfectly clear to me that I am not going to marry Henderson Hanes, no matter what else happens.

Jacky pulled at the reins and we turned off Pisgah Ridge Road. "Whoa now," he told Betty as she picked her way down a steep trail through thick mountain laurel, a trail I had never noticed before in all my three years of traveling that road to town. It was like going down a tunnel. We went a long way. Finally we came to a windy open field of blue trillium sloping down toward two tall pine trees and a rocky outcropping at the edge of the mountain. I have never seen anything so beautiful.

"Did you know this was here?" I called over the wind, and he hollered back that he remembered it from when he was little. "They call it Bone Valley," he said, "and over there is Manbone Rock." He pointed to a huge white rock which stood alone on its little hill. It was as big as a cabin.

"Why in the world do they call it <u>that?</u>" I asked him.

"I have heard it said that they found a man's bones up on top of it, long time ago. Of course they's a tale about everything." He stopped to grin at me. "We used to run these hills like bird dogs, me and BJ."

"Who's BJ?" I asked.

"BJ's my cousin," he said, helping me down. "You'll meet him directly."

"Well, I doubt that," I said.

Jacky just grinned at me, clicking to the horse as he led her down toward the rocks. The wind blew all around us, whipping my skirts and rippling the trillium. It reminded me of that line from the song, <u>Bow down ladies, bow down.</u>

"Whoa now." Jacky stopped at an outcropping of big white boulders that looked like playing blocks abandoned by some giant child. He took a rolled-up green blanket off the back of Betty's saddle and spread it out on one of the rocks to make a kind of bench, with another rock for us to lean against, while I stood looking off down the mountain toward Jefferson, or where I thought Jefferson ought to be. Hawks dipped and wheeled through the wide blue air. Nothing looked familiar to me. I felt like I was in another country. We were not on a cliff exactly, just a rocky point that the land fell away from in scrub brush. I felt funny out in the open like that, without the sheltering trees I had gotten so used to at Chattie's and the Bobcat School and even down in town, surrounded as it is by the mountains, like a town in the bottom of a teacup. Here I felt exposed, and a little bit afraid, and nervous. Anybody could see us, I thought, though I knew that nobody would. For a minute I thought I could hear their voices in the wind, singing church songs.

Jacky took my hand and sat me down on the green blanket, then sat Indian-style across from me, cocking his head like a gawky bird. He makes me laugh, Mary White.

"What's so funny?" he asked.

"Nothing," I said.

Then he leaned forward and put his mouth on my mouth, just lightly, once. He didn't touch any other part of my body.

"Now," he said. "Start talking. I want to know all about you. I want to know everything."

"First, I am engaged to be married," I said.

"I don't care nothing about that," he said. "That don't mean nothing to me. Where did you come from, anyway? What are you doing up here?"

So I started talking, slowly at first, then in a big rush like a creek running down off a mountain. I told him about Mama and Papa and the War and Spencer and Uncle Junius and Selena, and about going to the Gatewood Academy. I got hot and threw off my cloak, still talking. He nodded, chewing on a long piece of straw like an animal. I kept on talking. He acted like he had all the time in the world. So I kept on talking. I told him all about Agnes, and Chattie, and the Bobcat School, and Cicero Todd and the gun. He kept breaking in, asking more questions.

I feel like I have known him all my life.

"Now it's your turn," I said, despite the fact that the changeable weather was suddenly changing fast, the sun entirely gone now beneath a pile of gray clouds that were fast moving in from the west. I put my cloak back on and hugged it around myself.

"Me and my cousin, we run a store up on top of Rag Mountain. You can spit off the porch and hit Tennessee. We hold dances on top of the store. Daddy built it for that. But Mama don't dance, nor play music no more either, she's been crazy ever since the War and all the terrible things they done to her . . ." Jacky talked up a blue streak. He talked more in one afternoon than Henderson Hanes has talked in all the time I have known him. Jacky said they have about twenty family members living up at Plain View, "give or take some at any given time," and "some several" of them play music. Jacky himself started in on the piano at age two or three, taught by his uncle Blind Bill, who tuned pianos for a living, and played at dances. Jacky's mama played piano too, or used to, before the Home Guard came upon her when she was out washing clothes and tried to make her tell where Jacky's daddy and his uncle had hidden out, plunging her hands down into the boiling water when she refused. They hanged her from a sycamore tree too, but let her down before she died. She never told. "She hasn't never been the same since," Jacky said, and I said I'd imagine not. When the War was over, Jacky's daddy found the men that had tortured her, and killed them both—shot one man while he was out plowing in his cornfield, picked him off from the edge of the woods, and shot the other man as he came out of church with his wife on his arm. Big Jack Jarvis was never prosecuted for these murders, as there were no witnesses, and everybody figured they had it coming. He had gone on to live a long life, running the store and playing music.

Jacky had learned the banjo from an uncle who had learned it from a negro just before the War. He said his uncle traded a coon dog to the negro for the banjo, and called it his "coon dog banjo" ever after, playing it for years.

I started laughing, though thunder rolled in the distance.

"I want to go up there," I said, which I did, all of a sudden, more than anything. "I want to go dancing on top of the store."

"No mam," he said.

"Don't call me mam," I said immediately.

"Plain View ain't no place for a lady like you."

"I am not a real lady," I said.

"You're a schoolteacher, ain't you? You look like a lady to me. Shoot, you have even been to lady school."

"Well, maybe it didn't take," I said.

"Iffen it did or iffen it didn't, it sounds to me like you are fixing to be a real grand lady yourself soon enough."

"I'm not a lady." I don't know why I started crying. "I'm not a ghost girl either."

"Well, you sure as hell got that right." He pinched my waist. "You feel pretty solid to me."

The wind was blowing like crazy now. Jacky's horse whinnied and stomped her feet.

"Then take me up there." I grabbed his hand and squeezed it.

"Shoot, honey, I couldn't do that."

"Chicken!" I let go of his hand and jabbed him in the side. "Fraidy-cat! Fraidy-cat! Don't know where his tail is at!" This is what the children sing at the Bobcat School. I pushed him as hard as I could and then he pinned my arms behind me and I twisted him off of the rock onto the ground and together we rolled over and over down the steep hill through the scratchy weeds and sage grass. By the time we fetched up against another big rock, I had gotten to laughing too hard to quit.

"Shoot, you're a crazy girl, aren't you, you know that?" Jacky spoke in bursts, breathing hard.

We both lay on our backs, exhausted. But now the sky had turned dark. The light all around us was a pale, sickly green. A long deep roll of thunder, like a growl, came crawling across the sky, soon followed by a jagged bolt of lightning back up at the tree line not far away. Jacky's horse reared up, whinnying.

"Hellfire," he said, jumping up and pulling me after him. "Come on, I've got to turn her loose, and then we'll go over there and get up under the Manbone Rock, there is kind of an overhang if I remember right. Hit's fixing to come a big one."

The wind was against us as we struggled back up the hill. I waited while Jacky went over to the horse, still tied to the tallest pine. "Whoa, Betty, whoa, Betty," he said, but Betty kept on rearing up, her eyes rolling. She pulled her lips back so I could see her gums and her long yellow teeth. "Damn, Betty!"

Finally Jacky got her untied and gave her her head and she galloped back up the hill snorting toward the woods.

"Oh no, Jacky—," I cried, but he hollered, "Don't worry, she will come back," and I had to believe him.

"Now come on." He grabbed my hand as we ran hell for leather back up the hill toward the Manbone Rock which loomed up white and ghostly as a galleon in the dark stormy afternoon. Thunder boomed. We scrabbled up the hill, falling back again and again as the little loose rocks rolled under our feet. I felt like I was in one of those dreams where you run and run but you don't ever get anywhere. Jacky was pulling my hand. We had gotten almost to the rock when there came a sharp crack, as loud as a firing squad, which threw us both to the ground.

And then the first thing I knew, Jacky was leaning over me saying something. I could scarcely see him in the gray light which was all around us now, and scarcely hear him for the ringing sound in my ears. My mouth tasted coppery, like pennies. "Where are we?" I asked, and he said we were up under the Manbone Rock, and the storm was passing. Then it seemed like my eyes started working again and I saw the wide oval mouth of the cave and the gray slanting rain outside.

"What happened to us?" I asked next.

"I reckon we nearabout got hit by lightning," he said. "Iffen we'd of been any closer to that big tree, we'd most likely be dead now." He gestured toward the mouth of the cave. "Oh God, Molly, this is all my fault. I never should have brung you out here."

"I came on my own," I said. "I wanted to."

"Are you all right then, sure enough? Oh God. I didn't have no business getting you into something like this." Jacky sat cross-legged in the rocky dirt with my head in his lap. He pushed my hair back off my face.

It occurred to me to sit up too, and I did, and nothing happened. "I think I am all right," I said carefully, though my feet and legs were hurting and tingling like when they have been asleep.

Jacky took off his buckskin jacket and put it around me and set in to picking up wood from the corners of the cave and making a little fire which he got going in no time, he is good at things like that. We sat beside the fire getting warm and watching the firelight flicker on the cave walls. "I have to get back," I said, but he said, "Wait till it quits raining so hard. It's going to stop directly." How do you know, I almost said but didn't. By then I knew better than to ask.

"Looky here." Jacky moved his hands so that shadow animals went prancing across the red rocky walls of the cave. First a horse, then a deer, then a rabbit chased by a fox. He made animal noises with his mouth. I clapped my hands. "Molly, you swear you're all right?" He turned back and grabbed my hands.

"Yes," I said, "far as I can tell. Old Bess always said if you get hit by lightning yet live, you will have special powers," I told him.

"Well, I reckon we are going to need them," he said solemnly. We sat side by side leaning up against the cave wall holding hands like children at the end of the world. "I am not a good man," he said, "but I am not a bad man either, and by God, I'll be good to you. I swear it." We sat in silence while the rain gradually stopped and the sun came out again exactly like nothing had ever happened.

But it has, Mary White. It has.

Jacky stood up and stomped out the last of the fire. He helped me outside, steadying me, for at first I could scarcely see. Just when I was about to get scared, my eyes adjusted and then I saw the tallest pine tree blackened and leaning way over to the side, a long open tear down its trunk. While we watched, it cracked in two with a sound like a pistol shot and crashed onto the rocks below, the same rocks where we had been sitting earlier, completely covering up Jacky's blanket which we had left there, of course. It was a massive tree, its branches covered that whole outcropping. The branches shifted and settled with loud crackling noises.

"Damn," Jacky finally said when all was quiet again.

"Where is Betty?" I asked, for my legs still had pins and needles as we used to say, and I knew I could never walk all the way back.

Jacky grinned at me. "Don't worry. Watch this." He put two fingers in his mouth and whistled, a shriek that pierced the whole forest. He waited and whistled again and here she came bursting down from the treeline toward us, reins trailing. "Good girl, good girl," Jacky slapped her glistening wet side. "Well, it looks like I lost a pack someplace," he said to me. The banjo was still tied on. "But I reckon we are lucky to get off with our lives."

We were so lucky that I still couldn't believe it as we rode Betty back up the trail through the dripping laurel and across the Pisgah Bald and on up the road toward Bobcat. I felt like we had been saved for something. Twice Jacky stopped and jumped down to clear the road of fallen branches, for it had stormed heavily up here too. The sun was setting all red through the lacy trees by the time we pulled up in front of the Badgers' cabin. "They're not back yet." I was surprised.

"Chances are, they got rained on too. Who knows? All them Baptists might have got washed right down the river like the great flood."

"You better go." I jumped down but had to grab the fence as my knees threatened to buckle under me.

Jacky wheeled Betty around, then reined her in for a minute, both horse and rider black against the fiery sunset, like figures on a magic lantern. "I'll see you," is all he said before he rode away, yet those words seemed to enter my body.

I went in and took off my clothes and washed up and dressed again. I couldn't believe that I had left here only this morning, that I had been gone for only one day. It seemed like years. I opened the pie safe and ate everything I could get my hands on, old biscuits and a big hunk of cake and a handful of dried apples almost too tough to chew. I went out and got more wood for the fire which I had got blazing again by the time they all came trooping in, wet, exhausted, yet excited and full of stories. The storm had hit just as the invitation hymn was offered, according to Chattie, sending tens of people rushing forward to be saved. Agnes winked at me, then stared at me curiously. "What did you do all day, Molly?" she asked. "You look, I don't know, different."

"I went walking, and got rained on too," I said. Just then Granny Took made a snorting, strangling noise, so we all rushed over to her bedside where she was clutching her coverlet hard as she could with both little hands, her mouth working furiously. Yet no words came.

"Why, what is it?" Chattie cried. "Has she been all right today?" and I said, "She has been just fine."

I went off to my leanto with her little black eyes following me, hot and intense as coals.

WEDNESDAY

Today I was walking the Indian trail home from the Bobcat School alone—Agnes has gone down to Jefferson with Cicero Todd to pick up supplies—when out of the woods popped Jacky Jarvis. The sun came down through the trees, lighting up his hair. He was hatless and shirt-sleeved, as if he had joined up with spring. And I have to say that after all that has happened, I wasn't even surprised to see him, though I acted surprised.

"Why, what are you doing down here?" I asked. "Don't you have a job?"

"This here is my job," he said, falling right into step beside me. "I am getting to know you."

"Oh, you are!" I said, and he said, "Yes mam," which I hate, and said so, and then he walked me on home talking a mile a minute through these woods which are more beautiful right now than they have ever been. All the leaves are coming out now, with fiddlehead ferns popping and the May apples and bloodroot blooming. Two bluebirds flew through the trees keeping just ahead of us, I'll swear it was the same bluebirds though I didn't mention it, rattling on about my students and what all had happened that day in school.

But "Looky there!" Jacky said, pointing at them. "I reckon I am getting to know them too."

I had just started to say something else when I saw a flash of white moving on up the trail, and somehow I knew it was somebody's shirt. "Jacky," I turned to whisper, but he was already gone, vanished entirely into the forest as if he had never been, leaving me alone on the trail yet burning as if with a fever.

"Good afternoon, Miss Molly," said Horace Groats, awkward as ever, carrying a sack of coal down to the school, for which I thanked him kindly.

THURSDAY AFTERNOON AT THE BOBCAT SCHOOL

Today Felix came up to school bringing an "urgent" letter from Henderson's mother. I opened it on the spot. She wants to know my measurements, wondering if I can fit into her own wedding dress. "Isn't that sweet?" Agnes said. She is going to measure me tonight.

FRIDAY

Jacky came again

SATURDAY

And again, he says he is camping out like an Indian in a hollow tree down toward the river

SUNDAY NIGHT

Today I walked right out attracting no suspicion as the house was full of visitors, Badger cousins and such, everybody was eating cobbler. The weather has not changed yet, it is still pretty, the prettiest spring I can ever remember. The river shone like a distant mirror through the trees as I started down the path which I was not sure of, afraid I would get lost, and this is when I thought I saw your little red coat just ahead of me, Mary White, flitting through the trees, showing me the way. I walked faster and you walked faster. I know I can never catch you. But I was just so happy to see you, all the same. I was out of breath when I finally spotted the tree where he emerged like a forest sprite, grinning and waving, and then I started running down the hill toward him, I couldn't help it, and he ran out to meet me and picked me up and squeezed me, hard, and carried me into the tree where he had made a kind of nest with the thick leaves covered by a beautiful old quilt. "That's a wedding ring quilt," I said, and he said, "Is it?" and we fell down upon it. We stayed there all afternoon, Mary White, and I would be there still, but he woke me up saying, "Molly! Molly, you have to go home."

"No," I said.

"Yes mam."

"Don't call me that." I put on my clothes one piece at a time as slow as I could, watching his face all the while. You could never say Jacky is good looking, but I think he is beautiful.

"You better get a move on, girl," he said.

I stood up and pulled on my skirt.

"Take me with you," I said.

"I can't take you up there, crazy girl. Besides, he would come after you." Now Jacky was walking back and forth in front of the hollow tree, in and out of the sunlight, very agitated.

Jacky does not know that this is not true, because Henderson Hanes has never yet done one hard thing in his life.

Simon Black is the one who would come after me.

Jacky kept walking back and forth, then stopped right in front of me. He took both my hands in his. "Well Molly, I'd still like to get to know you, but I reckon I'm going to have to marry you to do it."

I looked up at him. The sun was in his hair, and on my face. "All right," I said.

At last this is my own true love story, for you, Mary White, though I will remain forever your own

Molly

Plain View

———

STATE OF NORTH CAROLINA, WILKES COUNTY

——◦◉◦——

This testimony made this 18th day of November 1907, by John Howard Willetts, aka "BJ" aka "Black Jack" Jarvis. Duly sworn before Coroner George Ragland, at Wilkesboro, and state of North Carolina.

——◦◉◦——

YES, I WILL SWEAR it on this Bible to tell the truth, the whole truth, and nothing but the truth, so help me God. I swear to God. May God strike me dead if this ain't the truth. She never done it. Molly Petree could not have done this thing if her life depended on it, which I reckon it does. But this is the truth, and the whole truth insofar as I know it, and I know more about it than anybody else in the world, for I was right there. I been right there all along. And it may be that Jacky Jarvis has had a bullet out there waiting for him all along too. Well I'm telling you whether it's necessary or not, it's the truth.

Start at the beginning? All right, I'll start at the beginning. But what is it? When did the beginning start? Did it start way back when me and Jacky was born six days apart to two sisters, and both of us named Jack? And him light complected and me dark, so that they took to calling us Yellow Jack and Black Jack right off the bat, for nicknames? Or did it start when I was two and Mama pitched forward in the fire carrying me, and you can see here what happened. Just go on and take a good look. Mama's own face was disfigured so bad that she never would let nobody see it but me, she got herself a black bonnet with a black veil, and walked with her head down. Daddy took off soon after, he was not from around here anyway. Come through selling sewing machines.

Well, Big Jack taken us in, that was Big Jack Jarvis, Jacky's daddy, and they all nursed Mama until her death which was not long in coming, and raised me like a son. So you see, sir, Jacky and me goes as far back as it gets. We were brothers, and more than brothers. He was like my other half.

When I first seen Molly? Jacky come riding up here with her, acrost the Rag Mountain bald. We can see folks coming from a long ways off. Now we live right out in the open, and the wind blows up here all the time, and there's a lot of folks that can't stand a wind like that, it will make them kindly nervous, and crazy-like. Why our uncle Calvin got himself the prettiest little redheaded wife one time, he found her over on Knox Creek, singing in a tavern. Anyhow, Calvin brung her up here, but she didn't stay no time, this wind gave her conniptions, she said, so she lit a rag for home. Then he got himself another one, now that's Clara, she's still here, a different kind of a woman entirely, she can work all day and then sit so still in one of them flour sack dresses, she looks like a sack of flour herself. That's the kind of woman you want up here, a woman that has got some gravity to her, so she won't blow off.

But Molly Petree is not that kind of a woman. No sir.

So when I first seen Jacky riding her acrost the mountain on that big horse of his, I thought, Well this ain't one for the books neither, I reckon, though she was the prettiest one yet, the prettiest one that had ever been brung up here, and just laughing to beat the band. Well, they was both of them laughing so hard, they liked to fell off of the horse. The porch was full of people, it being payday down at the mill, and the lot was full of horses and wagons and mules, with some men pitching horseshoes over at the side there, and everybody that was watching set up a holler.

BJ, BJ, come looky here, said Clara, and Calvin's little Jacob, and so I put down the hoop cheese after I finished cutting it, and stood back in the doorway wiping my hands on my apron, watching Jacky and her come acrost the bald. Jacky rode the horse right in among everybody, making a big commotion, the way he will.

BJ! Jacky hollered at the top of his lungs, BJ, get yourself out here! I have done it! I have gone and got me a wife.

Oh Lord, I thought. I reckon we are in for it now.

Because the truth is, and everybody around here knows it, Jacky Jarvis was not the marrying kind. Now I am his first cousin, and I growed up side by side with him closer than a brother, and I know him through and through, better than anybody. Jacky does not mean to be bad, but the fact is, he just loves women, the way he loves music and liquor and cards and traveling, why he wants everything there is, and he don't see any reason why he can't have it, either. Now you wouldn't think a woman would want a man like that, you would think they would rather have somebody reliable, such as myself, but they don't.

Nobody can hold a candle to Jack when it comes to women.

When he wasn't hardly out of shirttails, I reckon he was not but twelve or thirteen years old, he had him a girlfriend over the hill there, Bonnie Weaver, a good four or five years older than him, marrying age, and they done everything there was to do up until her mama sent her off to live with her aunt so as to get her away from Jacky. Now this was before Jacky's daddy—my uncle Big Jack—died, oh he beat Jacky with a belt over it, and Jacky cried and said he was sorry, but then it wasn't two months until it was another one, that sweet little Becky Pratt. Lord I can't even remember them all. They warned all the girls in the county about him, in church. From the pulpit! But Jacky didn't care, and it didn't do no good, either.

Mister George Elias himself came up here complaining that Jacky had been making eyes at his young wife—now that was a serious business, make no mistake about it, as he was a mean old son of a bitch if there ever was one, but Big Jack had a way about him too, and he set Mister Elias down and gave him a drink and then some several drinks of his good whisky, and convinced him he had made a mistake, and talked him plumb out of it! It were a marvel.

Big Jack was a big old man, what you might call a character. Used to could buck dance all night long, best dancer in these hills. He had the gift of gab too. Son, he said to Jacky when Mister George Elias left, a man that don't follow nothing but his cock will end up in Hell, and deserve it, now do you understand me?

Yes sir, Jacky said.

But then Big Jack died, and Jacky went back to his old ways. He was a back door man primarily, and it didn't even appear to be his fault. Seemed like he had to beat them off with a stick. Well he daddied some children round and about, and lived here and there, but he never married, or at least not so as you could tell it, though he got pretty cozy with that pretty young widow Icy Hinshaw, who lived down in the Ponder Cove. Her daddy used to play music with Roscoe and them, time was, and Icy was a fine little fiddler herself.

Jacky thought the world was there for the taking, that was the long and short of it. He liked to make people feel better, and he does make them feel better. He lights them up. When you talk to him about it, he's got a whole system figured out. According to this system, a lie is not a lie if it makes somebody feel better. The truth don't do you no good if it makes you feel bad. It's all relative, Jacky liked to say, a word he learned from a preacher's wife in Jellico, Tennessee. Everything is all right as long as you don't get caught. Getting caught is the problem, not whatever you done to get caught. And if you done it out of the county, you didn't do it, nor leastaways it don't count.

Now don't get me wrong here. Jacky wasn't bad, you understand. He didn't mean harm to a soul. He was sweet, and fun, and generous to a fault, why he would give anybody the shirt off his back, and done so. I couldn't make no money here at the store when Jacky was working. He'd give everything away if you didn't watch him like a hawk, even to folks like the Rumples who ain't never made good on a debt in their sorry lives. So it was a big relief whenever Jacky went off playing music somewheres with the rest of them, I done a lot better with him gone.

Me? It didn't bother me none. I loved him as good as the ladies, I reckon. Everything took on a kind of a glow when Jack was around. You never knew exactly what was going to happen, neither, which made things kindly exciting. It can get pretty dull up here when they're all out on the road and nothing much is going on and the wind blows all the time, whoo whoo whoo. It can spook you pretty good sometimes. Make you feel real lonesome away down inside of yourself. A man can get tired of it, I mean the same thing day after day, getting up in the dark at four thirty, going in and opening up, brewing the coffee, making biscuits—now I am a pretty fair biscuit cook, I'll admit it—then saying howdy to Rufus Butler and Old Joe Kapp and the rest of them that has been coming in here every morning for thirty years. It can get old, I'll tell you. Especially in the wintertime. A man needs a little spark. So I never got too mad at nothing Jacky done, I figured we would all live through it, whatever it was, but I have to say, it was a big surprise when he showed up here with the likes of Molly Petree.

LATER IT ALL COME out, of course, how it was that they had got married. He had up and gone for her in the middle of the night, over there where she was a living with Chattie Badger, and had come on in the house with no word beforehand to her nor anybody else, and Molly she had jumped right up out of a deep sleep and put on her clothes and gone with him directly. No talking about it, no bye-your-leave nor nothing. Went right with him. Didn't take a thing but the clothes on her back, and didn't care to! Jumped up behind him on that horse Betty and they took off in the light of the moon heading down toward Jefferson at a pretty fast clip.

Why, where are we going? she asked once, thinking they were headed the wrong way from Plain View, and he said, I done told you once. We are going to get married. Then they rode into town, straight down Main Street just as the first pretty streaks of dawn was showing in the sky, and turned up Perkins Lane into old Judge Worth's yard, riding around to the back of his big brick house.

Now it just so happened that the Judge hisself was standing on the back stoop in his purple satin robe smoking a cigarette while his hired girl Liz Ramey was fixing him some eggs for breakfast. They say he always ate four fried eggs for breakfast. He was a big man. Yessir. Big old belly, big old head of white hair.

Boy, what do you want? he said.

And Jacky said that they wanted to get married.

Well, you'll have to wait a while, then, the Judge said. You are welcome to come in the house while I have my breakfast, and then I will dress, and then we will get prepared for the ceremony, and then we will do it.

We thank you kindly, sir, Jacky said, and we just appreciate it ever so much, and we don't mean to put you out none, but the fact is that we are kindly in a rush here. So I am wondering . . . what if you was to marry us right now?

You mean, on the horse? The old Judge leaned over the rail to get a better look at them.

Yes sir, Jacky said. I've got some money here, sir, and I'll be happy to pay whatever it costs.

Well I'll be damned, the old Judge said. Then he said, And what about you, young lady? Is this your intention too?

Yes sir, Molly said.

Well then, I reckon we will just get on with it. Liz, he hollered. Liz, come out here, and she did, and she was the witness, and they were married in a minute, with the Judge not showing a sign of recognition at the sound of their names which was wrote down on the paper and give to them right away. They never even got off the horse. Jacky folded the paper up real little and put it in his shirt pocket and paid the Judge and off they went while the Judge went back inside the house and sat down to breakfast, and his eggs was still warm.

So Molly was real partial to Betty ever after, brushing her and patting on her all the time, and taking her a lump of maple sugar out to the barn ever day even when she got too old and broken down to ride, which was a time not long in coming. Oh, there was no question of giving Betty away, nor putting her out to pasture, Molly treated her like she was folks. Like she was company! Why she doted on that horse. Now maybe she wouldn't have, as Clara said one time, if they had of had any children, but they didn't. No, they was not blessed with children, you see, and that is the whole story. I'll tell it. Lord yes, I'll tell it all directly, but it is a long sad tale, and that is the heart of the thing.

Molly Petree is a fine lady, and we hadn't ever had us one of them up here before. Oh I don't mean she put on airs, nor nothing like it, but there was a quality about her, a way she had with everybody, I'd be hard-pressed to tell you what it was. She was just plain nice, for one thing. And she would set right beside you and listen to everything you had to say, for hours on end, asking stuff like where I got this or that for the store, and what all me and Jacky used to do when we was kids, and she didn't even seem to care what I look like. She'd look me square in the face and not flinch, for a fact, now. And she'd get down on the floor and play with the children like she was a child herself. She'd try to get Luvenie to talk, which she wouldn't, and she'd be real nice to Aunt Belle, who is crazy, and then she'd dote on Swannie—which is the way she really got around me, for Swannie was the sweetest one up here, and never complained, she was just like an angel.

Swannie is Jacky's sister, sir. Yes sir. I will try, sir.

I lived in the house right out back with Miss Luvenie and Belle and Swannie, that way I could slip in and out of the store real easy, for somebody had to be in there ready to trade at all hours whenever we was holding a dance, or somebody was spending the night out in the wagon yard. Came to where I didn't need hardly any sleep myself, just a catnap here and there.

Molly took to Swannie right off the bat, sitting down next to her despite of the smell on that very first day she come here, and saying, Why, how long has this leg been like this? and Can't anything be done? the answer being, of course, No, that Swannie would have to go down off the mountain for an operation, and then she might die anyway, and she didn't want to go, and all together it would cost more money than any of us was like to get together in one lifetime.

We've got that pasture land for sale, I told her, pointing out the window. Hell, we've got that whole mountain for sale, but it's not like anybody is coming around here banging down the door to buy it.

Oh my goodness. Molly pulled off the coverlet to look at Swannie's leg herself. I will do that, she said to old Aunt Belle, who was fixing to swab it with kerosene.

Good, said Belle in that highfalutin way of hers, because I have reason to believe that Mister George Roten will come calling for me shortly, and I must go to prepare myself.

Molly cut her eyes at me. It was a pleasure to meet you, she said politely, as Belle swept out of the room like a damn queen.

Now Belle is seventy if she is a day, and she ain't never had a sweetheart to her name, yet she claims she had one that was lost in the War, Morrison Maitland his name was, and she has been mourning him ever since, and trying to get another one. She will set her cap for first this one, then that one. Like this George Roten, from over at Lansing. Why he is not but about forty years old, and married. Everybody around here thinks it's a big joke, Miss Belle and her beaux. But it's real sad if you think about it, like Miss Luvenie is sad, not talking and running off in the woods the way she does, and Swannie, with that rotten leg.

Molly brightened things up, for a fact. Took over from Aunt Belle that minute with Swannie's leg. She used to say, Why Miss Belle, you haven't got any business doing this kind of dirty work. You look so pretty today. Why don't you just get yourself a drink out of the cooler, and go sit on the porch?

What's that, sir? Molly and Jack? They took over the house that used to belong to Big Jack, right out on the bald. It had stood empty for some several years, but Molly claimed she liked it. It's a nice big cabin with a big porch. And the way they was carrying on together, it looked like they would fill it up with children in no time. So we cleaned it up for them. It's real pretty out there. There's a lot of wind, a lot of sky. You can see all around you in ever direction, and I reckon Jacky liked that part of it too. Can't nobody sneak up on a man, now can they, brother? he said, and I said that no, it was not likely.

I did not say that I could understand how he might be worried about this.

It's a nice view anyway, over there toward Tennessee. To my mind, it's a prettier view than North Carolina, the mountains are higher and farther away, so that a feeling of distance and peace comes over a body, looking at Tennessee. Might be cause it was free in the War, I don't know. But Molly was happy in that house, I'll swear it. Ain't no use you trying to make out a case that she was not. She loved him, and she loved being up on Plain View with us. She purely did.

Molly was a hard worker too. Even that first day, her wedding day, she rolled up her sleeves as I said and then set about tending to Swannie and then went all around shaking hands with everybody in the store and out in the wagon yard. Hey Jacky! Have you gone and married a politician? somebody hollered, and Jacky he just grinned.

We were not beneath her, is what I mean. She was interested in us. She was interested in everybody. And she didn't even get mad when they came around serenading that night just like I figured they would, Jacky's old running mates Ernest Dollar and General Gentry and Jubal Smith and that whole bunch, banging on pots and pans and such, I believe you call it a shivaree.

Her and Jacky had already gone to bed over there in their new old house. Calvin's Clara had got up some bedding for them, and they had pulled the old rope four-poster bed over in front of the fire. I had helped them clean out the house, but then I got out of there. I couldn't afford to think too much about it, you know, them in the bed and the firelight jumping around on the walls which was covered with old newspaper pictures, pasted on. I had clean forgotten that until I went over there to help them. Uncle Hat Ashby helped too, and Biddle and Calvin. We made short work of it.

Good night! we all said, and Congratulations!

But then. Just after midnight, here come the shivaree, with pots and pans banging and them whooping and hollering, all liquored up. You might of thought she'd be scared or something, a educated, fancy woman like that. Jacky was mad, I'll tell you. He come out on the porch bare-chested, clutching his pants to his waist, and told them all to go to hell. But then she run out wearing her shift and her cloak, hair bouncing all around, and clapped her hands and said why didn't they all get off their horses and stay awhile? Can't you get some whisky or something from the store? she asked Jacky point-blank. So then he had to, and then we was in for it. It was a fine time, I'll tell you, the first time that porch had been full of people in twenty years, I'll bet, and not the last, either.

They sung the sun up, and her and Jacky was the last to go to bed. I fixed them some breakfast first, ham and eggs. They did not come out of their house until after noon the next day. Everybody in the store started clapping when they walked in. Molly smiled and curtsied to them all.

WITH ALL DUE RESPECT, sir, I don't know why you keep saying the scene of the crime, it wasn't no crime that I know of, leastways not involving her. It might well of been a robbery, now, that's what I've been saying all along . . . Yes sir. I am doing my best, sir. Okay.

The store? Well it's just a store, I reckon, same as any store, except it's got the dance hall up on top, like I said. There's two doors, see, and a staircase over here at the side, so you can go in that way if you're just coming in and out of the dance hall. Fine oak floor, top and bottom, Big Jack had the lumber milled and hauled up here from Mellicoo. Got those pressed tin ceilings from New Orleans. Yessir, it was a fine store.

That store was my whole life from the time I could walk until the incident we are talking about.

Well, not much, to be honest with you. Seems like I can't hardly work up an interest in anything these days, and then there's Uncle Hat and Aunt Belle to take care of, she has got up real old now. No sir. Belle aint never got married, to this day. But she is still hoping.

Yessir. The store. We sold near about everything you can think of, I reckon, from cradles to caskets, as Big Jack used to say. Matter of fact, Old Roscoe and his buddy Horace Kemp used to straddle two caskets piled up one on top of the other and play checkers between them. It weren't too reverent, I reckon, but then a store is not a reverent place. It is a place for playing cards, swapping stories, and talking politics, whittling and chewing and arguing religion, and griping about the rain, or no rain, and hiding out from your wife, and laying off of work.

We had two long display counters with shelves behind them and ceiling-high track ladders running the length of the store, so we could get up there to get things, now that was my first job when I was a little boy, not but about four or five years old.

Yes sir. It was my life, sir.

Well, let's see. We sold cloth, buttons, needle and thread, papers of straight pins, dye, candles, overhauls, gloves, boots, fancy combs and hair-pins, lamp oil and globes, wicks and those big old three-inch matches, octagon soap, scissors and razors, pots and pans, skillets and teakettles, tools, brooms, rope, cowbells, washboards, woodstoves and stovepipes, everything from straw hats to chamber pots. Had horse collars, leather saddles, bridles, and harnesses hung on the wall. Had a real pretty eight-sided revolving hardware cabinet up on the counter, the latest thing. Glass case for penny candy such as jawbreakers, red hots, gum drops, peppermint and horehound sticks, and those all-day suckers, now that was our most popular item. We carried tins of Lucky Strike tobacco along with Bull Durham and Sweet Caporal cigarettes, rolling papers, boxes of snuff, and plugs of chewing tobacco. Tobacco cutter and cheese cutter up on the counter along with them fancy brass scales from Germany. Soda, baking powder, salt, spices, cornstarch — then those big old sacks of sugar, flour, coffee beans, rice and dried beans on the floor. Six, eight, ten, and sixteen penny size nails, horseshoe nails, and carpet tacks — seems like those nail kegs would always end up around the stove where everybody liked to sit. We carried potted ham, sardines, cheese and johnnycrackers for eating on the spot. Old wagon seats and chairs over there too, and a big old peach can for a spittoon until Molly Petree allowed as how I ought to get a proper one, which I did.

Wasn't long before she was behind the counter herself, rolling up the prettiest little paper bags and packages you ever saw for sugar and salt and such, tying them off with string. She'd make a bow with the string. She'd draw a little animal on the paper, for the kids. Added up the sums in her head. She could do it with three, four, six, eight, twelve numbers. People came in from all over to see her do it, they'd check her on a piece of paper. She wasn't never wrong. At first folks didn't like it, you know, a woman working in a store like that, and then they kindly got adjusted, and then they took to it in a big way, and then later when she started up the storehouse school, why, everybody was plumb crazy about her.

Jacky was too. I'll have to hand it to him. Molly Petree was Jack's equal in everything, and he hadn't ever had an equal before, but he rose to the occasion, I have to say.

THEY CAME RIGHT UP here to get her, of course.

It was early morning, three or four days after he had brung her. First thing that happened was, a ragged little girl from up on Whitetail had come in with four Dominicker chickens, two in one hand and two in the other, tied together at the legs, squawking and flapping like crazy. She took them over to Molly, who jumped back. Why BJ, what in the world am I supposed to do with these? she asked.

Jacky was sitting on the wagon seat over there by the stove, fooling with a banjo and drinking coffee. He looked up and started laughing. Molly's scared of chickens, he said.

Why, I am not, she said.

Here, I'll take them. I came around the counter. I was going to put them in one of those cages back there, then Mister Cooper would pick them up and take them on to Damascus and sell them. But first I had to see how much they weighed, so I'd know how much the little girl could get for them. We pay a little more for Dominickers.

Mama wants some powder, the little girl said, and Granny needs some snuff, and we ain't got nothing to eat in the house.

Molly leaned down to her. Why, we will fix you up, honey, she said. What is your name?

Lucy Hill, the little girl said. She was still struggling to hold the chickens.

Here, I said.

But Molly snatched them up. She set one bunch up on the scale and managed to write down their weight before they flapped off. She threw those in the cage and came back with the second bunch, real proud of herself. Just a minute now, Lucy, she said over the squawking, this must have been about the time the door opened, I reckon, but we didn't none of us hear the bell. Molly was trying to weigh the second bunch when the string that was tying their legs together busted and both of them started flapping and squawking and we all jumped in to grab them. Jacky started laughing and the little girl started crying. Feathers was flying everywhere. The chickens were knocking everything off the counter into the floor—you never saw such a mess. Broke one of the candy jars and sent jawbreakers all over the place. One of the chickens went straight for Molly's hair, and then she started crying too. By the time Jacky and me got them all back there into the cage, the counter was plumb covered with feathers, it looked like snow.

Jacky came back and took Molly in his arms and kissed her real solid. I gave the little girl a biscuit.

It looks like you are having a busy morning, Mr. Felix Boykin said, and we all looked up to see him and Mrs. Todd—Miss Rutherford, that was back then—the other teacher down at Bobcat.

Yes we are, for a fact. Jacky didn't miss a beat, with his arms still around Molly. Welcome to Plain View. I'm Jacky Jarvis, and this here is Mrs. Jarvis.

Mrs. Jarvis squealed and ran over and flung her arms around Miss Rutherford, and then they both was crying. I hadn't had so many crying women in the store since that time those two Letcher sisters got in a fight over a man.

Why don't you all sit down over here by the stove? Jacky said, and we'll see if BJ can make some more coffee.

I was just fixing to do that, I said.

I parched the coffee beans, Molly sniffled, not letting go of Jacky. Didn't I, BJ?

She sure did, I said.

Oh Molly. Miss Rutherford was still crying but she let herself be led over to the stove and set down on the old wagon seat. She was a plain honest-looking kind of a woman with everything she felt wrote large upon her face, all the worry and disappointment she was going through. I didn't blame her none for it. In fact I thought highly of her.

I am so happy, Molly said to them all, standing up straight in spite of her tears. Believe me, Agnes, I had to do it.

Miss Agnes looked at her for a long time. I believe you. She smiled too. Mariah always said you were liable to do anything.

And it ain't no telling what she might do next. We are watching her like a hawk! Jacky said, and everybody laughed. He struck up a tune on the banjo, and I came around with some biscuits and some fresh coffee, and Lucy Hill climbed up onto Molly's lap. Before Lucy left, I got her everything she wanted for the Dominickers, plus some extra cash money, and then Mister Boykin loaded her down with the awfullest amount of things just for her, socks and combs and candy and the like.

I used to know your father, Mister Boykin said to Jacky. He was quite a man. I remember back when he had that pet bear tied up out there in front of the store—

Well, the upshot of it was that we set there until a whole big raft of people came in the store and we couldn't set there any longer, and then Molly took them over and showed them her and Jacky's house, all proud like, and Miss Agnes had Cicero Todd take her trunk of clothes out of the wagon and leave it there. Later they was to come back with books and I don't know what all else, for the storehouse school.

I reckon this was our heyday up on Plain View, looking back on it now. Heyday, now that's a funny word, ain't it? Part of a heyday is, you don't never know you are having yourself one till later when it's all over with, long gone. But that was our heyday for sure, and it lasted about three years.

IT WAS STILL GOING on when Mister Black come up here the first time.

Yes sir. That is Mister Simon Black, he was a right old man already by that time, walked with a silver-handled cane, but he had a way about him. A presence. He had this old Indian man with him too, or some kind of a thing, I don't know. They come in the store and stood there right still, both of them saying nary a word, looking all around.

Naturally I went over to them. Can I help you? I asked.

First he asked for a drink of water, and I went back and got them each a drink in a tin cup, I don't care if a Indian drinks out of one of my cups or not. They was here before I was, what I figure. But anyway, I come back, and now they was both standing over by the counter real still, and I felt—I don't hardly know how to tell it—like they had looked all around, or something. Like they knowed everything we carried, and everything about us. The old man had a presence, as I said. I gave them the water and stood while they drunk it down.

I am looking for Mrs. Jarvis, he said finally.

The Indian didn't say nothing.

We have got some several Mrs. Jarvises up here, I said. Which one was it that you wanted to see? Though somehow I knowed already.

Mrs. Jack Jarvis, he said, that is, the former Molly Petree from South Carolina. I was a friend of her father's.

Is that so? I said.

In the War.

The way he said it, you had to believe him. He had a kind of gravity himself, which a person needs up here, as I said.

She ain't here right now, I said, which was true. She had gone off gathering chestnuts with the rest of them, over in Crabtree Cove. I did not say that Jacky was not with them, having gone to play music at a wedding down in Bee.

We will wait, then, Mister Black said. Perhaps you will show us around. This is a beautiful country up here. It reminds me of Peru.

So I hollered for Calvin, and took off my apron, and toured them all over Rag Mountain. Now Mister Black was especially taken with the north slope that goes up there from Gum Branch where the old cabin is, and said it was good timber up there, as well as a fine prospect. I sat on the cabin steps smoking a cigarette while him and the Indian walked it from the tree line clear to the top. Once Mister Black stopped walking and made a big sweep of a gesture with his hands. I could hear them jabbering away to each other, him and the Indian, but I could not tell what they said because they were too far away and speaking in a language not American, I didn't know what kind of a language it was. It is real pretty up there, you forget what a pretty place it is if you live here all the time, you know a feller can get used to anything.

But still and all, it kindly took me by surprise when they come back down to the cabin and Mister Black asked me if any of this land was for sale.

I am something of a speculator, he said.

I sat there looking down the mountain. Why yes, sir, it is, I said.

And might I inquire the price?

Now we had not established a price, having never had a real offer before, but something got into me all of a sudden, and I quoted him a pure fortune, to my mind.

Sold, Mister Black said, sticking out his hand.

I will believe it when I see it, I thought, shaking hands.

But when we got back down to the store, Mister Black nodded to the Indian who took off one of those leather pouches he had slung around himself and got out a roll of money and started peeling off greenback hundred-dollar bills which he put out on the counter.

Whoa now, I said, Just hold your horses for a minute, sir, for I would have to talk to the rest of them, and get the deed drawed up, and so on. We would have to have us some lawyering.

This is earnest money, Mister Black said. You think about it. He had left it right there on the counter, and turned to go, when in the door came Molly all rosy-faced and kind of wild-looking, followed by Betsy and Biddle and Nancy and Clara and all the children, fresh from chestnut gathering. They had a cart full out front to show for it. That was the most money you could get for anything, even ginseng. Folks has been killed over chestnuts.

BJ, Molly started saying something to me, then she stopped dead, and crossed her arms. Why, Mister Black, she said in a different voice. What a surprise.

He bowed from the waist like a man in a play. Mrs. Jarvis, he said, very formal-like. I come to offer you my congratulations on your marriage and to inquire after your welfare.

Now everybody was looking at her and him.

Calvin had come out of the back of the store and grabbed up Mister Black's money off the counter and stood there holding it.

As for your congratulations, Mister Black, I don't need them, Molly spat out in a way that was not like her, that none of us had ever seen before. And as for my welfare, it is wonderful. In fact, I am going to have a baby.

Oh Lord! Nancy cried, hugging her, for none of us had knowed a thing about it. Everybody started talking at once.

Now who might this handsome gentleman be? Poor old Aunt Belle sailed out from the back with her hair standing out on one side of her head.

Molly! Calvin hollered, waving the money like a fan.

Mister Black inclined his head toward the Indian, then jerked it toward the door.

Molly! Calvin run out from behind the counter with the money in his hand. He is buying the mountain, Molly.

Molly looked down, and bit her lip, and then stepped forward like a soldier and reached for Mister Black's hand. I believe I owe you an apology, she said. You have always been very kind to me. I seem to have lost my manners somewhere along the way up this mountain, but perhaps it is not too late for me to find them again.

We kept looking back and forth between them. It was clear to all concerned that some water had passed under that bridge before.

No apology is necessary, Mister Black said. I apologize to you, as far as that goes. I am an awkward man, and a solitary one, with unusual habits. Social discourse is hard for me. I find it difficult to say or do the right thing, or anything. You must understand that I do not have—nor have I ever had—any intention of bothering you, nor of troubling you in any way.

It is simply that I have always had . . . an interest . . . in you and your family. I wish you well.

Molly nodded, her arms across her stomach. I understand that, she said.

The minute Simon Black and the Indian was out the door, Calvin started whooping and waving that money around like a kid.

And the upshot of it was, we bought new shoes for the kids, and overcoats, and a new wagon, and a new toupee for Uncle Hat.

Swannie got her leg took off down in Knoxville. Molly went with her, and stayed in a boardinghouse the whole time, Jacky visiting when he could, and bringing us the news.

Swannie? She got plumb well, and learned to walk real good on one leg and some crutches, and got married to a boy down in Warrensville and moved off the mountain, and had a passel of kids of her own. Had herself a life. Ain't that what we all want, I reckon? Some kind of a life of our own.

Mister Black? Well, he bought the mountain, of course, but he never done nothing with it. Fixed up the cabin some, and come up here from time to time, but very seldom, very irregular, and was always real cordial but never did mix with us none. Didn't seem to expect it, he was serious when he said he was a solitary man. At first, Clara swore it spooked her, and told the kids to stay away from the cabin, but it didn't spook me none, nor nothing like it. It seemed natural, that's all, like the bobcat that is seen on the mountain from time to time. Nothing more nor less than that. Fact is, I liked it when Mister Black was over there, I felt like he was watching over us, or something.

And by then we kindly needed some watching over, leastways, Molly did. For now we are coming into what I call the slipping down years, the hard years, when things gone from good to bad to worst.

HAVE I SAID HOW much Jacky loved children? which he did, and they loved him back, for he done endless tricks with them, finding a penny in their ear, and throwing their voices into them little hand dolls he used to make, and putting on shows, and such as that.

Well, we are all partial to children up here. But you never saw a man take on so as Jacky did that first time when she said she was going to have one.

Lord! Nothing was too good for Molly then, and I couldn't say I blamed him, I was near about as excited as them, watching her belly get big and her face get a little rounder, so that dimple appeared in her cheek. Jacky was a ball of fire, building the baby a cradle hisself and waiting on Molly hand and foot. He couldn't keep his hands off her neither, up until she got real big, and then he had to. Clara told him, in no uncertain terms. I come in upon her telling him, and left accordingly.

But as luck would have it, I was the one that was there when the baby come. We were closing up the store. Jacky had gone off playing music somewheres, trying to get them up some cash money to get ahead a little. I was putting up the mail, and Molly was straightening up the piece goods on that table in the middle, folding everything just so, the nice way she done, when all of a sudden she said BJ in a voice I had never heard before.

I looked over to see her clutching at the table with both hands while a pool of water spread out around her feet.

She is coming, BJ, Molly said.

I didn't ask how she knowed it was going to be a girl, but somehow it didn't surprise me none, her knowing. She was smart, smart, Molly—and then some.

What ought I to do? I asked her, running around the counter, but just then she moaned and sunk to her knees on the old oak floor, so I helped her over to this big old bag of rice we had there on the floor and stretched her out some. Help me, BJ, she said, and she pulled up her dress, and things commenced to happening real fast. I stayed right there so Molly could hold on to my arm, which she done so hard that her fingernails cut little bloody moons through my white shirt sleeves, now I was proud of that. See? I have still got these little scars to prove it.

Calvin run in at some time and said, Lord God, and run back out, and come back in with Clara and Nancy, and then I made to go, but Molly said, No, stay with me awhile, BJ, and so I did, and it were a miracle, sure enough, though it taken upward of five hours and we were all wore out when it happened, she came popping out all bloody and waxy into Clara's hands.

Now let me have her, Molly cried, her hair wet with sweat and her face so white in that lantern light, I wondered if all her blood had done seeped out between her legs. They had brung a ring of lanterns and put them all around us on the floor, and more of them up on the counter.

Clara cut the cord with those big old scissors we used to cut the wrapping paper, and handed her over to Molly, who held her to her breast, eyes jumping in the lantern light. Oh BJ, she said, isn't she beautiful? And though she weren't, naturally I said she was, and stuck to it until she was in fact, when her head had ceased being so pointy-like and her little eyes had turned blue.

Her birthing made a mess of my store, let me tell you! And that was a hundred-dollar sack of rice. Jacky had a fit when he came in a day later and heard all about it, and he called her his rice-baby ever after. They named her Christabel, after a poem, Molly said. She said she wanted her baby to have her own name, a name that nobody else had, which turned out to be true, at least up here. Jacky was crazy about Christabel and did not leave Molly's side from the day he got back until a good two months afterward but stayed underfoot in the store all day long, so we couldn't get a thing done.

It was the longest time I had ever seed Jacky stay put in his life time.

But everbody else carried on about Christabel too, now this was a baby that did not know a stranger. Molly kept the cradle over in the store where everybody could see her and marvel at how soon she was smiling back and cooing at them. Christabel was walking at a year, she used to follow me everplace, I don't know why, but she took to me, I have to say. And then she would take her nap on a pallet Molly had fixed up for her behind the counter. Pretty soon she was walking and saying Ma-ma and Da-da which tickled Jacky about to death.

She called me Bee.

Christabel was just over two when Calvin and Clara's little Dolly, age five, come down with the diphtheria, and died of it, and when we all come back down the mountain from the burying ground, why there was Molly on the porch with Christabel in her arms just a-screaming.

BJ, BJ! SHE HOLLERED. Jacky was gone then too. Come here! Oh, everybody come! Christy has got it too. Which turned out to be true, sure enough. She was struggling for breath with her face all red and her little eyes flat in her head.

We done everything we knowed to do. Clara swabbed her throat with turpentine, then blowed brimstone sulfur down it though Christabel cried so piteous that I had to go out and stand in the wagon yard. They lit pine tar torches all over the house. Christy's mouth was full of old gray stuff like spiderwebs which Molly in her desperation tried to scrape out with a spoon until the blood started running down her little chin and Molly couldn't stand it and had to quit. By the time Jacky got back, Christabel had yellow stuff coming out of her nose just as fast as you could wipe it off and was choking for air. Jacky snatched her up against his shoulder and walked her all night long singing "All the Pretty Little Horses" over and over. Molly sat on a chair and watched them. All over the store, you could hear Christabel trying to breathe.

Jacky carried her wrapped in her favorite little quilt that she dragged around everywhere, and rubbed the satin edging all the time with her fingers. She was the funniest, best little girl. She was dead by morning.

It took three of us to get the baby away from Jacky, so we could bury her. Oh, he carried on awful.

That is no way to act, Clara came right out and told him severely. Look to your wife, who sat still as could be, staring off at the mountains, at nothing.

Well, you know that sorrow will take over different people in different ways. And of course it is unnatural, the most unnatural thing that there is, for a child to die like that. They say there is no greater grief. When old Preacher Livesay come up here saying it was God's will, and suffer the little children to come unto him, why Jacky jumped on him like a bobcat, then run him plumb off. Everybody was scandalized including Clara and them who go down to his church pretty regular. That is the Welcome Home Baptist Church in Sweet Holler which me and Jacky never did attend. I ain't got no use for it, and Jacky didn't have no time for it.

Two of the Rumples children died too, and that little Hawks boy from up on Groundhog. It was a sad, sad time.

But even so, the body will take over after a while, you know. The body wants to live, and it is bound to do so. So because they was young—and naturally sparky, both of them—Molly and Jacky come back to theirselves after a time, or seemed to, though she said privately to me that she never would get over it, nor want to. We were sitting out on the store porch in the old rocking chairs, watching it rain.

I want to think about Christabel every hour of every day, she told me. There is a hole inside me now that will not be filled up, ever, nor do I want it to be, no matter how many children I might have. It is a place for me and Christabel to be together, like we used to be on those nights when Jacky was gone and I'd get up to nurse her. I remember the rain drumming so loud on the roof, and the moon shining out on the snow. It was like we were the only people awake in the world, just her and me.

I turned to look at her. You reckon you will have some more then, sure enough?

I never once thought I would want a child, she said real slow, but now I want it the worst in the world. I want it for Jacky. It is all I want.

Well, I hope you get another one then, I said, and she said, Thank you, BJ, and so summer came along and all, and her and Jacky took to sweet-hearting up a storm and carrying on silly the way they had done before, and to look at them, you couldn't have told that anything bad had ever come up in their life. Except that sometimes a look would come over Molly's face when she sat down alone for a minute, or come back in from the garden by herself, a real private look, not sad exactly, and I knew then that she had been there, in that place with little Christabel.

Then at the tail end of January 1889, Molly's second baby, named Spencer Jarvis, was pronounced dead at birth by Dr. Bowen who attended. I made the coffin myself. It was about the size of a toolbox. Jacky carried it. We all climbed up there in the snow except for Molly of course, some of the women stayed down at the house with her.

It was hard work digging in that frozen ground, but there was a lot of us up there, and we didn't have to go real deep, of course. We buried Spencer next to Christabel whose stone reads CHRISTABEL JARVIS, OUR DEAREST HEART, B. MARCH 9, 1885, D. MAY 12, 1887. Old Mister Crabtree carved it for them free, I swear it would just break your heart. Later he made Spencer one too, with just his name and the date on it, one date only, Jan. 29, 1889. We stood out on top of the mountain and took off our hats and said the Lord's Prayer, and that was that. It was a low heavy sky covered in clouds, looked like the underside of a quilt, and sure enough it started snowing on us as we went back down the mountain.

Later that same night, Molly ran out barefoot and rolled in the snow, over and over, in her grief. She did not know what she was doing then or for days to come. Ever time she'd lose a baby, seemed like it took her longer to come out of it.

Yes sir. I am doing the best I can, sir. But now we have got up to the hard part, and it is not an easy thing to tell. I will try to tell it a quick as I can.

Another stillborn baby, Junius, was to come in 1890, and then a beautiful little girl she named Mary Agnes, that lived for three weeks in 1893, long enough to get everybody's hopes up.

It was sometime in between the two of them that Jacky invented the rolling store. He bought a wagon, a mule, and a red bow tie for seventy-five dollars. I never did know where he got the idea, but I for one was glad to see him go. For Jacky did not have it in him to be sad for long, or sit still, or stay in one place, he had to get out and get moving. First we put sides and a good tin roof on the wagon, then we built shelves up against each side with a little space in between, just about big enough for one person to go in and see what was for sale, or for Jacky to get in there and find what somebody wanted. We put a regular house door on the back. Then he stocked it up with everthing he could cram in there, remedies in particular, such as castor oil, black draught sulfur, Epsom salts, mustard plasters, milk of magnesia, and Dr. LeGear's Cow and Horse Prescription, now that has always been a real big seller for us.

We all thought the rolling store was a crazy idea when Jacky first come up with it. Fact is, it was a good business decision. Damn good. Jacky hit the road and done great with it. Came back empty every time. Sold out. Me and Molly and Calvin kept on running the store, and Molly run the storehouse school too, in the mornings, and everybody loved her. Time passed as it will. Grandaddy Roscoe died, Aunt Luvenie died, God bless her. Biddle and Betsy had twins. Boys.

Molly had another boy herself, Washington, born dead three years after Mary Agnes, and another baby born real soon after that, and not natural. Not normal. Named her Eliza. Molly grieved so, and wouldn't let hardly anybody see that baby, but I seen her, poor little thing, and laid her out myself and then buried her up in the row. Put a rock on her grave the same as Washington and Junius. It had got to where it didn't seem right to let Mister Crabtree carve a stone for every one of them, and Jacky claimed there was no point in naming them anyway. Jacky himself would not take any part in naming them. But Molly insisted, and swore they could not go to Heaven without a name, I don't know where she got that from. She named every one of them.

Anyway, this time it was summer, and Jacky was drunk when we done it. Calvin and Biddle were holding him up by the shoulders on each side.

Looky here what a fine crop of babies I'm a raising, he said. Like cabbages all in a row.

You bastard, said Molly, shaking all over, leaning on me.

Jacky took off with the rolling store the minute we got down off the mountain and did not come back for a month and a half. Molly stayed in the bed for the longest time with her face turned to the wall, and would not even get up when Miss Agnes came to see her. Mister Black sent the Indian up here to inquire about her. But it seemed like it taken her longer and longer to get over it, ever time.

It was to happen once more, now that was Fannie, born Christmas Day 1900, you could not even hardly call that one a baby. And then that was the end of it. Just a row of rock babies up on the mountain like a little stone wall, and a husband with a red bow tie that had took up traveling in a rolling store, and a pretty wife alone on a windy bald. Well she wasn't really alone. Not strictly. For I was there too, right along, and the rest of us, and half the county still coming up here for the dances. But the situation of it, see, was what caught people's fancy, for people are interested in other people's business anyway, and so of course there was a lot of talk.

All kinds of stories started up about the two of them, as stories naturally will, kind of like that old love vine that grows all over Rag Mountain, it comes back every year, and you can't kill it. It was said that Jacky was mean to Miss Molly, as they all called her by then, and that he just liked to run around and never wanted no babies in the first place, and that he beat her to make her lose them. I am here to tell you, this was not true. Jacky loved her. And he mourned those babies something terrible and hollered from mountain to mountain every time she lost one. Other folks said <u>she</u> didn't want them, and done things to herself to get rid of them, and this is the meanest tale of all. I don't know what is wrong with people, to start such stuff as that. I reckon they have not got enough to do, or they have just got to believe that somebody else someplace is worse off than they are.

The only part of them stories that was true was the part about Jacky running around on her, a thing he could not help, it seemed, for he was bound to be a traveling man. I knew it, and it may be that Molly knew it, but I could not tell you that for sure. There's things a person can not bear to know. You can't never tell who somebody will love, you know, nor how fierce they can be about it. What I do believe is that she loved him anyway and could not stand to lose him. If she knowed anything about any other women, such as Ruby Coldiron or Icy Hinshaw, she did not let on. She kept cheerful, and held her head up with a smile. And every time he came home, she was always so glad to see him. She'd run out the door to fling herself on him and hug him, and Jacky he done the same, swinging her around in a big circle and kissing her in front of anybody, even at their age. For we was all getting on a little, you know. But Jacky always thought she hung the moon, and he loved her something terrible.

Now I kept a pretty close track of this myself, for I was watching over her, in my way, same as I always watched over Swannie and Miss Luvenie and Aunt Belle. I had to. Wasn't nobody else up there to do it.

Well, for an instance, I'd take me a walk around the place every night, pretty late, just checking on things. A patrol, you might say. Seeing that all them women was asleep and the horses was put up and the doors was latched and what-not, and I have to tell you, it was not a month before the end that I seen Molly and Jacky out waltzing on their porch in the middle of the night, him singing something into her ear. I couldn't hardly hear him, but she could hear him. And the moon so bright, you could see them as plain as day, swooping all around real graceful-like. I can't tell you how I felt, standing there in the shadows while they was dancing. And this was no time atall before it happened. Whatever that spark was between the two of them, it did not go out, not even after they got done farming that crop of stone babies.

So there is no way that she could have killed him. No sir. That is all talk, just a story, told by fools. I ought to know. I was right there.

Now THERE WAS ONE time not long before it happened that Icy Hinshaw come up to the store herself. It was a dark afternoon with a cold mean kind of a rain. Somebody had drove her up here in a wagon, some man, but I couldn't see who it was for the rain.

Can I help you? Molly went toward her when the bell rang and the door opened.

I come around the counter as quick as I could, as soon as I seen who it was.

She stood just inside and took off her wet scarf and shook her head like an animal so that her red hair sprung up and then settled all around her shoulders. She was wearing an old brown coat, a man's coat, which came down to her shoes. Old shoes, I noticed. Wore out. Now you could never say Icy Hinshaw was a pretty woman, not with that sharp nose and sharp chin and those sunk-down pale gray eyes. White eyes, almost. But there was something about her, for a fact. I remembered back when we was all young, and she'd run with the rest of them, and fiddle like a fool, all night long. She was a match for Jacky, sure enough.

I walked over to where she stood ignoring Molly.

Well Lord, if it ain't old BJ. Icy grinned the lopsided grin I remembered, so that just for a minute, she was beautiful. How are you doing, you old ugly thing?

Just fine, I said. It's good to see you, Icy. What can we do for you?

I'm looking for Jacky, she said.

He's not here, Molly spoke up quite plainly, like a schoolteacher talking to children.

You sure? You sure you ain't got him hid back there someplace? Icy squinted at us.

I am afraid not. Molly smiled at her. He's over in Tennessee with the rolling store.

Either Molly had turned into the best liar in the world, or she truly didn't know a thing. It was a curious moment as they stood there looking at each other in the dim gray light of that dark afternoon.

Maybe I can help you out, Icy, I said. Come on back here with me. I reckon this is something about that timber lease your daddy has up on the mountain, I said, making something up. She followed me back over to the counter where I gave her some money and some all-day suckers for the kids. I knew she would not have come up to Plain View unless she was desperate.

Molly busied herself with sweeping up, and then went over to stand on the cold porch and watch the wagon move across the bald and out of sight.

I came up behind her and put my arms around her waist and my face—my face—in her hair which smelled like lavender. Molly—I started, determined to say it all then, finally.

Oh BJ, she said, breaking my hold. She turned to face me. You know you will always be my best friend in the world. She stood up on tiptoe to kiss me, just once, on the mouth, then pulled back and put her finger to my lips the way you would shush a child, and ran down the steps and across the wagon yard to their house through the rain without her cloak.

So I WAS SURPRISED, to tell you the truth, when she asked me to take her over there right after the funeral which we held ourselves, up on the mountain where we buried him. Preacher Livesay had offered to come and preach, now that is the one Jacky jumped on, but Biddle just grinned and told him, Not hardly. If Jacky didn't want you up here when his baby died, he don't want you up here now. We turned down Felix Boykin and Reverend Graebner from down in Jefferson too. We bury our own, said Uncle Hat, who run the thing, and so we did. Grandaddy Roscoe would have liked it, he believed in the family doing for themselves and staying to themselves. So they tuned up and played "I am a Poor Wayfaring Stranger" and "Angel Band," Jacky's favorites. It was a hot sunny day in August—dog days, it was—with a little wind blowing across the black-eyed Susans and Queen Anne's lace and daisies that grow all around in the burying ground up there, flowers so thick on the ground that you couldn't hardly see some of them little baby rocks there in the row. Big spiky thistles and purple phlox. Orange and black butterflies everyplace.

Molly wore a bright blue satin dress, blue as the sky. Clara had tried to argue her out of it earlier, saying it was not a proper dress to wear to a funeral. I don't care, Molly told her. Jacky bought me this dress, and he liked it, and I am wearing it. Molly could be as stubborn as anybody when she took a mind to. She stood with her straw hat in her hands while the wind pulled at her yellow hair. I swear, she still looked like a girl, at least to me, like the very girl she was when she come riding acrost the bald with Jacky all those years ago.

At the end, she would not leave but stood to watch them shovel on the dirt with no change in her fierce bright face, though those around were crying. It was hard for us to lose Jacky, you know, even if he drove you crazy half the time, you had to love him. You had to enjoy him. It was hard to take in that he was gone for good. It was like somebody had blowed out the sun in the middle of the day. For I had always felt that Jacky was my brother, but closer than a brother. My other half.

BJ, Molly said to me while they was doing it, I don't know if I can stand this. I don't know if I can live without him or not. And the truth was, I didn't know if she could, neither.

Then all of a sudden at the very end Molly ran forward then stumbled and knelt down by the side of the grave, scooping up the dirt with her hand. She pressed it to her mouth and kissed it, then threw it on the grave. Goodbye honey, she said real clear, so all could hear her. Several people gasped. Molly bowed her head. When she got up and walked away, her face was streaked with dirt and tears, and dirt had got on her skirt too.

Now you tell me, you reckon she would have done that if she had killed him?

Molly held up her head looking neither right nor left when we come out into the open and saw that crowd of people stretched across the bald—Lord, it was the awfullest number of folks gathered up there you ever seen, there was even more of them by then than there was when we had left carrying Jacky, or what was left of Jacky, which was not much. We had not let nobody see the body. It must have been three hundred people up there.

Cousin Percy Allgood had not moved a muscle. He was still standing right there where the path goes into the woods, holding his rifle over his shoulder, staring down at the crowd so that no one would have thought of following us. Ernest Dollar and Jubal Smith stood beside him, and General Gentry with tears running down his face.

They took off their hats when we started coming out of the woods one by one, and the whole crowd stopped what they was doing and went silent. I swear, you could hear the wind through the balsams despite of all the people. Then Molly stepped out, and they all went Aaah as one. Some people leapt to their feet while others craned their necks, it seemed they all had to get a good look at her. They had been gathering for days, growing in number ever since the fire. You would think that they had never seen a fire before. Of course they had been going through the ashes with a fine tooth comb too, taking everything they could find that was any use to them, which was precious little.

Will the circle be unbroken bye and bye, Lord, bye and bye?
There's a better home a-waiting, in the sky, Lord, in the sky

Biddle started singing as we walked on down to the store, or where the store used to be, and all took it up as we walked along, stopping to shake hands and hug people, Molly too. Seemed like everybody wanted to touch her, for a fact, and stroke that shiny blue dress, kind of like Christabel used to stroke the edge of her little blanket. Everybody wanted to say they had been there and seen her, I reckon. Everybody we knew, everybody that had traded in the store or danced on top of it. It made me sick, to tell you the truth. This whole thing makes me sick. People can act so nice, bringing food and all, but in the end they are nothing but buzzards. Waiting to pick your bones.

Finally I got her back over there in the house. I thought she would want to lay down, and I was prepared to sit on the porch and keep folks away for the rest of the night if need be, seeing as I couldn't run the store no more. I had thought it all out ahead of time. I was going to guard her from everybody.

But Molly fooled me.

The first thing she done was get a jar of Jacky's corn liquor and pour out two glasses of it. One for her and one for me. She tossed her head back and drank hers down, while I sipped at mine.

BJ, she said, I want you to take me over there.

Over where? I asked.

You know, she said, looking me straight in the eye.

I did. I waited while she changed clothes, and then we slipped out the back door. I made to harness the mule but she said, No, I can ride, so I saddled the horses instead. I want to ride Jupiter, she said. That was Jacky's horse.

We rode out through the woods acrost the old pasture instead of acrost the bald, though several of them seen us, all the same. Still, nobody tried to stop us, though I knowed that Newt Letcher, the sheriff's deputy, was out there someplace in the crowd. He did not make to stop us. On we rode in silence acrost the mountain and headed toward Round Knob, crossing Little

Horse Creek at the mill, with Molly taking a sip every now and then from the silver flask Jacky always carried in his saddlebag.

We went to the Ponder Cove.

I had not been there in years, but I remembered right where it was. For I had gone there too, once upon a time, but that is another story. We reined in our horses at the head of the holler and stood looking down. The sun was fixing to set by then, so every tree and every rock and every thing cast a long, long shadow. It was still sunny up at the top where we were, but already getting dark down there at the house.

The cabin was set down in a little blind holler up against the side of a mountain. I had remembered it as a nice big cabin, but now it looked real small to me, and pitiful. Some kind of a building had fallen down right there at the back, a kitchen or a lean-to or something, and she had just let it lay there. Trash was scattered all around the yard where several children were playing, all of them blond as angels. Their cries barely reached us, like the sound of birds. There was no sign of Icy herself. Molly sucked in her breath, sitting Jacky's horse ramrod straight. A hot little breeze blew over us, lifting her hair. A bigger girl was taking wash off the line and putting it into a basket.

Then all of a sudden, a black and white spotted puppy came tearing around the side of the house and ran circles around the children, who screamed and tried to catch it. They rolled over and over in the weedy grass. The bigger girl carried the basket of wash into the house. After a while she came back out and called to the other children, a baby on her hip. She looked almost too slight to be holding the baby.

All right, Molly said to me without turning in her saddle. Let's go, then.

You don't want to go down there?

No, she said.

We turned and rode back through the gathering dark. She didn't say nothing more about it, so I didn't either. It was past midnight when we got home. We found the sheriff's deputy waiting for us, setting on the porch.

He stood up.

Hello, Newt, I said.

BJ, he said. Then, Mrs. Jarvis.

Then, Will Floyd found a pistol in the ashes this morning.

You know the rest of it.

YES SIR. THE FIRE, then. Again. Ain't you all got ears? How many times have I got to tell it? Yes sir.

It was August 25, 1907.

I had done made my patrol that I was telling you about, and gone to sleep. Well, we was all asleep, I reckon. That is, me and Aunt Belle in our house, and Molly over in her and Jacky's house, Calvin and Clara and them on up the hill. Uncle Hat and Biddle was up in West Virginia playing music. Everybody was asleep. It was a cool calm night in the dark of the moon.

Then Molly woke up out of a sweet dream for no good reason. She said she just laid there with her heart pounding, and wondering what was wrong, and why she had woke up in the first place. She couldn't figure it out. So she got up and walked through the front room and out on the porch and looked over at the store and seen it all lit up from inside by a red fiery glow and she set out running over there barefoot. She said she seen some big white flashes as she was running over there, which I have took to be the oil and kerosene tanks exploding, and then she seen Jacky's wagon, the rolling store, pulled up to the barn back there, and she knowed he had got home sometime in the night, and she got afraid he might be in the store.

She said she just knew he was in there. He often did this, you see, he'd come in late and go over there and get himself something to eat, or drink, you know, and put his money in the register, and such as that. Maybe pick on the banjo for a while to relax himself. Jacky never was one to sleep much of a night, you know. He was like a possum, he'd stay up all night, sleep all day long. So there was not hardly any doubt in Molly's mind where he would be.

She started screaming his name, over the sound of the fire, but the fire was so loud that she knowed he couldn't ever hear her. So she run up onto the burning porch.

It is the sorrow of my life that she did not come to get me first.

But you can't really watch over nobody, you know, no matter how hard you try to do it. You can't get them to do whatever it is that you want, and you can't get them not to do whatever it is that you don't want them to. You might as well not even try.

Yes sir. This is what happened when I woke up. Now I wake up kind of slow-like as a rule, and it taken me a minute to grasp that here was Aunt Belle a standing in my bedroom by my bed in her big old wrapper, whispering to herself and plucking at my covers. I don't know how long she had been standing there when I woke up.

What? I hollered. What is it? I jumped out of the bed and she commenced to picking at my sleeve. Still, I wasn't worried about anything in particular, just kindly mad at old Belle for coming in there and waking me up like that, even though I knowed she was crazy. I wanted to go back to bed but she kept picking at me, and backing up to the door like she was drawing me on or something. Her white hair flowed down past her waist.

All right, I thought. I will go see what this is about.

I no sooner stepped out of the bedroom than I seen the awful orange glow of the fire and smelled the smoke which filled our house too, by that time. I set old Belle down in a chair and told her to stay there, and went back and pulled on my boots and took off running.

I got over there just in time to see the whole front of the store cave in, porch and all, dance floor crashing down and sparks shooting up to the sky like fireworks. I seen the rolling store too, outen the corner of my eye. Uh-oh, I thought as I busted in through the back door that I have gone in and out of all day every day of my life. From where I stood, the front of the store was nothing but a wall of fire coming toward me, but right in front of me there was Molly all bent over and pulling on Jacky's legs, and there was Jacky a laying on his back all bloody and burned looking. His head was laying way over to the side and his mouth was open with blood coming out of it. It wasn't no question that he was dead.

Molly, I hollered, getting over there finally. Molly! I grabbed her from behind. She was trying to say something, but I couldn't hear her. The heat and the noise in there was terrible. You could not breathe. I figured I had about one minute to get her out of there or we would all be dead. I pried her hands off of Jacky and picked her up and carried her out, kicking and screaming, and held her back while the whole store fell in and the rest of it happened. By that time Calvin and Biddle and them had appeared, and it took all of us to hold her back. She didn't want nothing but to go in there and try to get him out, she didn't want nothing but to go to Jacky. To be with him. This is what she kept screaming, I want to be with my Jacky.

I was right there all along, and I am swearing to it. Yes sir. May God strike me dead too if this ain't the truth the whole truth and nothing but the truth, so help me God. Molly would have died too, a trying save Jacky, if we had let her. It was pitiful.

B. J. Jarvis
John Howard Willetts aka "BJ" or "Black Jack" Jarvis

George Ragland
George Carter Ragland, Coroner
Wilkes County, State of North Carolina

Mildred Hash
Mrs. Mildred Cooley Hash
Court Stenographer
Duly sworn, signed, and witnessed this 18th day of November 1907

• • •

MOLLY AND THE TRAVELING MAN
(Traditional Ballad, Ashe County, NC)

Gather round, ye young lovers, and I will tell
How a match struck in Heaven can end up in Hell.
They was two lovers met at a dance one night,
They fell in love by the fire's bright light.
Well, it burned them up, like a fire will do.
Now there ain't nothing left
But ashes and rue.
Lord, Lord,
Ashes and rue.
There ain't nothing left
But ashes and rue.

And a smoking ruin on a mountain top
And a gal who begged her traveling man to stop.
Then she shot him dead, and burnt up the store.
Said, "Honey, you ain't going off traveling no more."
For Jack was bound to wander, like a man will do.
Now there ain't nothing left
But ashes and rue.
Lord, Lord,
Ashes and rue.
There ain't nothing left
But ashes and rue.

She helt up her head, she looked left nor right
Her yellow hair hung down, and her eyes shone bright.
She come walking down the mountain so fancy and so free
And that big crowd it parted like the sea.
Lord, Lord,

That big crowd it parted like the sea.
She was all dressed up in satin blue.
Now there ain't nothing left
But ashes and rue.

Now the wind blows cold on that mountain so drear
For pretty Molly is gone far away from here.
And you can't buy love, nor hear the banjo ring
For the general store ain't selling anything.
Lord, Lord,
It's true. That store ain't selling nothing
But ashes and rue.

Another Country

Agate Hill

Dear Diary,

I can't remember anything about the weeks between the night of the fire—August 25, 1907—and the day before my coroner's inquest, which finally took place in Wilkesboro, not Jefferson, there being so much talk about it at the time.

It was almost Thanksgiving.

I had been held at the Wilkesboro jail for nearly three months, and frankly I had come to cherish the confines of my cell, ten by twelve feet, the single low hard bed, the dim hanging bulb which swung slightly on its chain through the still air every now and then for no good reason, the old green iron washstand in the corner, the high slitted window where I could glimpse a piece of the changing sky. It was all I could stand to see. I would not go out for exercise. Nor would I allow myself to be visited by the slimy pockmarked preacher or the fat old righteous preacher they sent in to see me, either one. I do not have time for preachers, I told them all, and turned my face to the wall.

I was too busy remembering Jacky, memorizing him, every inch of his body, every expression on his face, the way he threw his head back when he laughed, how his thumbs were double-jointed, the one-sided grin that always asked a question, the way he stared at me when he wanted me to come to him, his tawny eyes turning darker and darker. He had a rosy birthmark on his arm in the shape of the letter C, or a sickle moon. He was so skinny that I could feel his shoulder bones like folded wings, his hip bones like white china door knobs so close up underneath the skin it was scary. And the skin was so smooth right there, over his hip bones, smooth as a baby's, while over most of his body was spread a curly tangle of gold hair. I took him inch by inch, rib by rib, bone by bone. I remembered everything.

Memorizing Jacky took up all the time I had.

The jailor, Odell Cartwright, was a huge gruff man with a creaking gait and hair growing out of his nose. He walked heavily, his legs now stretched out straight in front of him like trees while he sat in a metal rolling chair looking at me as he ate cold fried chicken, one piece after another, which Martha Fickling had brought for me along with some clothes for my hearing. He had not let me see her. Odell Cartwright threw the bones in a pile on the floor where Tom Bright, the trusty, would have to pick them up later. Odell Cartwright liked to roll his chair over in front of my cell and sit there watching me, as if I were an animal at a zoo, and you know what? I didn't even care. I turned my face to the wall and memorized Jacky. Once or twice I had had to use the pot while Odell Cartwright was watching me. I looked him in the eye while I was doing it.

"Mrs. Cartwright will bath you off tomorry," he said to me—he always called his wife Mrs. Cartwright—"and then myself and some others will escort you over to the courthouse. They have finally got up a jury of six, by the hardest, the way I hear it. But you'd just as soon stay here now, wouldn't you? unless I miss my guess."

I nodded, sitting on my bed, surprised, for in general, Odell Cartwright was as dumb as a post.

"Well, you can't," he said. "Yer time is up, yer rent is due. Now I believe you done it, just fer the record, but I don't give a damn whether you done it or not. You could of done it, I'll say that, as you are a hard un, and you could of made yer time here a lot more pleasurable too, if you was not so high and mighty."

I looked up at my window while he finished eating the chicken and threw the last bone through the bars and out on the floor at my feet.

That night I scarcely slept but listened to my heart beating louder and louder in the prison cage of my ribs all night long. The moon was full. It shone white as day in the slit of my window for one half hour soon before dawn and then was gone from view. In spite of myself, I felt my body stirring, waking up. I felt a slow deep agitation.

Silent Mrs. Cartwright came for me at first light and led me to the wash-room where she had filled the tub with water hot enough that I gasped when she poured a panful of it over my head. I scrubbed myself with the hard old soap. It felt wonderful. "Thank you," I said.

She handed me the scratchy towel. "I wisht I got to go too." She bit her lip, and turned her narrow face away.

"Why, I'm sure you wouldn't want to go to court!" I said.

"I would ruther go anyplace atall than stay here with Mister Cartwright," she blurted out, then looked behind herself fearfully.

"But you could leave," I said, pulling on my underthings. "You could, Mrs. Cartwright. You're not in jail."

She snaked out a thin hand to pinch me suddenly, high up on the thigh where I could show no one. It hurt like blazes. "Bitch," she said. "You don't know nothing."

And in truth I knew only one thing as they cuffed my hands together and led me to the door. Jacky's gone, fare thee well, Jacky's gone. It came as a tune running through my head, Jacky on banjo. I wore the black suit and the white ironed blouse which Martha had brought me, my damp hair held back with two tortoiseshell combs she had stuck in the skirt pocket. I did not have a hat.

Though I had pulled up the hood of my old blue cloak, I gasped when they opened the door and the chilly wind hit me full in the face, bringing with it the smell of burning leaves which seemed to go straight into my body. November! Suddenly the world was all around me, bright and sharp. The sun shone, the wind blew. Red and yellow leaves flew past. They hustled me into a carriage.

The rest of that day is like a dream to me now, vivid disconnected moments, bright shiny bits of time jumbled together like the casket of mica chips here in this old box of phenomena at my feet.

First, the yellow blowing day itself. The sharp smell of wood smoke in the air. It made me think of all the fires we made in that stove at the Bobcat School, and the long walk over there from Chattie's on the Indian Trail with its quiet carpet of fallen leaves, the mountain laurel pressing close and green on either side.

But who was the girl who did that? I wondered. That girl who had not yet met Jacky.

I saw Mrs. Cartwright's lean dark face in the window as they drove me away.

It took only minutes to get there, or so it seemed, as we passed through the unreal town with its painted houses and busy people who stopped to gawk and point and stare as we went by.

"Standing room only," announced a man in the jostling crowd on the courthouse lawn when we arrived. A woman had set up a stand, selling sandwiches.

"Just look straight ahead, mam," the young deputy said, holding my elbow, and I did, all the way up the shallow scooped courthouse steps worn down in the center by thousands of feet before me. *And am I so different?* I thought, and knew that I was not. *Jacky's gone, fare thee well* played on in my mind.

Then the arch of the entrance, the sudden chill and dimness inside, the long narrow corridor, the echoing marble floor, the thick door, then the courtroom itself with its blue walls, blue as a robin's egg, the many little faces all turned to me like so many moons. The jury sat up in the front like a choir. We went in, and a murmuring rustle swept across the courtroom like a breeze.

The young deputy walked me over to the stand. "Oyez, oyez, oyez," said a man in a deep voice, and it began, and they swore me in and there was a lot of talking I did not hear, for just then I saw dear Agnes, wearing the close brown felt hat I knew so well, sitting in the second row with Cicero Todd, his hair plastered down unnaturally on either side of his uneven part and hanging into his rough red face. Just then Martha Fickling burst through the closed doors at the back of the crowded courtroom, past the deputy, nodding to everybody, and gave a great sigh as she took her seat and blew me a kiss. She put her finger under her chin and jerked her head up in a way that meant, Buck up, honey! Never let the bastards get you down. I had heard her say these words before, and found myself grinning back at her, the first time I had smiled in months, I believe. It made my face hurt. It caused a stir in the courtroom. But I didn't care—it felt good to smile. It felt like me.

Felix Boykin sat on Agnes's other side. Why, Felix is old! I thought. Somehow he had gotten so old. His old wife sat beside him.

But the coroner was younger than I would have expected, a thin pale man with a gleaming white forehead and wisps of blondish hair straggling way down over his collar. He bent low over the papers arranged before him, lost in his black robe. When he looked up, his eyes were as big as lakes behind the thick lenses of his gold framed glasses, with dark circles beneath them. He was very serious, his mouth pinched together as if in pain. Perhaps he was in pain. He seemed years older than he was, I thought, and this made me feel a kind of kinship with him suddenly, for ever since the fire, I had felt as old as the world.

Coroner Ragland called the court to order in a slow voice with an accent from the other side of the state, beyond the mountains. "Ladies, gentlemen, officers of the court and members of the inquest jury," he began, "I have summoned you here today to make inquiry as to the circumstances of the death of Jack Wesley Jarvis and to call witnesses as necessary to determine these circumstances, an affadavit having been duly filed by the Sheriff's Office of Ashe County, indicating blame. If it appears that the deceased was slain, or came to his death in such a manner as to indicate any person or persons guilty of a crime in connection with the said death, then this inquiry shall ascertain who was guilty, either as principal or accessory, or otherwise; and the exact cause and manner of the death. Whenever in such investigations it shall appear that any person or persons are culpable in the matter of such death, I shall forthwith issue my warrant—"

By then my eyes had found my dear ones, my family from up on Plain View seated all together in a row halfway back. They had come a long way to be here. How I ached to jump up and run across the courtroom and hug each one! How much Biddle looked like Jacky, it stopped my heart, how much I wanted Jacky to pick me up and swing me around the way he did whenever he came back home with the rolling store. <u>Jacky's gone, one more time, Jacky's gone.</u>

"Therefore we shall hear and examine any and all witnesses," the young coroner concluded. His voice was soft and measured.

And so it began, with Newt Letcher called up first to the stand, bent over to one side and shifty-looking as ever—Jacky used to say he moved "slaunch-ways"—yet all spruced up in his brown uniform, so closely shaved that his jaw was bleeding, grinning his sly one-sided grin and cutting his eyes over at me as if embarrassed. Jacky had never liked him.

Coroner Ragland asked Newt Letcher some questions which he answered one by one while I stared at all the Jarvises from Plain View, drinking them in with my eyes. Yet it was strange. They seemed utterly changed to me, sitting there. They looked like people in an old photograph, all dressed up in the way people dress up when the photographer is coming, in clothes they would never normally wear. They looked so country—Calvin in his high stiff collar and shiny brown suit, Clara with her plain lined face and hair pulled back like an old granny woman, Uncle Hat and Uncle Solomon like engravings from another century. Even Betsy, jolly Betsy, looked stiff and old fashioned as a doll, bright red spots of color on her fat cheeks, a silly lace collar foaming up under her chin. Thank goodness they had not brought Belle! Though I caught myself smiling to imagine Belle in that courtroom, preening and looking all around to see what men might be in love with her now. I tried to catch Biddle's eye, but could not for he looked straight ahead, with his jaw set in a way that almost made me cry, it was so familiar, like Jacky when he took a powerful notion to do something.

"Mrs. Jarvis," the coroner was saying.

Finally I caught Clara's eye, dear Clara, but to my surprise she turned red and looked down and would not look back up at me. I felt suddenly as if years had passed, not months, and they truly were people in another century, beyond some great divide.

"Have you ever seen this weapon before, Mrs. Jarvis?" The coroner leaned forward.

There it sat on the table, gleaming dully, drawing all eyes, its old oak handle charred black.

"Mrs. Jarvis?"

"Well, of course I have! I saw it every day," I said in a way that somehow occasioned laughter and did not advance my cause. "This is the pistol we kept underneath the counter at the store, anybody can tell you that. I imagine BJ has told you that already. Where is BJ anyway?" I looked all around.

People murmured throughout the courtroom.

The coroner tapped his gavel and said, "Order in the court. Now Mrs. Jarvis," he went on in his kindly, pained way, "Our purpose at this time is simply to establish what happened on the night in question, August 25, the night of the fire, and whether there is any proof of your probable guilt in a capital crime."

"That is ridiculous," I heard myself say, and then there was a lot of noise, and then several people came forward to testify that they had heard shots on the night of the fire and that they had seen the body, Jacky's body, and that he had not been burned to death but shot in the neck at close range.

Mrs. Carmel Reece, whose son Dean I had taught at the storehouse school, went on and on about this until I thought I would explode or go crazy. "The entire side of his head was gone," she said, "the entire side." She said some more things. She was all dressed up for the occasion in a fancy ecru lace blouse caught at the neck with a cameo pin featuring a cameo lady in profile so calm, so elegant, suddenly I would have given anything to be her, on her deep rose oval stone, surrounded by filigree.

But you can't be a cameo lady if you give your heart away, ran through my mind as a tune.

To this day, I remember that cameo pin better than anything else at my hearing.

I could not bear for them to talk about Jacky's body, and after a while I simply could not hear it though others were called, people I had waited upon at the store all these years, such as old Dwight Mahaffey who always came up short, buying medicine for his wife, and Mrs. Atkinson who drank vanilla.

Nobody looked at me except for Coroner Ragland, who looked at me steadily.

Finally they called BJ.

A hidden door in the other side of the wooden wall opened and there he was.

Before I knew it, I had jumped up and run halfway across the floor, I was so glad to see him. The deputies caught me, the judge called the court to order, they brought me back.

"You must sit down in order for Mr. Jarvis to testify, do you understand?" Coroner Ragland leaned forward to fix me with his huge pale eyes.

I knew that he was trying to help me.

"Yes, sir," I said.

But there was BJ, dear BJ, after so long, limping out in a badly fitting blue-striped suit—I could not imagine where he had gotten it—and a boiled white shirt, and a red bow tie, tied clumsily. One of Jacky's bow ties, I realized, understanding in the same moment that BJ must have gone into our house to get it, for Jacky kept all his ties in a willow basket on top of the chest. Then I felt so strange and agitated that I thought I would faint dead away or blow up in spontaneous combustion, as in Dickens, though I knew I must do nothing of the kind. For I understood what it cost BJ to dress up in a boiled white shirt and appear in a public court of law with his misshapen raspberry face on display before everyone. He placed his poor hand on the Bible.

"John Howard Willetts, do you swear to tell the truth, the whole truth, and nothing but the truth, so help you God?" the clerk asked.

"I do," BJ said in a surprisingly strong voice, staring at me, and I smiled back at him though the tears sprang into my eyes as I remembered all the hours we had spent in the store together. Why, I had probably spent as much time with BJ as I did with Jacky! But I remembered too how BJ had always hung back from the door, and nodded, and pointed, so as not to have to answer our customers.

I could never have imagined him here before all these people.

"Now go back, and start at the beginning," the coroner said.

Everyone leaned forward as BJ began to speak in his halting way, in bursts with long pauses between them. The coroner nodded, listening as if he had all the time in the world, asking a question from time to time. Sometimes they were surprising questions. Don't ask him that! I wanted to scream at the coroner, and You don't have to answer that! You don't have to tell him everything.

But of course I could not interrupt.

It was all beyond me now as BJ went on and on, laying bare his poor soul, as if he had been waiting for a chance to do so. Perhaps he had. He looked straight at me all the while though I had to look away from time to time, I couldn't stand it. I had known yet not known these things. I listened with a sinking, bursting heart, and a growing knowledge that soon I would go free and that then there would be no going back from any of it. I felt the walls of my cell close back around me, iron bars of love, and finally I bowed my head and sat waiting.

The sheriff's men took me straight back to Jefferson, turning me over to Willard Owens when we arrived. "Welcome home, Molly," old Willard said, helping me down the steps onto the wooden platform well after midnight. My knees nearly buckled out from under me. But there was Biddle, waiting with the wagon, sound asleep. It was coming on toward morning when we finally got home.

"Just leave my bag on the porch," I said, and watched him disappear into darkness across the scarred field which had been the store.

I sat down in my rocking chair—that same chair where once I had rocked my Christabel to feed her, years ago. She made a little sighing, gurgling sound as she nursed. I could still feel the steady pull of her mouth on my nipple, the sweet release in my breasts as the milk came down. There is nothing like that in the world. I thought of my other babies, too, Spencer and Junius and Mary Agnes and the rest, their sweet shallow breath and little curled fingers and rosy feet, all of them up on the mountain. Somehow

I could not go inside. I sat there chilled to the bone as dawn came on. First I could see the jagged outline of Three Top Mountain against the silver sky. Then all the dried gourds we'd hung from that crosspole out front, for purple martins. My rambler rose which had grown every whichaway all over the porch rail with no one here to cut it back, the roses now dead on the vine. The old swing teetering in the still cold air as if somebody had just got up from it, the poker table Calvin made, the cane-bottom chairs we used to clear away at the drop of a hat for dancing. The floorboards were worn down slick and silvery smooth by dancing. One of Jacky's cigarettes still lay on that old stump stool. He liked to sit tipped way back in the wicker chair with his feet up on the rail, barefooted, like a kid. You'll fall, I said. You'll fall, but he never did.

Jacky's gone, far from home, Jacky's gone. His banjo rang out in the morning air.

A rooster crowed. Smoke rose in a fine wavy line from Biddle and Betsy's chimney so I knew she was up, getting breakfast for the children, pouring milk from the old blue pitcher into their little cups. A door slammed, the rooster crowed again. The puffy clouds over top of the mountain turned red, then pink, and then yellow rays shot out from behind them like spokes on a wheel, like children coloring with crayons. The sun stretched across the long valley to touch the steps, then the rail, then my foot. A wagon made its slow way across the bald. "Hello there, Miss Molly," called old Mister Davenport. "Welcome home."

Home, I thought. Is that it?

I stood up and went inside where I saw that they had made me a fire which was almost gone. I stirred up the ashes and put a log on, then walked around in my cloak still shivering. Nothing had changed. I felt like we had never left, Jacky and me, like the story of the Three Bears which my schoolchildren had always loved. Jacky's prize banjos still hung on the wall, close to a dozen of them, including that old cheese box banjo and the coon dog banjo and the longneck gourd banjo that used to belong to Mister Thompson. Jacky's old guitar lay across the red-flowered chair in the bedroom, as if he had just put it down for a minute. His boots still stood by the bed, those hand-tooled black leather boots from Texas which I always loved, with the silver stars on the toes. Girl boots, Roscoe used to kid him, but they were not. His buckskin jacket hung on its peg by the door. A pile of his dirty shirts lay at the foot of the bed still waiting for me to wash them, fancy shirts, most of them, with satin piping and pearl buttons and neck studs and such as that. Jacky loved shirts. They all used to kid him about his shirts, he had so many. I leaned down and grabbed them up and sat on the bed and brought them up to my face and breathed him in, tobacco and cologne and whisky and sweat, a man will sweat out a shirt when he plays music all night long. I breathed him in, then fell back upon the bed holding the shirts to my face remembering all the nights that I had lain with him here and on the old rag rug in front of the fire and on the kitchen floor, I didn't care, and on a pallet on the porch and out on a quilt in the yard underneath the full moon and right out on the bald in the long sweet grass on the long slow curve of the earth itself. I knew I would never wash those shirts again. My fancy man. Who had ever thought I'd have a fancy man? but I had had him. I had. Jacky's gone, one more time, Jacky's gone.

There sat the basket on top of the dresser—red bow ties for the rolling store, string ties for playing music. Three unopened packs of Camel cigarettes, loose change, a buckeye for luck. Too bad he had left it behind. I lay on the bed with the yellow satin shirt against my face.

"Molly? Molly?" It was Clara and Betsy at the door, then in the kitchen, then I got up and went in and hugged them. Clara had brought me some of her apple stack cake which I love. "Why here now, let me make you some coffee to go with that," Betsy said, and so she did, and we all sat down and had some, and it was good, but it was not the same. Something had happened while I was in jail, something which nobody had expected or caused or meant to happen. The family had closed up again, the way they did, and I wasn't in it anymore. I had felt this in court but knew it now, sitting there in that kitchen, though they didn't know it yet, chattering like jaybirds to fill the time and distance between us. They said that Biddle and Calvin were going to rebuild the store, that Biddle had gotten a bank loan to do it, though

Uncle Hat had pitched a fit, as the family had never believed in bank loans. Betsy said that old Hat ought to think about which side his bread was buttered on, in her opinion.

By the time they left, I was exhausted. I put my forehead down on the cold slick enamel of the kitchen table and kept it there until I knew what I must do.

I got up and washed my face and put my hair up again and sat down in the big plaid armchair before the fire, Grandaddy Roscoe's old chair. Here Jacky had sat with Christabel on his knee playing that game she loved so much. "This is the way the lady rides," he'd start out jiggling her ever so gently, "trit, trot, trit, trot. This is the way the gentleman rides, boogety boogety boo," a little harder so that she'd start giggling, and harder still until "THIS IS THE WAY THE ROWDY BOY RIDES, GALLOPING, GALLOPING, GALLOP!" with Christabel bouncing high and waving her hands, collapsed in delight.

"Oh Jacky, that's too rough," I always said, and he always said, "Now goddamnit Molly, she loves it"—as she did—as she loved it when he tossed her way up in the air and caught her, a thing I could never stand to watch.

It seemed to me that I could hear her happy cries yet, up in the dark eaves of the loft. I put some more logs on the fire which blazed up crackling. I remembered how she used to sit on the old rag rug with her little clothespin dolls, walking them to and fro, putting them to bed in their shoe box house.

Though I had not yet been to bed myself, I felt as wide awake as I have ever been, looking all around my house which was not mine really, any more than it had ever been ours, any more than a person can lay claim to any place, for we are only passing through.

I sat there to wait for BJ, who was not long in coming. I watched him through the window, limping across the hill, picking his way through all the rubble. Gone was the white shirt, Jacky's red bowtie, the ill-fitting suit. Here was my own sweet BJ back again in his worn striped overhauls and old blue shirt and woolsey jacket, the same black hat jammed down on his head. First came his dragging step on the porch, then his red face in the wavy window. He saw me and froze. His face looked as I had never seen it, all lit up from within, and hopeful. A momentous thing had occurred. BJ had spoken, and it was clear that he was prepared to speak more.

I stood up.

He came in the door and stood there holding his hat, stopped by the look on my face, I guess, for I have never been able to pretend anything. After a minute he looked down, twisting the hat in his hands.

"Thank you, BJ," I said. I meant this from the bottom of my heart.

He nodded, still looking down. "It wasn't nothing," he said.

"It was," I said. "And I have one more favor to ask you," for suddenly I saw little Christabel running toward me across the rug, as in life, her plump arms outstretched, her face like a flower with its happy smile. She grabbed my skirt and hugged me so hard that I almost fell.

It came to me in that moment.

"BJ," I said, "I can't live here anymore, not after all that has happened. So I want you to promise me something. I want you to bring Icy and the children up here, and give them this house, and take care of them, for they are Jacky's. They are yours. Will you do that for me?"

He nodded, his Adam's apple moved up and down. He pulled the hat way down on his head, the way he always wore it, and left, shutting the door softly behind him.

Henry appeared three days later.

"Mrs. Jarvis." He inclined his head when I opened the door.

"Call me <u>Molly</u>," I corrected him, putting my hand out. "How are you, Henry?" He had not really changed, only shrunk and hardened somehow, as if carved from wood. He was dressed in a more regular fashion than before, brown pants and a woolen coat, his hair pulled back into a clasp beneath a black hat with a silver band that looked as if it might have belonged to Mister Black.

"And how is Mister Black?" I asked. It had occurred to me that I might move into his cabin at Gum Branch if I didn't move down to Jefferson. No one had used that cabin for years.

"He is not well." Henry's accent would be hard to place. He reached into his coat, handed me a plain white sealed envelope, then went to the end of the porch and stood looking out across the gap while I read the short note. Mister Black's familiar hand had grown crimped and shaky. He said that he had followed my situation with interest, and was pleased that justice had been served, and that he wished me well. He said that he knew it must have been an ordeal. He said he hoped it would not be an unwelcome imposition if he offered me some material assistance at this time, which Henry would be prepared to provide upon my request. The note was signed <u>Your faithful servant, Simon Black, Agate Hill, North Carolina.</u>

"Agate Hill!" I ran over to Henry. "What does he mean, Agate Hill?"

He smiled, his pointed teeth now dulled somewhat. Henry has a nice smile, actually, in spite of them. "Mister Black has owned Agate Hill ever since your departure. He purchased it for Mrs. Hall, feeling that your Uncle Junius would not want his wife and his unborn child to be cast out into such an uncertain future."

"Selena!" I cried. Everything tipped and whirled around me. "But did she stay on, then? Did she live there, with that—that—Nicky Eck?" I had never said his name before. "We heard that Agate Hill had been sold. Does she live there still?"

"Oh no. Mrs. Hall had a restless soul, as you may recall."

I laughed. "That's one way of putting it," I said. "But Mister Black is there now? And he is ill, you said?"

"Yes." Henry looked very grave. "He is there now. He took it in mind to come, in fact he insisted on coming, though it is not a place fit for a gentleman such as himself—or indeed, for anybody."

I took a deep breath of the cold mountain air—the air up there on Plain

View is the best in the world, Jacky always said. "Henry, have you got that money handy?"

"Yes, Mrs. Jarvis."

"<u>Molly</u>," I said. "Well, where is it?"

He withdrew a pouch from inside his coat—how well I remembered those pouches of his.

"I need it all," I said.

He took the sling off his neck and handed it to me.

"Thank you," I said. "Now come inside and wait while I pack up a few things, because I'm going back with you. I want to see Mister Black, and I want to visit Agate Hill again."

Henry's eyes flickered. "That will not be necessary, Mrs. Jarvis," he said. "In fact, it would be unwise. It is not a situation for a lady's visit."

I had to laugh. "I am not a lady," I said, "in spite of everything your master did to turn me into one. And now that I have gone through the fire, I believe I can do whatever I want."

This had just occurred to me. I have lived by it ever since.

"As you wish."

I sat Henry down and gave him some coffee and the last of the apple stack cake. I packed some clothes. I put the leather pouch with the money and a note for BJ in the middle of the kitchen table with a rock on top, so they would notice.

As we left, I twisted around on the carriage seat to look back just before we disappeared into the trees, for I have always fancied that I could see the whole wide curve of the earth at that moment, stretching across the bald. There it was. It was enough. I thought of my stone babies upon their mountain, and Jacky in his grave. The family would buy a stone for Jacky later, Calvin and Biddle would see to it, I knew, though I doubted that it would keep him put, for he was a traveling man. I had to smile. I remembered how, as a girl, I thought that I could not leave Agate Hill, that I could not leave my ghosts. Now I understood that love does not reside in places, neither in the Capulets' tomb nor the dales of Arcady nor the Kingdom by the Sea nor in any of those other poems that Mary White and I read so long ago, love lives not in places nor even bodies but in the spaces between them, the long and lovely sweep of air and sky, and in the living heart and memory until that is gone too, and we are all of us wanderers, as we have always been, upon the earth. I was free to go.

My heart beat like a hammer in my chest as we started up Agate Hill from the river on the last long leg of our journey. It was a cold, sunny late afternoon. I had insisted upon riding up on the seat next to Henry, so I could see better. Everything looked familiar and not familiar—all the fields entirely overgrown now so that the lane ran along through a thick woods like a wall on either side. The cedar grove was enormous, a pointy fairy tale forest like an immense dark pine-scented cathedral inside, with only a few dim rays of sunshine piercing the roof of branches.

"A person could live in here," I said to Henry, and he agreed. We had become very companionable during our journey, though as always he kept a certain distance.

We rode out blinking into the sunlight again. The big barn had fallen in upon itself into a pile of boards. The gin and the sawmill had disappeared entirely into a tangle of briers. The circle was all but overgrown with weeds. To my surprise, the house itself looked much smaller than I remembered, not a grand house at all but an ancient farmstead set upon its windswept ridge in the last of the sun, the brow of the hill rising behind it. My Indian Rock would still be warm from the sun. I was dying to run up there.

"Now you understand." Henry turned to me. "Agate Hill is almost gone."

"Why did he come, then?"

Henry smiled. "You will see."

No dogs barked, no one ran out as we approached. The urns had toppled and broken. "Are there no servants, then?" I asked, and Henry bared his pointed smile again. "You forget. I am the servant." He climbed down and tied the horses to the old iron ring.

I couldn't wait. I jumped down from the carriage and ran up on the piazza. The door gave inward groaning at my touch. "Mister Black!" I called into the dim and dusty hall, filled with its jumble of boxes and boots and old furniture and God knows what all, its staircase curving into the gloom above. "Mister Black!"

"Henry?" the low voice came from the middle room, Uncle Junius's old study.

I opened the door. Simon Black stood up slowly from the chair closest to the hearth where he had been sitting. His book slipped down to the floor. Despite Henry's dire predictions, he did not look much changed to me, wearing a loose white gaucho shirt and black trousers and carpet slippers, though I suppose I had never seen him before without those boots. His white hair flowed down to his shoulders, his white brows made a single formidable line across his forehead. He rubbed the back of his hand across his eyes. I was filled with a deep, thudding sense of anticipation. Well, I thought. I have been waiting for this. It was the last thing left to happen to me.

"Alice," he whispered.

"No. It is Molly," I said. "Her daughter."

"Of course. Mrs. Jarvis," he said, holding out his arms in the white flowing shirt, an entirely unexpected gesture. He looked like a saint in a stained-glass window. "Welcome. I had hoped to see you again."

"Thank you," I said. "I would have come sooner, if I had known. I don't believe that I have ever thanked you properly for what you have done for me over the years. For us," I said, meaning Jacky and everyone up at Plain View.

"It has been my pleasure," he said, "as well as my obligation. Fulfilling an obligation is the greatest pleasure a man like myself can take, so it is I who should be thanking you." This speech seemed to exhaust him, but before I could suggest that he sit back down, an extraordinary little personage darted past me and slipped under Simon Black's shoulder to support him.

At first I thought it was a girl, then a boy—then a child—then with a start I realized it was a grown man, though it was very hard to tell. He was quite short in stature, with short arms and stocky legs, like a baby doll or a gingerbread man. He had an unusually large round head covered all over by dark curls, and a round swarthy face with round eyes veiled by a kind of white film, like cotton. His eyes were shocking.

"Why, who in the world is this?" I cried—and he turned his head toward me, cocking it like a robin, the huge white eyes unblinking. I realized he was blind. Later I would learn that he is not totally blind, for he can see light, and distinguish movement. His hearing is extraordinary. That day, the day of my arrival, he wore muddy boots—the entire floor was muddy—and torn work jeans and Uncle Junius's old burgundy velvet smoking jacket which hung down to his knees.

"This is my little man," Simon Black said, my old fear of him falling away entirely in that instant.

"But who is he?" I asked.

"Selena's son. He has lived on this place all his life. His name is Juney."

"For Junius?" I asked.

"His full name is Solomon Junius Hall," Simon Black said, and Juney smiled at the sound of his name, a smile of incredible sweetness, like a small child. Now I remembered Selena's yellow vomit in the snow, how she had said, "You will have one yourself sometime," and how small her baby was, and how he had cried and cried.

I stepped closer.

"Hello Juney," I said. "I am Molly."

"Molly," he said like a parrot, still smiling, his blank eyes trained upon my face.

"Molly Petree," I said.

"Molly Petree," he said, then ran his hands quickly all over my face with the lightest skittering touch, like a hummingbird. I found myself closing my eyes, just for a second, giving myself over to it. I swayed and nearly fell. I felt entirely refreshed when I came back to myself.

"How long will you be with us, then? I am afraid that our accommodations—" Simon Black said, and I saw with a start that tears stood in his eyes. "That is, we have no accommodations. We are here only briefly. But pardon me, you must be exhausted. I am not sure what we have in the way of food, either—"

"Oh, nevermind." I took off my cloak. "I am a pretty fair cook myself. Surely we will find something. Henry, take my bag up wherever you can find a bed in one piece. And Juney, you come with me."

He turned his sweet radiant face back and forth between us in a question.

"To the kitchen," I said. "You will show me," and Simon Black, now settled again in his chair, gave him a little shove.

Thus we went out, me with my hand on Juney's solid shoulder, fingering the soft velvet, through the dark cold passage to a tiny ramshackle kitchen, indescribably filthy and cluttered, which had been built onto the platform at the back of the house. Whatever Henry's skills might be as a servant, apparently they did not extend to kitchen work. Liddy's old kitchen house stood abandoned in the back, its door ajar.

"Wood," I said to Juney, who showed me the woodbox. I started stuffing sticks into the stove. I pulled open a pantry door at random. "Where is—" I turned to ask Juney, but he had disappeared. I wondered—as I have often wondered since—if I would ever see him again. I found a pan, a pile of china plates, a big wooden bowl, two crystal goblets, and an old tin cup. Then suddenly there was Juney balancing a slab of bacon, a cabbage with the dirt still attached, and an apple pie, grinning his big grin. It was a perfect apple pie. I couldn't imagine where he had gotten it. It was as if he had produced it out of thin air, by magic. I clapped my hands. "Perfect!" I said. "This is wonderful!"

Juney put everything down on the table, and clapped his hands too.

• • •

May 2, 1927

That was twenty years ago, Dear Diary.

Are you surprised, old friend?

I'm still here, like Aunt Mitty who came to take supper with Mama Marie and never left, and for the same reason. Need is a powerful thing for a woman, maybe the most powerful thing that there is.

I have waited twenty years to come back into this cubbyhole, years which have passed in the twinkling of an eye, as in the Bible. But now the time has come for me to tell the rest of the story, for it is a love story too, as are all stories, in the end.

The time has come, and Juney knows it too, though we do not speak of these things.

The old green dress which hides the entrance to this cubbyhole fell apart at my touch—disintegrated! Oh now it is certainly time. I ducked through the low door feeling that I too might explode. Yet it was not as hard as you might think for I am such a little old woman now. I have shrunk to the size of a child again, I can still sit here in my fairy tale chair, and you may take Willie's little white chair, which you will remember. I had another friend too once, her name was Mary White, do you recall? But she is gone now, off into the world of light. Oh it was all so long ago. And yet here is that bad girl Molly stuck forever in this notebook, bursting from its pages. I thought I would not know her anymore, and yet I find that I am her, just as wild and full of spite and longing as ever, as I still am. For an old woman is like a child, but more than a child, for I know what I know yet I feel exactly the same in my heart. These young girls don't know that, do they? It would surprise them. But that thing does not wear out, I could tell them. I could tell those girls a thing or two.

Oh I know what they say about me in town. I know I am old and sick. Yet inside I am just the same and I'll swear it, still crazy with love and pain, still wanting who knows what. I am not sure whatever happened to that smart girl in between, the one who kept the Bobcat School and worked at the store wrapping parcels and adding up sums in her head. It seems like only yesterday that she walked out the door and got lost someplace down that old Indian trail.

But I would do it all again, every bit of it, I would lose him again just to have him again for an hour, for a minute, for even a second. I would do it all again just to see his face. My demon lover   my Jacky boy   my husband   sometimes I think I dreamed you up.

Oh Molly Petree, who were you? Strange and willful child

This is the box of her life

This is her diary

In fact everything in this cubbyhole is exactly the same, like the village in the paperweight Ben Valiant gave me so long ago, I don't know where that has got to now. I believe I left it at Chattie's house up on Bobcat. But here is the box containing our collection of phenomena, which you may recall—the man doll Robert E. Lee still vanquished, tossed in a heap with Margaret and Fleur those beautiful brides, all vanquished, and so long dead. The photograph of Simon Black (how young he was!) and my father (how handsome!) gone off to war. The filigree casket of mica chips, three poetry books, two catechisms, the green liqueur glass from Venice, my mother's silver hairbrush. A sizable number of animal bones, especially jawbones, skulls, and feet, though I gave the Yankee hand to Mary White, and where is it now? Ensconced in the world of light.

There is one new addition to this box of phenomena which you have not yet seen. Here. Isn't it heavy, surprisingly heavy? It is a heart-shaped stirrup forged by Simon Black for my mother, Alice Heart, years ago at Perdido, when they were about ten years old. Children. They were just children. I know all about it now. I know the whole story of Simon Black.

For soon after my return to Agate Hill, I woke up in the night and went down to lie beside him, a thing I could never have imagined doing in all my life. Yet I found there an indescribable sweetness and peace, a sort of joy, and I stayed with him until his death, flesh to flesh, bone to bone, pressing my body against his, the whole long fragile length of him, for it meant nothing now, and everything—it was the least that I could do. Sometimes I read poetry aloud from Uncle Junius's books, Shakespeare and Robert Burns and Byron and Wordsworth, and Simon Black seemed to like this, the sound of the words, though he was not an educated man. Henry and Juney took care of us. At the end, I don't believe Simon Black knew who I was, and I am not sure I knew who I was either.

I lay beside him as he died, early on a midsummer morning. First light, the birds going wild in the trees. He had lain unconscious for several days. The perfume of Fannie's Aurora rose filled the room, for it was blooming just outside the open window. I had noted it as I woke and slept and woke and slept throughout that whole long night, for I slept lightly then, my ear pressed against the bony cage of his ribs. The evening star still hung in the sky when I woke that last time to realize that Simon had slipped away. I lay beside him while the evening star faded and the yard filled with sunshine slanting in our window and across the bed. What a man he was. I lay beside him while all the changes took place, his ravaged body cooling, his thin arm growing stiff across my breast. We are like a sarcophagus, I thought, remembering the Etruscan tombs in Miss Lovinia Newberry's art class at Gatewood, so long ago. Now we are the sarcophagus itself. After a time, Juney came to stand beside the bed, for Juney always knows everything, and after some more time, he went for Henry. They had to help me break away from Simon's last embrace.

"Molly." Henry opened the drawer of the table beside the bed and took out the pigskin case which Simon had always kept there. "Open it," he said. "It is for you."

I took the case and sat up beside Simon and untied the leather strips which bound it. There was the stirrup, and there was this letter to me, penned in his careful hand.

• • •

January 1, 1907

My Darling Molly,

I shall be gone when you read these words, yet you shall know the high esteem in which I hold you, the love I have carried like a precious vessel for you always, a love perhaps more perfect still for its impossibility upon this ravaged earth. Time and again I have intended to explain myself to you, yet I am a man of actions, not words, as you may surmise. But the time draws nigh. It is my intention therefore to make a full accounting of myself humbly and forthrightly before you who remain the very center of my being, as I remain your obedient servant.

Let us go straight to the source and center of my greatest shame, the moment when your father lay dying in the yard of the Harper farmplace at Bentonville, one hand mangled and one leg amputated and his stomach pierced by a bullet meant for me. "Charlie," I said, "By God I am sorry, I did not mean to do it," for I had wheeled my horse on instinct as we proceeded up the muddy road through the incessant rain to join Hardee's command, myself at the head of the column, and he had taken the sharpshooter's fire. This I had done though Charles had saved my life at Trevillian Station, wounding himself at the time. "Charlie, can you hear me?" I kept saying into his ear, for the groans of the dying all around us and the screams of those undergoing amputation in the upstairs rooms of the Harper house were horrible. Legs came flying out the windows into a pile which grew as high as the smokehouse. A boy sitting next to me observed that it was easy to tell the leg of a cavalryman from that of an infantryman, the legs of the horsemen being thin and weak, while marching had made the legs of the foot soldiers muscular. Blood lay in puddles in the yard around us.

"Charlie," I said though his face was white as paper and his chest neither rose nor fell. But suddenly Charlie's eyelids flickered. I pressed my ear to his mouth so as to hear him if he should speak.

"You old cuss," he said. "Now go tell Alice . . ." Then he was gone.

I swore a sacred oath, then and there, to look after Alice and his children.

Still yet when the time of surrender finally came at the Bennett farmhouse scarcely one month later, I could not bring myself to dismount or go forward into the open where men of both armies milled about in fields and yard. There they stood, my brothers, hats in hand or pressed to chest, some of them weeping openly. Though many had fallen, I had been with a few of these boys since Edgefield. We had come down this long and terrible road together, and had got damn good at it too.

There stood William Halsey with his head hanging down in the sun and his mouth hanging open like a simpleton, though he had taken the highest prize at your father's school. I remembered him next to me in the line at Brandy Station, riding hell for leather, screaming the Rebel Yell. There stood Lonnie Ratchford and Porter Beaulieu who rode with me to steal the beef in Pennsylvania.

But somehow I could not dismount. Nor could I remove my hat. Nor could they see me plain, you understand, for I had stayed back in a little grove of willows there by the creek, a good distance back from the house. I could see Kilpatrick there in the yard, or a man I believed to be Kilpatrick, who had recently been caught in bed with his mistress and escaped capture in his shirt-tails. They said that General Hampton had caused his own horse to buck up yesterday, so as not to have to shake hands with Kilpatrick. General Hampton was not in evidence now. We all knew that General Joe Johnson was inside, where he had been for hours. But then the door of the house opened. General Sherman stepped forth and called a man, apparently his clerk, who sprang forward, papers in hand. The door closed behind him. Officers and men standing in the Bennetts' yard began plucking cherry blossoms as well as sprigs from the privet bushes for souvenirs. They carved pieces of bark from the large white oak tree in the yard. This sickened me.

I could not do it, no matter what sacred oath I had sworn. I accepted neither my ten days' rations nor my parole. Though I cannot condone my actions then or now, still I must say in my own defense that I knew Alice and her children had been taken in and provided for by Junius Hall at Agate Hill—far more than could be said for most widows and their children in that sad time. In any case I had no choice. Dark, broken, and in despair, I was not in a fit state of mind to help anyone, even had I the means to do so, which I did not. I had nothing.

I waited in the willows until cover of night then rode south down the Fayetteville road, one of hundreds scurrying down that rutted thoroughfare in the moonlight. No one stopped me or asked me any questions. Upon occasion it was necessary to ride around a person who had simply fallen in the road, whether dead or sleeping I could not say. The full moon sailed gaily through the puffy clouds all the while, and not for the first time I found myself thinking how beautiful the world is, how astonishingly beautiful, and yet it does not give a damn about any of us, nor any thing, nor does God, who would not be worth worshipping if he even existed, which He does not. For no god could condone such slaughter.

Thus I did not surrender—nor have I ever surrendered—but made my way south toward Perdido through scenes of unbelievable devastation along the way, the entire countryside plundered and destroyed. Railroads were torn up, schools and churches torn down. There seemed to be no work, as everybody—negro and white alike—roamed the countryside, most of them on foot, some of them pulling carts or wagons like a mule. One old man had simply stopped, sagging between the traces while the children in his cart cried and the rest of us surged on around him. Perhaps there were good Samaritans along that route, but if so, I did not encounter them, nor was I such a Samaritan myself, I am ashamed to say. Yet I could not help it. A vast blackness had descended upon me. I cared for no one. I passed children begging beside the road, I saw children picking through the cornrows in the field for even a kernel. I did not care. I kept a store of corn in my saddlebag for Atlas, feeding it to him out of my hand when we finally stopped for the night. I made a little fire and stirred my own ration into a thick gruel.

In three such days I reached the blackened heap of rubble and tall dreary chimneys which had been Columbia, its citizens all but disappeared, as if they had never existed. The few inhabitants I encountered were clad in little but rags and wore that blank stare I came to know well, the look of survivors of some enormous natural disaster, such as an earthquake.

I passed down through the ravaged countryside toward Perdido, now under a low sky with a softly falling rain, the earth itself covered in a gray blanket of despair. I found conditions there to be far, far worse than they had been here, for the war had been slow to come to North Carolina, you will recall, and it had not borne the trial of the armies crossing it again and again like locusts, back and forth, taking or devastating everything in their path.

I crossed the Saluda River on a badly constructed new bridge, the old one having been destroyed by the war, of course, as all had been destroyed by the war. I rode onto the other side remembering the days when your father and mother and I ran those woods like Indians, all day long. I remembered swimming in the black-water Saluda, I remembered the very day I taught your mother to float. We were in waist-high still black water just below the old bridge. I put my hand on the small of her back.

"Just lean back," I said. "Lean back, Alice, and close your eyes, and trust me. Lean far back. Let your feet rise up." And she did, going back and back and back into the dark water with her eyes wide open, holding me in them, so that I could see myself there, upside down. Her shift floated out around her body, her hair floated out around her head. Her legs were long and white and wavy.

"Now I'm going to move my hand," I said, and I did, and then she was floating for one minute, two minutes, three—I don't know how long—while the current took her downstream a little ways into deeper water and I swam to keep up, and then she was struggling and yelling, trying to put her feet down.

"Alice, I'm coming, I'm coming," I called. But she was furious and crying by the time I got there. I grabbed her and pulled her over toward the weedy shallows.

"Oh Simon, damn you," she said, but then I had her, and then I kissed her wet mouth, a kiss that she returned, twining her wet arms around my neck.

"Alice? Simon?" Charles was upstream yelling.

I kept on kissing her.

"Here," she called to him finally. "Down here, Charles," and he came, and we never mentioned this incident again.

Pieces of railroad track lay broken and twisted among the blooming wildflowers and thick grasses along the lush riverbank, and there on the other side I found an old countrywoman I had once known, Mrs. Hatch, who had helped in the kitchens at Perdido.

I rode over toward her and reined in Atlas. "Can I help you there, ma'am?" I called out to her.

She turned her worn red face up to me, blinking in the bright hot sun. Her eyes were wide and strange. "Why, he'll be coming back directly, won't he, sir?" she said. "I believe he will be coming home any day now."

"Yes ma'am, I am sure he will," I said, tipping my hat to her, as I rode on, cursing for all those boys including myself who had gone off to fight a rich man's war.

I reached Perdido at dark, riding down that long allee of live oaks with my heart in my throat to find nothing but a pile of rubble, only the huge white columns standing—five out of eight—across the front of what had once been the house. Bats flew round about, swooping low. I heard noise coming from the quarters, where I found an entire townful of people, both negro and white, disporting themselves in a lawless and lewd fashion everywhere in the light of burning flares. Perdido had become notorious, an outlaw haven along the levee. Not a man among them looked familiar as several met me at gunpoint.

Promising to take my leave, I did not, sleeping instead in the abandoned icehouse down by the river which I was fairly sure no one had yet discovered as it stood yawning dark and empty in the moonlight, vines growing across its door. I tethered Atlas inside with me, and slept with my gun in my hand. I got up before dawn and rode all about the place—my childhood's only home, as you will recall. Perdido was once an entire town unto itself, it encompassed a whole civilization, now vanished, as if it had never been.

I went out to the meadow where the barns and stables had stood, where I had shod so many horses, and trained others; there had been the oval track, the beautiful jumps and fences. Here I had led your mother around and around on her little gray pony Lucy, teaching her to ride. Here I had trained Desperado for Charles, from here I had ridden with him to victories at Charleston and Camden and even up in Virginia.

My father's blacksmith shop was still standing, again in some sort of use. Despite the risk I dismounted and ducked inside. Here I could see him yet, my huge cruel silent father, hammer raised above the glowing forge. May the Devil take him! I thought. Here I had dodged his blows yet learned my craft, and it came back to me then that in fact I had once had a craft, other than war I mean, for war will take a man over utterly, especially if one is good at it, as I had proved to be. Upon impulse I lifted up a rock in the hearth and there it was, Alice's little stirrup in the place where I had hid it years before. I put it in my pocket and was leaving as an old man appeared in the doorway to ask what I was doing there, and I said I had used to live on the place, and he said I had best be on my way then. So I left, in fact I could not leave fast enough, suddenly, spurring Atlas straight down the middle of the long allee of oaks, and be damned. The hell with it.

I would never go back. I had never been a member of that family, no matter how much I had willed it so. I had been neither brother nor sister nor lover, I had been more like a body slave with no knowledge of his enslavement, little more than the negroes on this place. And I had remained enslaved by it, by the very idea of Perdido, all these years. Such a child had I been, such a boy, and then I had gone to war and become another thing altogether, a horrible thing. I could not believe I was still alive. I had no wish to be alive. I carried Alice's little stirrup in my pocket as I headed down the levee and into the world, suddenly resolved to find another country altogether. For I had no hope and nothing to lose—a condition of total freedom, as I came to realize.

I was headed for Texas, from whence I planned to travel to Mexico—an idea much in the air at that time, put forward by many of our most illustrious leaders such as General Jo Shelby of Kentucky and our own General Wade Hampton himself, who had reputedly offered to take President Jefferson Davis with him.

Such was my plan until I fell in with a man at a public house who was bound for Brazil, his saddlebags full of rattlesnake watermelon seeds, a fruit he planned to introduce there in partnership with his brother, already established and farming. He gave me an article written by his brother which described Brazil in the most glowing terms, which somehow burned their way into my perhaps fevered brain: "Who can picture, who can paint nature as here exhibited? With wonder, admiration, and reverential awe, one may contemplate the vastness with which he finds himself here surrounded, the profusion of nature's bounties, and sublimity of scenery, but to describe them, to picture them as they are, is beyond the scope of human capacity. Here we behold the great Amazon, by far the largest river in the world, located in the center of the world, with its vast tributaries embracing more than two million square miles, teeming with animal and vegetable life; a world of eternal verdure and perennial spring, of whose grandeur and splendor it is impossible to speak in fitting terms."

Another country indeed. My resolve rose to meet such eloquence.

Consequently I turned south to New Orleans, a city which swallowed me for a time, as I was susceptible then to drink and to all manner of other vices, emerging however with a pocketful of cash and a set of blacksmithing tools for the journey.

At that time it was not necessary to join a colony. I secured passage on a large British sailing ship, the *Marmion,* carrying double the load of passengers for which it had been intended, most of them men from the Confederate Army, such as myself, also cattlemen from Texas and planters from

Alabama. The ship had been stripped bare during the war. We sailed without furniture, sleeping in canvas hammocks hung three deep, though I could not sleep much under those conditions. I stood at the rail for hours as we departed down the delta of the Mississippi River, my heart rising with every mile of muddy water that slid under our bow as I stood looking out at the long shining spread of water and sky before me. A storm came up just as we reached the Gulf of Mexico, driving us onto a giant sandbar already occupied by a grounded pirate ship—wreckers, they called them then. Seeing us, some of the men rushed out across the sand with their cups extended, begging piteously for water.

"Water be damned!" cried Jess Crocker, a big redheaded Texas planter standing beside me. "Get back!" They did not. He drew a pistol from his belt and shot the closest man twice in the stomach. This pirate died a screaming, writhing death upon the sands before us, while his compatriots turned back to their wretched ship.

"Shame! For shame!" The outcry rose all about us, but Jess Crocker was unrepentant, threatening to shoot anybody on the *Marmion* who disagreed with him. No one did. Apparently the captain was of the same mind, for Crocker was never chastised or disciplined in any way. As our journey continued, Crocker and I grew to be friends, or something like it, playing poker nightly, a game in which Crocker dealt with all disagreements strictly, in much the same fashion as he had handled the pirates.

Our meals were served from tin pans—boiled potatoes, bean soup, and salted beef. I had lived on worse. A woman and two children died and were buried at sea, unceremoniously, as the only minister on board stayed drunk the whole time, his private cure for seasickness.

The mouth of the Amazon turned the ocean a reddish brown sixty miles off the coast of Brazil. You could dip a bucket down into it and come up with fresh water. At dusk we anchored outside the city in view of the Raza lighthouse, the fort at the entrance to the harbor, and the lush green mountains which went right down to the Bay of Guanabara. Our fifty-six-hundred-mile voyage was at an end. By the light of the moon, we could see Sugarloaf Mountain rising above all. I stayed awake that entire night, sitting on the bare deck, my heart brimming with fear, memories, and anticipation—a sensation oddly similar to the nights I had experienced before a battle.

We raised anchor at sunrise and steamed up to the city with its bright colors, tiled-roof buildings, and iron-railed balconies, not unlike New Orleans. I could fashion such railings myself. We disembarked and walked up huge white paving stones through an open iron gate. Here I parted company with Jess Crocker and most of my compatriots, for I had chosen to continue upriver to the village of Rio Doce, two days and two nights of further travel in wide canoes poled by men who walked up and down the runways on either side of the craft. Though plagued by mosquitoes, I was enthralled by the variety of handmade crafts on the river, the strange trees and vines beside us, the bright loud birds and big snakes sliding into the water.

The town of Rio Doce featured a beautiful river of the same name, as well as the large Lake Juparana with its broad sandy beach. Everyone set in to the work of settlement immediately, the men digging ditches, clearing fields, and building houses in the native manner, with palm roofs and dirt floors. These soldiers had truly "turned their swords to plowshares." Women who had never performed manual labor in their lives were cooking, sewing, and washing clothes in the river. People have said that the Confederados, as they called us, came to Brazil because slavery still existed there, at least until 1888, but in my experience, this was not entirely so, for few could afford slaves, depending instead upon free negroes who were present in an astonishing variety of color and were treated as the equal of whites. Though this was upsetting to many Confederados at first, especially the women, soon all grew accustomed to it, feeling that at least these negroes were preferable to Yankees. A tribe of Botacudo Indians, naked except for belts and knives hung around their necks, caused the women more consternation than the free negroes whenever they came running into town drunk on cachaca, the local rum. Their faces were grotesque, earlobes and lips distended by wooden discs.

One morning at first light, following a fearsome storm, I was setting up my blacksmith shop, my forge having at last arrived with the greatest of trouble and expense, when I heard the Botacudos' unmistakable clamor outside. I came to the door just in time to witness two of them circling each other in the muddy street, knives drawn, and chanting—or so it seemed to me—in their incomprehensible language. One thrust into the other's shoulder, the other slashed a spurting cut down his opponent's forearm. I turned back for my pistol, returning in time to see a third man rush forward to cut off one of the combatants' heads with a swinging machete. The head rolled into the filthy rushing gutter; the others chased it, yelling, snatching it up. I fired repeatedly into the air to dispel them, then drank myself into a stupor—all before eight o'clock.

I awoke sometime in the afternoon, disoriented, head pounding. For a moment I thought I was on a lane in Virginia, marching toward Fredericksburg. I was eating an apple, incredibly sweet and tart at the same time, the best apple I had ever eaten, and I remember thinking, Well, this is a fine country, just before the guns began to roar in the distance ahead.

I sat up carefully on the dirt floor of my hut in Rio Doce.

"Senhor."

I looked around.

Crouching not four feet away was an Indian boy holding out an animal bladder filled with—what? In that moment I did not know or care, recklessly seizing it and upending the contents into my mouth. It could have killed me, of course. But it was only water, blessed water. I drank my fill, then poured the remainder over my head while the boy squatted like a little ape, watching me with no expression on his face, or in his long light eyes.

"Obrigado," I said.

He said nothing.

Finally I succeeded in standing up. He did not stand up.

"Obrigado," I said again.

He did not move.

"You will have to leave now," I said. "Go on, vai embora." He scuttled backward like a crab, fetching up against my cot.

"Sai d'aqui," I said.

Instead he grabbed a cobertor, pulling it down over his head until he had covered himself completely. I almost laughed. Since he couldn't see me, he imagined that I couldn't see him either. I picked him up and threw him out into the street, cobertor and all, latching the door behind him.

The next morning he was back at dawn, crouched against the door. He fell into the hut when I opened it, then handed me a banana.

"Obrigado," I said.

He nodded.

"Como se chama?" I asked.

The boy shrugged, then shook his head.

This was Henry, whose father had been decapitated before my door the previous day, and he has been with me ever since, as you know. I named him myself, then set about schooling him, finding him both intelligent and industrious, unlike most of them.

At Rio Doce, Henry immediately became my helper, then my right hand man at the forge and indeed, in all enterprises. I needed such a helper, as it turned out. Though I had thought to return to a simpler life shoeing horses, soon we were overtaken by the extreme need for plows, spades, harrows, and rakes, iron tools never having been employed in Brazil before our arrival. It was hard to believe, but it was true. I moved to a larger space, hired on four more Indians, and we sold iron plows as fast as we could make them. A line formed outside my door every morning, Confederados and Brazilians alike, white and Indian and negro, and I made no distinction among them. We worked like demons.

Until I came down with malaria, that is, almost an occupational disease in that climate. But I had rather a rough go of it, ending up in a tent clinic at Santarem where Henry and I had gone to deliver a load of tools for a new mining venture. First I was freezing, then burning up, beset with pains and vomiting, my mind filled with a host of phantoms, chattering and laughing endlessly until I thought they would drive me mad.

Finally my fever broke, and I awoke to find myself drenched all over in sweat, as wet as if I had fallen into the Rio Doce. A vision in white gave me a dose of cinchona then held a tin cup of water up to my rough lips.

"É agua?" I asked.

A beautiful white smile lit up her dark face. "Sím," she said. "Aqui. Bebe." Her hair was a black cloud around her large black eyes. An otherworldly sweetness seemed to envelop her. She poured the cool water down my sore throat, and then she disappeared, and then I slept, deeply and truly, awakening after another twelve hours in another sort of fever, wild to find my nurse. I did so despite all good advice to the contrary. For what did I care about good advice? Nothing ruled me save my own appetites and desires.

Her name was Maria Conceicão and she was the daughter of a free negro who ran a sawmill in the interior. I gave her father a sum of money, and we were married on the spot by an outlaw whisky priest. I brought her back to Rio Doce as my bride.

Maria was a sweet, docile girl with a natural sense of grace and composure, a true lady as compared with the Confederado women who shunned her—and me—forcing their husbands to do the same. I was astonished! For here we were in Brazil, where all had come to find the freedom to live as they chose, or so it had been said. Apparently this freedom did not extend to befriending my Maria, who was just a girl, after all, suffering these slights, and missing her family. My friends all but disappeared. We could not hire a servant.

Now with child, my beautiful Maria wept every day. I was at my wit's end when Jess Crocker, the Texan from the Marmion, appeared in Rio Doce on a business matter. He came to visit me at the shop, and left impressed by my business. A deal was soon struck. Within two weeks time we were all en route to Americana, the town where Jess Crocker proposed to back me in the establishment of a tool factory—all of us, that is, Maria and myself and two of the Indians, with Henry and more Indians bringing the forge and other equipment separately, under some duress. We built our Fabrica de Arados and four other houses, one for Maria and myself, one for Henry, one for the

Indians, one for the servants. "It is a city!" Maria exclaimed. I bought her fine dresses, a pearl necklace, silver candlesticks, an arara in an ivory cage, fine china from England. "Simon." She said my name like a caress.

I called her Minha Nega, my darling.

Maria gave birth to our twin sons whom I named Simon and Charles, in hopes that they would enjoy such a friendship as your father and I had had at Perdido. Maria proved to be a lovely mother, a natural mother, endlessly patient with the little boys, laughing in delight at their antics. Of course she was not much more than a child herself. Her sister Leonilde came to live with us, affording Maria both help and companionship. The boys grew. The factory expanded, successful even beyond Crocker's wildcat expectations. Orders poured in, stacked up. Soon we were employing thirty men.

Almost despite myself, I was fast becoming a wealthy man. I developed certain ambitions, in keeping with my station—or perhaps to spite those who had been so cruel to Maria in Rio Doce. Though she loved our simple, low house with its courtyard and gardens, I ordered up a grand stone house to be built, with tower and parapets. I insisted on it.

With construction under way, Maria and Leonilde took the two little boys and set off for a visit to their family. The boys were wildly excited. There would be cousins, and dogs, and a donkey cart. Though they were over three years old, their hair still hung in curly black ringlets to their shoulders, for no one could bear to cut it. Their mother had dressed them in matching white linen suits. Minha Nega wore a blue cotton peasant dress that day, embroidered with all manner of fanciful beasts and flowers, and a straw hat. One of the most trustworthy of my Indians—though not Henry—drove the carriage, and it has never been explained to my satisfaction what could have caused those fine horses—personally trained by myself—to run away on the mountain road, plunging over the rocky cliff and into the waters of Lago Azul. Only Maria's sister's body was ever found, the lake being too deep to drag.

In an instant, I became a shattered, broken man, consigned forever to my former darkness, the outer circle of despair. *Yes,* I thought. Such is my fate, such is my punishment for assaying even a shred of hope, a moment of pride and optimism.

I left it all—the factory, Henry, my mansion in progress—and went back to Rio de Janeiro for a time, seeking to lose myself in all the ways a man may do that there. I returned to Americana some months later to find Jesse on his deathbed and the fabrica a roaring success. I buried Jesse, then sold the factory. This was the first of my fortunes, my dear, for ever since that time, I am like the fabled King Midas—everything I touch turns to gold. It has meant nothing to me.

Henry and I set off on a series of travels—first to Peru, then to Lisbon, to London and Paris and Rome. We traveled for two years, and then I was ready to come back, resolved if nothing else to visit Agate Hill again and look in upon Alice and her children. You know the rest, my dear. Please do not misunderstand me. I was at that time long past any hope of personal happiness, or any notion that my presence could be of any use to anyone.

And yet there you were, your mother's child—but your mother before she was diminished by age and disappointment, your mother before she had chosen Charles, your mother before she had even become a woman, when we were all children together, playing in the river at Perdido. And your predicament was so dire, so extraordinary, that I seized upon it; I resolved to help you, whether you wanted me to or not. For I had carried Alice's little stirrup all these years. The truth is that I needed you at that point, my dear, far more than you needed me. You and your concerns have afforded me a life, of sorts. An involvement. A purpose. For a man must have a purpose in this world. Therefore I give you now my deepest gratitude. It has been my privilege to know you and your family, my privilege to cherish and serve you; and if such a place as the afterlife exists, I shall be there serving you still, and this task will continue in death to afford me my greatest joy, as it has in life.

Yrs.
Simon Black

❧

I read this letter straight through immediately, then again, while Henry and Juney waited patiently. The letter was everything that I might have hoped from Simon, an extraordinary man, and I am pleased to have it though I required nothing from him, as he required nothing from me. I folded it back up and replaced it in the pigskin case, tying the leather strings.

"We should tell—," I began, but they both shook their heads, no, for Simon had been ours and ours alone.

"Then we will take him out to Four Oaks," I said, "for this is where all our dead are buried." I took a bath and washed my hair while they rolled him up in Henry's cobertor and hitched up the mules and put him in the wagon. It was a beautiful, blowing morning—the kind of day we don't usually have here in midsummer—as we rode out to Four Oaks, Henry at the reins.

Of course I knew that the house had been sold long ago, but I had not been there for years, and no one had told me that it had become a golf club. FOUR OAKS COUNTRY CLUB read the sign on the old stone arch. The graveled driveway led to a parking lot filled with automobiles. The house had been painted glistening white. Men and women lounged on the wide porch and sat on wrought iron benches beneath the giant oaks. A man in knickers bent over the little white ball on the putting green over to the left, while two other men watched intently, and a flag waved gaily on a stick. Beyond the house, green grass stretched over the hill, dotted with golfers and caddies.

A beautiful blond girl in sunglasses stood leaning against the nearest oak, one knee raised, her bare foot against the rough bark, talking to a man in a wrought iron chair. She was laughing and smoking a cigarette, then paused, blowing smoke out, to stare at us coming along the road in our wagon, approaching the arch.

I clutched Henry's elbow. "Just keep on going straight." I was already anticipating the PRIVATE PROPERTY sign which appeared on the closed gate of the old road leading up to the cemetery. "Turn around when you can," I told Henry.

It was a long day's journey out to Four Oaks and then back home; we buried Simon at dusk in the garden plot beside Liddy's kitchen house at Agate Hill, Henry and Juney taking turns at the shovel. They were making short work of it when suddenly Henry said something in his language, throwing the shovel aside. He knelt reaching into the hole to sift the dirt with both hands, finally drawing forth a long human leg bone attached to a foot. Then he paused, still kneeling, to look at me. Lightning bugs rose from the overgrown garden all around us.

Of course I knew immediately. It was Mister Vogell, Selena's husband who had disappeared. She had done it, she had killed him so that she could have poor old Uncle Junius. Of course she had! Selena would have done anything. I was not surprised, I believe I had known it all along. Perhaps this is why I hated her so much, because I knew—even then—that I was exactly like her, skin and bone, tooth and claw. I would have done anything at all to have my Jacky.

Juney cocked his head toward me, but this was a love story too long and too hard to tell. And in the end it didn't matter.

"Put him back," I said, and so they dug another grave for Simon, over there by the miller's stone where those sunflowers are growing now. There is no stone.

Just look.

Have you ever seen any sunflowers so big? Nobody else has either. They come back bigger every year. I swear, they are pretty as a picture.

July 21, 1927

Upon Simon's death, I got up and took charge. We cleaned out the tenant house and moved in there, Juney and myself, while Henry took Liddy's kitchen, thus giving Agate Hill over to its ghosts for good. Now they rush through the passage, up the stairs and down, up and down, they have the run of this house. The foundation is crumbling, the roof of the parlor is falling in.

But we don't care. We are done with all that.

Henry and Juney dug up the big field beside Liddy's kitchen. Here. You can see them out there working in the garden right now, through this chink of a window.

Just look!

What a garden!

Now in midsummer we have row upon row of tall rustling corn with silk at the tops of the ears and morning glories climbing all over the sturdy stalks, potatoes and cabbage and onions and beets, big old pie plants and shiny elegant eggplant, hill after riotous hill of squash—Hubbard, pittypat, yellow, and green—with their yellow flowers blooming. Beans climb up the strings laced between their poles like Jacob's ladders. Skinny orange carrots stand in the dirt with their lacy tops waving. Gourds and watermelons hide among their vines growing bigger and bigger. In spring we have early greens and little butter lettuce and also ruffly lettuce, like crinolines. Pumpkins and mustard and curly kale in the fall, and collards with their huge veiny leaves.

But look.

Juney moves across the garden on his hands and knees as the sun moves across the sky, pulling radishes like jewels out of the earth, onions and potatoes with dirt clinging to them. Henry follows, holding the old flat basket, both of them unhurried, for they know they have all the time in the world. Here we've got nothing but time! Juney wears a pale blue shirt and an old straw hat. His fingers scurry like spiders, finding sweet peas. Henry goes away with his basket full and comes back with another basket. Now Juney stands and moves among the corn rows, lost to view. Juney can tell a perfect full ear by the feel of it, he is never wrong.

On Saturday we will take all these vegetables to market in town along with some eggs and some flowers stuck into old coffee cans that Mister Jordan gives us from the coffee shop every Saturday. We like to go to market. We sit on the bench outside the old courthouse until everything is sold. Then

Juney will play us a tune on Spencer's old harmonica, he plays "Shortnin' Bread" and "John Henry" and "Sometimes I Feel Like a Motherless Child." Juney learned these tunes from negroes when he lived in the woods and on the place by himself for so long like an animal. The negroes called him the Big-Headed Boy.

"Stagolee and Billy, two men who gambled late, Stagolee threw a seven and he swore that he threw eight," Juney will sing while everybody gathers round. One time a nice young man came out here and recorded Juney singing into a machine. Another time some bad boys from town came out here and picked him up in a car and took him to sing at a party. They dumped him back onto the piazza the next day and he was hurt, he ran into the woods and was gone for days, I do not know what happened to him. Their mothers came out from town to apologize. "Stagolee shot Billy, Billy fall down on the floor—" Whenever Juney sings and plays the harmonica, a good-sized crowd will gather.

Oh I know what they say about us in town, and I say, the hell with them! I tell you, I don't give a damn. I have got to be an old woman in the twinkling of an eye, and it is sort of a relief, I can tell you. I do what I want to now. Last week I traded all our eggs for ice cream at Holden's Grocery. Now that I have shrunk down little as a child, I figure I might as well act like one. I don't care. I like ice cream. Juney does too. We like to put bourbon in it, and make ourselves a milkshake.

Look at him out there in the hot hot sun, moving so slow along the rows. He is as good as he can be. Two negro women have come now to sit patiently on the bench over there under the tulip tree, one of them is reading a magazine, perhaps she will leave it for me. I like to find out what they are up to, all these girls. These two have come to consult Juney, and I know they will wait all day long if they have to. One of them looks to be pregnant, though it is hard to tell from up here. A little split oak basket sits between them, covered by a red cloth, so I know we will have something nice for supper.

I hope it is salmon cakes. We like salmon cakes too.

We love it when people bring their babies, which they often do, Juney has a way with babies. They quit screaming the minute he lays them flat on their tummies across his knees. His fingers are so little and quick, he can get out splinters, thorns, and fishbones in an instant, in the twinkling of an eye. He blows down their throats to cure thrush. He says something into their ears for earache—who knows what Juney says?—and uses spiderwebs to stop bleeding. He did this to me one day when I had cut my finger with the kitchen knife, and it stopped immediately.

Juney is sweet as pie, my little man, as Simon called him. It kills me to think of him running wild in the woods all those years, it's amazing he's still alive. Or maybe not. But I wish so much that I had been here to find him and catch him and hold him tight. That's all he needs. So I can't die, for then who will do it? I think about this all the time. He won't come to Henry. Sometimes Juney just sits like a sweet potato, with no more going on in his mind than that, his face so sweet and blank, but at other times he still takes off through the woods and no one can find him though he always comes home eventually. He is so tired then, he sleeps for days.

Juney moves along the rows while the negro girls fan themselves with their magazine. They have been joined by a white man in a white suit. It is not uncommon for people to drive miles to speak to Juney, though he does not really talk much. "No," he'll say, or "Yes," or "Something like that." It seems to be enough. Mostly he just listens and touches them, or touches something that they have brought with them, such as a handkerchief from somebody sick, or somebody they love or hate or something. There is no end to the kinds of trouble that people get into. There is no end to the terrible things that happen to them. Not a day passes that we don't have somebody. They wait as long as they need to. They bring what they can. Sometimes it is a cake or a pie or a loaf of bread or a pretty rock or a feather or a hundred dollars or a bottle of bourbon. We like bourbon. Sometimes it is nothing. It doesn't matter. It is a gift, as Juney's illness, if it is an illness, has left him with certain gifts.

Now Juney moves across the garden on his hands and knees like a bug, lifting tomatoes up one by one to Henry who places them carefully in the basket so that they will not bruise. Our tomatoes are the best at the market, people always line up before we get there and we always sell out in fifteen minutes, or just as long as it takes me to weigh out the tomatoes and make the change, doing the sums in my head. It's a funny thing. Sometimes these days I can't remember people's names, or whether I had breakfast or not, or what I was going to do when I went over to the stove. But I can still add the sums up lickety-split in my head, and recite most of "Hiawatha's Childhood" for Juney. This is his favorite poem. He loves to say "Gitchee gumee" and "the shining Big-Sea-Water." He also loves

Half a league, half a league,
Half a league onward,
All in the valley of Death
Rode the six hundred

and "Quoth the Raven, Nevermore." Juney loves poems, and he loves stories too.

"Say it, Mammalee," he begs. Over the years he has gone from calling me Molly, or something like Molly, to Ma, to Mamma, to Mammalee. "Say it, Mammalee," he begs, and I do, telling him, for instance, the story of the time Spencer caught the big fish, or the time the ghost horse galloped around the circle, or the time Old Bess and Virgil flew away over the snow, or the time Mary White and me saw the fairies, for I remember everything. "Say it, Mammalee," Juney says, and I do. I say the world for him.

So I am the one who adds up the sums and tells the stories. Henry is the one who drives the car, for we have got a blue humpbacked car now, brought out to us from town by little Russ Grady, the son of old Russell Grady who was Simon's attorney. We go to market in the car, Henry driving, me wearing Mitty's old black hat, I know it scares the children, but you know what? I like to scare the children! And I believe they like it too.

•   •   •

❧

July 22

I have forgot to say that twice lately I have waked to find myself in the passage, then last night I woke up out on the hill in the moonlight, you know I used to sleepwalk as a girl. The full moon cast shadows behind every tree and the night breeze blew my nightgown around my legs. I had no memory of how I got out there, or even of going to bed, or what we ate for supper, or anything. But there I was on the hill, and then there was Juney too, he held out his little hand which did not surprise me, for Juney knows everything. Oftentimes he will answer questions before I even ask them, such as once I was wondering whatever became of Nicky Eck and he said, "Kilted, Mammalee, kilted." His illness, if it is an illness, has left him with certain gifts. Sometimes I think he sees all our lives as if we are the people in the village in the paperweight Ben Valiant gave me so long ago, he sees our comings and goings to and fro, he sees me nursing Christabel deep in the night while the rain drums so loud on the roof and there's nobody awake but us, he sees Simon's Minha Nega and his twin boys caught forever in the water at the bottom of the lake with the skirt of her blue embroidered peasant dress swirling all around them.

I took Juney's hand and we walked out of the woods and across the yard together past the big garden with our shadows going out in front of us like giants. "Look Mammalee," said Juney, waving his arms, and then both of us waved our arms up and down and our shadows waved back, we were both laughing so hard it was so funny though it was the middle of the night, I could not do without my little man.

He was working out in the garden with Henry when I woke up in my small iron bed in the tenant's house, this used to be Selena's house, and this was the children's bed. Somehow it had already got to be afternoon.

I have forgot to tell you that Godfrey came back here once in the wintertime, snooping around in a big black car, he said that Blanche has been dead of tuberculosis for lo these many years and that Victoria had become a famous whore in San Francisco, then a rich man's wife. She lives in a hotel now and wears an evening dress to dinner every night. Well I was glad to hear this! But all my life I have wondered, whatever became of Mary White? Godfrey of course did not know. Godfrey himself is a fatcat. He did not stay long or even get out of the car for Henry stood right there beside me holding the ax as he had been chopping firewood when they drove up. Godfrey had a lady in the car with him who kept saying, "Honey, let's get out of here! This place is giving me the creeps!" Later we learned that he went on into town to look up the title on this property, but little Russ Grady handled that! "You are not to worry," big Russell Grady always told us. "Mister Black has taken very good care of you."

Washington came back too, years ago. He had become a lawyer with gray hair, in a three-piece suit. We sat in the parlor and visited, and looked at photographs of his wife and his five children, two boys and three girls, all of them dressed up. One of the boys looked exactly like Washington used to. He tried to give us money but we refused. "We don't need a thing!" I said, while Juney nodded up and down. Juney liked Washington right off. Washington's name was Elijah Washington Hall. He was in the Legislature in Pennsylvania then but he is dead now, a card came in the mail, edged in black. Washington had a big gold watch on a golden chain it told the time in six different places in the world but not the time out here at Agate Hill, we are on different time here.

So much has happened, and yet nothing has happened, for each day moves so slow, the way we like it on this place, Juney and Henry and me, the seasons as they come and go   the days the hours   each with its appointed task for we are creatures of the seasons here, like rabbits and whistle pigs, snakes and catfish. We keep chickens and bees and raise vegetables. We are a part of the earth and the sky, the living and the dead, and we make no distinction between them. One great war has come, and another is likely, Juney says. So it will happen. Now there are electric lights in town, and many cars on the road.

Tomorrow we will go to market. I must not let my little man play marbles with the little boys. He always wants to play but their mothers jerk them away   oh nevermind, that was years ago. These years have passed as in the twinkling of an eye as in the Bible, a book I have never much cared for.

Now Juney is lining up the coffee cans on the bench in front of Liddy's kitchen and Henry is cutting the flowers to put in them, so I had better get down there. Henry does not have an eye for it, and Juney can't see worth a damn. So I am the one who arranges the flowers I will say them aloud to Juney, "Red zinnia, orange chrysanthemum, purple aster, sunflower, sunflower, rose."

"Say it, say it, Mammalee," Juney says.

I am the one who arranges the flowers. Henry is the one who will drive the car.

July 23

And today is the day we will go to market if this morning ever comes! I have been awake all night long   I believe I have got my days and nights turned around now but nevermind it is all the same to me   I will sleep when I'm dead anyway! So why worry about it!

The moonlight is beautiful, shining bright as day in the yard, falling upon this page upon this diary and the box that contains my life. Agate Hill is a magical place again, as it was when Fannie was still alive, for they are all still alive now, all of them including Mary White, see there she is in her red coat at the edge of the trees I am going down to her now. We will climb up the hill in the moonlight together it is bright as day but look, I cast no shadow. Oh why must she run ahead? Why will she not wait for me? We are going up to our Indian Rock   we will dance and yell when the storm comes closer, first the thunder then the lightning   you can count in between them   one thousand foot soldiers, two thousand foot soldiers, three thousand foot soldiers   to see how many miles away the storm is. The lightning is striking, the thunder rolls. It comes closer and closer.

But there up the hill is the Manbone Rock, thank God, and the cave, and the shadows Jacky makes with his fingers, and the jumping fire. "Molly," he said when I came into the store with the lantern. "For God's sake, Molly," he said. He lay half on the floor and half across our big sack of flour which was covered with his blood for he had been gutshot, his stomach open. "Help me," he said. "For God's sake." Jacky lay outstretched reaching for BJ's gun which lay on the floor where he had dropped it, but now he could not get to it, the blood was coming too fast.

"Help me, Molly," Jacky said.

All around us the store was in perfect order as we had left it, BJ and me, waiting for the morrow, with the piece goods all folded and the sums all totaled and the new round of hoop cheese under its glass dome.

"What must I do?" I asked, knowing the answer already.

"Honey, for God's sake help me. Get. The gun."

I went over and got it and put it into his hand which fell open, he could not hold it. "Who did this?" I said, but he shook his head and smiled at me all of a sudden, that sweet old crooked smile while his heart's blood pooled on the floor. I was walking in Jacky's blood. "Please, honey," he said, and I took the gun in both hands and shot him in the neck so that his head fell over to the side with his eyes wide open and the smile still on his face and then I lay down there beside him, I would have done anything for my Jacky.

I was still there when BJ came in through the door hollering, for he had heard the shot, and came over to us and jerked me up though I wanted to stay, stay stay right there with my Jacky. But BJ jerked me up and thrust me toward the door and said, "Get over there, Molly, or I will kill you too." He tossed the gun out the door and opened the big cans of kerosene and threw it all over the back of his beloved store all over the clothes and the groceries and the piece goods and held me tight when I tried to stop him for I saw what he was going to do. Then BJ threw the lantern into the clothes and flames sprang up like an explosion lighting up BJ's poor face as he thrust it into mine.

"Now listen to me, Molly," he said, pinning my arms behind me. "You woke up, and you smelled smoke, and you came out here, and you found this fire, and Jacky was already shot, and you tried to save him, but you could not. You could not!" as the yellow flames licked Jacky's face and lit up his yellow hair. I realized that it was BJ's intention to let Jacky burn, in order to save me. But somehow I got free and grabbed Jacky's leg and then finally BJ started helping me too and then somehow we dragged him outside just as the dance floor fell in.

Oh Mary White, don't you remember how we danced and danced as the storm came on, what did we know then of lightning? Jacky's gone, one more time, Jacky's gone. His banjo rings yet in my mind. Oh Mary White, I am glad I gave all my heart   I would do it again   I will tell all these young girls. And don't you remember how we used to sneak up and lie on our Indian Rock at night? It was still warm from the sun, its heat went all through our bodies, and sometimes we fell asleep there as my stone babies sleep now on their mountain up at Plain View. Why here is Christabel, child of my heart, why here she comes running toward me with arms wide open, her face like a flower. I am the one who arranges the flowers. Zinnia   chrysanthemum   New York ironweed   purple aster   goldenrod   sunflower   rose. It is time to go to market. It is time. I am the one who tells the stories, Henry is the one who drives the car, and Juney is the one who holds the basket of eggs still warm on his lap while the land flows past on each side, tree and rock and fence and flower, all the hours, all the days, Juney is waving at everybody. Oh I could not do without my little man.

TUSCANY MILLER
30-B Peachtree Court Apts.
1900 Court Blvd.
Atlanta, GA 30039

Dear Dr. F:

And that is THE END! The end of the diary, that is all she wrote. Her death certificate at the courthouse says July 23, 1927. So I don't guess they ever made it to the market, do you? Or maybe they went on without her, Henry and Juney, what do you think? They were all so crazy. This is all pretty crazy but it is so sad too, it really gets to me, I have to say. I start crying every time I read the end.

I interviewed old Mr. Grady (the lawyer) who says that nobody here knew anything about Molly's court case or the ballad associated with her. He was just amazed to hear about it. According to him, Molly was buried at Four Oaks with her family. I did not see the grave because they were having the Member / Guest Tournament on the day I went out there, and the cemetery is right in the middle of the fairway on the 7th hole. Henry either died or disappeared, nobody knows which. After that, they put Juney into Dorothea Dix Mental Hospital in Raleigh, where he died and was buried with only a little metal marker that has his patient number on it, 04139. It is up on a hill though, and it is real pretty up there.

The house was sold at auction, then changed hands repeatedly until Daddy and Michael bought it in 2003.

I have not been able to find out one thing about Mary White, though she is my favorite person in this whole box. This just kills me. But I have this idea that her terrible grandmother died, and her real mother came to get her, and she got up out of that contraption and got well, and went out West, and lived happily ever after. Do you think this is possible?

Well, after reading all this stuff I guess anything *is possible!*

So Dr. Ferrell, what do you think? I know all this is way too much stuff but I am hoping I can find a thesis in here someplace like Michaelangelo said he would look at a big chunk of marble and then just cut away everything that wasn't David. But I will tell you something else. Even if you don't let me back into the program, I don't care. I will confess to you now that the only reason I ever got into it in the first place was because I was involved with your assistant Eric Ringle the one with the tattoos, I thought he looked so hot in those big clodhopper boots. What did I know. Then he went off to get a PHD in Austin, TX, and I got married to a jerk under a bare hanging lightbulb in Dillon, SC. So I admit I was not a big student back when you knew me but I will be now, I swear.

The other thing you might be interested to know is that Daddy and Michael's bed and breakfast is a huge success. They have renovated it and decorated it and named the different rooms for different people in the diary such as Victoria's Room, Uncle Junius's Study, Aunt Fannie's Sewing Room, Mary White's Room, Molly Petree's Cubbyhole, etc. The cabins are so cute, they are condos now. The Tenant House is a duplex, and Liddy's Kitchen is the honeymoon house. It is very romantic in there with the original brick walls, the big fireplace, a hot tub, and a gorgeous antique bed with canopies and 400-count sheets. The Carriage Barn is a fancy restaurant with a hot young cook that Michael stole from the Magnolia Grill in Durham. And now they have even brought in some fancy decorator cows (Belted Galloways) and put them to grazing out in the fields.

You can view it all at www.agatehillplantation.com.

But I just want you to know, I am coming back to school regardless. I do not intend to be a hostess forever.

Daddy and Michael are back in my life now. To be honest, Michael helped me figure out the order of these documents, and Daddy sprang for typing. They have said I can have a job at Agate Hill, maybe Event Planning, weddings and parties and such, when I finish school. I have always been good with the public, I can talk to anybody. Michael thinks I have a real flair for design too.

In conclusion, my horizons have been expanded by the contents of this box. I realize that it is completely true what Martha Fickling says, that "sometimes there can come an attraction between two people, even people as unlikely as we was, that is going to last though all hell breaks loose and longer than death." I have thought about this a lot, Dr. Ferrell. This was true of Molly and Simon Black, in fact it is true of a lot of people in this box. I believe it is true of Michael and Daddy too. In fact I have a much better relationship with Daddy now than I have ever had with her before.

I forgot to say, I hope you are well, and that your family is just fine too. I look forward to hearing from you soon.

Yours Truly,
Tuscany Miller

ACKNOWLEDGMENTS

MY DEEPEST GRATITUDE TO Mona Sinquefield for her help with research and manuscript preparation; to my editor, Shannon Ravenel, for her expertise and patience; and to Hal Crowther, my husband, for his love and support during the writing of this novel.

The title of this book was suggested to me by Alice Gerrard's haunting song "Agate Hill." The first section is deeply informed by Mary Alves Long's memoir *High Time to Tell It* (Durham, NC: Duke University Press, 1950) about her Reconstruction childhood in piedmont North Carolina, with visits to Hillsborough. Here I found details of house and countryside, daily life, children's chores, and activities of the day such as "Baltimore work" and knitting a "man doll." Information and inspiration came from visits to historic Stagville Plantation and Bennett Place, both in Durham, North Carolina. I am indebted to Darnell Arnoult, Marshall Chapman, Morgan Moylan, and Tom Rankin for their various suggestions; to Walt Wolfram and Connie Eble for their help with appropriate diction; to Dale Reed for her help with Southern music of this period; and above all, to historian Ernest Dollar, past head of the Orange County Historical Museum, for his expertise and wise counsel throughout the writing of this novel.

Though my own Mariah Snow is entirely a fictional character, I got the idea for her by reading the estimable Mrs. Anna Burwell's diary, which is to be found at the Burwell School Historic Site in Hillsborough, North Carolina, where I was ably aided in my research by Katherine Malone-France and Lauren A. Mikruk. Here and there, I have used Mrs. Burwell's own words: for example, her dictum, "Have communion with *few*, Be intimate with *one*, Deal justly by *all*, Speak evil of *none*." My Gatewood Academy is a fictional combination of Peace Institute in Raleigh, the Nash-Pollack School in Hillsborough, and the Burwell School itself. Especially helpful were Kathleen Johnson, ed., "Nineteenth Century Reflections on Life, Love, and Loss in the Diary of Clay Dillard," *North Carolina Historical Review* (April 2004); and Ann Strudwick Nash, *Ladies in the Making* (Durham, NC: Seeman Printing, 1964).

Later sections of this novel are informed by the following books: Zeta Barker Hamby, *Memoirs of Grassy Creek: Growing Up in the Mountains on the Virginia–North Carolina Line* (Jefferson, NC: McFarland, 1998); Karen Cecil Smith, *Orlean Puckett: The Life of a Mountain Midwife, 1844–1939* (Boone, NC: Parkway, 2003); John Houck, Clarice Weaver, and Carol Williams, *Images of Ashe County Revisited* (Mount Pleasant, SC: Arcadia Publishing, 2004); Martin Crawford, *Ashe County's Civil War* (Chalottesville: University Press of Virginia, 2001); Cecelia Conway, *African Banjo Echoes in Appalachia: A Study of Folk Traditions* (Knoxville:

University of Tennessee Press, 1995); Sean Wilenz and Greil Marcus, eds., *The Rose and the Briar: Death, Love, and Liberty in the American Ballad* (New York: W. W. Norton, 2004); William A. Link, *A Hard Country and a Lonely Place: Schooling, Society, and Reform in Rural Virgnia, 1870–1920* (Chapel Hill: University of North Carolina Press, 1986); Andrew Gulliford, *America's Country Schools* (Washington, DC: Preservation Press, 1991); William R. Trotter, *Bushwhackers* (Winston-Salem, NC: John F. Blair, 1991); and Londa L. Woody, *All in a Day's Work: Historic General Stores of Macon and Surrounding North Carolina Counties* (Boone, NC: Parkway, 2000).

Thanks to the late Frank Colvard for his suggestions in Ashe County; to Leland R. Cooper and Mary Lee Cooper for the books *The Pond Mountain Chronicle: Self-Portrait of a Southern Appalachian Community* (Jefferson, NC: McFarland, 1998), and *The People of the New River: Oral Histories from the Ashe, Alleghany, and Watauga Counties of North Carolina* (Jefferson, NC: McFarland, 2001); and very special gratitude to Clarice Weaver, longtime children's librarian and educator whose remarkable oral history project may be found in its entirety at the Ashe County Public Library in West Jefferson, NC.

Thanks to attorney Cyrus D. Hogue III for his legal knowledge and to Sally Cook and Bruce Cormier of Castine, Maine, for their expertise in Portuguese, Confederados, and life in Brazil. I found Eugene C. Harter's *Lost Colony of the Confederacy* (College Station: Texas A&M Press, 2000) to be especially insightful on this fascinating topic.

Other helpful books include:

Mary Elizabeth Massey, *Refugee Life in the Confederacy* (Baton Rouge: Louisiana State University Press, 1964); Judith McGuire, *Diary of a Southern Refugee during the War (1867)* (New York: Arno Press, 1974); U. R. Brooks, *Butler and His Cavalry* (Germantown, TN: Guilded Bindery Press, repr. 1994); Drew Gilpin Faust, *Mothers of Invention: Women in the Slaveholding South in the American Civil War* (Chapel Hill: University of North Carolina Press, 1996); Jane H. Pease and William Henry Pease, *A Family of Women: The Carolina Petigrus in Peace and War* (Chapel Hill: University of North Carolina Press, 1999); Walter Sullivan, *The War the Women Lived: Female Voices from the Confederate South* (Nashville, TN: J. S. Sanders, 1995); Michael J. Varhola, *Everyday Life during the Civil War* (Cincinnati, OH: Writers Digest Books, 1999); Manly Wade Wellman, *Giant in Gray* (Dayton, OH: Press of Morningside Bookshop, 1980); Clint Johnson, *Touring the Carolinas' Civil War Sites* (Winston-Salem, NC: John F. Blair, 1996); John Gilchrist Barrett, *North Carolina as a Civil War Battleground, 1861–1865* (Raleigh:

Division of Archives and History, North Carolina Department of Cultural Resources, 1987); Richard L. Zuber, *North Carolina during Reconstruction* (Raleigh: Division of Archives and History, North Carolina Department of Cultural Resources, 1969); Mark L. Bradley, *This Astounding Close: The Road to Bennett Place* (Chapel Hill: University of North Carolina Press, 2000).